DECEPTION

SOUL SEER CHRONICLES, BOOK 2

S.J. CAIRNS

Black Thumb
Publishing

Cover design by Getcovers
Logo created by S.J. Cairns
Logo image by CNuisin depositphotos.com ID 265803116
Tree vector by Nikhomtreevector depositphotos.com
ID 391693140

ebook: 978-1-7782426-3-2
paperback: 978-1-7782426-4-9
hardcover: 978-1-7782426-5-6

Previous edition printed 2018

Black Thumb Publishing
Ontario, Canada
www.sjcairns.com

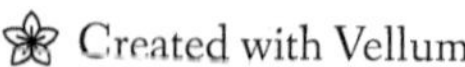 Created with Vellum

ACKNOWLEDGMENTS

Much has changed since Book 1 of the Soul Seer Chronicles was published including the closing of its original publisher and the second publisher a year later. Once the sobbing and panicked freak-outs abated, friends with big hearts became a lighthouse in the darkness and helped me find my way. I can't thank them enough for having faith in Sophie's story.

Thank you to every reader of *Discovery*, Book 1, for sticking it out with me and for reading *Deception*, Book 2. I hope I have exceeded your expectations.

As always, I owe a tip of the hat to my writing group The Quillies. They hold a special place in my heart. With loyal support like theirs, I have already found success.

To my husband:
You have lost countless hours of my time to my never-ending desire to create worlds on the dark side of reality, but your love provides me the greatest inspiration of all. Your support, understanding, and yummy food-making has not gone unnoticed.

1

COVEN LIAISON

More heavy-duty cleaner, more polishing, and still the light hit a stubborn smudge on the bar top. Disintegrate the whole damn thing with innate power passed down for generations? Abso-freaking-lutely. Erase all signs of dried-on BBQ wing sauce? Not a bloody chance.

Hiding my powers from the Blind, the non-magic patrons of The Lush's, busy poisoning their livers with cheap drinks and their colons with deep-fried everything, was a pain in the ass.

"You hedging for a tip?" my co-worker Eddie asked. "Because I'm pretty sure the bar top is the wrong kind of wood for rubbing that hard."

I chucked the cloth at his face. A wet slap smacked him before he could get his tattooed hands up.

"Touchy much?" He tossed the cloth onto the lower counter out of my reach. "Your attitude's been flipped to max bitch since you came in. Clear tables and burn off some energy. You're freakin' me out."

"Pfft. Freaking you out," I muttered.

If Eddie only knew about the real world. That he wasn't the top of the food chain. That with the help of a coven, I saved the life of a guy I met in my nightmares from a sleeping curse? Ha! Then he'd freak out. Hell, I freaked out. We still didn't know the reason behind why Caine Berisford was stuck in the sleeping curse to begin with, though we knew an evil fucker, Loring, was somehow involved. I had already gained too much of his attention and expected to see him again soon.

While all the lifesaving and near life-losing turned out in Caine and I's favour, all I wanted was to keep busy and pretend I was just another Blind human like Eddie who had no idea how dangerous the world really was.

Dish bin in hand, I rounded the bar and caught sight of a familiar redhead in my peripherals coming through the door. My feet didn't stop. I cleared beer bottles while their previous lightweight sippers flirted with a couple of guys at the pool table.

"Hey! Sophie, slow your roll."

Stopping wasn't going to happen.

"You can't get away from me." Kim followed and grabbed empty bottles and glasses and dropped them in the bin as we moved around the crowd. "What are you doing here?"

"Taking a crochet for dummies class."

She wasn't thrown by my deadpan sarcasm. "Why are you working? Why tonight? Caine's awake now."

"Confirmed alive and healthy."

"Yes." She lowered her voice. "But considering what happened to you while you were under—"

I spun around so quick her green-blue eyes widened. "You don't have to remind me, Kim."

"Got it."

"I was there."

"I know."

I broke the tension and kept going.

Kim followed.

"What's going on, Soph? You were fine at the hospital and then went mute on the ride home. You said you were going to bed, but then you left."

"You're keeping tabs on me? Do I need to worry about waking up to you staring at me and wearing my underwear on your head?"

"No," she said with forced calm. "We're neighbours, it's impossible to miss Bosco wailing when you leave." She lowered her voice again. "I figured out where you went with a location beacon."

"A what?" She gave me a look and I understood it was a magic thing. "Whatever. I'm busy Kim."

I spun away from her and knocked over a pint of beer, the whole thing splashing down my leg, the glass shattering on the hardwood.

"Watch it!" The college-aged patron yelled at me over the sound of the top 40 hits and loud enough to bring the attention of more than half the bar. "Work much? It's your job to pour drinks, not dump them."

I ground my teeth. "I'm sorry—"

"You're headed to the bar to fetch me another fucking drink, is what you are."

A flush of magic raged to the surface of my skin and crawled up the back of my neck before I registered the power surge. This punk had no clue what I was capable of. Hell, I didn't know what I was capable of, and it was burning to let loose.

Something grabbed my attention over the guy's shoulder. Another patron raising his arm to take a swig of dark liquid from a short glass, his profile visible to me across the room, his soul glow unmistakable. He was a stranger to me, but his dark soul glow told me everything I needed to know.

A Tainted, evil Magic was in the bar.

The pissed off and drink-less college prick snapped his fingers in my line of sight. "Hey! Get me another drink. I'm not paying for it either."

Refraining from taking the broken glass and shoving it into the prick's neck, I smiled and headed back to the bar. Dragging Kim with me, I dropped the bin of glasses on the bar top with a loud clang.

"Did you break something?" My boss, Drew, with impeccable hearing unless you're asking for fair wages and legal break times, came out of the back office.

"Yes, Drew," I said without patience, wanting to tell Kim what I saw. "Take it out of my pay as well as funds for a pint."

Drew sneered and went back into the office, saving me from further argument. Since I threatened him with the authorities for his shady dealings, he's backed off by a crotch hair.

Eddie laughed. "He's going to double it for you being a bitch."

"Let him."

"What about you?" Eddie asked Kim, stopping me again. "How 'bout I make it up to you and buy you a drink?"

"Oh...." Kim looked at me surprised.

I turned to Eddie. "Shouldn't you be making it up to me?"

He gave me a withering look.

"Vodka martini," Kim ordered. My expression turned on Kim. "What?"

"Coming up." Eddie slapped the bar top and got working on the drink.

"Kim, we have a big problem."

"Eddie? Why? He's super cute. I'm not turning down a free drink. Or do you mean the freak-out you're having about Caine because that's definitely a problem."

"Neither." I quieted my voice. "That guy has a dark soul glow."

Kim gasped. "Eddie?"

"Ugh, no, get your mind off clearing your cobwebs." She pouted. "The guy in the back. He's one of Loring's goons."

She tried to see who I meant, but he wasn't visible from the bar through the crowd unless you could see his filthy soul.

"He was at Aunt Lacey's when Loring attacked."

She gasped. "No way!"

"Yes way. Call Aunt Lacey and get her to—"

"Here you go." A chipper-voiced Eddie interrupted and served Kim's drink with four extra olives.

"Thanks, handsome." Kim beamed at Eddie and took a sip of her drink still looking at him over the edge of her martini glass.

"Call her!"

"Ah!" She sloshed her drink. "Okay, okay!"

"Call who?" Eddie asked.

"No one," I snapped at him.

"Fine." He pulled back. "Jesus fuck. You still have to serve that asshat his drink and clean up the mess."

Kim used the natural power of her blue-green eyes and trained them on Eddie. "And I would be eternally grateful if you could do it for Sophie." She even tacked on a head-tilt which caused her long red hair to fall over her shoulder. "I still need her for a quick moment. Please?"

He huffed. "Fine. You can at least pour the guy's drink."

"Got it." At least that way, I didn't have to interact with the college prick or get close to the Tainted Magic, even if it meant Kim's shameless flirting.

"Thanks bunches." Kim slapped on an extra wide smile as Eddie passed with the mop and bucket. She then called Aunt Lacey as I poured a pint of Rickard's Red and put it on the bar top.

Kim was still on the phone talking as she searched through her purse for something, silent as I presumed Aunt Lacey was talking. She took out a vial of something and pinched a bit into her palm before sprinkling it into the pint I poured.

A quick check of the room showed no one noticed, too enthralled with their night out. "Are you planning on date-raping that douche-nozzle?"

She shushed me.

Before I could dump it, Eddie returned and took it to serve to the college prick.

The thumbs-up from Kim was discomforting.

The Lush's doors opened and in walked a man that had me saying "Holy shit" and gripping Kim's arm before I could stop myself.

His blond head turned to me, but I was too busy checking out his bright soul colour to remember basic manners.

Kim spun to see what I reacted to as the blond man approached us.

"Do I know you?" he asked.

"Umm...."

"Who are you?" Kim spoke for me, her phone still to her ear.

He scanned the bar. I followed his gaze and noticed the Tainted Magic was no longer polluting the back table with his dark soul. Was the blond stranger looking for him? Before I could ask, he said, "I'm tasked with welcoming—"

"Hold up." Kim raised a finger to him and went back to her phone, listening as myself and the blond man stood in awkward silence. He checked over his shoulder at the bar patrons. Disappointment evident in his furrowed brow and the downturn in the edges of his lips.

Whoever he was, his soul was nothing I had ever seen before. No other Magic at Aunt Lacey's party emitted a similar soul glow: a bright white with a glimmer of metallic pink. The shimmer captivated me as I tried to train my eyes to take in what I was seeing.

"Sure." Kim's high-pitched tone stole me from my gawking as she thrust her phone towards the blond man. "Aunt Lacey wants to talk to you."

He took the phone with less surprise than I would have. "Elder?" He listened. "My apologies." More silence. "Understood." He gave Kim back her phone. "As I was saying, I am a Coven Liaison tasked with welcoming new inductees and had a moment to stop by this establishment to do so."

"Bullshit." I couldn't help myself.

"I beg your pardon?"

"Coven Liaison?"

"That is what I said."

I kept his gaze and leaned into the bar top. "Your visit has nothing to do with some welcoming task any more than it does the half-price beer bucket. The dark-souled motherfucker who happened to disappear when you showed up isn't a coincidence."

He opened his mouth to speak, but he looked like he was going to lie, so I saved him the trouble.

"Loring's man, right?"

He nodded. "How would you know, Sophie?"

I crossed my arms. "If you know my name, then you know how."

He half-smiled before saying, "Indeed." He took a seat at the bar. "Families with the Soul Seeing trait exist in the tomes, though I had my doubts any bloodlines remained active. Quite a gift."

"Then you know more than I do." I knew nothing about my bloodline or the power I inherited. Family was useless. My Grandma Lizzie was too busy making it her mission to condemn me for giving into the "Devil's charms" by practicing. I couldn't even shut my Soul Seer ability off, which cast Mr. Pink-Sparkly-Soul in a perpetual haze of princess glitter.

He moved on. "Our Elder informed me of your identity which explains your overreaction at my entry."

"I didn't overreact."

"You did." He looked over his shoulder. "And tipped-off my target who seems to have disappeared. I admit 'Coven Liaison' was a weak cover, though it has worked on those without your talents to call me out."

"I'm not a fan of liars. The fact you're quick to give one says a lot."

The man held my gaze for a moment, something like guilt shining through his dark blue eyes. A sadness contrasting with his glittery soul glow. Though he never apologized.

"Why were you following him?" Kim broke our staring contest.

The man took a breath and considered before responding. "He's within territory he knows better than to cross. After speaking with our Elder and finding the Soul Seer he attempted to snatch at the Elder's gathering, the question of why is easily answered." He looked at me. "Why no wards?"

"Wards?"

"Safety measures. You work among the Blind. Simple wards would safeguard against those such as my target. Or provide a basic warning of their entry."

"Safeguard? He's the first evil fucker to come in here."

"Please." Eddie came around the counter. "We've had plenty of assholes in here. Evil is a bit much though, don't you think?" Thinking back to Jack, my neighbour who tried to kill me feet from where we stood, I had to disagree with Eddie.

A screech and commotion had us looking towards the customers. The college prick bent over his table vomiting on the floor as his girl-friend was freaking out and gagging. The others around them squealed and raced out of the splash zone. The college prick's stomach contents continued to waterfall onto the hardwood as his friends stood around. One ever so helpful sack-pimple pulled out their phone and started live-streaming.

"I take it back," Eddie said. "That motherfucker is pure evil."

"Umm...." I looked at my co-worker but didn't have to finish.

"Yes! I'll clean it." He cursed and grabbed cleaning tools.

Eddie stormed over to the guy, hoisted him off his knees by his arm, and dragged him outside. His girlfriend followed, covering her mouth and nose, as if she would rather leave him than have the bar know they were together.

So much for loyalty.

"He could have at least made it to the bathroom," Kim said.

The blond man turned to her. "You're responsible?"

Kim's eyes went wide with obvious guilt. I don't know how he knew, and Kim looked terrified that he did.

"No permanent harm," the man stated. "I'm certain he deserved it."

"He did," she was quick to justify.

"All right." He stood up. "Since the question of why my target crossed into this territory is solved, I'll take my leave." He took a few steps towards the door before turning around. "Coffee grounds work best. Maybe save your co-worker from contributing to the mess."

Eddie's screwed up face as he tried to use a dustpan to scoop up the nachos and beer we served college prick was enough to tell me he was close to losing it. His gag reflex had onlookers still dry-heaving with him or laughing. I grabbed a bag of coffee grounds and raced over to save Eddie before heading back to Kim, surprised at how well the coffee masked the vomit.

"I love/hate you right now," I told her. "And why the fuck would you carry around something to make assholes vomit? Do you meet that many a day?"

She shrugged and smiled. "I'm a Kitchen Witch. I'm well-prepared."

I sagged against the bar top.

"Why don't we get back to discussing Caine?" Kim said. "He's leaving the hospital tomorrow, against doctor's orders, and wants to see you."

"Or we could focus on the grittier topic of why the evil dude border-jumped to hang out here and who the pink flamingo who came in after him is."

"Pink flamingo?"

"Blond dude with the pink glittery soul. Who was he?"

"Weird. Maybe it's a lineage thing."

"No idea." The fact no one was around to ask about it was frustrating.

We still had to follow the Olive lead too. I hated thinking my grandmother's institutionalized sister had answers I might not be able to salvage from a warped mind.

"Aunt Lacey said his name was Ranlyn. A Coven Elite by the sounds of it. He's right about the safeguards. I should've thought about that sooner."

A flash of heat hit me, and the sensation of my power made my arms itch as I attempted to rein it in. Having a Tainted Magic show up where I worked was bad, especially if it tipped off a Coven Elite to chase after him. Joining the Coven was supposed to iron out life's speed bumps, not create extra. The sense things were about to turn from complex to chaotic gave me hot flashes.

Panic, not power, reared its ugly head and roiled in my stomach, threatening to add to Eddie's vomit cleanup. Kim was right. After all that happened, I shouldn't be at work right now. Especially not if I was leading people like dark-souled guy around a bunch of the Blind trying to have some fun and maybe get laid. Drew would be pissed, but since the college prick unloaded, many cleared out. A few customers remained and it was Eddie's night to close anyway.

———

The whole drive home, Kim pestered me with questions about Caine: what was I going to do? Would I invite him to a coven meeting so he could meet the people that saved him? Would I help him re-assimilate to life outside the sleeping curse? Would I meet up with him like I promised? I must have been on autopilot at the hospital because I didn't remember promising anything.

Ugh. I should have walked, but Kim insisted on driving. By the time we got onto the elevator, I had tuned her out.

The elevator lights went out, dropping us into pitch black darkness, the car stopping with a jerk. Quiet overpowered the small space. Neither of us moved or spoke.

I reached out in the darkness until my hand touched her arm. "Kim, you got any special Kitchen Witch powders for this?"

Her hand clutched mine. "A downer in case you're claustrophobic."

Kim grabbed her cell phone and used the flashlight app to find the emergency call button. It didn't work. Nothing did, including her cell service.

"Sometimes the signal drops out in here," she said as I kept trying to push buttons and ended up pounding on them.

"Stupid fucking, goat's ass, shit-bug building. Of course, there's no emergency phone. Wouldn't want to spend a dollar more than—"

Kim shrieked as a loud grinding sound had my voice stuck in my throat.

"What the—?"

Our hands covered our ears as the sound reverberated off the elevator walls.

Kim pointed her phone light at the doors, the light vibrating with her nerves.

The steel opened an inch, and then another.

With a grunt of someone on the outside, the doors widened with another ear-piercing squeal and stopped halfway. A hand shot through the opening, lit by Kim's shaky light and the red haze of the emergency exit signs in the hall.

Stuck between levels, I braced a foot on the cement wall and grabbed the hand. With a strong grip, I looked up to our savior and my stomach dropped.

Those eyes.

I gasped and let go of the hand. He snatched my sleeve. My scream punctuated the rip of fabric. The other hand grabbed a chunk of my hair and pulled me up off the elevator floor. Kim clung to my waist. We were both lifted off the ground, but she couldn't keep hold of me.

My spine dragged across the metal lip of the threshold of the elevator until it hit carpet.

Kim screamed my name. The slap of her shoes hit the elevator floor as if she jumped, unable to get out.

"Let me go!" I screamed, hoping someone would come out of their apartment.

No one did.

My nails dug into cold skin without reaction from the hand attached to my scalp as my power grew with immense pressure in my chest. Between screams, I whimpered, the panic and fear so blinding I saw nothing of the dark hallway the fucker dragged me down. A dose of post-traumatic stress dropped me into another scene altogether.

Flashes of the attack from Jack sprung tears to my eyes. His snarling face, the stench of alcohol-soaked breath turning my stomach, pain, helplessness, despair. A flush of heat suffocated me. The pressure in my chest so heavy my ribs might cave in. When my magic grew to the point my bones peaked with fireworks of agony, an explosion of power burst from my body and ignited the hallway with light.

I hit the floor. Immense relief and unshakable pain flowed through me. I rolled into the fetal position and gripped my body until my lungs expanded with gasping pulls. Loring's man was on his ass against the wall at the end of the hall holding his chest. His dark soul now streaked with grey and lighter tones as he roared, his face cramped in fury.

Grey eyes snapped open and fixed on mine. My stomach seized. The moment hung as he sat there. We stared at each other, my scalp and temples throbbing. Kim's screams were an echo in the background as his dark soul pulsated between light and dark tones. Darkness regained its footing, drowned out the lightened streaks of his soul, and left him panting.

The release of power left me empty. Even in my panic of what would happen next, no itch of my skin or vibration came forth to save me as he regained his strength.

On his feet, a heavy breath left his lungs as I froze in place. Shitfuckshitfuck!

He reached out his hand and yanked me to my feet without touching me or moving from where he stood more than ten feet away. I dangled from his telekinetic grip, unable to fight back, and crying out when he pulled me across the carpet towards him.

Bright light flashed in the adjoining hallway, throwing my kidnapper off his feet, and slamming him into someone's apartment door. He dropped me. Rug burns thrashed the skin up the left side of my face, palms, and elbow. Grunts from fighting filled the hallway, but tears from the sting of my face blurred my vision.

The fuzzy glimpse of someone rushing towards me had me scrambling to get away, bracing for more pain. Whoever it was, bypassed me and took off.

"Sophie?!" A familiar voice called, another blur in the darkness in front of me.

I blinked my eyesight clear of tears and saw the blond man from the bar. I couldn't remember his name but his face equalled safety. There were not enough expletives to express the relief I felt.

"Kim's still—"

"I know. Let's get you up first."

I reached up, he grabbed my arm to support me. His fingers dug into my damaged skin, and I pulled out of his painful grip before I was steady. I cried out, falling back on my ass.

"Hey!" A new angry voice called out.

Donovan.

Bright light. Flurry of movement. Grunts of pain.

Donovan tossed the man from the bar aside and hit him with a shot of power in the back. I flung myself at Donovan. Both of us crashed into the wall and then to the ground. I scrambled on top of him and bore my weight down on his shoulders, his dark eyes wide, his mouth agape.

"He was saving me!" I yelled and watched Donovan's expression narrow and his nostrils flare.

2

———

BAD TIMING

Electricity was restored to the building. I recoiled against the onslaught of retina-burning overhead light and then looked back at Donovan still beneath me.

His dark eyes softened for a moment, warm black tar too deep to fathom, before they hardened and acid poured into his voice. "Off. Now."

His tone was so harsh and his eyes so cold I cringed, quick to stand up. On his feet, as soon as I backed off, he looked everywhere but at me, as I fretted about why he was pissed.

"Are you okay?" Kim ran to me after the blond man helped her out of the elevator, while Donovan acted like I was patient zero and kept his distance. Kim stopped short and looked me over, then reached into her bag. "You're bleeding."

That's when I noticed blood dripping down my arm onto my hand and dotting the carpet.

Kim pulled out sheets from a tissue packet and handed them over. I thanked her and did what I could to clean up the gash on my elbow.

The blond man approached with a hard look at Donovan whose jaw flexed as he stood with his arms crossed. "Donovan."

"Ranlyn." Donovan matched Ranlyn's intensity.

"Try assessing the scene before attacking next time," Ranlyn said. "You know what kind of damage you could have caused her."

"And you know I would've killed you if I'd thought you were a true threat. My attack *was* my assessment."

They stood in silent challenge. Donovan's dark eyes so hard he looked like a stranger, and although he seemed reluctant, Ranlyn looked away and asked me if I was okay.

"Scraped up and pissed off," I answered. "Someone's gotta teach me some offensive moves. This white knight shit is ancient and everyday self-defence doesn't cut it when they can laser blast you."

"Laser blast?" Kim's sculpted brow peaked. "What did I miss?"

"Another failed kidnapping attempt," Ranlyn stated.

"One you'd think someone would have intervened on. So much for neighbourly camaraderie," I said, then muttered, "Piss bucket sippers."

Ranlyn's face twitched with disgust. "The Blind are privy to only what Magic's allow. Loring and anyone working for him would make sure no one would hear a thing."

"Yeah? Well, Loring's an empty dickbag who needs to pick up a hobby. Like lawn bowling or erotic asphyxiation. Or maybe his donger doesn't work and he's pissed at the world because not even his power can give him wood."

"He's an empty dickbag who could cleanly end your life or send someone else to do it for him as he's more apt to do. Again." Donovan concentrated on Ranlyn. "What the fuck are you doing about it?"

"Riiight," I interjected while Kim passed over more tissues for me to bleed through, "'cuz ol' sparkles here scared off the guy for the second time tonight."

Ranlyn tilted his head to look at me. "Sparkles?"

Donovan's attention spun to me so fast I cringed. "Do you enjoy playing the bait? Because that's what he's using you as." His intensity shifted back at Ranlyn. "Your timing is astounding. Waited long enough to ensure Loring's man was too distracted with trying to drag her off before attacking."

"Bait!" I turned on Ranlyn, no longer seeing him as a glittery white knight. He shot a glare of resentment at Donovan. "Shouldn't the bait know they're bait so they'll be in on the con? What if he got me before you could swoop in? I had no back-up plan, and my James Bond skills are a tad rusty."

"You're a Seedling with zero cognitive defences. Unprotected thoughts would have betrayed my efforts."

"Oh, I'm sorry. Next time I'll pack contraceptives."

"Contraceptives?"

"Yeah, you know, for my unprotected thoughts. Wouldn't want to get knocked up by a deadbeat thought-daddy."

"Thought-daddy?"

"Well, thought-father doesn't roll off the tongue as well, does it?"

His voice dropped as he said, "Soul Seer...."

I crossed my arms. "So, you stick me in information blackout to protect your efforts? What efforts? You already know he tried to get me at Aunt Lacey's. Clearly, he thought he could trap me at work, and since he failed, he followed me home." Ranlyn stared at me without a hint of apology.

"Fine." I pulled my ripped sleeve over my still bleeding elbow. "You've earned yourself 'round the clock guard duty." I pushed passed him and hooked my non-bleeding arm around Kim's to take her away with me.

"You don't have authority to modify my orders," Ranlyn called from behind us as we made our way to the stairwell. No way was I taking the elevator.

"A call to Aunt Lacey should do it. Modify this, buddy." I shot him the finger over my shoulder.

After climbing two flights to get to my apartment, Kim helped clean my wounds. She used some Kitchen Witch ingredients while I talked to Aunt Lacey, praying she backed me up in securing Ranlyn as my guard. She did and apologized for his actions. I didn't need the apology, not from her, but I felt better knowing she hadn't put him up to it.

My guard remained out of sight. I contemplated taking a night walk to test him, see how he liked being bait. The memory of the Tainted guy dragging me down the hall by my hair had me heading to bed instead.

————

Sleep was no friend of mine. The Sandman stopped by for short increments to laugh at me and grace me with a host of faces I didn't want stalking me in my brief dreams. Loring in a dapper suit, the hair-gripper from the hallway with his grey eyes too similar to Caine's, and Jack, my shithead ex-neighbour who thought ending my life on the end of his blade was a swell idea.

Surrender came with an echoing "Fuckballsandwich" after the fourth time waking up in a cold sweat.

With nothing else to do in the middle of the night, I worked on a paper on the differences between Freud's Psychosexual and Erikson's Psychosocial Personality Development theories. Even after Aunt Lacey's tea leaf reading and the rest of the Covener's assessments deeming my seeking a higher education to be useless because I was "destined" for other things, I refused to drop out. Chaos dictated my past, not my future. My plan to get my shit together and find a path of my own still took precedence.

The victory cry was earned, as was the vertigo after the air guitar and head banging, when I hit send on the finished document to submit it along to my professor. An invisible pin fell into place. A mocking laugh and blazing middle fingers in the face of whatever Loring was cooking up.

————

An early morning knock at my door interrupted me making a snack as music pumped from my computer down the hall. I shook my hips to a rock and hip-hop mash-up, my good mood still thrumming as I walked to the door. Bosco was too busy lapping at the peanut butter stuck to the roof of his mouth to beat me there. When I opened up, I was hit with a dose of white-blue soul glow. The shock made me drop the peanut-butter-caked knife with a clang.

Caine.

"Sorry." He picked up the knife, holding it out for me as I gawked at him. When he realized I wasn't taking the knife, he lowered it. "I should have called."

"No, no. Fuck. Okay. Um, right, can you wait a second?"

"S-sure."

"One sec."

"Okay."

I closed the door, raced to cut the music, and ran to change out of my pyjamas.

"Duckfarts!" Why didn't I look through the peephole? Having Caine see me without a bra and my hair in a messy bun thing more like a tangled rat's nest was not acceptable for a second-time meeting. How did he find me? Plus, Ranlyn might be out there on guard duty, but what if he wasn't and I opened the door to another kidnapper? I needed to get my shit together.

Bosco was licking the peanut butter from where I dropped the knife when I made it back. I shooed him away, looked through the peephole to see if Caine was still there, and then opened the door for him.

The hit of seeing Caine engulfed by his white and blue soul glow outside my door was as dumbfounding as the first. Clad in a pair of beige cargo shorts and a plain white tee, he stood, eyes of a winter sky starring back at me, and I lost my ability to speak.

"Mind if I come in?"

"Shit. Yes, sorry." I motioned him inside. "You surprised me—"

"This is yours." He held up my peanut-butter-swathed knife.

"Yup, it is." I took the knife, tossed it in the sink, and jumped along with Bosco at the loud clang.

"And this must be Bosco." Caine kneeled and upturned his palm. My pug companion went right over to him and sniffed his fingers, licked them, then rubbed his face folds against his knuckles. Caine laughed and made a comical sound of disgust at his wet hand. "Is face grime a sign we're friends?"

"Well, the real test is if you let him lick dog food out of your belly button." Caine looked up at me and blinked. "Not your thing? That's cool." I tossed him a paper towel. "You're Bosco and pet owner-approved."

Caine stood and took in a deep breath, and I felt another apology evident in the slight tension in his lips as he averted his eyes.

"It's fine. I wasn't expecting you at my door, so it's your fault you got the full glamour of me in my PJ's."

"Wouldn't be the first time." He gave me a bright smile and put his hands in his pockets. I immediately wanted to jump him.

"Right. Again, your fault."

He smiled bigger before it disappeared. "You seemed a little... overwhelmed at the hospital yesterday so I didn't want to push right away. I thought maybe we could hang out or go for a walk and talk for a bit. If you have time since I barged in on your day."

"Sure."

The air was thick with the day's humidity, and the sun beat down through a clear sky. Caine squinted and shaded his eyes.

"Where'd you like to go?" I asked him. "This street isn't the greatest for a leisurely walk."

"That's okay. I wanted to go to the park. You said it was by your place?"

"The park? Like, *the park*?" He nodded. "Why? You didn't spend enough time there already?" My judgment was out before I could bite it back.

"I want to see it in the light."

My chest squeezed a little.

We crossed the street, and I led him to the railway tie steps that descended into the park where Caine spent almost four years trapped in a sleeping curse. Only then did I realize I hadn't told him that's what it was. The Awakening Ritual was too important to add another layer of weird. He still believed the accident with his brother caused his coma.

I wasn't as ready for this walk as I had thought.

Caine descended first, slow in the beginning and then pulling out ahead of me with long strides and skipping steps. The toe of my sandal clipped a stair as I tried to follow and I saved myself from going tits up. I concentrated on the mouth-watering image of Caine's sculpted back. His shirt stretched and contoured to his body. No amount of distraction kept me from breaking out into a sweat having nothing to do with the heat.

Expectation weighed on my nerves. I hadn't dated for a long time. Even though he made no attempt to label this walk, the familiar anticipation of an awkward first date hit me anyway. We spent months together in the nightmare landscape of the park, most of the time without a clue who the other was. Now, the situation had changed from those dreams into the real world. It was a stadium I was ironically far less comfortable in. The park from my nightmares now somehow seemed easier.

I snuck a discreet whiff of my pits, happy I opted for an extra layer of deodorant and body spray before we left. The sun was already baking me. What wafted back was my favorite mix of freesia, casaba melon, and plums. I took deep breaths hoping for a calming effect. Then put my arms down, realizing I was huffing my armpits in public, grateful Caine's attention was ahead of him and not behind.

Caine stopped at the bottom of the stairs.

"You okay?" I asked and watched him survey the park.

"I feel like a tourist." He didn't explain if this was a good thing.

"Let me know if it becomes too much and we'll leave. I don't mind."

He nodded and started down the path.

No amount of distraction relieved the edge to my anxiety, though

I tried and chatted as we walked. "I used to love it down here. Bosco likes to run off leash and play with other dogs."

He didn't respond, busy scanning his surrounding with fresh eyes.

The gravel path brought us to where it all started.

"It's weird here for me," I said. "This is where all my dreams happened. It was a place of complete fear for a long time."

The sound of the lazy creek filtered up beyond the trees, the level of the water tame and no longer threatening to drown us. The willows where we escaped the rain swayed serenely instead of thrashing around in the storm. The spot in the lush grass where we made the willow circle during the ritual was nothing more than grass.

A tear escaped from behind my sunglasses. I was quick to wipe it away, but not quick enough. Caine's hand on my back was difficult to accept. The need to be consoled by him made me uncomfortable. Overprotective of my heart, I knew it was my way of pushing him away, even though I was at war with myself on why I should. His show of comfort made my composure slip even more while I struggled against a flight or fight response.

Caine rubbed my back and walked us to a park bench never included in my dreams. A puzzle for another time. Embarrassed by the weak display, I kept my head hung while collecting myself, wishing I had my hair loose to shield my face better.

I stole a few deep breathes. "I promise I'm not usually such a crybaby. You caught me at a crazy time in my life." Removing my sunglasses to wipe my eyes I glanced over at him. "Feel free to pop a tear duct and make me feel less of an idiot." My giggle was an attempt to lessen my grief while Caine sat, expression impassive. Either he was used to tears or was freaked and didn't know what to do.

"I assumed you were an emotional person." He turned his body towards mine. "Instead, you've been broken down by how much I've unloaded on you."

"Sorry. It'll pass, but don't make this about me. You have so much to process. Lived through horrors I can't imagine."

He held my hands and rubbed remaining wetness from my tears into my skin as he attempted to soothe through touch. A part of me sunk into his caress while another part cringed. I looked straight into his eyes lightened by the sun and melted.

"Sophie, I'm out of the dream and sitting here because of you. I never expected to find you, or whatever happened. I promise, I'll do everything so you'll never shed another tear over me."

My heart dropped, my mind reeling at his idealistic sentiments. I wrapped my arms around him as he held me tight and left thoughts of why I initiated the embrace for later. Keeping such a broad promise was unrealistic as well as unneeded, but without a doubt, I could tell he meant to keep his word.

When I pulled back, I tucked my emotions away with a promise to never allow Caine's time in the park affect me. Instead, I'd reminisce about the park as the place we first met, complete with the summer breeze flowing through the trees, the calming sound of the dark-water creek, and the intimate privacy it created from the rest of the world. The romanticized version of the nightmare was what I chose to hold close.

In that moment, I gave Caine a piece of my heart I never wanted back.

Light shifting in the trees pulled my attention away from Caine.

"Your humble guard at your service," I heard Ranlyn's voice in my head. *"You trying to make my job difficult by being out in public with another Seedling?"*

Seedling? Fuck, I still hadn't told Caine what he was or the truth of his coma.

"You okay?" Caine asked.

"Yes," I answered too fast. "Yeah, I'm fine. What about you? Also, how'd you know where to find me?"

The wayward question gave me wiggle room to stay quiet as he went on about it being the only high rise around where he crashed into the park, and then something about someone letting him in and then complaining about my noisy dog.

"Why can't you hide better?" I mentally said hoping Ranlyn would catch it. I didn't know how this mind-reading thing worked or if he could hear me.

"I hear you," Ranlyn confirmed as Caine went on about how his mother wasn't happy about him leaving the hospital so soon. *"I've warded your apartment door, though you need most work on your internal mechanisms."*

"My door? What'd you do to my door? And without asking. If it was anything like Aunt Lacey's, it may go off when my brother came in with the intent on making me tap-out from whatever wrestling move he decided to pin me in that day. How would I know what crossed the line into evil intent?"

"You insisted on me guarding you, which includes your place of residence. Consider yourself safe."

"Would that be okay with you?" Caine asked me.

"Ah, sure," I said having no clue what I agreed to.

"Dinner date." Ranlyn filled me in.

"Fuck! You dong-duster. What's the matter with you? See what you made me do? A date?"

"Tonight."

"Wonderful."

Thoughts of Donovan sprung forward before I could stop them. He in Aunt Lacey's backyard filling me in on our past life together, holding my hand as I went under to save Caine, and the unending snark I still found myself conflicted about.

"Should you be daydreaming about dimples and dark eyes right now? And what's a dong-duster?"

My irritation peaked as I pictured beating Ranlyn with a moss-slick rock from the creek.

"Nice," he commented. *"Sophie, careful, your power."*

I hadn't noticed the crawl across my skin until the warning in his voice caught me off guard.

Caine looked around himself in question. Did he feel it?

"Of course he did. Control yourself before I'm forced to take you out."

"Take me out? You pissed me off in the first place!"

"You okay?" Caine asked.

"First and last warning, Soul Seer. Make good use of it."

Controlling myself wasn't so easy and I had to rely on hard-earned tactics. I looked for visual distraction in a few birds flying overhead, then focusing on what I heard around me, then how I felt a slight breeze on my skin to chase away the burn of the sun, and so on. Engaging my senses to pull me out of my thoughts and grounding back into the world around me.

By the time I smelled fresh cut grass, I had leashed my power and was back to a low thrum of anxiousness I'd felt since Caine showed up at my door. After that, I ignored Ranlyn. Besides a periodic glimpse of my bodyguard's frilly-colored soul in the trees, he remained scarce.

To further the avoidance of telling Caine the truth about his power and sleeping curse, we talked about the superficial essentials about our lives like jobs and family. Caine had worked as a Project Manager at a small IT company, though mentioned he would rather "work at McDick's then go back."

"I've got time to figure it out," he concluded. "A benefit for Cole and I left me some resources. Insurance payout, too. Either way, I'll be good."

I nodded, happy Caine had some time before returning to the grind. I looked over at the sound of a light splash in the creek. More than one soul glow moved in the trees. Ranlyn's glittery soul and then another much darker of a Tainted Magic. The rustle of bodies in the trees became louder, and the last thing I wanted was Caine starting to look around and ask questions, so I mentioned I wasn't made for the sun and offered Caine lunch at my place to get us moving in the opposite direction. He was unaccustomed to the weather as well, so it was an easy sell.

"What the hell is that?" he asked as we approached my apartment and the hallway filled with noise.

"Bosco."

"Is someone beating him?"

"Nah. It's normal."

Once inside, Bosco's yaps and yips continued, a good sign for Caine since in Bosco terms you got the barking treatment if he liked you.

Caine played more vigorously than I would have with Bosco. He looked like an oversized kid on the floor. By the end, my pug companion was wheezing with his tongue hanging out of his mouth.

Ecstatic my tomatoes hadn't gone bad, I made toasted tomatoes sandwiches, a staple in my house as a kid and foolproof: toasted bread, mayo, sliced tomatoes, and salt and pepper.

While Caine was in the bathroom, I called Kim and told her about Ranlyn fighting the dark-souled Magic in the park so she could call Aunt Lacey. Since my bodyguard would have stayed in the hall if he did get back, I didn't know what happened to him. As we ate and watched a Manchester United soccer game, I worried that he was dead in the park where I left him.

Another thought hit of how much I needed to tell Caine and how I was ill-equipped to tell him. Dammit, I still had to invite him to the next coven meeting. I wondered if Donovan would train him like he did with me. Maybe that was his role in the Coven, though the thought of them in a room together was daunting. Maybe Kim could help instead?

As way of an ice breaker into the magic subject, I roused my power while his attention was on his meal, bringing it to simmer at a safe intensity.

He paused mid-chew, and I upped the dose of energy. Caine swallowed, touched the center of his chest, and cleared his throat.

"It's—"

A knock on the door snapped my concentration, sending my power retreating into me.

"If that's you Ranlyn, I'm as happy as a tickled clit you're alive, but I'm going to find a way to give you the magic-laden atomic wedgie you deserve."

I whipped the door open to find Kim standing there.

"Whoa, everything okay?"

"Sure. Why not." I opened the door wider and stepped aside so she could see Caine on my couch.

"Hey, Kim," Caine called out, smiling.

"Hi," Kim replied and then lowered her voice. "Bad timing?"

When I made the S.O.S call for Ranlyn, I left out the bit about me and Caine being in the park together.

"Yup."

"I can—"

"Nope. Get in here."

"Ranlyn?" I whispered before she came all the way in.

She shook her head.

Damn. That asshat better be alive.

Kim immediately drew Caine into conversation with an ease I envied. After a few minutes, the conversation turned to things he had missed while in the coma. I noticed people at the hospital glossed over details about their lives, anything he may have missed or would have been involved in. They were afraid to upset him, but I found it unsettling. So, when we had the chance to fill him in on the world he missed, we didn't hold back.

Obviously, we knew nothing about any family or friends, but we covered everything from environmental bans, polymer money, planetary discoveries and expeditions, and even sports. Those we needed to Google search as neither Kim nor I were football fans.

Conversation ate up a few hours until Caine announced he was leaving. "My mom picked these clothes since mine are still in storage. Last time she dressed me she was still cutting off the crust of my bread. I was lucky she skipped on dinosaurs and trucks, but I'll need to hit up a shop before our date tonight."

"Date?" Kim asked with a lascivious leer.

"I'll walk you out," I told him, shooting Kim a glare.

At the door, I reached up and hugged him, enjoying the feel of his arms wrapped around me. Even if I didn't get the opportunity to tell him about the power and his sleeping curse, I still chalked it up as a successful visit.

When the door closed, I sighed and wilted against the back of it. Kim laughed but Caine's visit exhausted me.

The door pushed open.

"Yo!" I called out and jumped away as Ranlyn squeezed in and closed the door behind him. "Didn't you hear me? Magic-laden—"

"Atomic wedgie, yes, I heard you quite well."

"Good. Now bend over and take it."

"What's going on?" Kim asked.

"You're alive? What happened?" I added without pointing out the mud and schmutz on his pressed khakis.

"Do you really plan on going on a date while Loring has a bounty out on you?"

All worry about him disappeared. "It's your fault I agreed to the date in the first place."

"A bounty?" Kim asked.

"Yes," Ranlyn answered her though he still looked at me. "I assumed you possessed the ability to alter plans given the severity of the danger our enemy possesses if he manages to get a hold of you. An attack in broad daylight, again, is testimony to the level of danger you are putting yourself, Caine, and all those who watch over you in."

I crossed my arms. "I thought you were my badass bodyguard, ready to vanquish evil in a single bound? You managed in the park."

"I don't bound. I'm not Superman."

"Clearly," I muttered, and his blond brows cinched together.

"It was one assailant. Loring will dispatch more."

The mention of Loring's name made me squeamish despite my bravado.

"Caine's going clothes shopping. I can't cancel. Plus, I still have a lot to tell him about all this magic stuff, and apparently, it can't wait. Didn't you hear? High threat level these days."

He may not have appreciated the snark, but I wasn't bailing on Caine now.

"Fine. I will escort you to the venue as well as be present inside the establishment while you eat at a table of my choosing dependent on access to multiple exits. Deal?"

"Only if you make it a booth."

He glowered at me. "Fine."

"Good. Now piss off. I need to get ready."

"A thank you would suffice."

"I bet it would, but thank yous are for people who don't trap me in the position to be thankful for in the first place." I opened the door and waved goodbye as he left to continue guarding the hall.

———

Kim the fashionista decided on an outfit for me. A turquoise v-neck satin tank with crystal embellishments, under a long-sleeved black dress shirt that clung to my dark jean clad hips. After glamming up my make-up, straightening my hair, and adding a crystal beaded bracelet and long silver dangling earrings, I was ready.

And sweating balls. The realization I was about to go on a date blindsided me.

I contemplated bailing when the kitten heels Kim lent me slipped on my kitchen tile. Heels were not an everyday accessory, and if Ranlyn wasn't being so damn impatient, I would have switched them out for flip-flops. Caine wouldn't care what my feet looked like anyway, and if he did, he could wear them himself.

"Ready?" Ranlyn asked with increasing impatience.

"Yes, Jeeves. Bring the carriage around before it turns into a pumpkin."

3

WATERWORKS

The cracked window saved me from Ranlyn's high-speed driving. Not only was I nauseous, but the prospect of a date was freaking me out.

"If I make a fool of myself and end up running out of the restaurant, I'll make sure you get that atomic wedgie you deserve before hibernating for the rest of my life."

Ranlyn turned off his dark sedan, released his seatbelt, and turned to me. "You're more afraid of conversation and a meal than the danger this date poses to your life?"

"Humiliation ends with death, living through it is my concern."

He raised a questioning blond brow and my ears burned as my fear shifted into anger.

"Save your words, Seer. I've heard them already and they don't alter the variables of this situation."

I blew out a breath I didn't realize I was holding in preparation to berate him.

"The hostess will lead you to the booth I've selected, and I'll remain under a cover spell unless needed. If anything, this may reveal more of Loring's followers, which is the primary reason I allowed this."

"Allowed?"

"Yes, allowed. You're putting yourself, Caine, and not to mention me, in danger and Caine doesn't even know why. Now get out and accept your flowers gracefully."

"Flowers?"

He pointed behind me out the window. Caine sat on a wooden bench outside of the restaurant, his knee bopping as he held a bouquet of lilies.

"Shitballs."

I heard murmuring behind me. When I looked, Ranlyn had disappeared. "What the fuck" was the only thing on my brain as I got out and slammed the door shut. When the doors locked on their own, I realized Ranlyn hadn't disappeared, but had went ghost and used a cover spell to remain unseen.

Too many things were knocking me off-kilter tonight. How was I supposed to concentrate on dating etiquette when an invisible, glittery-souled version of a driving instructor, was supervising from whatever corner he perched in?

"*Smiling helps,*" I heard Ranlyn say in my mind.

Fucker.

When Caine caught sight of me, he stood and smoothed out his shirt. Dressed to impress, I drank in his six-foot-four body, surprised he had even styled his hair. With a bouquet of glitter-dusted white lilies in hand, he was a GQ cover-shot making my pulse flutter as I prayed not to twist an ankle or vomit on his casual-but-nice shoes. He flashed me a big grin, and I couldn't help but reciprocate.

"Hi." He handed me the bouquet, leaned in for a quick hug, and kissed my cheek.

"Thank you." I blushed. "Now I feel empty-handed. I didn't get you anything."

"It's not customary for women to bring men gifts on a first date."

"Don't you wish it was?" I quipped and smelled the flowers.

"Actually, yes. Next time I expect a little something."

"Yeah, I bet you do." When I realized I'd tripped over the threshold from quippy to suggestive, I headed inside and tried not to chew through my cheek.

"*Nice job*," I heard Ranlyn in my head and envisioned the atomic wedgie, this time with spike-filled underwear.

Outside, the air was too warm for what I wore, but I bet on the restaurant's central air. A blast of cold confirmed it and helped deepen my breath as the hostess lead us to a booth near the back. It was next to the hallway that led to the bathrooms and the back exit. So far, Ranlyn had delivered. Same with being scarce. After his comment, he became radio silent, and his blond head and glittery soul were nowhere in sight.

So far, so good, I thought about ten minutes into the date. The relaxed setting along with my glass of liquid courage, and carefree conversation was perfect for inflicting the least amount of pressure on already strained circumstances, even though I couldn't help survey the restaurant for dark souls and shady side-eyes. Someone was hell-bent on kidnapping me, and Loring had goons I've never met. Ranlyn couldn't follow me everywhere, not into the bathroom, though I couldn't see him so maybe—

"*No windows.*" I heard Ranlyn say in my mind. "*Though a female counterpart will follow if needed.*"

All right then. He was around.

I had no idea who his female counterpart was or where she was, but chances were she was playing the masterful blending in game, too. I stopped looking for them when Caine took a sip of his drink and saw the guarded look in his eyes. He thought I was bored and looking to the crowd for a better conversationalist.

"Perfect, it's still here." Caine dug into their house bread with some type of oil and balsamic dipping sauce with child-like clumsiness, excited for something left unchanged from his time asleep.

This refocused me on him and away from the potential dangers.

I asked Caine thoughtful questions and kept eye contact to prove interest. Through the shared bruschetta appetizer and flatbread Caine craved, we continued easy conversation, safe in our isolated booth.

Unfortunately, not isolated enough.

Caine became animated about a hilarious childhood event involving his brother and a squirrel, when his eyes flickered over my shoulder. Thinking some Tainted Magic was behind me, I followed his line of sight and saw a blonde woman standing in the hallway outside the bathrooms. No soul glow.

I looked back at Caine. The muscles of his jaw flexed, crossing his arms as he sat back in his chair, his grey eyes a hard gaze of a wolf as he chewed over his thoughts.

"Caine...?"

"Caine." The woman's voice was a mad combination of shocked, apologetic, and seductive. She came right over. "I never thought you'd wake up. I'm so sorry."

She bent to wrap her arms around him, but this set him off. "Don't touch me, Tracey."

"Who's Tracey?"

"His girlfriend from before the sleeping curse." I filled Ranlyn in.

Caine raised his hands to stop hers from touching him, she dropped her arms with a look of shock. He stood, forcing distance between them.

Tracey had a shadow of crocodile tears in her eyes without mustering the actual waterworks as she took a step toward him. They looked at each other, leaving me to sit uncomfortably on the sidelines. Her attempt to use her saddest puppy dog face to soften his rock-hard stare failed. Totally. Defeated, Tracey shifted her weight back on her four-inch heels and acknowledged my existence. All grief vanished from her blue eyes, her stare souring, filling with judgment.

"Who are you?"

Surprise at her audacity made my power surge to the surface of my skin. I fought the impulse to punch her pretty little freckled nose as the tingle built and begged me to follow through.

Instead, I reciprocated with the same smile she gave me and refused to engage in her game, pissing her off more and delighting me to a sick level of immaturity.

"Please leave." Caine was politer than I could have been.

Tracey popped her hips and planted manicured hands on them, looking down her nose at me before back at Caine. "You've been awake for, like, a day and already you're with some hussy? Slimy, Caine, even for you."

Unaware of the people I dealt with at work, this pixie bitch with perfect lips was nothing in comparison.

"You have bigger issues at hand, Seer. Control yourself. Her display is garnering too much attention."

Ranlyn was right, but Tracey's comment opened up questions about the person Caine was before the accident. Besides, who uses the word "hussy" anyway?

Caine leaned in and said, "How long did you wait before you became someone else's *hussy,* Tracey? A month?" Her tight expression fell, her blue eyes round and wounded, a layer of manipulation she pulled up. I was so proud it wasn't working on him. "We were having fun, but it shows how wrong I was about you."

"Caine, I...I...." Tracey stammered.

A flicker of true shame flashed in Caine's ex's eyes, and my fury morphed into dread. This was a train wreck. Tracey was a stranger to me, and the chick had earned every moment of this, but I kept praying she would leave or return to her table. Anything to lessen the embarrassment, if only my own. My power remained at the surface as anxiousness took over.

Caine remained merciless. "There's nothing you can say to me to make what you did any better, and even if you could, I don't care enough to listen."

Tracey's expression reverted to her vengeful state like she had ripped off the mask. A flash of something else changed within her as silver began to ring her blue eyes.

Silver?

"Sophie!" Ranlyn screamed out loud. He appeared out of nowhere and lunged forward at the same time as Tracey grabbed a knife and thrust it at Caine.

I tried to shove Tracey away. I wasn't fast enough. Her body flew to the ground before my hands touched her and before Ranlyn reached her. Was it him? Was that me? Whose power had done that shit?

Caine sucked in a shocked breath as Tracey attacked. He looked from Tracey to Ranlyn, who had grabbed my arm.

Tracey jumped from her sprawl on the ground and growled as she dipped into a defensive stance.

"What's going on?" Caine demanded.

"We need to go," Ranlyn snapped.

The room sparked with soul glows, one dark enough for me to dig my heels in and pull away from Ranlyn who was dragging me in their direction.

Heeding my sudden reaction, Ranlyn grabbed Caine and shoved both of us behind him.

"Hey!" Caine shouted at Ranlyn when I toppled sideways, having to grab Caine's sleeve. "I don't know what's wrong with her, but Tracey—"

"Shut up and look." I pointed at the room.

People ate and laughed without any concern for the crazy, growling, silver-eyed blonde woman. No one noticed the people who stood next to their tables, blocking our way, and surrounding us with murderous intent.

"They can't see them," I explained to Caine, who was staring in shock at the scene before us. "You know that magic stuff that woke you up?" He nodded numbly, still looking around him. "Yeah, well, it's a bit more dangerous than I let on. You're one of us, meaning me and Ranlyn, and Ranlyn is the only one on our side right now."

"Not the only one," Ranlyn stated with cold confidence. Empty chairs and barstools lit up with white soul glows. Magic's sat, braced to pounce on their dark-souled targets now winding around oblivious restaurant patrons.

I didn't want to see what came next, didn't want this to be Caine's official introduction into this world, so I grabbed Caine's sleeve and went to race down the hallway to the back exit. A Tainted Magic wearing an opportunistic smile blocked our way out and geared up for an attack. It was too late for me to back pedal or shove us into one of the bathrooms behind us.

The back door blew open, and the Tainted Magic crumbled to his knees with a shriek of pain. The bolt of burning magic meant for us hit the ceiling instead and rained down charred pieces of wood and insulation. When I looked up again, the figure standing fifteen feet away shocked me.

"Donovan." I nearly sobbed his name in relief.

He looked up from the body on the ground in front of him, his brows pinched together, as stunned as I was to see him there.

Aunt Lacey came in behind Donovan and did little more than wave her hand and the door fixed back on his hinges and closed. Loud banging from the other side said it wasn't moving. Then she did something to the man on the floor. He wasn't getting up. I didn't ask why, but I didn't think he was dead as his dark soul glow still swirled around him.

"I don't have the skills for this," I told Aunt Lacey. "What do we do?"

She looked at Donovan instead and said, "Stay vigilant." She walked past me into the room adding her brand of magic to the fight by raising her hands. Darkness cloaked the room. No screams rang out, so I assumed the Blind were still literally blind, enjoying their meals like people weren't dropping blood and screaming war cries inches from their appetizer salads.

Soul glows and blasts of magic were my only source of light so I knew it was worse for Caine who couldn't see what I could. I soon envied him as the lights became so intense I had to close my eyes.

"Move!" Donovan yelled, followed by protests from Caine. I didn't know what was happening until Donovan's strong grip circled my arm and my legs were hitting the bench of the booth. He pushed me into the booth itself, Caine into the opposite side, and then stood next to my side so no one could get to me.

I squinted around Donovan the best I could to get a sense of the room. Bodies flew, Magics screamed, Tracey lay on the ground—her fate unknown. I recognized the Elders in the mix. Those with dark souls didn't care and fought with mad abandon.

"Don't look!" Donovan turned to me and panted.

Before I could respond, he dove into the strobing magic light of the room. I lost sight of his green soul, my scream lost in the din of violence.

Someone dragged me from my hiding spot. I tried to wrap my feet around the table leg and lost my shoes. The room went black. My eyes were open, nothing over my head, but I couldn't see. Cold tile scraped my now bare feet when someone threw me to the ground and the din of fighting sounded further away.

Kitchen? Judging by the strong scent of food, it was my best guess.

I scrambled to my feet, refusing to lay there and die. My open eyes struggled to see something, anything, but still I saw nothing. With my arms out around me, I felt for anything I could grab. If this was a kitchen, there had to be something I could use to defend myself. A knife wouldn't be much use against Tainted Magics, but the black-souled bastards were still human and could bleed with the best of them, that is if I could find a knife in this messy darkness.

Power buzzed in my bones, but I still had no clue what to do with it. Growing weeds wasn't going to save me right now and that was the only power I knew.

A hard, flat surface grazed my spread fingers. Happy it wasn't a sizzling stove I was shoving my hands at, I found something heavy and metal to grab onto. My attacker's gaze landed on my back with a heavy satisfaction at seeing their helpless prey, the sense of being watched unmistakable.

I gave them what they wanted by leaning into the countertop and slumped my shoulders in feigned defeat.

My attacker stalked across the kitchen. Whoever they were, he or she had no clue how used to this sensation I was. I endured it for months while stuck in Caine's sleeping curse before I knew who he was, and all I had to work with was darkness and fear.

When a hand grabbed my shoulder, I gripped my weapon and spun, accelerated by my power. My strike landed with a dull thud, and the restaurant kitchen sparkled into view as my attacker bent over grabbing his head.

I looked at the waffle iron in my hands and then back at my enemy as he stood, and I watched the gash bleeding onto his shoulder magically heal.

"Loring."

A smile stretched across his face, showing the same deep creases around his mouth and eyes I had seen when he killed a Covener on Aunt Lacey's doorstep in a show of arrogant power.

He shoved me onto the countertop without touching me, his power doing all the heavy lifting. Three feet away was a Blind cook chopping sweet peppers, oblivious to my struggle trapped in Loring's telekinetic hold. I tried to kick him, my legs doing nothing more than flail at empty air as he forced me backward in a painful arch over the counter.

Loring pinned me, again without touching me, stopping me from moving and stepped between my knees. Unable to close them, he made himself comfortable and hinged his short-statured body to lay over mine.

"Fuck you," I spat, at least able to speak. He thought this was funny and that pompous smile resurfaced.

Leaning closer to smell my neck, I thought I might hurl. I hoped I would. Right into his fucking face.

"So much trouble," he said with a heavy gravel voice as his dark soul pressed in around me.

I couldn't take it.

I looked at the Blind man chopping peppers and willed something to happen. Anything. My power buzzed until my head pounded with my pulse. My right hand was a few inches from the prep cook's knife. I prayed for it to cooperate.

Loring's breath scorched a line from my collarbone to my ear, and I felt his tongue graze my lobe. Resisting the urge to break down into tears while he dragged out whatever he planned to do, I kept my sights focused on that knife.

Changing tactics, I pulled my power from that buzzing uncontrolled extra layer doing fuck-all for me into my right hand and directed it out to the cook's arm. The man's chopping stopped as Loring's teeth clamped down on my lobe, piercing the skin, causing me to scream.

The surge of pain gave me what I needed.

The prep cook's face pinched in confusion and then shock as his knife-wielding hand raised to the side and thrust down into Loring's back. My enemy roared. The prep cook scrambled backwards into another cook at the stove, knocking the frying pan out of his co-worker's hand. Yelling echoed off the steel surroundings, but I was too focused on Loring.

He staggered and wheezed, his expression twisted. Free of whatever spell had me pinned, I braced the countertop and booted the black-souled sonofabitch in the chest, sending him backwards into stainless steel fridges. Loring's knees buckled and he crumbled to the ground, the knife shoved deeper into his back.

I watched his dark soul spill out from his body and slither along the ground like toxic fog before dissipating.

"Holy shit, you killed him," the cook said.

"I didn't...." I couldn't finish.

Then the prep cook backed up behind his co-worker, both pointing and cursing at the body on the ground with renewed fear.

Now, I saw what they did. Loring's dark hair disappeared, leaving a lighter brush cut in its wake. His face changed to that of a much younger man with tanned skinned wearing jeans and a leather jacket. The opposite of Loring's tailored suit.

Not Loring. Another lackey using tricks I was too much of a Seedling to anticipate.

"Sophie?"

Donovan stood at the entrance of the galley kitchen, his face and hands bloodied, his expression lost in sadness at the sight of me. Without looking away, he reached up for something on the wall and fire alarms went off, the sprinklers turning on.

The cooks ran, as did the customers. Screams from more than Magics. The patrons were no longer covered by whatever spell kept them Blind.

As water soaked me through, Donovan bypassed the body on the floor and wrapped his arms around me. I stayed there a moment, drinking in his calm amid chaos.

When he pulled away, streaks of blood and water ran down his face from his hair. Without thinking, I touched his cheek and his eyes fluttered shut. I pulled away with silent apology, forgiven with a set of dimples. Unfortunately, the smile never made it to his eyes.

Movement caught my attention at the entrance again, Ranlyn and Caine, both in a terrible state and drenched. A flicker of question lit within Caine's eyes as he saw Donovan and registered our closeness. Before this added any further drama to our night, I followed them out of the restaurant and met out front with the rest of the patrons. Most seemed panicked but not as much as I assumed they would be.

I wrapped my arms around myself, happy for the summer heat.

"Are you okay?" Caine stopped and asked me.

I nodded, unable to find my words in the moment, not even to ask the same of him.

When I realized this was more than speechlessness, I lifted a finger to hold him off and walked away back towards the building. He called my name, and I raised a hand without looking back, hoping he wouldn't follow me.

Beside the building, in the darkness next to a dumpster that smelled of rotting potatoes, I vomited the meal Caine and I had shared, the face of the man I killed before my eyes.

4

ASSUMPTIONS ARE EASY

I hadn't intended on throwing Caine into the deep end with the whole magic subject. He knew it existed, but seeing the danger it posed and to find out he was one of them? That needed more finesse, and instead he had it shoved in his face.

Ranlyn and Donovan fought over who would bring me home, until Aunt Lacey stepped in and Ranlyn ushered me to his car. I blanked out somewhere in between the restaurant and home, not realizing Caine wasn't with us until Ranlyn parked in my apartment's lot. I was too overwhelmed by the face of the dead guy from the kitchen and how easily I was taken over to track where I was or who I was with.

Ranlyn explained another Magic brought Caine home and I felt like a dickhole for not talking to him before he left. Or did I? I couldn't remember, but it had to be a record-breaking worst end to a date.

I lay in bed replaying the night, fighting with myself over small details including if Tracey's presence was mere coincidence or a set up like the ambush itself until I finally passed out.

————

In the twenty-four hours after the restaurant debacle, I didn't go out and test Ranlyn's bodyguard skills unless necessary. Bosco's walks were short and tense and I drained the day's hours by focusing on school assignments until Caine came over with a pizza in hand.

"You don't scare easy," I said, surprised to see him.

He smiled. "Nope. Maybe we can finish a meal without someone dying and you can explain a few things before the coven meeting."

"Magic things?"

"Magic things."

We sat on my old couch with plates on our laps as I decided to start with what went down at the restaurant and then about his sleeping curse.

Caine was still processing the fact he wasn't asleep for almost four years by accident when a knock on my door made me jump with a quick inhale that lodged the pizza crust in my mouth in my windpipe. While I coughed it up, Caine answered my door.

"You two ready to go?" Kim asked, all big smiles and bubbly anticipation. Apparently, she was raring to get to the coven meeting.

"Yo, Jeeves!" I called out with half-chewed food in my cheek. "You ready to go?"

Ranlyn dropped his cloaking spell and popped up next to Kim outside my door, scaring the shit out of her.

"Jeeves?" he questioned.

"Yeah." I swallowed. "You're either the chauffeur or the stalker tailing us. Bodyguard's choice."

Kim called "Shotgun" before I could. The relief in Ranlyn's shoulders was a tad insulting.

Riding his patience like a mechanical bull, he masked his annoyance and took the choice I knew he would.

————

Caine and I stood in Aunt Lacey's foyer as Ranlyn and Kim left us to head to the basement, she putting Bosco out back before heading down. I didn't want to leave him at home alone and Aunt Lacey's was the safest place. Since Caine was a new face to the Coveners, they would be reminded of the rules for when guests are present. He was quiet and apprehensive as we waited.

"At least you're not alone like I was." I elbowed him and gained a genuine smile before he looked back at the masks hanging on the wall. I remembered from my first visit to the mansion. Now that I knew Aunt Lacey's history, I knew they weren't replicas and realized Caine still knew nothing about my Coven Leader he would soon meet.

Kim returned to escort us downstairs. Caine walked in front of me with ten times the confidence I had my first time. The Coveners were sitting in a circle, eyes sparkling with intrigue, everyone appearing ultra-exuberant tonight.

Avoiding eye contact with Donovan was difficult, especially when he was drilling a hole straight through the room's oxygen in my direction. My sunglasses shielded me from the intense soul glows of Aunt Lacey and the others, but I had no escape from Donovan's burning stare.

"Welcome to my home, Caine," Aunt Lacey said as we took a seat in the circle. "Merry meet from myself and those within my Sect, who all, in their own way, were responsible for your awakening."

Before he could respond, the Coveners introduced themselves using their birth names instead of Coven names since Caine was a guest. When it came time, Donovan said his name while staring at me instead of Caine, leaning back onto his hands, a cocky smirk in place.

Civility was hanging on by its fingernails.

Aunt Lacey held off the Coveners' questions as she invited Kim, Caine, and myself to the back table where I had my first tea leaf reading. I knew what was coming, but let Caine experience it as I had, grinning when he turned down the tea Aunt Lacey offered. Nervous shifting followed the explanation before he accepted the teacup, a tiny piece of porcelain in his large hand.

Kim prepared to transcribe the reading. I was familiar with this as she had written down my reading, too, but why the hell was I here? Who knew what Aunt Lacey might say? I didn't need to know the gritty details.

He must have sensed this because he looked over, smiled, and grasped my hands clasped in my lap. This was the only reason I stayed.

Before Aunt Lacey began, Caine said his piece. "First, I wanted to thank you for going to such lengths to help me. I don't know if you realize what you saved me from, but I appreciate it."

Details of the Awakening Ritual used to wake him up from his sleeping curse weren't covered again since he was there, though now I was thinking I should have told him the Coveners got a full dose of the world he was stuck in through a spell Elder Roon fixed.

"*Details, Sophie. Details,*" I heard Ranlyn's voice in my head. With my back to the room, I couldn't see him, but I understood his point. In Caine's position, I would insist on every detail. Caine should get the same.

Aunt Lacey smiled at Caine and held his hand on the tabletop. The dim lighting shone off the eccentric jewelry around her wrist and fingers. "Sophie's nightmares introduced us to your plight. Leaving you imprisoned wasn't an option for any within this room. While I accept your thanks, I feel it is I who will thank you one day." She patted Caine's hand and said no more of it.

As Aunt Lacey's ancient eyes searched the tea granules for a long time. Kim and I exchanged a look of apprehension.

"Is something wrong?" Caine masked his nervousness with a smile.

Aunt Lacey replaced the cup onto its saucer and folded her hands on the table. "Not wrong, nor right. Not yet."

"Meaning?" Caine urged her to continue.

"Your future and the actions which pave your path are wrapped in a choice beyond me to read."

"Beyond you?" I asked.

Caine squeezed my hand tighter. "Choice? What choice?"

"I cannot tell. In my experience, a wrong choice brings consequences, some foreseen, others ignored." The stare she fixed on Caine when she said "ignored" shot steel into my every muscle. "With restored life beyond your sleeping curse, uncertainty will rule as you war with what came before and what lies ahead. This war blinds you to important truths.

"To be frank, Caine, I see you faced with decisions. I cannot see how they arise, who they involve, when they occur, and most important, how you intend to handle them. If reckless, you will fall to negative practices, and I'm afraid, would have been better off left in your sleeping curse. One to which you *will* be returned to if necessary."

Well, Jesus on a tortilla. I waited for the seriousness to bleed from her features and be replaced by the grandmotherly wisdom, but it didn't. Her threat was real. I was floored.

"I know the coma was a sleeping curse." Caine's voice was a hint above a whisper. "Someone did this to me."

"No, Caine. You were born a Magic to a bloodline of Magics as most are. They slipped you into the sleeping curse and held you under, but power came to you as a babe. You have yet to seek answers as to where the power within you stems or what happened to you and your brother. You know what Sophie sees of your soul."

Caine remained quiet.

"You may choose to sidestep answers surrounding the sleeping curse and why someone would suspend you within the prison of the park when you knew nothing of our world, but therein lies the potential for negative consequences. Future decisions write their ending the moment you dip the quill. The choices made with clear intent leads to your future. As does the neglect to make choices. You cannot outrun what comes from within."

Aunt Lacey reached for Caine's hand again. This time he tensed. When she reached for mine next, I recoiled, relenting when Aunt

Lacey's expression shifted. Her mask of warning thinned until it exposed a hint of fear evident in the crease of her brows. She may have been ancient, but she was still human, and something about all this was freaking her out.

"A path of awe and excitement lay ahead of the both of you. Honesty forces me to point out I also see pain and misfortune along your journey. Unable to see why or when any of this occurs, I fear my sight has failed to assist you. Hold strong together, trust your instincts, and you'll accomplish more than any foretelling I could serve you with."

Aunt Lacey's gift allowed her a keen sense of future, but this triggered my distaste for any future set in stone. In my opinion, this was impossible unless you considered freewill a farce. For someone who could read my thoughts, Aunt Lacey didn't comment on my less than enthusiastic opinions. When I glanced at Caine and saw his delighted expression, my inner monologue soured like sun-spoiled cheese. I didn't understand why until I realized he thought this would erase my indecisiveness about our relationship. As if I would listen to her telling us to stick together and forget my personal reasons. If anything, it strengthened my resistance.

His smile and the grip of his hand around mine told me all I needed to know. He focused was on us and I was stuck on the fact Mrs. Matchmaker also threatened him.

"Caine, I would like to extend to you an invitation to be one among the Coven." Whoa, quick subject change. Aunt Lacey went on. "I understand this is beyond your natural element, but I see potential and wish to be a part of the discovery and strengthening of your talents. We may prevent those outcomes I fear. Do you accept my invitation?"

Caine looked at me. I offered him no expression to sway his decision. We never covered the question of how I would feel if he became a member, though I knew it was coming. He met the Elders outside of the restaurant, knows where Aunt Lacey lives, and has now met the Coveners. That's not knowledge you walk away from.

I didn't want our relationship, or lack of one, to play a factor. Either he wanted aboard this leaking life raft, or he was good to swim these waters alone.

His thumb caressed the back of my hand. "I'd love to be a part of the Coven."

All right. Leaking life raft it was.

A shiver rocked his body and tightened his grip on my hand. I saw this and looked to Kim and Aunt Lacey who tried to hide her smile at his reaction. I remembered it happening to me as well. Add this to the list of things Aunt Lacey was keeping to herself. Caine thanked Aunt Lacey without questioning the shiver. My thoughts were a tangled mass that stole my focus from the table and those around it.

I moved to stand, needing to get away. My flight-or-flight response activated. Half-way to my feet, Caine tugged on my hand he still held, and I stopped fleeing.

His eyes searched mine with a plea, while mine must have reflected consternation or something far bitchier. "This isn't worth doing without you," he said to me.

"The added pressure isn't helping."

"You need to be okay with this."

"No, I don't. Your choices, your consequences, remember?" I was too close to this, too clouded by my own baggage for an appropriate response. Using Aunt Lacey's words was the best I could do. Somehow, it helped, because he smiled and looked content with his decision.

Regardless of some connection or whatever hokey shit Aunt Lacey was peddling, I reminded myself I agreed to be in the Coven. I told myself I would do everything to observe and learn. Now that it appeared I'd be a contributing member, you would think this would have made me happy. Tomorrow, it might have. Right then, Caine was joining the Coven, and that wasn't happy shit. Not really.

"We are lucky to have you, Caine." Aunt Lacey and Caine stood, and they shared a quick hug. When Aunt Lacey pulled away, she said, "Now, I meant it when I said not making a choice was still a choice. For the both of you." She speared me with a look. "Looking into the past may be the ticket to your future."

"I'd only have my mother to ask, and I can't," Caine said. "She doesn't know anything."

Aunt Lacey crossed her arms, pulling her beaded shawl tighter around her. "No question gone unasked can be answered, correct? Assumptions are easy. As you can tell from your experience within the sleeping curse and the restaurant, this way of life is anything but easy. The difficulties and complexities will grow as each day passes. Anything to ease your journey is worth pursuing. You too, Sophie."

The only person I could think of was my grandmother.

"The only one?" Aunt Lacey questioned, this time pulling the thought from my head.

Olive.

Her brow raised. An answer, yet not quite. She smiled, gave a gentle squeeze to Caine's arm, and moved to the side of the room to speak with Ranlyn.

Caine moved toward me and panic rose, my throat clenching in anticipation of how I might respond to whatever he wanted to say. Probably something too serious right now. I was full of serious and needed a moment.

"Well, Caine," Kim said with renewed excitement after being silent during the whole exchange as she took notes. "Now that you're a new member and not a guest, let's make your first meeting experience whole by getting in some readings. The Coveners need to polish their skills on someone they don't know every little thing about already."

My voice roared back to life. "Yes, let's do that." Anything to get us moving from the table.

We stayed away from the palm reading like it came with a side of the plague. Not that Caine was aware of this, and I was thankful Kim didn't press to venture to Donovan's spot on the floor. Avoidance techniques? Hell yeah! And I didn't feel a ball hair bad about it.

They would meet one day, more than in passing, and things would unfold, but not tonight. I couldn't deal tonight.

The side-eyed glares from Donovan were more than enough, which of course meant I was keeping tabs on him too. Anger simmered behind his locked down expression. I saw betrayal and anger flash along the surface of his dark eyes. He had made his feelings for me clear, and here I was, parading Caine to the Coveners like a newborn fresh from the hospital. I'd be pissed too.

Everyone else was happy to hear Caine was joining the Coven and snuck in a question or two about the park. Caine answered, even the far-too-personal questions. I must admit that hearing he never ate, drank, or slept while inside the park was interesting. Made perfect sense since sleeping curses were a form of torture. I never thought the day-to-day elements of human upkeep he had missed out on could be a nightmare in itself.

Near the end of the night, Aunt Lacey called for the attention of the room. "There's been questions of the Lughnasadh celebrations at Diluculo and if they will take place this year in light of recent security concerns—"

"No one can get inside Diluculo." A muscle-head named Blake cut off Aunt Lacey. He sounded confident about wherever this place was. Others agreed. I had no idea what the celebration was about or where it was held as no one had mentioned it before, but Donovan's smirk called out their naiveté.

Aunt Lacey's half-hearted smile led me to believe Donovan might be right. "Our best are ensuring Diluculo earns such trust, so at this point, the celebration will commence as planned." Blake and his towering friend Jared celebrated with an exuberant high five. They struck me as the chest-bumping type, so I guessed this display was subdued for them.

Aunt Lacey went on. "Ensure you clear the August first weekend for the occasion. I expect to see all your faces around the fire. Plan well, those of you with Blind spouses or families, since communication will be impossible. And until then, remain vigilant. Safeguard yourselves. Never leave yourself open for attack or subversion. If you suspect or see anything, contact me day or night and expect assistance."

I didn't require the warning, but I realized I was lucky to have the security I did. Did any of the others? If not, it didn't seem fair.

"If Loring showed interest in anyone of them, they would." Ranlyn popped up at my side.

"Don't do that. And stay out of my head. If I had a question for you, I'd ask it."

"You had a question, I answered it. Ready to go?"

"Maybe I'll lend you out to those two," I thought and looked over at Blake and Jared who made good on my chest-bumping assumptions.

The expression Ranlyn returned was enough of a response. "See? Could be worse. Let's go, Jeeves."

The eye roll was priceless.

———

All the way home, Caine was tense and chewing on his thumbnail while focused out the window. Kim and Ranlyn were discussing something about the properties of hyssop. Not that it wasn't riveting conversation, but I was stuck in observation mode, wondering what Caine was thinking.

Back at the building, I harnessed Bosco and Caine and I took him for a walk. He plodded across the street, too tired from all the attention at Aunt Lacey's to pull on the leash.

"What is it, Caine? Ranlyn can pretty well hear whatever we're talking about, but I doubt he gives a shit."

"I really don't," he confirmed. *"I'll stay out of it. Don't go far."*

This time, I knew Caine heard Ranlyn telepathically as well, evident by Caine's darting glance towards the Magic across the street sitting on the plastic bench out front of the building. I didn't know how my bodyguard pulled it off, but hoped I could figure out the whole telepathy thing one day.

Caine stuck his hands in the pockets of his cargo shorts. I kept my attention on Bosco as we walked, but I was sweating over what he might be gearing up to say.

"What's with you and Donovan?" he asked first. "I realize it's none of my business, but I get the sense there's a lot I don't know, and I can't figure it out. Is he your ex?"

Maybe I wanted to test him, to see if Caine would back away once he knew. I don't know, but I told him the truth about Donovan and I and our blissful marriage in a past life.

"How's that possible?" Caine asked once I finished. "You're saying that reincarnation is real?"

"I'm not saying anything. I'm just telling you what Donovan told me."

"Then how do you know he's telling the truth?" I stopped and gave him a look. "Aunt Lacey," he said after a moment, finally understanding.

Instead of pressuring Bosco to get things over with, I let him explore the trees across the street within Ranlyn's view while Caine processed this new information.

"I don't care," he said.

I laughed, the sound punchy in the quiet and without humor. "No, eh?"

"Not if you don't."

"I never said either way."

"No, you didn't, but I have a feeling you've had the opportunity to be in a relationship with him again and you're not."

He was right on that one.

"Hold up." He touched my arm and I stopped as Bosco sniffed the grass. I didn't want to look up at him, but I forced myself to because Caine earned my full attention, even if I wanted to cower away. "I realize this might sound ridiculous to you, maybe even inappropriate given the circumstances." He glanced back at Ranlyn. "But

I know there's more to us than a dream and that park. No one can tell me different. No one. If what you say about you and Donovan is true and even possible, then he'll be around when you want. In the Coven, in your life, your memories—"

"His memories, not mine."

"Okay, his memories. Regardless there's history. I'm not looking for history, I'm looking for a future. Up until recently I thought that park was all I had to look forward to. Then you pop up, and all this Magic stuff is...."

"I know what you mean." He looked down at me with his wolf-grey eyes, and I added. "About the spontaneity of life. The agenda you planned means nothing, not when stuff like curses and evil fuckers come into play." He gave a small laugh. "Get to the point before I explode. I don't need a speech; I need to know what's on your brain before I get Ranlyn to search it for me."

"Okay," he laughed. "Sorry, my point is that I want you to give *us* a try before you explore whatever it is you and Donovan used to have. Like I said, there's a past there I can't compete with, but let me try and show you what a future might look like with me instead."

"Donovan isn't the reason I'm not in a relationship right now."

He blinked. "All right."

I smoothed my hair behind my ear, wishing I had shut my mouth a few seconds sooner. "I can't get into all that now, but it has nothing to do with Donovan."

"Does it mean you're unwilling to try?"

Bosco started kicking at the grass after peeing on a tree, and I knew this conversation needed to end.

"No, I didn't say that. I-I want to. I actually do." The truth of this surprised me. "But I have a feeling this isn't going to end well and you're going to get annoyed with...me...with everything—"

"Annoyed?"

I let out a heavy breath.

"Fine, I get it," Caine said. "You've got baggage that weighs more than you're equipped for."

"For starters," I muttered.

"Well, I spent years in a sleeping curse set by God knows who. I'm unemployed, homeless, and have no big life plans to make you feel an ounce better, which means I've got baggage too. I'd like a chance for us to figure this out with each other without outside distractions."

"Distractions? You mean ones with dimples?"

He smiled. "Yes, those ones."

I nodded, trying for a more playful side since things got too serious. While I realized this was classic avoidance mixed with my commitment issues, I surprised myself by saying, "Okay."

His disbelief was proof in his raised eyebrows.

"Nah, I changed my mind," I said to mess with him, then immediately smiled and shook my head to let him know it was a joke. "I can promise I'm not looking to complicate my life any further, even if *you* count as a complication, but I won't add to the fucked up left-turn my life has taken by dating both you and Donovan."

He nodded.

"And I won't promise this will work out," I added. "It's been a while for me, and I'm shit at the dating game. I can be blunt and flighty, and I might freak out and end the whole thing, but I'll do my best to not be a total dickhole."

A white-toothed grin broke through his hesitation, and he surprised me by wrapping me up in a big bear hug and picking me up off the ground. I squealed and laughed.

"The giggle was worth the possibility of you booting me in the balls," he said after he put me back down.

"Yeah, well, you might regret this decision once you get to know me."

"Not likely. A bigger issue will be the day Donovan gets sick of cross-room glowers and figures out I'm not going anywhere."

"Ugh," I grunted as we made our way back across the street towards the building.

How do I show up to the next coven meeting with Caine

knowing my ex from a past life is holding onto a future with us reuniting? One I haven't ruled out?

"*Try being a dickhole,*" I heard Ranlyn's voice as he stood up from the bench at our approach. "*Seems to work for you.*"

"*Atomic wedgie, Jeeves. Atomic.*"

5

NO PUNCH LINE

The phone rang. My least favorite way to wake up. I expected it to be Caine. He was an early riser and had fallen into a routine of calling me in the mornings since we solidified our relationship. Which was fine, unless I had worked late the night before.

"If you ever plan on getting me naked, you gotta drop the early calls, Caine."

Pause. "Who's Caine and why is he trying to see my daughter naked?"

Oops. "Hey mom."

"Sophie, wanna answer the question?"

"Nope."

Loud sigh into the phone. "Fine. Make sure he's worth it and use a condom."

"Thanks, mom."

"You're welcome, now get dressed. It's been many years since your Grandma Lizzie has seen you naked. You'll make the woman jealous."

"Grandma Lizzie?"

"Yes. You're helping me with family reunion stuff today, remember?"

"No."

"Well, you are. Serena and I will be there soon."

"You didn't con Adam into this?"

"He has band practice."

"My ass."

"Sophie Olivia," she chastised.

"Fine. See you soon."

"Love you," she was saying as I hung up.

While I was getting dressed, the phone rang. This time it was Caine.

"Knew you were trying to see me naked," I joked as I searched for something to wear.

"What?"

"Nothing. What's up?"

"Know anyone selling their house?"

"Pfft. You're implying I know people who own their own houses."

The line went silent.

"Caine?"

"My mom's having trouble adjusting. Not the change in routine, but changes in me. Of course, she's ecstatic to see me upright, but since I can't tell her about the sleeping curse, she doesn't understand. She thinks I'm being an asshole, but doing everything possible to make me feel like an ungrateful son."

"Did you think maybe you're being one?" My abrasiveness was intentional. He had to realize it could be him.

"I thought so at first, but she's been cruel. Granted, I'm not the best son. I know she sat next to me while I was under, stopped speaking to friends, put her life on hold, but all she's doing is making me feel like I owe her. She's my mother and she actually said Cole would have treated her better."

"Ouch. I'm sorry."

"You didn't do anything wrong, but thanks. You'd think she'd worry about my survivor's guilt, not making me feel worse."

"You know the accident wasn't your fault, Caine."

"I know, and maybe she's dealing with everything now, like she's also been in limbo the last few years, but I've suffered enough. She doesn't know what that means, but still."

"She misses Cole. You woke up like nothing happened and continued living your life. Maybe a case of the empty nest syndrome, amplified since one son will never return."

"Yeah, maybe." He didn't elaborate further, and I dropped the subject, hoping he and Joyce would find a way to bypass the hostility.

"Any chance you have nothing to do today? I have to find somewhere else to live and don't want to figure that out while I'm under my mother's roof."

"Sorry, I'm headed to my grandmother's. I'd rather shave my head than be there all day. I'll be at the bar tonight too, but I have a few hours between. Any chance you have friends?"

He laughed. "Yes, I have friends. You met the guys at the hospital. They would take me in a heartbeat, but I can't. I can't answer their questions. I can't hit the bars and live it up. And with all the magic stuff, I don't think I can deal with lying to them while living on their couch. Seems disrespectful. Plus, I don't want to put them in danger."

"Isn't your mother in danger too?"

"Nah, Ranlyn put someone on the house, but I can't have a bodyguard everywhere I go."

"What? You don't love having a stalker?"

"Not by the sasquatch Ranlyn's got watching me. I think he resents the fact I'm stealing his free time. Plus, I'm pretty sure he can pop my skull like a grape and smiling is something he charges extra for. I asked." He breathed heavy into the phone. "It's fine. Hotels are always available, and I'll enjoy the room service and pool access."

"Except that it's as dangerous for you and the other hotel guests. Too many places to take you down. I think my apartment is giving

Ranlyn cluster headaches. Why don't you stay here? You can keep Bosco company while I'm at work."

"You're kidding."

"I'd like to think I'm wittier than that."

"Sophie."

"What?"

"You've kept me at arm's length. I'm sure for good reason. We've only known each other a short time and you're upping the relation-ship stakes pretty high with that invitation. Unless it's not a big deal to you, which I would think it would be."

"Well, yeah, I guess it's a big deal."

"You guess?"

"I'm not asking you to tattoo my name on your neck."

"Right. Because neck tattoos are a sign of true commitment."

I exhaled in frustration, happy he wasn't in front of me to see me cringe at the word "commitment". "It's a temporary couch to sleep on since you have no clue how dangerous things are right now."

"Not just a couch. I'll be alone in your place...for hours."

"I'm sure you'll find something to do. Plus, I'll need a dog-sitter."

He laughed a little and the tension relief I sought let go a notch.

"He likes you and I hate leaving him. Win-win."

"Right."

"And if you rummage through my underwear drawer or sell Bosco to a puppy mill, my tips will go towards paying Aunt Lacey to deal with you."

"Stellar threat," he said with some levity in his tone.

After a goodbye, my hand shook as I hung up. What was wrong with me? As soon as I let go and travelled beyond my comfort zone, an immediate foreboding hit me. It was as if this giant new step paved the way for a shitstorm to balance everything out. My twisted thinking landed me back into the web of skepticism about Caine and I as a successful couple since the nightmares began. My shaking hands settled. Caution always kept me level and I wouldn't let the decision to host Caine on my couch knock me off course of taking control of my life.

Caine arrived soon after, duffle bag over his shoulder, rolled up sleeping bag and pillow under his arm, and inextinguishable excitement all over him.

"I won't be here long," he said above Bosco's wailing when I opened my door.

"Oh, I know you won't," I responded, but smiled to soften the harshness.

A knock at the door accented the end of the conversation. Assuming it was Ranlyn, who I failed to make aware of our new arrangement, I found Serena instead.

Fuckstains. "Hey cuz, how'd you get in the building?"

"Slid in behind someone. I wanted to borrow your purple clutch for..." Her question floundered as she eyed Caine standing with his duffle and sleeping bag.

With no way out, I made introductions. They exchanged pleasantries as I ran to retrieve the clutch.

Before leaving I handed Caine my keys. "I'll be back before work, contact numbers are on the fridge, call if you need, and...yeah...I'll see you later."

"Nice to meet you Serena," he said with a wave.

"You too," she returned with a laugh.

I pushed Serena out the door. I felt awkward leaving Caine in my apartment but reminded myself it was my idea and was happy not to hear Bosco wailing as I left.

"What's he like?" Mom pried Serena for details once in the car.

I sat annoyed in the passenger seat. "You can ask me, mom. I'm right here."

Serena leaned in from the back seat and gushed about Caine's height, long hair, and weird eyes.

"Nice going," Mom mocked in a sorority girl tone.

The forty-five-minute car ride consisted of unrelenting questions about Caine. I couldn't answer many of them because I didn't know.

After my mom asked again about how we got together and why now and not before.

"He was in a coma for almost four years," I blurted in frustration.

The car fell silent. When it was clear no punch line was imminent, the questions started over and grew more serious in nature.

I explained the accident and followed up with a white lie by saying we met up in the park as I was walking Bosco. Then spent another fifteen minutes fielding questions about whether he was appealing to my compassion with a sob story. I challenged them to check out the article I found and added I'd seen him in the hospital without adding when or why I never told anybody.

When we arrived at my grandmother's converted old barn, they knew everything I could tell them about since my mother was still Blind. Stepping foot out of the car pulled me back to the reality I would soon be in the presence of a woman who detested me.

My chest tightened.

The last thing I wanted was to spend the day around someone who hated me. It would be the first time since she told me I was humping the Devil all the way to eternal hellfire by using my powers. Ones she must have had, as well, of all the ironies. She had to be a Soul Seer or she wouldn't have known I had released my powers. Every memory about that woman from the moment after that visit was coloured with disgust. The family reunion couldn't happen and be over soon enough.

Getting my hands into garden dirt was a good excuse to ignore the woman. Instead, Serena and I went straight to the backyard and got busy taking measurements for my mother and figuring out where the tables would be set up.

"What are we going to do?" Serena asked me after sketching a rough version of the backyard schematics.

"About what?"

She dropped her arms, the clipboard in her hand slapping against her leg.

"What?"

"You know what. About Grandma Lizzie, what do we do?"

I shrugged. "You wanna find a place to hide the body?"

Her face scrunched up.

"Oh, you didn't mean murder?"

"Avoiding her won't last. She'll come outside at some point. You might be able to stay away, but my mom and Hunter live here. And we still don't know enough about Olive. Gram put her own sister in a mental institution and no one knows anything about it. I bet Olive's like you. Why else would Gram get rid of her?"

"I get it, but what—"

"I can find out."

I jumped. "Fuck!"

"What?!" Serena yelled.

"Don't do that, I can't even see you."

Serena's blonde brows cinched together as she motioned to herself. "Um...."

"Not you." Fucking Ranlyn.

She put her arms out and turned around, seeing no one else. "Are you losing it? I was joking about you being like Olive."

"No, I—"

"You!" my grandmother's voice trilled across the backyard.

My head snapped her way and I gasped. Redness in her round cheeks looked more menacing by a soul glow I never expected to find.

She clutched a garden trowel, but paired with her anger as she stomped across the yard, it may as well have been a butcher knife. "Get out of my yard!"

"Sophie?" Serena started.

"She's coming at me, not you," Ranlyn said as my grandmother's fury speared at the empty space where I presumed Ranlyn stood.

"Ranlyn," I murmured, "how can she see you?"

"See who?" Serena screeched.

"Interesting," was all he answered. I didn't have time to answer my cousin.

"Who did you bring onto my property?" My grandmother was

inches from me, her eyes wide with rage as she looked from myself to over my right shoulder.

"Does it matter? You can tell he's not Tainted. His pink, frilly glow is a little weird, but it's not nice to make him self-conscious about it."

"This is no joke, girl." She didn't bother looking at me. "Whoever you are, you leave before I make you."

Ranlyn popped into view, scaring the shit out of Serena. "How do you plan on that, Elizabeth?" He questioned my grandmother with her real name, one I never gave him, somehow retaining a respectful tone. "You no longer practice. You have fallen into disuse, have turned your back on your essence. A sickly fate you've sentenced your soul to as evident in what I see in Sophie's thoughts as she wilts at the sight of your soul glow." He leaned a few inches towards her. "You no longer have the ability to mask your mind." My grandmother crossed her arms, her face screwed up with disgust. "Your fear is palpable, madam, but I don't pose a threat." He straightened. "You harm your kin far more than I ever could."

"Evil filth!" Grandmother seethed.

"Is that what you thought of Olive?"

A twitch of a smile hit my lips as my grandmother's face drained of all anger at the mention of Olive's name. Ranlyn may as well have slapped her. After a tense moment, she recovered, and her anger resurfaced with flared nostrils and gritted teeth.

"I have what I need," Ranlyn clipped before she could say anything. "I'll see myself out but will be close by." He looked at me. "We'll speak later."

My grandmother watched him as he sauntered across the backyard and left, waiting until he was out of sight before turning on me. A slow step in my direction coupled with her blatant disgust had me fighting the urge to slink away. I refused to absorb the shame she meant for me to accept. Hate had settled deep within the woman who told me she would always love me, always have her arms open for when I needed love. How easily promises of "always" adopted conditions.

"Chick...." my Aunt Karen called across the backyard as she came out of the house using her nickname for Serena. "Do you have the measuring tape?"

I lifted the tape to show my aunt I had it and would be there in a second, then looked back at my grandmother. "Olive is no longer a secret. Soon, I'll know whatever it is you've done to her and the rest of the family to make us Blind. And you can bet it won't stay that way."

Something in my gut told me Olive needed me. A stranger, but still my blood, and I couldn't wait to leave and find out what Ranlyn plucked from my grandmother's snarling brain.

———

After an uncomfortable visit avoiding my grandmother, we arrived at my apartment. Mom insisted she needed to use my bathroom after the long drive. I called her out for her impatience to see Caine, but she insisted her bladder was her main concern.

We smelled something familiar before we got to my door.

Food!

"That's coming from your place?"

All I could do was shrug.

I opened the door to find Caine in a fog of delectable-smelling steam rising from various pots on the stove. Bosco at his feet waiting from something to drop on the floor.

"We're back." I wanted him to realize I wasn't alone. "Something smells good."

"Hey, Sophie, you're early." Caine turned and looked from me to my mom.

"Yeah, we are. Umm, Caine this is my mother, Lucinda. Mom, this is Caine." I stepped out of the way so Caine could step forward to shake my mom's hand.

Caine was enthusiastic, his large hand grasping hers. "Great to meet you, ma'am."

"Call me Lu." She shook his hand in turn. "Nice to meet you too, Caine. I see you can cook. I doubt that stove has ever seen so much action without fire alarms going off."

"You're welcome to come over and cook for me anytime," I told her.

Caine thought I was funny. "It's only spaghetti and meatballs. Easy to be humble when it's my mom's recipe."

"Oh, nice. Us mothers will have to meet one day."

Caine smiled and nodded, looking about as happy about it as I did.

While my mother's confidence in a long-term relationship came from a desperate place for her daughter to be happy, I gave her a look that hinted she was lingering too long. So, she said her goodbyes and wished me a safe work shift at the bar before leaving.

So much for needing to use the bathroom.

"It amazes me how much your family looks alike," Caine said, smiling and shaking his head. "Not your cousin, but your mom and brothers. My family's a cluster of misfits compared to you guys."

"How do you know what my brothers look like?"

"Picture in your room."

"Rummaging through my underwear after all?"

"Yup. Don't worry. I didn't take any trophies."

I tsked. "Missed opportunity."

"I won't miss it again," he promised.

"This smells amazing, Caine," I commented and sat on the counter beside the stove.

He looked at me perched on the edge and laughed. "No biggy. I thought it'd be nice to have something to eat before you worked most of the night."

"You're helping me with Bosco. Shouldn't I be cooking *you* dinner?"

"From what I've heard, that might be detrimental to my health."

He earned himself a hearty swat on the meat of his bicep.

———

I was so busy eating and chatting with Caine before getting ready for work, that I forgot about the update from Ranlyn. Once I was behind the bar taking orders, my frilly-souled guardian removed his cloaking spell and got comfy on a stool with a scotch and a burger.

After filling an order for nachos, I did a round of the room to clean up tables.

"She's alive," I heard Ranlyn in my head.

I froze mid-step.

Since I couldn't hide my thoughts, Ranlyn must have heard I was chomping at the bit to learn what he knew about Olive.

"You're sure?" I asked in my thoughts.

"No. But as far as your grandmother knows, she is."

I started moving again, sprayed down a table, and took my time wiping it down.

"What else did you find out?"

"She's a patient at The Royal City Wellness Centre in Guelph."

"And?"

"And you need to find some things out for yourself."

"That's unhelpful." I scrubbed the table harder.

"You know she's alive and where to find her. The rest isn't for me to reveal."

I supposed he was right, but I needed to know. *"Does she deserve to be in there?"*

A few moments passed before he said, *"No."*

6

NO COMPASSION FOR THE BLIND

Bosco's barking and the sound of my front door closing woke me with a gasp. I sprinted out of bed in defensive mode. It took my brain a second to catch up to the possible threats. I reached the hallway as Caine kicked off his sandals.

Fuck. I forgot he was staying with me.

"You scared the ever-loving shit out of me!" I gasped and dropped onto the couch, burying my face into his pillow, dizzy and exhausted by the sudden burst of energy.

He laughed. "And you were going to go fisticuffs with an intruder?"

"Turtling also occurred to me."

"Big, bad witches turtle in the face of danger?" I felt a quick peck on the top of my head before he sat on the couch. It was comfortable and had me inwardly questioning if it was too comfortable before I groaned into his pillow, breathing the scent of him into my lungs.

"They should if the intruder got by Ranlyn or whoever else is out there. I'm not so with it in the morning, so the only weapon I really have is death by morning breath."

"So I've learned." I looked up from the pillow and glared at him. "It's okay, you're adorable, morning breath and all."

"Aww, your first blatant lie," I said with heavy sarcasm. "Now you can make up for it by grabbing me a bottle of water to douse my dragon breath before I singe your eyelashes."

I felt a little bad it worked, until I guzzled half the bottle he handed me and the cold water hit my belly.

"I found an apartment," Caine said.

I stared at him, waiting for him to add, "That I want to look at," or "That has great gym access," but he didn't go on. "You found an apartment?"

"Yup."

"You did not."

His eyebrow twitched. "I did."

"How?"

"The internet genie."

"The internet genie?"

"Yeah. It's that wondrous invention hooked up to the shiny box in your office."

My shoulder sagged, and I speared him with a look.

"What?" I didn't buy his innocent laugh. "I called a number and checked out the Portside Place Apartments on Geneva Street. Nice place with anything you could ever want."

I gasped. "There's a waiting list to get in there." I found out real quick they were out of my reach when I was looking for my current apartment.

He shrugged. "Six months rent in advance...in cash...they tend to overlook the list."

"Caine!"

"What?"

"That's a lot of money to throw at someone. Did you get receipts?"

"I was unconscious for four years, not forty. I know how to avoid shady landlords."

"No, I know, but holy shit, money *does* talk. When do you move in?"

"As soon as the landlord fixes the bathroom sink and paints the kitchen. So, couple of days? I'm not locked into a lease, so there won't be any issues if I end up moving sooner."

The phone ringing interrupted us. Before I answered, I said, "Remind me to get you to negotiate my next raise. The sexual favours route is driving me into early knee replacements."

A raised brow and tilted head told me he couldn't tell if I was joking or not and wasn't happy about it. His pillow chucked at his face solved the mystery for him as I picked up the phone.

"I found her!" Serena screamed into the phone.

"Who? Your inner child?"

"What? No. Olive!"

"Olive? How?" Especially since I hadn't told her about the information I got from Ranlyn.

"A lot of calls. She's been in The Royal City Wellness Centre in Guelph since 1974. Well, it wasn't called that then, but the family, our family, said she was having delusions and that she was aggressive towards them. Plus, she keeps telling everyone she's an all-powerful witch. Which isn't that crazy, but she displayed violent outbursts that led them to believe what the family reported about her was true.

"Of course, they think she's crazy," Serena went on. "Says she has power to do awesome things, but can't even break out of the place? Even if she has power like you and gram, why not lie and give the docs what they wanna hear? It doesn't make sense and doesn't sound dangerous enough to keep her there."

"It's not."

Olive's claims of power and aggression explained why someone might have committed her, especially back in the 70's. This still left a school bus-sized gaping hole in the logic of why she couldn't leave. She had power. My grandmother's reactions to seeing my soul confirmed that.

Plus, The Royal changed from an institution to a wellness center over the years. When the change occurred, the residents had their cases reviewed and many were released. I had learned as much through my schooling, so why was Olive still there?

"Can you believe *our* family would do that to her?" Serena's voice sounded fierce. "Put her in a place like that to fuckin' rot. She's in her sixties. What the fuck's she gonna do with her life now?"

I didn't know what to say. I had so many questions, and Serena wasn't the person to ask.

"Please say you don't work on Monday," Serena asked. "It's the only day I have off when we can visit her for a couple hours."

Forcing myself to snap out of my internal hamster wheel of angry questioning and suspicion was difficult, but I managed. "No, I don't work. Geez, Serena, you're on the ball. I can't believe they confirmed she was even there." Serena's tenacity was ever impressive. When she was passionate about something there was no stopping her, but privacy laws were a real thing not even persistence could break.

"She didn't have any restrictions in her file and gave permission for family to be able to find her if they came looking, so confidentiality wasn't an issue. And come on, when does anything like this ever happen to us? I mean our family has its screwballs, but this is epic. Maybe she *is* insane, I don't even care. It'd still be interesting to see what crazy shit she says. Psychotic freak-out I can handle. If she pees herself, she's all yours."

I laughed at my cousin while feeling the weight of so many people suffering from mental health symptoms they had no control over, knowing Serena's intention wasn't to be insensitive as she knew nothing about the struggles Olive could be facing.

I hung-up feeling conflicted about visiting Olive. The ability and willpower to keep my expectations in check were non-existent. One thing I was certain of: regardless of if Olive was a Soul Seer or not, she needed help.

———

The pop of my knuckles cut through Kim's lesson on dangerous mixtures, my fingers achy from writing so much trying to keep up with her. She stopped talking and her face screwed up with disgust.

"Don't eyeball me," I protested. I sat back into my couch and rested my neck. "You talk like if you were fast enough it might save us all from global annihilation. You're killing me."

"Skip on the word for word and pick out the important parts."

I looked at Caine. "Do you know which parts are important?"

"I...um...."

"No, because we know nothing, which makes it all important. Or we risk turning ourselves into ravenous, flesh-eating ducks or some shit."

"Flesh-eating ducks? Toadflax is for protection and hex breaking."

"Not if I get a hold of it," I mumbled and rubbed my creaky finger joints.

Ranlyn walked in.

"We're beyond the knocking phase? How domestic."

"We've got a problem."

"Is it flesh-eating ducks?" I fake gasped. "See, Kim. Told you I'm dangerous."

"Ducks?" Ranlyn questioned, his attitude screaming this-is-not-the-time-for-inappropriate-humor. "No. Loring. His devotees took a Mother Coven member. One of the ones working on safety protocols for outside Diluculo in prep for the Lughnasadh celebration."

"Devotees? Creepy and cult-like. Good fit." I lifted my hand like he was a schoolteacher. "Where is Diluculo again? I've never heard of it."

"Hours away. Undetectable by the Blind."

"But the Tainted can find it?" Caine asked.

"They're not supposed to." Ranlyn looked at his phone a moment after it buzzed in his hand.

The crease between his eyes deepened as the three of us sat in quiet, waiting for more.

"Ranlyn," I said when he stayed quiet, reading whatever was coming through, and looking more worried by the moment.

"Ranlyn," I said again and instead of waiting got up and went to him to look at his phone myself. The word "INCOMING!" popped up on the screen and my stomach clenched.

"Fuck-buckets." I grabbed Bosco.

"What? What's happening?" Kim and Caine said simultaneously.

"We have to get out of here!" I yelled at them.

We scrambled, Bosco in my arms. I shoved on my Chucks, folding the backs down beneath my heels and hoping I could run in them. Ranlyn pulled the door open and whipped his arm up in front of me to stop as someone was in our path. A neighbour. An overseas university student who lived down the other wing of the hall.

"Sophie?" The girl asked with a heavy Asian accent.

I hesitated. "Yes?"

With my confirmation, her expression morphed from casual to furious. She sprang forward. I yelped and jumped back.

My neighbour raged forward and hit an invisible wall that spread across my doorway. Light sparked from the threshold into my apartment and encased the young woman where she stood, driving her into a seizure.

"It's killing her!" I screamed.

"The ward's not strong enough to kill her," Ranlyn said.

"Move!" Caine yelled, pushing us both out of the way and throwing yellow powder at my frothing-from-the-mouth neighbour. As soon as the powder hit her, she collapsed onto my apartment floor, the seizing completely stopped.

"What the tits, Caine? What'd you do?"

"Powdered and concentrated Datura seeds knock you out. If she's unconscious, she can't think of hurting you."

"Deactivating the ward. Good job," Ranlyn praised him.

"At least one of you was listening," Kim quipped.

"You have anymore, Kim?" Ranlyn asked.

"In my apartment. Why?"

"We're going to need more." Judging by the fear he was trying to mask and the sound of shuffling feet down the hall, a whole lot more neighbours intended to make a house call.

"Ranlyn, can we—?" Kim started to ask.

"No time."

"Then what—?"

The door across the hall opened.

The innocent face of a six-year-old boy took a few steps towards us. "Sophie?" he asked with a lisp.

Tightness. In my throat. My gut. Disgust. How could they?

"A kid?" I heard Caine from behind me.

"Loring has no compassion for the Blind regardless of age."

This time I kept my pie-hole shut. Child or not, I didn't want to see anyone else hurt by the ward meant to protect me.

When the kid took a step towards my door and then another, the tightness keeping me rooted in spot let go in a wave of panic. "No!" I pitched forward and slammed the door shut. The sickening sound of bone meeting wood shook the door as I turned the deadbolt.

If bashing the neighbour kid's noggin in didn't earn me some negative Karma, I wasn't sure what would.

Pounding vibrated my door. I flinched but managed to hide my yelp as I backed away as if they could reach through it. Another voice called my name, one I didn't know. More pounding followed and then my name again. Knock, name, knock, name, over and over again.

"I'm officially changing my name to Betty."

"Well, Betty, do you have a security deposit?" Ranlyn asked.

"Yes. Why?"

Power enveloped the room to the point of choking me. It punched out of Ranlyn and through the wall with brilliant light. The whole apartment wall shattered. Shards of bricks and drywall flew into us in a violent upchucking of eighties architecture. Hunched over to protect Bosco in my arms, I heard Ranlyn's order to get running, but when I looked up all I saw was a fog of dust.

When my apartment door collapsed under the pressure, bodies fell onto my broken tiles as others crawled atop them. I stretched my arm out to guide myself through the floating dust and passed Bosco to Caine through a jagged hole that provided us a second exit.

Though Kim was my neighbour our apartments didn't share a wall as a staircase was between. Jumping out of the hole onto the steps had me skating on debris. I strangled the metal railing before my hands slipped off and I went flying tits-first down our escape route.

Descending two steps at a time wasn't enough. One of my neighbours burst through the fourth-floor entrance and grabbed Kim by the hair. Her scream reverberated up the stairwell. Punctuating foot stomps of people coming down the stairs behind us, had us retreating for Kim in a panic.

Before greedy hands could drag Kim away, Caine and I shoved the people back into the fourth-floor hallway and tried to slam the door on them. One still had a hold of Kim's hair. She screamed as we pressed our weight into the door to keep it closed.

The small window in the fourth-floor door gave me a view of recognizable faces. No names came to mind, but the old man who sneers at Bosco and every other animal he sees, the Asian university student I've shared the elevator with, my Superintendent who hates me for always losing my keys, and even Theresa whose husband tried to kill me all pushed to get through the door with mirrored passion for their mission.

They wouldn't stop.

Caine pulled away as someone's nails scraped his arm. Blood beaded the surface like seeping tears. With Bosco under one arm, I could only throw my back into the job.

My feet kept slipping.

"Ranlyn!" I screamed.

"Hold on!" he screamed back.

"No! Hurry the fuck up or Kim's gonna be scalped!"

Whoever had the chunk of Kim's hair wasn't letting go.

My power rose. I knew I could hurt them, disintegrate the hand holding onto Kim, but I might kill them as well as Kim. I had no control. Plus, this wasn't their fault. Loring's devotees were responsible. The fucker knew I would see them as neighbours and not drones.

Sadistic prick.

Ranlyn sprinted up the stairs, pushed against the door with us, and grabbed Kim's hair with one hand. "Prepare to lose some strands," he warned, and Kim squeezed her eyes shut and whimpered.

Those coming from upstairs finally reached us before he could free Kim.

"Incoming!" I yelled.

Ranlyn cursed under his breath in another language and turned with an outstretched hand. Power telekinetically knocked the descending bodies over like dominoes. He took too much weight off the door and the gap widened enough for my Superintendent to squeeze half-way through. We scrambled, pushing back with everything we had. Ranlyn let go of Kim to keep back those flooding into the stairwell.

The stairwell was too tight, stuffed with people, and we were about to drown beneath them. I refused to let Bosco down. With my power enacted and antagonized by Ranlyn's sparks of power, I was close to losing it.

Caine shoved my Superintendent back though the door, but one of them still had a hold of Kim's hair. "Jesus fuck," Caine yelled. "Let go!"

When the door slammed shut, I bounced off it with jarring impact, stunned until I realized Kim was free.

"Come on," she said with a note of shock and took off down the stairs.

I took off with Caine and Kim, checking back to make sure Ranlyn was on our heels. He was and we found the exit seconds later.

"Where now?" Kim asked Ranlyn as I breathed in a hit of stifling humidity.

Dark-lit souls spotted us from the parking lot and started after us. "Shit. Not that way."

"Come on," Ranlyn said. We followed him across the street. Seeing where he was going, I let Bosco down as we hit the railway steps. My arms ached from trying to hold up his fifteen-pound body for so long.

We reached the trees across the open field by the time I saw dark souls following us.

"Caine!" No! Cole's voice.

Caine stopped behind us. If I didn't know Cole was long dead, I'd think the voice was real too.

"It's not him," Ranlyn called to Caine. "Keep moving."

I grabbed Caine's arm and dragged him away from the bleating voice. Whether Loring thought Caine was naive enough to fall for this or if he planned to piss Caine off enough he would go straight for them, I didn't know.

Rounding a bend in the path, we went into the thick of trees and crossed the shallow creek across moss covered rocks, to gain ground. I couldn't see the souls anymore, and stopped and let the others know. My lungs burned. The progress report also a chance to catch my breath.

"I can still hear them," Ranlyn said. "We need to keep going."

"Hear their footsteps?" Kim asked. "How?"

"Not their feet, their thoughts," Ranlyn clarified.

"This park is long, the creek longer," I said between phlegm-filled breathes, "but we'll hit a road if we keep going this way. They could be waiting for us there."

"Fine. Hide us," Ranlyn said to me.

"How? I don't know any cover spells."

"Come here." We followed him a few feet towards a willow amongst small trees and broken-down foliage as Cole's voice still cried out for help.

When Ranlyn told me what he wanted me to do, I laughed. After some convincing and his promise of pending capture otherwise, I agreed to try.

Kim held Bosco. After a moment to strategize, I used my power to elongate and thicken the willow vines until they pooled onto the park floor. Then I grew long, wild grass around the outskirts of the section that kept us hidden, the grass beneath our feet left short. The smell of fresh cut grass and earth filled my nose as the greenery responded to my magic.

Once I finished, we couldn't see out except for the days dying light at the top, which meant no one else could see in.

"What about our thoughts?" Caine asked. "Can they hear ours?"

"How about a high-five for this boss set-up, first?"

From the look I got from everyone, it wasn't happening.

"Fine." I crossed my arms. "What about our thoughts?" I asked as Bosco lifted a leg to our new walls. "Good boy," I told him. "Next time on Jeeves." Bosco looked up at me and then kicked his feet at his mess.

"Yours are already temporarily concealed."

"How?" Kim asked.

"Slipped into your drinks."

"Smart," Kim said.

"Smart? Dose me again and you'll be Bosco's butler from now on. Slipped in," I scoffed and mumbled, "Asshole."

Since our little haven wasn't soundproof, we sat quiet and waited for rescue. I had no clue who. Ranlyn texted someone who instructed us to wait and remain hidden.

Sleeping would have been nice, but I had a hard enough time trying to keep Bosco awake so the bad guys wouldn't hear him snore.

We didn't talk, but Caine sat with his knees pulled up wearing the same expression as he had in the sleeping curse. Too many times had this park held him captive, and now, he was replaying the reel of his brother's terror.

I didn't know if Loring was out there, but at some point, he was going to pay for fucking with the people I cared about.

———

Hours later, Ranlyn gave the word that we could break down our willow cage.

"What does that mean?" Kim asked him as she brushed her butt of forest debris.

"It means the imminent threat has dissipated, and we must erase signs of our time here."

"Dissipated, but not gone," Caine pointed out.

Ranlyn huffed with impatience and turned to him. "You're a Magic. You will forever be in the midst of a threat. For now, yes, the threat had dissipated."

Wired yet exhausted, we left it at that. After making the willow and grass look more natural, we made our way back through the brush, across the creek, and up the railway tie steps.

Getting off the elevator, I was amazed to see the hallway looked normal. A glimpse through the window of the stairwell door next to my apartment proved it was.

"No way." I flung my apartment door open in search of a gaping hole in my wall and was stopped short by someone who grabbed the door to stop it from hitting them.

Someone peered around the door, a moment passing before their dark eyes softened. Donovan. He opened the door wider. Passing him was awkward as I felt him glare at me, but I was too astonished by what else I saw to really care. My wall, back the way it was before Ranlyn destroyed it, down to the pictures hanging on it.

I was torn between gratitude and disgust for living through the terrifying possibility of capture by Loring's imaginative evil, then seeing the evidence of his creativity obliterated.

Aunt Lacey came to my side, holding Bosco in her arms. I hadn't noticed she was there.

"Guess I get to keep my security deposit." My smile was natural yet half-hearted.

"Yes. If I believed leaving evidence of Loring's presence would in some way assist our cause, I would have kept it."

"I can imagine how many damaged places there would be if Loring's presence wasn't erased each time."

A small sound of agreement. "Scars across this nation and others aplenty." She handed Bosco to Donovan, my sidekick slathering him in a good helping of puppy kisses. "Loring's flock will not relinquish the hunt for you and others he deems worthy of taking. An invitation to remain within my home is always open, though I won't ask now as I know the answer." She was right, I didn't want to leave my home. "Instead, I will increase security."

"Security didn't make a difference."

"Much occurred outside the building as well as within and while you were in your willow den. Ranlyn and many others kept you all safe."

"I know that." I didn't mean to sound ungrateful.

"Plus," Donovan snapped. "You can continue to use Sophie as bait, right?" His damning expression sparked shame in Aunt Lacey's hazel eyes.

I didn't need her to explain. "I get it. Bait is an easy job, but I have an actual job to do, one that pays, and I'll be visiting Olive. I can't have Loring's devotees putting my customers at risk or following me to see Olive."

"They won't," Aunt Lacey promised. I didn't know how she could be certain, but she looked it.

Fingertips pressed on my lower back, and I turned to see Caine. "That's one good part of us Berisfords being a small family. I only have my mom to worry about."

Aunt Lacey clasped her hands in front of her. "Yes, I will—"

"Berisford?" Donovan cut her off and looked between Caine and Aunt Lacey and then stepped closer to our Coven Leader. "He's a Berisford?"

"Hey," Caine snapped.

"Wend...." Aunt Lacey tried to settle him.

"What if he's—"

Aunt Lacey snapped her fingers with a sharp, "Enough" and shut Donovan up immediately and against his will. "Leave. Everyone." She raised her voice. "Outside."

Kim didn't want to go, but she obeyed with a look of concern no doubt mirrored on my own face. Donovan set Bosco on the couch and did as he was told, anger emanating from his every step out the door.

7

MOVING FORWARD

Once we were alone, I thought Caine was going to attack Aunt Lacey with a flood of questions, but like with Donovan, she controlled the thread of conversation.

Aunt Lacey took a breath before reaching up to place her hands on Caine's shoulders. "As much as the information I possess would answer all that makes you resentful of me, they are not my secrets to reveal. I've encouraged you to seek out certain truths, and for your own reasons, you have resisted. With respect for your justifications, I again, press the importance of such discovery." She paused as if waiting for a reply. When Caine stayed quiet, she moved around him to leave.

I had expected him to refuse to accept her explanation and continue to demand answers. Instead, he stood still and thoughtful as we watched Aunt Lacey leave.

"What the fuck, Caine? You're not going after her?"

He remained silent without looking at me.

"Caine?" I touched his arm.

"It's been the three of us," he said, eyes unblinking, gaze and attention distant.

"What?"

"Donovan knows something."

This time he did move. Faster than I expected, straight out my door and into the hall. The yelling started before I caught up.

"Tell me!" Caine screamed as Donovan stood, shoulders squared, dimples caved. He refused to say a word, as if he knew the priceless-ness of whatever it was he knew. The haughty laugh depleted the last of Caine's patience. Caine pushed him against the wall, his hand at Donovan's throat. When Donovan's eyes became heavy hooded, his lips falling apart in a slight gasp, I realize what was happening and shoved Caine away from him.

Donovan snapped out his trance.

"What?" Caine looked at me and then Donovan. "Did you get something from me?"

Donovan attempted to leave, but Caine got in his way.

"Move. Now." Donovan's voice was hard, his fists clenched.

"Caine," I warned, watching Donovan's fists.

"Tell me what you saw," Caine demanded.

As he asked, the sensation of power rippled across my skin.

"I saw the crash," Donovan answered, his voice flat. "I saw your brother drown. Then I saw you run, panicked through the rain like a frightened child." Caine straightened in shock. "You wanna know more?"

Caine had heard enough and stepped aside. Donovan left, but the altercation had done its damage.

"How could you do that to him? What the fuck's the matter with you?" The hallway was far from empty, but no one stepped in. Not even Aunt Lacey, who stood observing by the elevator.

Caine followed me as I stormed back into my apartment, slamming the door behind us.

"You don't think it's weird he hides his gifts from everyone, but he tells you all his secrets? He's manipulating you." Caine paced restlessly across the room.

"And this is you telling me I'm a moron?" If I could growl like Bosco, I would have.

"I didn't—"

"You did."

"Sophie—"

"I've dealt with a lot of shit from labia munchers worse than Donovan. Aunt Lacey told you to find out yourself and you didn't. You don't get to be pissed Donovan knows things you don't. Pushing up on him did nothing but make yourself look like a—."

"Labia muncher?"

"Yes."

"I don't know what that is, but a little teeth never hurt anyone."

"I'll remember that."

He gave me a look that would make me fake fan myself if I wasn't still mad at him.

Caine wrapped his arms around me, holding me close. "I don't want to fight. The last thing I want to do is make you upset. I don't like how he's playing you, and I wanted to know what he knew."

I kept my arms crossed. "Did you notice anything while you were being the schoolyard bully?" Caine's eyes narrowed and he dropped his hold. "Power. Didn't you feel it?"

"Well, yeah, I did. You were pissed, I'm sure you—"

"Nope. Not me. I felt it *around* me not from *inside* of me. I've done it enough now to know."

"Maybe it was Donovan."

I gave him a look that silently called him a creative expletive for me. I was too exhausted to make the effort to say it out loud, not sure if it was worse—or better—than "labia muncher."

"I'm moving, and then there's the Initiation...a lot is going on. I don't have it in me to delve into family shit right now." Caine raked his fingers through his hair.

"Whatever. If you want to take a squat in a tub of denial that's your business. Right now, I need a shower, food, and sleep. In that order."

"Might be difficult while I'm squatting in your tub."

"Luckily, I'm flexible," I called over my shoulder and closed the bathroom door behind me.

———

"Morning," I said as Caine was rolling up his sleeping bag for the last time. "Ready to get your life back together?"

"I've already started to get back my life because of you." Caine's side-eyed wistful stare had me smiling.

"At least you'll get your couch back. I know me being here was difficult for you."

"Difficult? I asked you to stay, remember?"

"Yeah, but it was above your comfort level."

I crossed my arms. "Is that why you took the apartment so quick?"

"No, no—"

"Cuz' I wasn't trying to kick you out."

"I didn't say you were, Sophie."

"You can stay longer if you need to."

"Sophie, stop." Caine put his hands on my shoulders, and I fought not to shrug him off. "I knew this was a short-term arrangement and I had no intention of hunkering down. I took the apartment because I scored an amazing deal. I'm not taking off. I'm just living somewhere else. And I'm hoping you'll be there often." I stared up at him as he paused. "Okay?"

"Yeah, okay."

"Sure?"

"Yes."

"Okay," he repeated and kissed my forehead.

I evaded any further talk of it by heading to the fridge for a water bottle. He followed me into the kitchen and planted a kiss on my lips that had me flushed with desire. I hated that he knew what I needed to hear and because of that would try and slink away from him. The fact he wouldn't let me was so sweet I needed a minute alone to process.

I took my water into my room, relished the cold drink, and then dressed in sturdy moving clothes for the hot day—jean shorts and a white v-neck tee—and pulled my hair into a low, messy braid. As I re-entered the living room, Caine's eyes widened.

"You look great." The tips of his fingers brushed my thighs below the hem of my jean shorts.

"I'm in old clothes."

"You're beautiful. And the braid is adorable." He tugged on it as I, again, took his compliment with an avoidant snort that told him to shut up.

Saved by Kim's strong knock, she was brimming with excitement when I opened the door. Her mood continued all the way downstairs in the elevator.

"Were you a professional mover in a previous life, Kim?" Caine joked as the three of us climbed into Ranlyn's car, our bodyguard's mood nowhere close to Kim's enthusiasm.

"Nope. Great weather, and I don't have to work, so no matter what, it'll be an awesome weekend."

I groaned. "You exhaust me when you're in these moods." I was never jovial, working or not.

"Oh, Soph, give in to mornings. You know deep inside you love 'em."

"As if. Mornings cause me misery, Kim." I affixed my sunglasses to my face. "You're a strange breed. Like a glow-worm, all that sunshine out your ass."

Caine laughed as Ranlyn pulled onto the road.

"Me? *You're* the weirdo. I think you're the only who enjoys working late nights. What are you gonna do when you graduate and need to work a day job like the rest of the world?"

"It's not my fault the world doesn't cater to night owls. I could be a night-time therapist."

"I'm pretty sure they call those sex trade workers."

"Hybrid services? Would earn me a pretty penny."

"Umm," Caine piped up, "I vote against the hooker idea."

We ignored him.

"You could make your own hours and free up time for coven meetings," Kim added.

"True," I agreed. "Plus, give me extra bucks for a car so Jeeves here can hang out in the back seat every once in a while." Ranlyn glared at me in the rear-view mirror.

"The back seat does allow for the most room, considering you've gathered a menagerie of sex trade worker-therapist co-workers."

"No thanks," was Ranlyn's deadpan response.

"You sure?" I asked him. "I can get you a discount."

Ranlyn huffed with annoyance and turned up the radio as we dropped the game.

Caine put his arm over my shoulders. "You two get sick pleasure out of torturing us, don't you?"

"Totally. But it'll cost you extra once my sex trade worker-therapist business gets up and running."

"What? No discounts?"

"How would I make enough money for a car for Ranlyn to get nookie in the back of? Use your head."

He laughed, pulled me close to plant a kiss on my forehead as we made our way to the opposite side of town. As much as my sex trade worker-therapist business was a flaccid idea, buying a car was a motivating incentive to making my overall life plan work amongst the craziness of all this Loring bullshit. Our morning banter brought with it the levity I needed, but Ranlyn scanning the streets as if danger was a lurking sexually transmitted infection, brought the fun down a few notches and reminded me comfort was a long way off.

As we pulled into the lot of Caine's new building, Kim turned down the radio and spun in her seat to talk to him. "I don't know how you skipped to the head of the line on the waiting list, but you better make use of the pools and sauna. You realize you could afford to mortgage a house with the rent they charge, right?"

"That's the plan," he said. "Gives me a few months or so to buy a house I can grow into."

Kim looked at me. "Well, isn't that nice." Her voice rang with suggestion.

I rolled my eyes, but realized it was less than effective from behind my sunglasses.

Ranlyn headed around back and parked in visitor's parking where a small flock of men cheered as if they had been waiting for ages, giving Caine hugs and handshakes as he got out.

After the barrage of welcomes, Caine made introductions. "Some of you've already met. This is Sophie and her friend's Kim and Ranlyn." All the guys smiled and waved. I never thought about how we'd explain Ranlyn's presence, but helpful friend would do. "And this is Dom, Reid, Frog, Lee, and the ginger in the back is Teddy."

The ginger, Teddy, smirked, enjoying having Caine back to make fun of him again. His short orange-red hair gleamed in the sun. Lee was the quiet one of the bunch standing in the back, an all-around average guy with dark eyes behind a pair of glasses.

"Okay! Let's see our new party palace!" Dom, a wide-shouldered boulder of a man with a shaved head, and dark skin, slapped Caine on the shoulder pushing him along.

Caine shot a look back at me as if to say I should ignore his over-eager friend. I had figured Caine was a much-changed man since the accident, and spending the day with his people solidified that fact.

Everything from the Jacuzzi fit for two, the blond hardwood floors, to the open concept design edged with crown molding, screamed elegance. Kim ambled through Caine's inflated idea of a turn-key apartment, mouth agape noting every detail like an architectural virtuoso.

As beautiful and spacious as the apartment was, it fell opposite of my personal style; modern to the point of sterility with zero personality of its own. I would never have pictured Caine living in this place, temporary digs or not. Did he rent it because he could afford it?

Shocked out of my confusion by Kim testing the trash compactor,

I looked away from Ranlyn who was looking at me like he knew what I was thinking, even though I knew he couldn't have since whatever he dosed me with shielded my thoughts. Maybe he thought the same.

"What now, buddy?" Reid asked, his sculpted faux-hawk unmoving as his lean, muscular body bounded into the room like a child on a sugar high.

"Now that I've got the key, furniture delivery is set for this afternoon. The rest is at my mom's, so we'll head there." His dread was evident. "Frog, did you bring your truck?"

"You didn't see her? She's pure sex."

The only man present that stood nose-to-nose in terms of height with Caine, but sporting blond hair and light eyes, spoke in detail about the truck as if describing his first love. After twenty minutes of the guys slobbering over Frog's re-painted black and orange pick-up, we made our way to what I assumed would be an angry Joyce.

Pulling up and parking along the curb in front of the house, Joyce caught me in an acidic stare from the front window.

"I'm not going in," I announced, my eyes on Joyce's in an unintentional school yard staring contest.

Caine muttered something profane. "The guys can handle the heavy lifting. Wait here. Ranlyn?"

"I'm staying too," he told Caine who nodded.

Conceding the winning title of the staring contest with Joyce, I spun to the back seat before he left. "Keep me out of the conversation. It'll piss her off if you defend me."

He grimaced in reply and left to collect his pre-packed belongings.

I chastised myself for tagging along. One of his friends could have squeezed Caine into their vehicles if they needed to make another trip. Leaning against the headrest, I exhaled, irked by how Joyce's aversion for me could have burrowed so deep and reflecting on how it was going to affect us going forward.

Joyce was experiencing emotional torment over both of her sons and deflecting her pain to someone easier to blame. Since she would blame anyone but her sons, one being dead and the other suffering years as result of it, she blamed me. That I understood. Nothing could resurrect Joyce's idyllic life before the accident. I accepted the normalcy of her behaviour, but wished I could find a way to help the woman deal with the tragedy.

"The eagle's on approach, Seer."

I looked to Ranlyn finding him pointing out my window. Before I had the opportunity to look for myself, a hard knock on the glass made me recoil with a yelp.

"What are you gonna do?" Kim asked.

"Talk like adults, I suppose."

We all stepped out of the car, Joyce leaving me only enough room to squeeze out of my seat and onto the curb. Joyce had made her way down the front lawn in her purple Crocs. Her lips pursed, white with anger as her stare beat me down.

Kim stayed on her side of the car, and Ranlyn hung back as well.

"Joyce...." I began.

"He never had an eye for the right woman. You think you're any better?"

Wow. Joyce did hate me. She shook her stubby finger in my face, then crossed her arms as if restraining herself from doing more than yell.

"Joyce, I won't pretend to understand how much you're hurting—
"

"He's so much like his father," Joyce interrupted again, clearly uninterested in anything I had to say. "Maybe too much."

"I'm sure there's a lot of you in him as well. You should trust him."

"Should I? Like I trusted you? You're a liar. You didn't know him before the coma. I should've turned you two away the first time I saw you." She glanced over my shoulder at Kim.

"It would've stopped nothing." Ranlyn stated from behind me.

I shot him a 'You're not helping' glare and felt a tingle of my power swell with my frustration over being unable to control the situation. This can't be happening now. Get your shit together, you fucking freak, I berated myself until it subsided. I tried to be subtle about taking a deep breath to stave off my rising panic.

Nervously, I pushed my hair behind my ears, and I noticed that Joyce was staring at the ring on my finger. It was the one Aunt Lacey had given me. Aunt Lacey told me the teardrop smoky quartz surrounded in diamonds belonged to her daughter-in-law, Nya, who burned at the stake with Aunt Lacey's son, Gareth. Too disillusioned with their immortality to live on, Nya and Gareth gave themselves to the Witchburners. Did Joyce know this?

"You...." Joyce started before her voice trailed off.

"Joyce?"

Fixated on the ring, Joyce's expression turned from anger to revulsion as she looked up at me. "You are poison! I *will* find a way to get my son away from you. You can't have him."

With that, Joyce turned her back on me and stalked back into the house.

We got back in the car, dumbfounded by Joyce's intense reaction.

"Could she have thought it was an engagement ring? That would make sense, right?" I was grasping at straws to make sense of the encounter.

"Wrong finger," Kim objected. "Plus, it's not like it's a huge diamond or something."

"Not all engagement rings are diamonds. It has diamonds on it. Maybe she didn't see which finger it was on."

Kim shook her head, unconvinced. "Come on, Soph, you saw her face. She was thinking of more than her son marrying someone she hates."

"Fucked if I know what, though. What about you Ranlyn, what'd you hear?"

His expression was too blank. "I wasn't listening in."

I smirked. "Now who's the liar?"

"You'll found out soon enough."

The guys, minus Caine, exited the house moments later. I

assumed Caine was stuck inside getting an earful. I both wanted and dreaded to find out what Joyce had to say.

Reid held up a black garbage bag in each hand, while Lee carried two large boxes. Dom carried nothing but a light, tall CD rack. They loaded everything onto the flatbed of Frog's snazzy truck and Lee's old, light blue Buick. You could sneak a minimum of three bodies into the Buick's enormous trunk, but even with its size, the door was still tied down.

After many trips in and out of the basement, and taking full advantage of everyone's laps and bungee cords to hold in precarious boxes, we fit all of Caine's belongings into Frog's truck and Ranlyn and Lee's cars.

Caine was tense and silent on the way back to his apartment and I didn't want to push him for information in front of Kim and Ranlyn.

When we arrived, Kim and I helped carry things into the new apartment, setting them into their assigned rooms. I couldn't help but curl my lip at the way every box was labelled in Joyce's fancy scroll. With everyone pulling their weight, we were done pretty quickly, and even the beating sun making us sweat balls didn't seem so bad. With everything inside, we rested and waited for Caine's furniture delivery.

I found a moment and slipped into the smaller second bedroom with Caine to talk. "Did your mom tell you she talked to me?"

His expression dropped from contentment to simmering fury. "She said she had words with you."

"Words?" That was putting it mildly.

"Doesn't matter." He laid a tender hand on my arm.

"What'd she say about the ring?"

"The ring?" Caine asked, puzzled. I held up my hand as reference. He studied it and said, "What'd she say to you?"

I sat down on a large box, my legs aching, and told him every word. "I thought she assumed it was an engagement ring, but Kim thinks it's something more. Ranlyn wouldn't tell me whatever he overheard in her head, so clearly it's something important."

"Like what?" He knelt in front of me, his arms resting on my thighs, winding around me.

I shrugged. "Like maybe she knows."

"Knows what?" I gave him a telling look to clue him into my meaning. "No way. There's no way she knows anything about that stuff. No possible way."

"Why else would she look at the ring like the stone meant something to her? Aunt Lacey said the Berisford name carried a past and told you to dig into your family history. Your mom might know about the ring, and might know about that magic stuff."

"No. I think you're right, and she assumed it was an engagement ring."

"She would've said something specific to you if she thought you were getting married. Try and talk you out of it. What exactly *did* she say?"

"You're wrong for me. I needed to look closer at what you were. You're trouble." He gave a small laugh and shook his head, sending a chunk of his hair falling into his face. I tucked it back. "I don't know, Sophie. My mom hates all my girlfriends. Doesn't mean she knows anything about that world."

"Fine, but I think you need to ask her about your father."

Caine's brows pinched together.

"I'm sorry, Caine. I realize I'm doing the Irish jig on a fragile relationship, but your mom said something about you being like your father."

He pushed to his feet. "My mother's handling things all wrong, but talking about my father, a man I don't remember, don't even know his name, would push her over the edge. Moving out is bad enough."

I stood up, too, toe-to-toe with him now. "I get that, I do. But what if there's something—"

Reid yelled out from the other room, "Dude, truck's here!"

What kid never pushed the subject of a missing father growing up? To me, this smacked of something weirder than a taboo subject.

Whatever excuse Joyce supplied had worked, but it was unacceptable considering everything that had happened.

The delivery truck was a seventeen-footer accompanied by two strong furniture movers girdled with back braces and non-slip gloves. As they lifted the hatch, I saw a couch, bedroom set, and a dining table with smaller pieces as well.

Kim and I took in a matching set of tall lamps and night tables for the bedroom, which also mirrored the end tables for the living room.

She got some extra help from Frog while I dropped an end table into place a little too roughly. With a raised brow and slight smirk, Ranlyn silently took the lamp from my hand so I could fix it and check for damage as an over-exuberant laugh escaped Kim from across the room. Instead of asking for her help with the next load, I let her be and watched her and Frog head out together.

Heavy plastic, tape, and packaging made a small mountain in the corner. The mess was the only sore sight in the room now filled with dark, sturdy, masculine furniture that made the expansive space feel a tad cozier. The furniture I loved and could picture myself with a book in hand on a lazy night, but the rest of the space I still didn't understand.

With the furniture in place it was time for Caine to buy the tradi-tional payment to his company for helping him move: pizza, wings, and beer for everyone. He and Lee took the blue Buick. Frog didn't want his truck to smell like pizza, which doubled as an excuse to stay behind and chat up Kim. He leaned over the black speckled granite of the kitchen island as she ripped plastic off the new pots and pans set.

I sank into Caine's over-sized dark-chocolate suede chair, my legs curled beneath me, and looked out the windows, thinking of Joyce and her reaction to the ring. Obsessive and stubborn were two traits I possessed and did my best to overcome them when I was proved wrong, but this time, I knew I was right.

Dom came into the room after christening the bathroom and

plopped himself down on the matching couch. "Nice place he got himself here, huh?"

"Crazy beautiful," I said. "Trumps my apartment by a long shot."

"Oh yeah? Where do you live?"

I told him and earned a look of wary surprise. I shrugged and answered his unspoken question, "I know, I know, bad area for a girl like me, right?"

"Bad area for a guy like me." He laughed. "You must be fearless."

"Meh. Caine doesn't complain."

"Yeah, I bet he doesn't."

Dom and Caine seemed the closest, so I thought it might be worth asking him about something that had been on my mind. "Do you think Caine's different since the accident?"

"Well, you knew him before too, right?" While warranted, since I maintained the lie Kim and I made up to get access to him in the hospital, his confusion still tripped me up.

"Yeah, but you don't tell the chick you're trying to fuck that you're a piece of shit trying to catch a piece of ass. You play it nice and sweet."

He howled until his eyes teared and then thought for a moment and answered a little mournful. "Yeah, he's different." He shifted and leaned toward me. "To be honest, he's a whole new guy." I nodded, assuming as much. "Don't get me wrong, new is good. Before, he was a little wilder, more confident, arrogant actually." A reminiscent smirk turned up the edges of his lips. "It's like he matured without living the years to get that way. A new-and-improved version of himself." He swiped a meaty palm over his shaved head. "He gets this jacked-up place, talkin' 'bout buying a house." He paused. "Plus, you."

"Me?"

"You're not his usual type. Chicks were always...well, chicks. His last girl, Tracey, was a flake and bar-hag skank by twenty. But who cares 'cuz she's disposable, right? He coulda picked up a handful of Tracey's every night."

I agreed I was no bar-hag skank, even if I worked at a bar, and was grateful for Dom's ability to distinguish the difference.

"I heard you and Tracey met. Wish I'd been there. Good for you for not taking her bullshit."

Caine never told me what he said to his buddies, considering the one time I met Tracey she was overtaken by dark Magics and tried to kill us. We never saw her after the restaurant cleared out.

"Not the cat fight you're imagining, but thanks."

Dom smiled then said, "You're a relationship girl. The kind you introduce to family, cook romantic dinners for without expecting sex. More than a fuck and chuck."

"Wonderful." I rolled my eyes.

"Tell me you're that girl, Sophie." His tone was abrupt with worry.

His sudden intensity surprised me.

He perched on the edge of the couch, his body squared to mine. "I have *never* seen him like this. I mean with anybody. He dated this girl in college for a while, and they were tight, but even that doesn't touch whatever's going on with you guys. Honestly, I don't get where it came from. We've never met before and he's been under a long time, but he talks about you like it's permanent."

If his point was to freak me out, Dom was doing a great job of it. "How would you know?"

"He was in a coma, but he can still work a phone," he teased. "You were topic number one, especially after he jumped your bones in front of a room full of people at the hospital. PDA? Not a Caine-before-the-coma thing. Not ever."

I covered my face in embarrassment. "You're exaggerating."

"Believe me, it was Baywatch-worthy and I harassed him about it for hours." His expression turned serious again. "If you have no inten-tions of being 'that girl' please walk away now. I'd rather it stops here before it gets serious. With Cole and the coma, I don't know if he could take it."

"Don't worry." I was reluctant, but added, "I'm serious about him, too."

Dom's shoulders relaxed with relief he had performed his duty by asking, so I took the opportunity to do the same about Frog and Kim. "Is he a relationship guy or should Kim expect a fuck and chuck?"

We looked over at our friends in the kitchen, standing close in conversation. "Frog isn't a gentleman, but they're getting along for now."

"So, he's a for now kinda guy?"

He shrugged. "He still has this on and off thing with his ex you might want to warn her about, but he wouldn't play both. His ex's a dog anyway. At least Kim can see her feet."

"Damn. Big girls need love too."

"Hey, I'm all about a little cushion, but I meant her nose. Jody's got a beak you wouldn't believe." He pitched his fingers to illustrate a Toucan Sam.

"Hey!"

"Being honest." He wore an unrestrained smile without a hint of apology.

I also asked for the story behind Frog's name.

"With a last name like Froggen, our eight-year-old minds naturally went for Frog. After a year of pitchin' a fit, he got used to it. Never call him Wesley. It's Wes or Frog, or you'll hear it."

Made perfect sense.

Teddy joined us and slinked onto the other side the couch, his checks red from sun exposure. Dom leaned over and gave him a hefty punch in the arm, and Teddy winced at the surprise attack and rubbed the spot.

"I'll beat your bitch-ass later when I have the energy," Teddy promised.

Dom laughed. "Doubt it. You couldn't sneak up on me if my eyes and ears fell off."

I laughed while they bickered. Teddy, scholarly about speed versus strength, placed himself in the winner's category since Dom fought with brawn. Dom had his own piece to counter, sounding much less cerebral than Teddy's university-educated-in-Health-Sciences response.

The rest of the night consisted of cold beer, buckets of fried chicken, honey garlic chicken wings, potato wedges, and three monster sized pizzas loaded with toppings I had never had on a pizza before. I tried it all and found I liked the Italian sausage, broccoli, and even the cheese-filled crust. By ten o'clock, everyone's energy was at the greasy-food-level low, and the garbage overflowed with sauce-stained paper towels and food containers.

I went to the bathroom to rinse my face before the grease could attach to my pores. After checking my braid and tucking loose hairs behind my ears, I turned to leave and jumped at the sight of the man leaning against the door frame.

"What the fizz, Caine?" I pressed against my pounding heart.

"Sorry. A little eager." His smile was apprehensive. I waited as he gathered the gumption to say whatever made him impatient enough to scare the shit out of me. "Can you stay the night?"

"Oh...um..."

"I'll take the couch."

"What? You don't plan to sneak in and grope me in the middle of the night?"

"Don't tempt me." He became serious. "I haven't spent a night alone since leaving the hospital. I was either at my mom's or your place. When you worked, I had Bosco." I nodded. "As needy and unsexy as it sounds, I don't want to be alone."

Admitting what he saw as weakness was difficult. I reminded myself how fresh from his sleeping curse he still was, and how long he spent every waking moment alone while trapped.

"I'll have to get Bosco. With so much new stuff for him to destroy or mark, it's a risk."

"Well...." A hint of deviousness morphed his expression. "Kim offered to babysit."

"Oh, she did, did she?" So, Kim was in on it. I caught my friend's guilty leer over his shoulder. Bosco would be in safe hands with Kim, but their collusion was a bit bothersome.

"Sure, I'll stay."

"Thank you." He grabbed my head with both hands and planted a big kiss on my forehead. His smile was pure relief as we rejoined the party.

Caine stopped at the kitchen to grab us drinks, and I squeezed in next to Kim on the end of the couch.

"What's the going rate for colluding babysitters these days?"

"Am I in trouble?" she asked too low for Frog beside her to hear. "Caine was so nervous and begged for me to let him ask first. I can't say no when he gets all intense. Plus, he was adorable as hell."

"I'll forgive the conspiracy this time. Next time bring me into the know."

"We can also work on training tomorrow before heading to Aunt Lacey's."

"Hmm? Looks like you've got it all worked out."

Kim smiled. "Looks like."

―――――――

As the time came for everyone to leave, the guys all shook hands or hugged, each with a hug for me as well as they welcomed me into their group. Their sweetness was a world of difference from my experience, considering my ex-boyfriend's friends. Made me miss my own friends, who I hadn't got together with in far too long, and I made a mental note to mention it to Serena who would get on rounding out the plans for the girls' night we started to plan.

"If Bosco wrecks your stuff, you deserve it." I warned Kim, making sure she had my apartment keys, along with my second-hand knowledge of Frog's ex, Jody with the big schnoz.

Ranlyn wasn't the happiest about the sudden venue change but made arrangements. He planned on staying for a few hours before trading off with someone else, making sure to ward Caine's balcony before falling under a cloaking spell and heading into the hall.

A deep kiss surprised me the moment we were alone. Caine squeezing me against him in what felt like a desperate thank you.

"Do you want to go through some of your stuff?" I asked as we pulled apart. "You have a lot of boxes."

"Sure. It's gonna be weird. I haven't seen any of this stuff in so long."

I found generic office supplies in one box: stapler, mouse pad, paper clips, sticky notes, and binders with paper. In the same box was a picture frame, hand decorated with leopard print paper and cut-out magazine letters that spelled '4-EVER' glued to the frame. Caine's grey eyes shone in a ray of sunshine, his smile small as Tracey planted a red lipped kiss on his cheek. Her outreached arm captured them selfie-style.

"Lord love a duck." I clamped down the belly laugh threatening to erupt. "Tracey was a crafty girl."

I passed it to Caine. He sneered. "Unfortunately. I hid it in the drawer when she wasn't over."

"Note to self, cheesy framed picture gift idea already taken."

"Stay away from the glue gun and animal print, and we're golden." The crash the frame made as it hit the garbage pile punctuated his request.

I was more than a little happy as I watched him dispose of Tracey.

———

We decided to leave some work for the morning and get some sleep. The deep green sheets and comforter he gave me for the night smelled of the packaging Caine removed them from. Department store scent wafted every time I tossed around in discomfort without my duvet and snoring canine company. The clothes Caine lent me twisted, and I had to readjust the dark basketball shorts tied as tight as they would allow, though they still hung past my knees. The old Pittsburgh Steelers t-shirt was more a dress than anything.

Another twist and Caine's smell crashed my senses. Pressing the shirt into my face, I breathed in his cologne. I focused on the scent mixed with some deep breathing, finding comfort and familiarity to ease me into sleep.

———

An odd sound infiltrated my sleep. A muffled scream and moan brought me back to the room. I panicked from the initial confusion of where I was until my night vision revealed a floor of marked boxes with Caine's name on them.

The sound came again.

I tip-toed into the living room fearing what I might walk into. Caine laid out on the couch, making those noises with beads of sweat down his face. He was in the middle of a nightmare. I knelt beside him and called his name. He didn't wake up, so I shook him until he snapped awake. A gasp of breath and a clenched fist came at me. My quick reflexes had me shooting backwards into the stiff wood of the coffee table, but saved me from a busted face.

"Fuckballsoup!" I yelled.

Caine's eyes went wide. "Holy shit!" He unclenched his fist and collapsed back onto his pillow in exasperation, resting his hand on my knee, the other pressing into his eyes.

The threat of violence over now, I could focus on being concerned. "You were having a nightmare?"

"I'm sorry." He panted and ran trembling fingers through soaked hair. "Usually you don't hear me."

8

———

THE CYCLE

"Usually?"

He sat up. "I'm fine. Go back to sleep."

I sat on the edge of the couch. "What are they about?"

"Nothing."

After all the dreams I went through with him it took me a moment to brush off the snub and decide the middle of the night was not the time to pick a fight.

"Come sleep in your own bed."

He laid back down. "I'm fine."

"Perfect, then we'll sit and chat."

His exhale heavy. "You're being ridiculous."

"I know, right?" I shovelled on the sarcasm. "Trying to convince a guy to get into bed with me? Makes me such a twatburger."

He laughed. "Fine, lead the way, twatburger."

Surrendering to me allowed him to remain mute about the dream, but he laid down in bed and nudged closer, wrapping an arm over me as we lay on our side. Instead of creating distance, I pulled him tighter around me.

Time passed. I could tell he wasn't sleeping. Everything in me wanted to make him give in and talk about the dream, thinking of tactics I would use on future clients to get them to open up, but I skipped on the experiment and gave the space I promised.

———

The sun's rays shone pink through my eyelids, its warmth my alarm clock. Caine's arm was draped heavily across my stomach as he slept. I stared at his strong features at rest. Before my sleepy brain rejected the thought, I pressed my lips to his, a quick moment passed before he responded. When I pulled away a minute later, he opened his eyes for the first time of the day.

"Mmm." His chest rumbled. "I'll take that wakeup call every morning."

I giggled and kissed him again.

This kiss went deeper. I wrapped my arms around him, and his hand in my hair to pull me closer. When his tongue grazed mine, I melted and searched for it again as his weight pressed me into the mattress. *Did I moan?* Tracking my actions was impossible at this point. My focus fixed on his lips and how his intensity managed to be gentle yet forceful while allowing me to dictate the pace.

When things started picking up, the muscles of his back flexed beneath my palms and he broke the kiss.

"Don't say it," I told him.

"Say what?"

"Whatever gentlemanly thing you think you have to say."

A breathy laugh. "I'd be stupid to—"

"You'd be stupid to ask questions. Yes, I want this. No, I won't regret it. And yes, I have issues that might complicate things later. We're adults and I'm not letting any of that get in the way. A more important question is if you happen to have any condoms within their expiry date among your shit?" I smiled and brought my lips back to his with a roll of my hips that contacted the part of him ready and willing to comply.

Caine reached to the nightstand drawer without pulling his body off mine to grab a single gold-package.

"Hmm," I hummed as my fingers dug into his lower back then down to his ass beneath his shorts. "You're quite prepared for someone who just 'didn't want to be alone'."

"Not me. Dom." My arched brow made him laugh. He dropped a kiss with light suction on my throat. "When he heard you were staying, he thought they might come in handy. No way in hell did I anticipate using them."

"Them? I get a double feature?"

"A trilogy if you're lucky, and we take a nourishment break."

"Be sure to thank him for me when you tell him all about it." I pulled him close for another kiss as my body flushed with a dizzying heat.

He pushed up, whipped his shirt off, and I moved to remove mine.

"You're giving me permission to tell?" He laughed.

"Sure." I undid my bra, pulled it off my arms with an inward celebration cheer at the lustful look I received. "If you think Kim won't be first to know, you're delusional."

A low moan escaped him as leaned in to kiss me and then my breasts. I lost all sassiness to the rush of my pulse as Caine took over and made good on Dom's thoughtful supply.

———

Caine found me dressed in my moving clothes from the day before drinking a can of pop I hid in his fridge from the guys. Breakfast be damned, I had built up a driving thirst over the last hour. Caine snuck behind me and snatched the can for himself.

Awake and invigorated with plenty of time to sift through boxes before Kim would be by for our training, I floated on a fragile high from the morning's activities. Any kind of intimacy had been a long time ago for both of us and the exploration of those sensations and vulnerabilities was scary as fuck as well as freeing.

We sat on the living room floor, surrounded by Caine's belongings. I handed him things, and he separated them into piles to keep, donate, or chuck. A jersey of a team I would never guess for a million dollar question had an autograph on the left shoulder.

I held up the jersey. "Is this an important player?"

Caine looked up from the box in front of him and froze. He snatched the fabric, stuffed it back into the box, and carted it to his room, muttering about looking through it later. Alone and taken aback, I waited for him to return. When he didn't right away, I found him standing in front of the closet, box at his feet, jersey in hand.

I kept my distance, remaining by the door. "Something you want to talk about?"

"No." His voice was flat as he returned the jersey to the box and kicked it in the closet. He walked past me as he left the room and started to open other boxes.

"You sure?"

"I'd rather you didn't push."

I chose not to take offence. I also chose not to heed his wishes. Who would I be if I refused to push? "Caine, you don't need to fill me in with every aspect of your life, like that fact you ordered a house-load of new furniture, or that your friends know all about me. That's your business. But last night and today, something heavy happens and you decide it's better I don't know anything. Omitting things isn't exactly helping my trust issues, especially when things are happening right in front of me."

His hard grey eyes looked up at me. "You don't tell me everything. You were stabbed at work and played it off as nothing. Plus, I know nothing about who hurt you or what they did to make you guarded. Seems pretty damn important. Everyone has things they're not comfortable talking about, including you, so when you're ready to tell all, maybe I'll do the same."

"If you thought a defensive stance was enough to get me to back off, you don't know me at all." His expression begged me to drop it. "I wasn't too guarded to fuck you," I tacked on.

Shock value has its uses.

"Sex isn't the same thing as opening up."

"So, it was sex?"

"Don't twist my words. If that's what you want to hear to make it easier to walk away, than that's an issue I'll have to contend with. I don't have it in me to share right now, especially when you're not talking either."

"Look, it's not my style to let things fester. Backing off when, in the past, I should've pressed is how I got myself in the mess I'm in in the first place." I sat on the couch. "Sex and true openness *are* different. And neither of us held back while creasing the sheets, so I'll let self-sacrifice make a good example."

His voice flooded with anger. "Sophie please, I didn't mean now."

"A neighbour is married to this prick." I continued without missing a beat. "I stood up to him. He caught me alone and cleaning up after the bar closed. I forgot to lock the door. He was polluted and pissed at me for refusing to serve him earlier and for getting between him beating his wife again."

Caine met my stare, the DVD 'Rudy' in his hand.

"He broke my jaw, fractured my skull, and stabbed me. When I didn't die fast enough, he strangled me until I stopped breathing. Aunt Lacey and Kim found me, and the Coven healed me. I got the impression I survived with a lot of help from Donovan." Caine looked down and picked at the plastic edging of the DVD case while I went on.

"I didn't tell you because I didn't want you to worry about me. No one else but those who were there knows for that same reason. You were still in the sleeping curse, going through far more than I was. They healed me and dealt with the guy who did it. He'll be in a mental institution for the rest of his life, so I had my revenge before you were even awake."

He stayed quiet for a few moments after I finished. "Well, I feel hideous." He paused again. "You died. That's no Mickey Mouse situation."

"I never said it wasn't serious. It happened, the Coven healed me, and then they healed you. Everything's happening so quick, and I didn't want to rehash it."

He gave a slow nod with the DVD still in hand.

"And the guy thing...." I continued.

"Stop." He dropped the DVD back in box and raised his hands. "It doesn't matter. I lost my point and went too far."

"Yeah, you did, but I still want to tell you." A quick pep talk and a check to my emotions and I was pushing through to recall the story I never admitted to anyone in full.

"We were together quite a few years. Brock—the douchebag—was the charismatic type everyone loved, including most of my family. He hid his problems like a seasoned magician. Handed his dick out like free carnival pie, stole from me, and controlled our money as if he worked for every dime. Manipulated who I saw and when. I made excuses so friends and family wouldn't know. Pawned anything nice I did have for what I found out was drugs, cocaine being his preference."

Caine was stone-faced. "I can tell it doesn't stop there."

"I wish. Instead of leaving, I focused on the type of person I believed he could be and not the reality, and things got worse. Physical." Caine's jaw muscles clenched and I figured the details were unnecessary. "The kicker? He left me. On a normal piece of shit day, he disappeared, again, but this time he took Bosco. Talk about sending me into freak out mode. I banged on the door of every drug den and trap house I'd pulled him out of until I found Bosco and stole him back. Fucker had pawned him and left town to flee a debt to a dangerous guy."

I took in a steadying breath that felt anything but. "People question how it's possible, not knowing a person you live with, someone...I...agreed to marry...could do things like that under your nose. For the longest time I had no clue. I thought something was maybe going on, but not that. Couldn't see what he was capable of. When the truth reared up and flashed its pock-marked ass at me, I was too ashamed to tell anyone, and he took advantage of my pride. When you're caught in the cycle after years of manipulation, you shift into survival mode and that's what you do day in, day out.

"After becoming educated on the cycle of abuse and addiction, I conditioned myself to be cautious because I couldn't trust my instincts. I won't be that girl again. This morning was about me making a choice knowing we could land in happily-ever-after territory or drown in regret. I've survived worse so I took a chance. Some walls are still up, and others might spring up at any time, but I'm still in control. And after all we've been through, I think we both needed it."

Silence grew as Caine absorbed my story. "I assumed something like a cheating ex, but nothing so involved. Engaged? That blows my mind."

I shrugged. "I got a pretty penny for the ring considering it was stolen."

"Stolen?"

I nodded.

He shook his head.

"Told ya. Douchebag."

He sat on the cushion closer to me, and I stiffened to disguise the effect of recalling my past which had me trembling. "I know you're trying, Sophie. This morning proved that."

"Even if there was no emotional connection, it's been a while since I've gotten any."

He didn't find my humour amusing. I hated the look he was giving me. As if I had morphed into some fragile thing he had to protect. This was also why I didn't like telling people.

"I appreciate the fact that every time you're with me, you're pushing yourself to pretend you were never affected by all that. In the future, please let me know what I can do to make it easier."

I gave a small smile and fought against coursing adrenaline. "Trusting implicitly is not my thing. Now you know why."

He nodded and held my hand, his thumb rubbing the back of it, soothing my nerves.

"So, I guess it's my turn," he said, and I gave an encouraging smile. "I feel stupid now. Nothing I have is close to that."

He took a breath as I waited.

"I've been dreaming about the accident every night since I woke up from the sleeping curse."

"Shit, Caine. That's horrible." The park was his version of war and the PTSD would stick with him for a long time.

"It's the crash itself, then after as I'm looking for Cole. Pretty much what Donovan saw. Of course, it couldn't end with seeing you. At least it'd be worth dreaming about."

"A chick screaming at you half-naked is certainly memorable."

"Sometimes fully naked."

"Perfect." I laughed, but he wasn't done with serious yet.

"The dreams are vivid. I'm in the driver's seat. The weather sucks and it's freezing. Cole's cheap ass cologne is in my nose. Something's on the road, and the car veers into the trees. I don't remember locking the brakes or maneuvering around it. I think I turned, but I don't remember. Then I crawl out of the wreckage and Cole's gone. I run around trying to find him, knowing I can't leave him there and having no idea if he's hurt or why he'd leave me alone."

"I'm sorry you have to relive that."

"It's like the curse hasn't let go. I thought of telling Aunt Lacey about it. Maybe she's got a trick to give me a full night's sleep without waking up in a pool of sweat."

"As sexy as that sounds, I'm sure she can. After the stabbing, she gave me something so I wouldn't dream at all. That might be better."

"Dreaming of nothing is better than nightmares. I'll talk to her tonight."

Relief we had found new understanding had me soaring, but I wasn't quite done. "So, the box. Cole's stuff, right?"

"Yeah." He cleared his throat. "Cole wanted an autograph. We couldn't afford to actually get into the stadium to watch the game, but he insisted, so I waited around in the cold with him afterwards." Caine shook his head and ran his hand through his hair. "I didn't expect my mom to put his stuff with mine, though she would have known he'd want me to have it. I'm leaving it where it is for now."

"It'll be there when you're ready. I'll help if you need it," I offered, knowing he would process alone. He smiled and wrapped me up in a hug.

As exciting and emotional as the morning had been, I was anything but tired. In fact, I was now so wired, I ripped through boxes at light speed. Caine was the same, and we made as much progress with his boxes as we did with each other.

———

Later that afternoon, Kim picked us up to head back to my apartment for whatever she had planned. Our guard followed in behind while another camped out at Caine's.

"How was he?" I asked about Bosco as he jumped on my lap with a barrage of kisses in Kim's car.

"He has a weird thing for showers."

I laughed. "He jumped in with you?"

"Sure did, wouldn't take no for an answer."

The image of Kim struggling to keep him out was hilarious. It was impossible unless you shut the door against his unmatched lust for water.

Back at my apartment, I showered—door closed—and did all the things I couldn't at Caine's. The memory of his hands on me, the unexpected passion, and his attentiveness to my pleasure was enough to reignite the ache between my thighs and keep me under the pelting water longer than necessary.

Instead of training in the apartment, we decided to head to Aunt Lacey's. Ranlyn was happy for it as it was easier to guard.

We found our Coven Leader with her head in the fridge searching for something. Donovan sat at the kitchen island, eating a sandwich.

"Caine," Aunt Lacey's said, emerging from the fridge with a carton of lemonade. "You have yet to follow through with the details of our last conversation. Only action will secure your advancement." She poured herself a glass.

"Seems pointless when you already know." Caine's tone bordered on disrespectful.

"Why?" Aunt Lacey said with caring eyes. "Your power's existence remained a secret to you, though you were born to it. As with Salix, fear on the part of close-minded individuals left you Blind. You crave to know why, even if you deny it." She sipped her drink. "Do you not feel the need to speak of it? If I spoke when there was something I did not know, I would hardly speak a word. I may have been around for centuries, but I still understand basic human curiosity."

Caine's mouth dropped and he looked at me to confirm if Aunt Lacey had been joking as she scooped up Bosco and went outside, coddling him on the way.

"I forgot to mention the whole immortality part," I answered with a rueful grin.

"What? You didn't test him with that question? Guess that one was only for me." Donovan's condescension was thick as he dropped his plate into the sink with a clang and turned to lean on the counter. I had asked him once if he was hanging around with Aunt Lacey all the time because of her immortality. He said it was loyalty, but I never found out the full reason.

My patience with Donovan's bullshit was already exhausted. "Is this how it's gonna be all day, Donovan?"

He pegged me with a hard stare. "Figured it'd be an important question."

"It doesn't change anything," Caine said.

"No? Being powerful, so powerful that one day you stop aging, makes no difference?"

"No."

"Unbe-fucking-lievable. You could at least be honest, man." He moved forward and leaned into his elbows on the kitchen island. "Tall order to fill, don't you think? All this talk about Sophie and her power mixed with Nya's. Aunt Lacey's daughter-in law was no Seedling and Sophie being the vessel for Nya's power equals a long life." His dark stare slid to mine. "You won't age past thirty-five. I'd put money on it." I squirmed under his stare until he looked back at Caine. "Where does that leave you if you can't follow? Or what if you can? You ready to shadow her through the years without finding someone else?"

"That's enough!" I snapped. His implication was insulting and not only to Caine.

Caine responded anyway. "Wouldn't you follow her if she wanted you to?" This quieted Donovan and had me and Kim exchanging a look of ragged discomfort. "You claim to care about her and then put her through your bullshit. If I'm a lemon, wait for your opportunity, but you're a coward to cause her pain to get at me, and you know it. I'm going to see what Aunt Lacey and Bosco are up. Excuse me."

After giving me a kiss on the cheek, he left the room the bigger man.

"Me too," Kim said awkwardly and quickly followed Caine.

I went to join them.

"Please. Wait."

I did but wanted to make Donovan wish I hadn't. "What the fuck-flavours-of-the-month is the matter with you? Truly. Acting like a child will not get you what you want no matter who usually gives into your grousing."

"Sorry about that."

"No, you're not. Not even a little. You don't want to look like an asshole. I'd think you'd be used to it."

He took a step towards me, his expression smooth and for once free of arrogance, gifting me a view into something honest within him. I don't know what I saw, but what I experienced was more than anything I ever had before. Something perceptible, yet difficult to pinpoint, and my anger fell away.

"I know you don't hate me, babe. A part of you wishes you could be two people to appease the sides of you that care for both me and Caine, but you can't. I'll try to respect that, for now, but like Caine said, I'll be waiting when you change your mind, since I know you will."

As much as he fascinated me, I shook my head at his assumptions. "You can't know any of that."

He broke his stare. "Unfortunately, I can."

Donovan headed towards the living room. Guilt chilled me, while something else I couldn't identify weighed me down, holding me in place, and wishing he would come back. Being two people to test his theory would answer some questions. Questions I, too, wanted answered.

Both Caine and Donovan came into my life under extraordinary circumstances. I wasn't the daytime TV soap opera type and refused to play both men, or keep one on the side for a rainy day. I hated my duplicity, questioning my relationship with Caine because of something Donovan said. More likely, he was manipulating me with another trick that I was still too fucked up to see and might fall for.

Caine returned to the kitchen. "Everything okay?"

"No." The word fell from my lips in a desperate whisper.

Caine touched my shoulder. "What'd he do?" His intensity pulled me from thoughts of Donovan.

"Nothing." I smoothed my hair behind my ears. "I think he just needed to get that off his chest."

Caine's smile was hollow, and I went into the backyard before he could ask anything more.

9

TWO OF A KIND

Caine

Worry about the Initiation didn't hit until we were waiting for the other Coveners. My mind was too wrapped up in whatever Donovan said to Sophie to get her wound so tight. She moved around the backyard and then the house as if on autopilot. Getting things ready for the night, busying herself with whatever she could. As much as the kid hated my guts, he cared about Sophie, or at least thought he did, so I can't imagine he was rude to her. Which meant the opposite.

Goddammit.

Whatever Donovan said got her thinking about him, about them. Was she that close to dropping me already? I thought we were making headway.

I put my arm around her shoulders hoping this would relax us both. Instead, I saw her eyes through the side of her sunglasses flicker to Donovan sitting across from us as he leaned against the wall. He wore a bored expression, but I had no real clue what the guy was thinking.

"What do I have to do?" I asked Sophie to gain her attention.

She stared up at me, her brows all bunched up. Did I sound that transparent about my desire to have her choose to stay with me?

"During the Initiation?" I clarified.

"Nothing," Kim answered when Sophie didn't. "Follow whatever Aunt Lacey tells you and you'll be fine."

I ran fingers over Sophie's shoulder, this working better to gain her attention.

"Hope you get a cool name," Kim added.

"Great." I forgot naming was part of the coven experience.

"Oh, shit," Sophie said too loud. "I didn't get you a gift."

"Please, you don't have to get me anything. It's weird they give gifts anyway."

"Hope you're not being polite because I forgot too," Kim apologized. "I've been busy with the whole bad guy thing and you moving."

"Seriously, Kim, it's fine."

"Good," Donovan said. "I also seemed to have forgotten."

"Like I said, it's fine." I wanted to punch Donovan's pompous smile through the back of his teeth. That would have been the best gift ever.

The Initiation was as confusing as Sophie said it would be. I'm a water sign, a Pisces. I knew this, had even used it as a conversation topic on a lonely night, but I didn't expect this.

All around me was a water effect created by some type of illusion magic. Gentle movement hit the dim lighting of the basement and made the floor around me shimmer as if I was ankle deep in water at night, though nothing like the park. This was clear and soothing, more bath water than immanent lake monster attack. Cool, but I had no clue how Aunt Lacey did it.

If any of the guys knew I was doing this, they would think I had brain damage from the coma. Old me would have never believed in this stuff let alone participated, but with all I knew, and all I had to gain, there was no walking away.

The seriousness with which Aunt Lacey spoke of deities and elements with a burning blue candle in front of me along with a huge old book, was nerve-wracking. If she tested me later, I was sunk.

Kim and Sophie stood next to Aunt Lacey. I tried not to look at Sophie too much and seem like I wasn't paying attention, but I couldn't help it. Even if I couldn't see her beautiful eyes watching me, I knew she was. At least more than she watched Donovan, who bugged the shit out of me by sitting just on the edge of my peripheral vision so I could see how he wasn't paying any attention to the ceremony.

Once Aunt Lacey moved on to her history, I booted Donovan from my brain. The woman had been through the wringer. If she was telling the truth, she was old. Ancient. From the faces of everyone around me, no one questioned this.

She moved on to speak about her son.

"Gareth's strength was inspiring. Yet, he and his wife, Nya, were overtaken by the grief of the extended life we choose to live as immortals." The room went eerie silent, and from those faces, I could tell whatever was coming next wasn't good. "When unable to endure the demise of so many as they lived on, they chose to give themselves to the Witchburners. Those who scoured the lands, purifying people of what they feared plagued their towns with pestilence and heathenism. The ignorant prided themselves for the discovery, never admitting to townsfolk of the surrender, claiming a righteous capture. Gareth and Nya were the only true mystics burned in our town. All others were innocents, yet they burned no different."

Sophie and Donovan didn't react to hearing about the facets of the deaths of Aunt Lacey's family. I knew a bit about Sophie being Nya's vessel, but she didn't get into extreme detail. Details, it looks like, most others didn't know anything about.

A large intake of breath preceded her next words. "Before they died, they relinquished their powers bound to their physical bodies, freed their souls to live on in search of new vessels in which to carry them into the future. I pray one day they find each other again and this time live with peace of mind." Speaking of their death spliced her expression with sadness, as if she saw their deaths firsthand. I got the feeling she had.

The room adopted a mournful atmosphere. Even Donovan bowed his head, his eyes closed as if he was deeply affected by this piece of history. Instead of going on with the ceremony, Aunt Lacey excused us for a break, looking like she needed it most. As she stood, my water effect disappeared, and the loss was jarring. I didn't realize how much of a difference it made until it was gone.

Grabbing Sophie's hand helped, especially knowing it was something Donovan couldn't do.

"How much longer?" I asked as we gathered in the kitchen with the crowd.

Kim talked around the mouthful of disgusting-looking marshmallow salad. "Naming and presents still, so buckle up for the long haul."

I groaned, thankful it was a onetime occasion. "Kind of messed up Nya and Gareth burned to death."

"They did it together at least," Sophie said, surprising me she thought of it as romantic. "Though it's a nonsense way to die considering the unfathomable pain. Poison or something else less excruciating would've been smarter."

That sounded more like her.

After filling and draining our bellies, we returned to our spots in the basement for the Naming Ritual. A thrill ran through me as my water effect returned when I stepped into the circle. Corners and Deities were called to witness again, though I had no clue who they were. Kim handed Aunt Lacey an old bowl full of water with coloured stones and floating flower petals. She walked around me as she spoke and flicked water at me.

She stopped in front of me and said, "In front of this coven, the collective universe, and with all your consent, I hereby assign you, Caine, with the coven name 'Leith'."

I peeked at Sophie, she smiled with approval as Aunt Lacey

continued.

"Water is a powerful and unstoppable force when given proper momentum." She ran her finger over the water effect around me as it moved around her as well. "Water was the physical result of your anguish as it fell from the park skies in your worst moments. Yet, it allowed you to endure the pain in which I pray you will overcome. With the power of the water and your innate perseverance, you will create great success for yourself and those you allow within your waters."

Kim held Sophie's hand now. Not in excitement but for support. I didn't expect Aunt Lacey to bring up the park. It brought me to this room, but still. Speaking of the park in front of the others made my shoulders tighten. I fought against clearing my throat.

"Does anyone object to this name?" Aunt Lacey asked the group as I fought not to react.

"We acknowledge thee as Leith," declared the Coveners.

Sophie's lips didn't move.

Equipped with my new name, Aunt Lacey said farewell to our invisible guests and then had the group introduce themselves with their coven names.

I sat on the couch for the gift segment, rubbing sweaty palms on my jeans ready to get home or at least out of here.

Sophie removed her sunglasses. "You okay?"

"Better than your bloodshot eyes. Put those back on." She did but waited for an answer. "At least the name's okay. I'm pretty sure I went to school with a kid named Leith."

My answer didn't satisfy her, but someone handed Sophie a gift to pass to me, ending the conversation. When we got down to the last one, Sophie paused with a lingering look at it before handing it over. I removed the paper to find a small rectangular box with carvings on it that looked a lot like one Sophie had on her dresser.

When I opened the box, I thought I heard a small gasp from Sophie. A ring? "Oh, it's like yours," I said to Sophie, her attention fixated on the jewelry. The ring nestled in a plush setting, the thick band the same vintage white gold and smoky quartz as Sophie's with one small diamond on each side of the recessed gem. "Thanks, Aunt Lacey."

What else do you say when a recent acquaintance gives you a ring? I don't even wear rings. Never have. Right now, I couldn't care less about if Aunt Lacey thought I accepted the gift with grace. Sophie wasn't happy. Anger radiated off her like a heat lamp, her sunglasses hiding her eyes that would tell me much more than her clenched fists in her lap.

"You're welcome, Leith." Aunt Lacey clapped her hands. "Okay everyone, you're all welcome to stay and socialize or practice. Please do not forget the fast-approaching Lughnasadh celebration. For now, I need a moment with our guest of honour. Leith. Salix, Wiccum, you too."

The crowd migrated into groups. We joined Aunt Lacey at the back table where all serious conversations took place.

"Matching rings, huh?" Sophie said to Aunt Lacey in a clipped tone I rarely heard.

"Your rings are two of a kind, this is true. Forged simultaneously and gifted to yourselves with purpose."

"They're Gareth and Nya's rings," Sophie's voice was edged with insult. "I knew mine was Nya's, but you decided to keep the whole Caine-is-a-vessel thing a secret until now? And this brings up a few questions about why you gifted them and hid this from the beginning."

"As I said, my son and his wife relinquished their powers in hopes to find their way into the future, to gift them to others capable of carrying the strength of their magic. Individuals with power born into their blood, since Gareth and Nya had been so strong." No one spoke as she paused, but I knew what came next. "As I told you, Salix, I saw Nya's power buried within you before we met. Once I learned of Caine and heard of his plight, I knew my Gareth was within him as well. Surviving the Awakening Ritual and allowing me to glimpse you in person solidified what I knew to be true."

Gareth is in me? I would have laughed if Sophie didn't look so pissed.

"I feared you would recognize me. A ridiculous notion...." Aunt Lacey shook her head and laughed sadly. "You see, Gareth and Nya themselves are not within you. You are not a reincarnation of a person by any means. However, their powers were so intertwined that a shadow of them has survived. One I recognize. Without understanding the power and its capabilities you would not have understood if I had revealed any of this sooner."

The table was quiet. Kim hadn't said a word and cast nervous glances at Sophie.

"Your path can be different," Aunt Lacey responded to Sophie's thoughts with a hint of fear that alarmed me. What did she hear? "I told you, these powers are yours to do with as you choose, not bound to their fate, bound to no one, not even each other. Intertwined as they are, they will prove more potent when used in conjunction with the other, but it doesn't require a romantic bond."

We sat speechless. How could Gareth's power be in me? When did it happen? Why was Sophie so pissed? I wanted to ask her questions but not at the table. She wouldn't give me a full answer in front of the others.

"This is amazing," Kim said, clearly sharing Aunt Lacey's perspective. Sophie lips were in a hard line as if restraining herself from lashing out.

"Seek me out with questions when you can articulate them. For this night, Leith, I am proud you are amongst the fold. Understand this power of my son's is not the only one within your arsenal. Discovering your true lineage is still a venture that you *must* make a priority."

I nodded. Crazy lady or not, she believed in this power inside me. She saved me from the park. The chances she was right was bigger than the prospect of her being wrong.

I didn't want to admit it, but I needed to know.

10

MISGUIDED

Happy my sunglasses hid my rage from the Coveners who side-eyed me as I left the table, I didn't stop when Aunt Lacey held Caine back to discuss gaining a hold over his power. I couldn't talk to him yet. I wanted to get out of the basement before I started kicking people. Hard. Kim followed me upstairs. I slid my sunglasses to the top of my head since her low glimmer was easier to handle and only a few others were around.

"Heavy shit, huh?" Kim loaded another plate of marshmallow salad.

"Keeps piling up and gathering flies. Maggot orgy any moment now."

Kim's raised spoonful, stopped part-way to her mouth, grossed out. She ate the goo on the spoon anyway. "No offense, Soph, but you're overreacting. I get the rings have your commitment issues tying your shoes and pushing you down the stairs, but Aunt Lacey said they don't mean you're connected to each other in a romantic sense."

I leaned against the counter. "This is destiny shit she's peddling down there. The word implies an ingrained path without a future of our own."

"No one else but you is using the word."

"Please. She's thinking it and you know it."

Kim put her plate down and held onto my crossed arms. "Nothing's changed. Don't let tonight mess up what you've been working towards."

I pursed my lips. Kim must have taken this as a sign of agreement as she smiled and left for the bathroom, but my expression meant everything but satisfaction. She hadn't known me long enough to know the difference. Right now, I was fuming.

"Tell me you don't buy into it." I spun to see Donovan standing inside the kitchen, the backyard door sliding behind him. "Nya and Gareth. Tell me."

"Why do you—?"

"Sophie." His intensity shocked me as much as the usage of my name instead of calling me "babe".

We stood captive in this moment; me in my shock, he desperate for an answer.

"You ready to go?" Ranlyn asked, stealing my attention for a moment.

I turned back to Donovan and said, "No." My voice stronger than I expected. Then I turned back to Ranlyn. "Kim's in the bathroom."

When I looked back at Donovan, he was sitting at the kitchen table, staring into the abyss of his thoughts. He and I knew who my original answer was for, yet neither of us knew what it meant.

Caine asked me to stay over again that night. Aunt Lacey worked some knot magic with a complicated array of thread and knots meant to help Caine with his nightmares. After seeing what he had gone through in the sleeping curse, I couldn't leave him to test it out alone.

Ranlyn kept what happened between me and Donovan to himself, but he looked at me funny in the rear-view mirror as if he knew something. His attention made me wonder if whatever he dosed me with to cover my thoughts wore off yet.

"So...immortality, huh?" Caine asked as we sunk into his couch.

I shrugged. "If you're strong enough."

"Do you want to be strong enough?"

I shrugged again. "I'm not planning for it. I'd rather leave it to chance without the pressure of expectation."

He nodded. The conversation made me uncomfortable. I couldn't pinpoint why, but I was happy with leaving it alone.

"Do you mind if I bogart your shower? I don't want to go to sleep all gross."

"You're not even close to gross but of course you can." He leaned over for a quick kiss, which I accepted before I jumped into the most luxurious shower I'd ever set foot in. Water rained down on me from jets positioned from the walls and the showerhead above allowed the water to rain down on top of me. I had to admit I turned off most of the wall jets. They were excessive and no amount of luxury would get my head straight after Caine's Initiation.

A powerful surge of magic pulsed through my body while mid-shampoo. I raced out of the shower and into the living room as someone burst through the front door. My scream echoed off Caine's walls as I tried to cover myself from the white-and-yellow souled Magic standing wide-eyed in Caine's foyer.

Caine jumped in front of me to shield me from the Magic.

"It's fine! We're fine!" he yelled. "I was just practicing." Now that I could breathe again, I realized the Magic in the foyer was part of our security detail. Ranlyn was probably off getting some beauty sleep to restore his pink sparkly soul. The Magic nodded at Caine and disappeared back into the hallway.

"You okay?" I asked.

He looked down at me standing in a puddle and smiled. "Better than okay."

I shot him a cheeky look, then squealed and ran back under the water, as shampoo dripped into my eyes.

Ten minutes later, the surge of power rippled through me again. I smiled at the thought of Caine practicing. Hopefully, Bosco wasn't hiding under a table somewhere or turned into some kind of ten-foot-tall monster pug.

Another surge slammed against my chest as I opened the bathroom door. I found Caine sitting on his living room floor, legs folded, eyes closed tight.

"Don't force it." I bent down to kiss him on the cheek before sitting on the couch.

He exhaled, looking defeated. "It's so much harder than you make it look."

"It gets easier." I remembered the same pessimism as Donovan made the dandelion grow without looking at it. "Let it come from you as you're relaxed, not frustrated. At least you know how the power feels."

"I scared the shit out of myself. Bosco, too. Feeling it had me pumped, then it kept getting stronger. It's like pushing a stalled car that hits a downslope and takes off. I don't see how you stop it from doing that."

I sympathized. I asked all the same questions not long ago but had someone experienced to answer them. Having Donovan over was out of question, so I promised we would work on it together.

"Are you sure you don't want to have a shower before bed? It's tits-gold and then some."

"Nah, I'm more of a morning shower person."

"You morning people, I don't know," I joked as we crawled into bed.

I suddenly found myself sitting up in Caine's bed looking around the dark room in a daze. An actual daze. My dopey stare moved over the room, sluggish as my head swam like I had consumed ten drinks. My mind was everywhere.

Emotional.

One second I was as exhausted as I had been before I went to sleep, then the next moment overwhelmed with seething anger, right before sliding into gripping depression that brought tears to my eyes. I walked on unsteady feet to Caine's couch, Bosco following. I covered myself with the wool throw as he jumped in next to me. All I wanted to do was sob and beat the living shit out of someone at the same time.

Had I been dreaming? I couldn't remember. Sometimes my dreams were so vivid they stalked me even in my awakened state, but I would have remembered something about a dream overloaded with such frightening sensations.

Without reason or remedy, I curled up, blanket to chin, Bosco in the crook of my knees, and forced myself into sleep.

———

I sat up in confusion, wondering why I was on the couch before my memory kicked in of how I got there.

"Mornin' princess."

When I looked over the back of Caine's couch towards the kitchen, I found Caine, Kim, and Serena staring at me, eager to get the day started.

Caine came over and pecked me on the cheek, I blushed with embarrassment in front of Serena. "You okay? Why'd you sleep out here?"

"Umm, just got too hot. Your body is a furnace." I didn't want to lie but I had no explanation for whatever that was last night and didn't want to worry him. "Holy shit, guys." I smoothed my hair and rubbed under my eyes. "I didn't expect everyone to be so lively this morning."

"Hurry your skinny ass up and get ready," Serena demanded.

"Where's Ranlyn?"

"Who?" Serena asked. "Oh! The weird disappearing dude. Does he sleep here too?"

"No," I said, quick to remove the image I knew was rolling around in my cousin's head.

"He'll be around," Kim answered.

With Bosco safely stowed at Aunt Lacey's, we headed on our way to Guelph. We parked across the street from the institution about an hour-and-a-half later.

The colonial masterpiece of a building was as beautiful as it was welcoming. The closer we got to the surrounding wilderness, soaring white columns, red brick, and freshly painted white walls, the more incredible it became. It was a picture-on-a-postcard kind of glorious.

In my mind, The Royal City Wellness Center was supposed to be an oppressive monstrosity like a prison with barred windows, barbed wire fences, and armed guards roaming for escapees. Not only was there no barbed wire, The Royal could have been a small college campus. I tried to imagine the day the family forced Olive into this beautiful place. What a facade! Veneers on rotted, poison-seeping teeth. After the first initial captivating glance at the intimidating structure, I knew I still hated it.

"This place has been a sanatorium since 1902," Serena explained. "Its fifty acres has tennis courts and even a bowling alley. Can you fuckin' imagine? I wanna live here!"

Caine's thumb brushed the back of my hand as we walked across original hardwood floors. I sneered at the vaulted ceilings accented with crown molding and chandeliers wondering how much dirty money it took to bankroll the institution's interior designer.

The front desk receptionist's long black curls bounced as she spoke to Serena. "I'm sorry, ma'am. Visiting hours are at four o'clock. You will have to return later."

"Nah, thanks, honey." Serena's tone got sweeter as her patience got thinner. "Get up and walk your pedicured toes to your supervisor's office. I know he's here because I spoke to him. We're expected."

A German accent in an expensive navy-blue suit introduced

himself as Director of Operations, Herman Kleinfeld. We hurried to keep pace with the short man's quick steps as he walked toward a greenhouse on the grounds where he was confident we would find Olive.

"She's quite special to us," he remarked as we walked a stone pathway.

"Why's that?" I wondered.

"Olive has been with us the longest." Herman's hand gestures were expressive as he spoke. "We no longer house patients for such extensive time periods, most discharged within weeks or months. Nonetheless, Olive was grandfathered in from the old system. This seemed appropriate though the Board was much against it."

"Why did they keep her?" Kim asked. "Other facilities could have housed her long-term, no?"

"The Royal is Olive's home. The family argued a transfer would be detrimental to Olive's progress. An argument I fully supported and fought to win."

"Family, meaning her sister?" Serena asked what we assumed.

"Yes," Herman confirmed.

"How is her mental state?" I chimed in, trying not to trip on the cobblestone in my sandals.

"Olive is high-functioning," Herman said. "Like many others, she exhibits good days and bad. Most of her time is spent tending to her plants. Frankly, it surprised me to hear she had visitors."

"She doesn't have many?" Kim asked.

"None since her admission. Even when her sister fought for her continuance within the facility, to my knowledge, she did not visit Olive. For fear you may not show, I did not want to give Olive false hope."

"She doesn't know we're coming," I concluded. He shook his head no. Depending on how accurate he was about her headspace, this could prove a mistake. "Does Olive have an official diagnosis?"

He tsked. "A few depending on the age of the assessment."

"They evolve over time, and it's been near thirty years. I get that.

But are we talking an adjustment disorder, a personality disorder, or something more complex like D.I.D.?"

He stopped and lifted his thick, bushy brows at me.

"Sorry, psychology student. I thought a diagnosis might give me insight into why she's been here all these years."

"Ah." He continued to walk as we followed.

Serena raised her hand. "And for the non-psychology students?"

"Dissociative Identity Disorder," Kim answered and received a look of shock from the rest of us. "What? I watch television."

"Yes, well, nothing as complex as D.I.D." Herman sounded somewhat irritable. "Olive does not present with a host of other personalities as with D.I.D. No, Olive is very much herself, a strong-willed and unique woman with healthy self-awareness and drive for personal happiness."

"So, she *is* making progress?" I asked hopeful as well as relieved at no D.I.D., though he was elusive about her clinical diagnosis.

"Oh, yes. She has long since ceased her outbursts and destructive behaviours. Those most likely came from frustration with rules and sheer boredom. Sometimes improper or overmedication. Once the construction of the greenhouse occurred, Olive directed her efforts to bringing things to life instead of destroying them in aggravation. Good thing. With our non-violence policies, lobbying to prevent her discharge became dicey in times of triggered unrest."

We reached a building sided and roofed with glass to allow the sun free rein, though greenery blocked the view inside. Herman led us through a leafy maze where he said Olive was re-potting some sickly ivy found on the grounds.

"Olive, dear, you have visitors," Herman announced, his voice full of optimistic apprehension.

"Always pleasant to see you, Herm-Germ, but you don't qualify as a visitor," a husky, musical voice answered with a hint of humour.

"Ever the card, Olive. I mean actual visitors. Family."

Serena's shaky voice spoke next. "Sorry to interrupt your gardening. My name's Serena. I'm your great-niece?"

Silence bloomed.

"Who is your mother, darling?"

"Karen. Oh, and this is Sophie, Lucinda's daughter."

I was still stuck behind Herman, whose body, though short, combined with the greenery, hid me from a proper introduction.

"Come around to face me, dear." I stepped around the Director without damaging our fragile surroundings.

When I saw her, I froze.

"Oh, my word!" Olive gasped as her eyes glassed over.

Brilliant streaks of white highlighted Olive's chocolate hair. Those eyes. I saw the same colour and shape reflected back at me every morning in the mirror. Olive was a future version of myself, as shocked at our uncanny resemblance as I was.

Not only was I overwhelmed by emotion as I stared at my aged doppelganger, but by Olive's white and green soul glow.

"W-we didn't know...about you," I stammered, swallowing before saying, "Sorry to drop in. We...." Words failed me as I watched tears fall down her cheeks.

Olive ripped off her soiled gardening gloves and wrapped her arms around me, sobbing, then drew Serena in for a three-way embrace. As I held my great-aunt, all emotion from my first night in the Coven rose up, released itself, and reduced me to tears. Olive was my link to the magical realm, not Nya or whoever I was in Donovan's past or even Caine's. This was my lineage, my blood. The relief at this connection was truly magical.

Herman cleared his throat and excused himself as Olive was content with her visitors.

I pulled back and asked Olive, "Can you *see* me?"

She understood my true question. Could she see my soul?

Olive nodded, wiping a tear from my cheek before holding us close again. She would be able to tell that Serena wasn't a Magic, at least not yet, but she was no less one of us.

"Oh!" Olive's voice edged a few octaves higher as she looked over my shoulder. "Who are your talented friends, Firefly?" Of course, she would notice Caine and Kim's radiating souls.

Kim's smile was exuberant, her eyes glistening as she introduced herself with an outstretched hand Olive grasped with both her own. Reaching past Kim in the limited space, Caine also extended his hand, but I took it upon myself to make the introduction.

"This is my boyfriend, Caine."

It was the first time I used the label. The sentiment did not go unnoticed, and he flashed a gleaming white-toothed smile at Olive.

"It's great to meet you, ma'am."

"Please, call me Olive," she insisted and gave me a playful elbow. "Aren't you a lucky girl for trapping yourself a good-looking man with the gift." Her eyes never left Caine, she making no attempts to hide the lingering once over she gave him.

I laughed at Olive's overt observation. Apparently, we were alike in more ways than one. "Actually, he sort of trapped me, but that's a long story." I eyed Caine, mimicking my great-aunt's slightly salacious glance. He gave me that heart-flipping crooked smile from the park.

"And you back there? Show yourself or leave." The snap in Olive's voice was unexpected.

We looked behind us as Ranlyn popped into view.

"Why does he keep doing that?" Serena asked.

"Good day, ma'am," Ranlyn said with respect. "I'm tasked to watch over this lot. Remaining out of view allows me to do this."

"Fine. Be a ghost all you like." She looked back at me and Serena. "Oh, this is marvellous. Scoot outside. We need more room for you to tell me everything!"

Brilliant flowers peppered the colourful grounds. The grass was country-club-perfection until it met the edge of the forest ringing the institution. Other residents ambled or sat with orderlies. Comfortable wrought iron garden furniture with thick, pale-yellow seat covers and matching sun umbrellas sheltered us from the beating sun.

Questions flooded as we caught up on a lifetime of absence while

Ranlyn remained invisible and on guard. The topics started light as Olive tried to grasp her connection to us girls. We went over our birthdays, the city we grew up in, professions, and justifying why none of us had children or husbands. Olive was younger than us when they committed her. She never had the opportunity to have children, though always wanted to carry on the bloodline.

One thing was clear to all of us, including a novice psychology student like me; Olive was sane. No signs of instability roared up after the shock of relatives and Magics, seen and unseen, showing up on her doorstep. Of course, her mental state could spiral into a dark hole of fear and paranoia, but from what Herman explained, it wasn't how Olive coped. No, I was more certain than ever of my grandmother's treachery, but had to admit I was scared shitless to find out why.

Olive reached out to clasp my hand, examining it in the sun. "Why the rings if you're not married? Anniversary? Promise tokens?" It was the first time that Serena saw the matching rings since Caine received his the night before. She and Olive waited for an explanation. Serena with a hint more impatience evident in her tight, blank expression.

Caine looked at me, as if willing to follow my lead. I told them everything. Serena took it as she did everything else, with radiant excitement.

"All those years Gareth and Nya's power searched for their place in the world again," Olive shook her head in amazement. "What distinguishes you two as vessels?"

"Wish we knew," Caine answered. "Aunt Lacey never said, though we had to be Magics to qualify. One's strong enough to contain their power."

"Strength you're still uncovering," Kim added. "You're babies still. Seedlings to a Coven you have no clue how powerful they are yet. Don't worry. Aunt Lacey and the rest of the Coven will get you there."

Olive's expression darkened. "While I do find comfort someone is taking a Magic of my blood under their guidance, I must say, it surprises me you would resort to an alternate coven in the first place."

Serena looked to me and then asked, "Alternate to what?"

Olive sat forward in her chair and glared at us before sitting back in her chair. "If you don't know what I speak of, then the Ballard Family Coven has disbanded."

"Ballard Family Coven?" Serena echoed. "Ballard as in Grandma Lizzie's maiden name?"

"And mine," Olive added.

"Okay, yeah, but a coven? Our family has a coven?"

"Maybe we haven't learned about it yet," I suggested.

"No, Firefly." Olive's attentions refocused on me. "They would have recruited you by now. Few remained when I was an initiate: my cousin Leon and his wife Tapi, Iris and Gloria, and of course my sister. Some new ones had yet to be inducted, but had shown great promise." She picked invisible lint from her skirt. "The Coven's demise should be no shock, especially if you knew nothing of me. I suppose I thought they would have fought harder."

"Iris and Gloria? Magics?" Serena laughed. Olive didn't. I could see why Serena would. The twins were odd. We didn't know them well, but they looked out of this century and acted kooky.

"Actually, being Magics sort of makes sense, now that I think of it," I said to her.

"I guess," Serena said in half-hearted agreement. "But what's with the secrets? Your Coven, our family's coven, everyone sits around and lies about all this power. We've seen Iris and Gloria at countless family things and they never said anything to you."

"My powers weren't released back then. Maybe they couldn't tell."

Olive gave a humourless laugh and crossed her arms, the foot of her crossed leg kicking in restrained anger as she looked off away from us.

Quiet spread, along with my worry. As the chirp of birds in a stone bath grew louder in our silence, the questions started stacking up, and treading lightly was no longer possible.

"Olive, why don't you leave?"

"I can't." Her reply was robotic, and she didn't look at me.

Serena wanted more. "Have you ever tried?"

"Of course!" Her harsh tone causing us to flinch as she glared at us. "I've spent more years at The Royal than you've had birthdays. Every opportunity I take to escape, I'm overcome by some kind of raving hysterics, incapacitating me, and they drag me back. Because of it, I haven't attempted it in years. The fallout of my inevitable failure isn't worth it." Our imaginations had to fill in the blanks of what Olive's consequences were, but I assumed it involved a high dose of chemical restraints.

"A Binding," Kim said.

Olive nodded.

"Someone can do that?" I questioned.

"Your sister." Kim was confident, again Olive nodding.

"Wait a sec," Serena had her hands up. "Binding, like, bound here? Forever?"

"Forever." The dread in Olive's voice was heartbreaking.

"One strong enough to force you into hysterics when you try and leave the property boundary," Kim added. "No wonder she fought for you to stay here when The Royal shifted into a wellness center. Would be difficult to replicate somewhere else. This is the perfect place. You're out in the middle of nowhere."

"Kitchen Witch?" Olive asked.

Kim found it difficult to suppress her smile as it was her turn to nod.

"Good for you." Olive told her. "If more of your kind existed, Magics wouldn't need to hide in the first place."

"I can't believe it," Serena interjected. "How could Grandma Lizzie do this to you?"

Olive scoffed and sat forward in her chair. "Do you know a different woman than I do, child?" Serena's blonde brows stitched together. "Elizabeth's always wanted the estate for herself. Always thought she deserved it because she was older." She wagged her finger. "Birth order doesn't dictate an heir, and she knew it. For centuries, the Magic with superior power gained status to ensure even if the name changes, the strongest bloodline lived on. Elizabeth couldn't accept that. She used the Blind to commit me to enjoy the estate in peace. Jealous. Always jealous!"

Olive's tangent answered as many questions as it created. Picturing our grandmother's house, it didn't seem worthy of such betrayal. Nothing grand or able to withstand centuries.

I didn't understand. "Are you talking about the house on Taffeta Street?"

Olive looked at me, then to Serena, her bird-like movements unsettling. "Elizabeth doesn't live on the family estate?"

"If the family estate is on Taffeta Street, then, yes, she does," Serena answered.

"Are you mad, girl?" Olive shot to her feet, surprising us all, even Ranlyn whose power rose to a perceptible level in warning. If I felt it, so did Olive. "Is the estate on Taffeta Street?" Olive mocked, continuing without acknowledging Ranlyn's threat. "Sure, when chickens grow lips." She huffed, shocked by our obliviousness and paced in the grass. "The Ballard Family Estate rests on Elegy Road where it has stood since before the town was even a town!" She crossed her arms and leaned toward us. "Elizabeth does not live on the estate?"

We shook our heads, concerned about her reaction. Olive collected herself, returned to her chair yet stayed silent, then slapped the arm of the chair making us all cringe. A flutter of Olive's power rippled against me. I looked to Caine as he exhaled from the same sensation. A roaming orderly stood watchful but kept his distance, business as usual.

Olive shot forward and grabbed my and Serena's hands. "Promise me girls, even if I'm meant to die a Royal captive, you will find out if the Ballard Family Estate is still standing. If it is, you need to take it into your possession, Sophie." I attempted to protest. Olive spoke over me, her eyes wide and severe as she pleaded. "Find out if you're this generation's heir and take possession of the estate. Others may be in hiding. The house *was* mine, and I spent not even a year in it before my sister stole it from me. It needs to be the cradle for the power in your blood. It can protect you more than this jokester." She looked at the negative space where Ranlyn stood behind me. She fixed her gaze at his invisible eye level and spoke to him. "Not one Magic can save them from whatever you're skulking around for. Try as you might, you're nothing more than a chaperone."

"I call him Jeeves. More a chauffeur than a chaperone," I muttered.

Olive's intense expression softened.

I placed my hand over hers in a move meant to express tenderness as well as keep her calm. "Olive, I won't need to take over the house. We're here to get you back to it. I don't know how, not yet, but we'll figure it out."

She exhaled a breath and I couldn't tell if she trusted me or thought it was worthless to continue arguing. Either way, a hell of a lot happened to her. Serena and I needed to find out who owned the estate and if it still existed.

The hard issues tackled, the intensity of the visit lessened, and we were now able to spend quality time together. To our surprise, Olive enjoyed living at The Royal. Once it changed over to a wellness center, she said it became a place she loved, spending most days in the greenhouse with her plants. Serena insisted I show off my new talent. Olive laughed and laughed as she watched me grow her ivy an extra three feet.

"Once I get out, you bet that's my first test. What a treat." Olive looked her ivy over with pride and placed it upon a higher shelf, letting its leaves hang down.

I found the trick easy now. I even kept my eyes open while evoking my power. Aunt Lacey did say it would be like that, I reminded myself.

"My admission date was the last day I experienced true power,"

Olive stated. "Seems my sister covered all her bases by ensuring escape was impossible."

"It's still there. Plus, you can see Ranlyn's glow when he's invisible. I can't even do that."

"Our power never disappears, as I'm sure my sister and others of the family coven have found."

"She told me the power came from the Devil, like it was a family curse. I've come across some pretty evil fu— bad guys, recently." I censored myself. "So, I could see why she thinks that, even if she's wrong for hiding it from us."

"Oh, Firefly," Olive chuckled. I enjoyed the nickname even if I didn't understand where it came from. "Elizabeth has always looked down her nose at what didn't serve her as she wished. Weakness be damned, she found ways to use it to her advantage. Instead of enjoying our innate gifts like a companion, she used the power as her slave to do her bidding. Never has she embraced it, pulled it within herself, and experienced its purity. Before she put me in here, she started with that devil nonsense, and her soul suffered. Yes, our power can do horrible things, monstrous things if used with such intent. I fear that is how my sister sees us all. She's clouded by envy and hate, but not like the evil fuckers you speak of, only misguided."

I had to laugh.

Olive's lack of disgust for her sister was surprising. Describing her as "misguided" was more than generous.

Visiting hours were until nine o'clock, so we stayed to eat and hangout. Olive gave us the grand tour of the grounds including her private room. She had years to create a homey space and beamed as she pointed out a family quilt large enough to cover a king size mattress with overhang. Patches covered the front, each in the shape of a butterfly inside a square, each different colours and patterns. One in particular caught my eye, deep burgundy with a small floral design on its square background.

"Your great-grandmother and her sisters, Eleanor and Opal, stitched this quilt by hand using old clothing, sheets, and rags. It's holding up quite well. Every now and then needing a stitch added to ensure the butterflies don't escape. They, too, would be appalled at the family's condition."

Black and white pictures crowded her dresser and window ledge, capturing faces only Olive knew. She went ahead and gave a name to each face, pointing out the others who were once in the now-dissolved family coven. Then, I found a picture of my grandmother. Why Olive would keep a photograph of a person who caused her so much pain was beyond me. When Serena asked about it, our great-aunt explained the photograph was taken when they were inseparable. They spent hours in their family stables, gardening, and sharing each other's deepest secrets. Yet somehow, differing opinions regarding their power came between them.

How could I not immediately think of Serena? Deep down, this was what caused me pause when contemplating Serena joining Aunt Lacey's Coven. I didn't want us to end up resenting each other for one reason or another. I cared too much about her to imagine one day hating her.

The heartbreak in Olive's eyes choked me up when visiting hours ended. The notion it would be the first and last visit was a palpable fear for all of us. We did our best to assuage this by promising her a return visit, along with the promise of breaking the Binding and looking into the status of the Ballard Family Estate.

For her sake, I hoped we could follow through.

The goodbye hug couldn't last long enough. We lingered until the nurse insisted we get going with a pleasant smile and an edge in her tone. It killed me to leave without smuggling her out, but with the Binding intact, we wouldn't get far.

"Where does your grandmother live?"

I stared at Kim, catching the implication behind the question. "It's too late to go there."

Serena turned to Ranlyn. "Haul ass and I'll pay for gas."

"Serena!"

"You tell me where to go and I'll drive." Ranlyn didn't seem bored by the idea, just complacent.

"I asked, Soph," Kim persisted. "Old people don't sleep much anyway."

"I'm game," Caine added.

"Caine, please. It's a weak excuse for barging into our grandmother's house this late."

"Neither of us are in her good graces anymore," Serena justified. "And Olive's sleeping in an institution tonight. I can't sleep comfortably after knowing she doesn't deserve to be there."

Fucknuggets. Serena was right. Olive had suffered enough, and we were the key to her freedom.

11

HIDDEN AWAY

The ride was long, too long for me, my stomach queasy from watching the trees in the darkness blur by. I tried to focus ahead of the car, but it was foggy, leaving nothing to see. Serena recognized the signs I was beginning to lose it as I slumped in my seat, one hand propping my head up, zero conversation. She had Ranlyn pull over so I could lay my head on Caine's lap in the back seat.

"Close your eyes. We'll be there soon." His voice was tender as he brushed my hair from my face and rubbed my back. I concentrated on the motion of his hand, and my stomach began to settle.

Light shaking woke me. Sitting up, I was surprised to find we had reached my grandmother's, but the quick motion had my head spinning.

"You okay?" Caine asked.

"I need air." I wrenched open the car door and stuck my foot out onto the gravel.

"Wait," Caine warned, running around to meet me at my door.

Before he got to me, I hauled myself fully out of the vehicle but ended up staggering against the window, unable to regain control of my weak knees. Caine saved me from toppling over and helped me lean back against the car for support.

"You're going to hurt yourself," he said.

Too stubborn to wait for my equilibrium to stop swimming, I used Caine to pull myself upright. "Serena's already in the house. I need to stop whatever tirade she's on."

Raised voices rang out before I even made it my grandmother's kitchen. Staying calm while her emotions were raging was impossible for Serena. She'd have to take it down a notch for all our sakes. Her mother and brother were one floor away in the top suite and knew nothing about Olive or our family's magic link. Ranlyn was there to protect us, but it didn't mean he wouldn't shut her up if Serena was risking exposure of Magics to her Blind mom and brother. Wherever he was, he remained invisible, but was no doubt close or at least listening in.

My grandmother gasped as Caine and I rushed in, looking both of us over.

I studied my grandmother's soul glow, my angry protests gagged in my throat at the sight of it. Her light was more akin to a flashlight smothered beneath a thick blanket. Not Tainted. Her soul was drowning, suffering as she damned it as evil.

"I knew it! This is your fault!" She pointed an arthritic finger at Caine.

"Ah, it's actually my fault," Kim chimed in, raising her hand like a schoolgirl. "But it doesn't change what your family is. Why punish Olive after all these years? Don't you think it's time to let her go free?"

My grandmother stared bug-eyed at Kim as we waited for her answer. Instead, she remained silent. Her lips pressed together as she stood in her dusty-pink nightgown and robe.

"You're sisters," I tried. "You loved each other, but because you didn't get the family estate...a fucking house...you lock her away forever? Please tell me there's more to it than four fucking walls." Nothing but silence. "You don't even live in the damn house which makes it *that* much more ridiculous. So, you're not the strongest. Big deal. Stop being a sore loser and let her go."

Clutching the robe tighter around her, my grandmother spoke through her teeth. "Olive turned on me. Wanted to leave me with nothing. She wasn't stronger than me, not by a wheat grain. She sidled up to our aunt, the heir until that point. It was pure and simple favouritism. It didn't have anything to do with the concentration of power, as they claimed.

"Olive should have known better than to attack me in front of the Blind. She was dangerous, and they saw this." Her tone softened yet remained smug. "I don't live in that house because it's dripping in the same evil as the rest of you. No human should possess such God-like abilities."

"All those years," Serena said. "You preached righteousness, faith for the good in people...all a bunch of bull. You want us to pretend we don't know the truth? Hide away our power like you did? Well, fuck that. You don't get to decide how we live anymore. I don't care what happened back then, you make this right. Now!"

Stubbornness ran through our family's veins more than any magic. My grandmother clamped her lips shut and raised her chin. Disappointment coursed through me. This was an opportunity for her to redeem herself, and she let it slip by.

"We know you trapped her using the magic you'll never get rid of no matter how much you hate it," I said when Serena's plea failed. "How unfair it is we Soul Seers can't see our own souls, yet others are visible to us whether we want to see them or not. Have you seen a soul that's been hidden away, kept a secret, and cursed for being strong?" She remained impassive. "You look sick. You're a Magic, born a Magic. Hate yourself because of it, suffocate your soul in the process, and pray your God will still want you when you're rotting, but it doesn't have to be like that. Others realize the immense good our power can do. And you know what? You don't deserve it. Our mothers are Blind. They may never accept the power or us. All because you're a hypocritical bigot and a bitter old lady."

I paused, overwhelmed by my own words, and tortured by needing to speak like this to a woman I once revered. "If you hate Olive so much, then let this evil take her over. She doesn't need to be in The Royal for God to damn her soul, right?" No answer. "Let her go. Your plan to bury the power was an epic fail. If we burn, that's our fate. You don't get to choose that for us."

I couldn't talk anymore. Still nauseous from the drive, my throat gave an involuntary squeeze. All I wanted to do was heave a gnarly chunk of The Royal's shepherd's pie special on the kitchen tile. In a sick way, it would be evidence that Olive was real. Yet, I refused to lose it in front of this woman.

When my grandmother left the kitchen, I released a lung full of air. Leaning into the table while collecting myself, Caine hovered, and the kitchen was too quiet. Too much time passed before I realized my grandmother could have been brewing up a spell against us. When she did return, she threw an old, heavy-looking metal key on the table.

"Eleven Elegy Road," she said.

The key for the Ballard Family Estate.

"What about Olive?" She was more important to me than a house.

She hesitated. "I'll take care of it."

"Tonight!"

"Tonight," she agreed with disdain. "All of you will make fine companions for the Father of Lies."

Zero happiness filled me at my grandmother conceding a fight I shouldn't have had to step into the ring for. Not only did she betray her sister, but she believed when she trapped Olive, her sister would never step outside the gates again. That she would die strapped to some gurney after going mad about the power she used to have and the family that abandoned her. Disgust for this woman chased away my nausea. Turning my back without a thank you was easy.

In the backseat of Kim's car, I fought against angry tears. She didn't deserve it, but I couldn't help feeling the loss of my Grandma

Lizzie, a woman who only approved of me when I was stripped of my essence and molded into her version of cured.

Ranlyn pulled out of the driveway. "Where's Elegy Road?"

After visiting Olive and emotionally beating down my grandmother, why not continue to the house that pioneered the entire tragedy?

I vaguely heard Serena's answer. Caine wrapped his arms around me. I couldn't relax or sink into his comfort. It wasn't what I wanted right now. Anything less than taking every family member that collaborated with my grandmother and setting them up like a whack-a-mole game with me using a sledgehammer wasn't going to cut it.

We turned onto Elegy Road, which ran through the town cemetery where our great-grandparents and other family members were buried. The cemetery was old and large considering the small size of the town. I strained to see my great-grandparents gravestones lost in the haze of the night, envisioning the stone carved with music notes and horses.

Trees began where the gravestones ended. An earthy gate ushered us in, hiding the blackened starry sky as the paved road deteriorated into loose gravel.

"Can you see that?" Serena's excitement peaked.

We leaned forward at where she pointed. The trees pulled back at the mouth of the property, allowing brilliant moonlight to shine through.

The old, English-style mansion had a grey stone facade. I was no architecture buff, but I didn't need to be to fall in love with every last detail: butter cream banisters on the wraparound porch, antique windowpanes, thick and decorative corbels, and the columns that led the way to the arched wooden double doors. Everything was faded and cracked from years of inattention.

Standing in the driveway, looking over the wild lawn, which reached up the sides of the moss-covered stone house, I realized I was happy Serena pushed for the adventure, even though I was exhausted. I wanted to see everything the large bay windows hid behind dark curtains. Or maybe the secrets inside were too deep for the moon to touch.

Ranlyn had a couple of emergency flashlights and both Serena and Caine utilized an app on their phones. Our ever-accommodating chauffeur didn't look so chill with the idea of exploring the large home and went invisible to do his own sweep of the exterior, though admitted he didn't think anyone was around. Something about him was off and I hoped it was paranoia and hyper-vigilance his security detail entailed.

Each step groaned as I climbed the few to the porch, clutching the flashlight ready to use as a weapon against rabid raccoons or squatters. The old key worked in the lock, but the door took Caine's muscled shoulder to open. Once we were in, we shone our lights into the darkness. Dark red curtains covered the windows. Caine pulled them open to allow the moonlight in and got a dust-laden cobweb shower for his efforts.

The first room was a time warp into a parlour of Victorian furniture. Hand-carved details covered the wood of every end table, chair, and in the frame around the marble mantel and the bricked fireplace. A dusty film made everything greasy to the touch. The stale air settled in my sinuses. I ran my flashlight over the faded wallpapered walls, some of it peeling and hanging down like paper tongues.

An oblong chandelier hung from the ceiling in the middle of the room. Small lights, dripping crystals, and chains caused a kaleidoscope of colours to sparkle along the walls when my flashlight hit it. Grimy dust turned all the crystals grey. I wanted to reach up and give it a polish. In its glory, it would have shone like diamonds.

A prickling sensation brushed the skin of my arm, travelled up to my shoulder, and then down my back. It had the pressure of an exploring touch. I ruled out a chill or a breeze. Other explanations had the impossible bumping heads with the rational in my brain.

Before I could shake it off, the sensation happened again, this time stronger, like a palm laid on my chest, the ticklish feeling seeping into my lungs.

I inhaled deeply. In the dead quiet, it sounded much louder and attracted the attention of the others, their flashlights blinding me as I put my hand over the center of the sensation in my chest.

"What's wrong?" Caine's voice was panicked. He rushed over and placed his hand on mine, made a sound of surprise, and pulled away, cursing.

"What? What happened?" Kim demanded.

I couldn't answer. Without realizing it, I had closed my eyes. The sensation no longer stopped at my skin. It delved into me to explore. Fear had my blood pumping hard, but I couldn't move, couldn't respond to the other's questions, or find my ears to hear them. Whatever this was pulled me inward with it. Power began to simmer inside of me, rising up to match the strength of this new sensation.

Confusion warred with my curiosity. I wanted to know more, understand what it was, and find a way to communicate with it. I needed answers, and before I could learn more, the tingle dissipated. What began a shocking invasion morphed into something protective. As if this unknown feeling knew me, and what I needed to feel safe.

I trusted it.

"Don't go," I heard myself say in a desperate whisper.

"Don't go where? Sophie?" Caine voice broke through my fog, and the sensation vanished.

"Maybe we should come back during the day," Serena suggested.

The silence was crushing. I didn't want to leave. I wanted to re-enter the estate a thousand times to chase the feeling again and again.

"Soph?" Kim touched my arm.

I nodded and let them lead the way out back to Ranlyn's vehicle. He didn't ask about why we left so quickly and I, again, wondered if he knew without me telling him.

Whatever I sensed inside, it filled me with something I needed and now ached for.

No one spoke again until we were through the graveyard and headed towards home.

"Are you okay?" Caine asked.

"Yeah, spill it," Serena said. "You went all buggy, wouldn't stop touching yourself, and zapped Caine. What gives?"

I opened my mouth to explain, but instead asked Caine if he was all right.

"I'm fine. It was more like a vibration, or a warning. Like you didn't want me to touch you."

"It wasn't me."

"Your power was switched on."

"I didn't do it on purpose. I don't know how to explain what I felt. It was... Yeah, I don't know. Just hard to explain."

Caine nodded and was cut off from asking more questions.

"Damn, girl. Can you believe it?" Serena asked, turning her whole body to look at me in the back seat. "Freaky, zappy ghosts aside, you could be heir one day. The estate would be yours. How kick-ass is that?"

"It wasn't a ghost." Was it? "And the estate's not mine. We have no idea who else has the power in the family. Maybe cousin Liana gets the house. Or you once your power's released."

"Please," Serena sneered. "Liana could out-dumb a goldfish. No way she has power let alone more than you. She still wears feety pyjamas."

"Maybe it's a ruse and she's a closet Einstein."

Serena burst into laughter, but in my mind, the estate was Olive's, and I couldn't wait for her to be back as the rightful heir.

"No idea how we're going to find out," I said. "It's not like we run into family on the street. We avoid Liana like swine flu." Too many young summers forced to play nice-nice.

A light in my head went on, and I gasped. Everyone switched into alert-mode thinking something else sinister was happening. "The family reunion!"

"I forgot." Serena groaned. "How much is that gonna suck."

"No, it's perfect. I'll get a look at everybody and see if anyone else has power." Now I was impatient for the day.

"What about grandma?" Serena raised a crucial concern.

"What about her? I seriously doubt she'll say anything. Plus, our mothers are Blind, so they won't understand why things are suddenly different. We have to treat grandma like we used to."

Serena rolled her eyes. "Great. More secrets."

"Yup. Hone your acting skills, cuz. We Magic's are all about our secrets."

Serena abhorred the thought. I didn't like it, but I had my mind set on answers. If it meant kissing ass, I'd pucker up and add some cherry ChapStick.

We reached my place by two-thirty in the morning, totally exhausted. I invited Caine to stay over, and we walked Bosco in the still of night. My ever-watchful bodyguard was no longer invisible but gave some personal space as he had the whole night waiting for us to get back inside before switching off with another guard to get some rest himself.

As we crawled into bed, I longed to fill the emptiness left and recreate the wholeness of what affected me in the estate, seeking this in Caine's touch. While replicating the feeling was impossible, Caine's body and keen attention to my need for distraction and stress management left me breathless.

12

CONSUMING THOUGHTS

Caine

I choked on a sharp intake of breath as knocking on Sophie's bedroom door jarred me awake. I bolted upright as soon as I heard it, seeing Ranlyn open the door and motion for me to come out into the hall. Sophie could sleep through anything, and after her difficult night and the fact we passed out after sex two hours ago, she was dead to the world.

I pulled on a pair of shorts and met Ranlyn in the living room. "What's up?"

"I need you to head to your place with me."

"Now?"

"Right now."

"Why?"

"A break-in occurred."

"What? Where was the security guy?"

"We don't know. He's missing."

"Missing as in kidnapped or missing as in he was the one who stole my stuff?"

Ranlyn's jaw flexed. "We don't know."

"For fuck's sake," I muttered. "What'd they take?"

"We're hoping you can tell us."

"Of course you are." What could I say? My brain was too foggy to think.

Back in the room I pulled some clothing on and tried to wake Sophie. Slight acknowledgment tricked me into thinking she was awake, but she was back to snoring before I could respond to her sleepy questions. It was clear she wasn't waking up. I knew I had to leave but worried about her safety. What if the guard outside was an undercover Loring sympathizer waiting for an opportunity to get her alone? In the case the other guard was out-manned, how—

"They're loyal to me," Ranlyn said overhearing my thoughts. Guess the mind shield wore off. "You have my word. I wouldn't leave them in charge of Sophie without trusting that I'll find her in the pristine condition we left her." Ranlyn had stationed a guard inside the apartment, two in the hall, and more around the building's perimeter, but I still felt uneasy leaving her.

When we got to my place, I saw a new guard standing by the door. Ranlyn stopped me before we went in.

"Remember, damage is fixable. Pay close attention to anything stolen since we don't know what they were looking for."

Damage? Great.

When I opened the door, I expected a mess, but not this bad.

We stepped over items and tripped over more. Coats and shoes ripped out of the hall closet, the linen closet, kitchen cabinets, and dresser drawers all emptied. White stuffing from my shredded couch covered my living room like the beginnings of a Christmas scene. Same with my mattress, which was off its frame and in the middle of the room in the bedroom.

"The walls...." I whispered. Drywall dust covered the floor below a gaping hole in the wall.

"Do you see anything missing?" Ranlyn asked me.

I ran a hand through my hair in a state of shock. "How could I tell? Some stuff was still boxed up from moving."

My mind went to Cole's stuff. I raced to the closet. The whole box was gone.

"What was in it?" Ranlyn asked, freaking me out by answering my thoughts again.

"No clue. I didn't get to checking it out besides an autographed jersey on the top. Unless a bunch of Magics were looking for a boost in eBay sales, I doubt that's what they tossed my pad for."

"No, they wouldn't. Was it just the one box?"

"I don't know, man. Sifting through my dead brother's stuff wasn't high on my priority list. One for sure, but there could've been more."

"Take your time," Ranlyn encouraged. "We'll work on getting things back together. Order may help you see better. We're also checking any camera sources in the area in case they slipped up."

He clapped me on the shoulder in show of support, but I wished Sophie was here. She may have remembered what was in the box. Plus, she makes me calmer. Cole's box was all I had left of my brother, and some evil asshole steals it? For what?

Anger hit me so fast I was sweating from the heat.

Questions I couldn't answer had me caged in this sense of help-lessness. While Kim's lessons were informative, they were Kitchen Witch stuff. I had true power and wanted to use it for something other than freaking out the neighbours with uncontrolled bursts.

Aunt Lacey's words to find my own replayed a dozen times as I looked around at the wreckage of my apartment. I wasn't being diffi-cult. If Aunt Lacey was right about my mom having answers, the knot in my stomach at pushing for them was what stopped me. She couldn't know. I couldn't believe it she would lie to me my entire life. To both Cole and I. Was she capable?

What worried me most was hurting her. I protected her my whole life. And now that Cole was gone, how could I do that to her? On the other hand, considering how big all this was getting, why did I care if I pissed her off? She was happy to voice her opinion, what was I protecting her from?

One thing Sophie was right about was how weird it was Cole and I never questioned who our dad was. Or if we did, I didn't remember it. Was that a hint at something shady or the outcome of growing up in a single parent household?

"I've got to go."

Ranlyn looked up from shoving the insides back into my couch. "No problem, I can take you back to Sophie's."

"No." Ranlyn's expression was evidence of my harsh tone. "No, I need to go to my mother's without a brigade of bodyguards on my ass."

"You know the dangers."

"I still need to go."

Ranlyn grabbed my arm when I went to leave and asked, "What about Sophie?"

"Don't tell her anything. I'll explain things if I get what I'm looking for."

"I won't lie to her for you."

We squared off. "Ranlyn," I said with as much calm as I was capable of considering my head was pounding with fury. "Stay here and investigate. I don't need guards. Don't tell Sophie anything about this or where I've gone. I shouldn't be long, and I don't want to worry her. I've got this."

Ranlyn paused a moment, then stepped back.

"Thank you." I was out the door and calling a cab before I could formulate a plan.

———

Knocking on the door of my childhood home was odd, regardless of the time, but walking in uninvited would piss my mom off from the get-go. My mother's severe expression as she registered my face told me it was a good choice, but I was screwed either way.

"I have questions about my father."

The crease between her eyes deepened in anger. No matter how old I was or what father-son events I missed out on, I never made her talk about him. Maybe I was being protective. Now I felt less inclined to be complacent without answers, pictures, or even a name. There had only been one accidental comment about how I resembled him while I was growing up.

My mother let the screen door stand between us until I said, "I'm not leaving without answers. Please let me in."

I sat at the wooden kitchen table where I ate my mom's special meatloaf whenever I asked for it or when she thought I needed it. Mom leaned against the counter with her hands folded as I repeated myself. "I have questions about my father."

"Why?"

"Because I can't find him to ask myself. You kept everything from Cole and I." I took a breath to refocus. "I don't care about the past or whose fault it was. I need to find him."

"I have no idea where he is." Her answer was too quick.

"You know something. His friends, his family, anyone." She shook her head as I talked. "How about his name? Tell me his name."

She stared at the floor, crossing her arms, and refusing to speak. The chair screeched across the linoleum as I stood, took a step towards her, and held her shoulders as I got down on one knee at her feet. Still, she refused, now closing her eyes.

I spoke in a soft plea. "I know you disagree with how I'm living my life by being with Sophie—"

"She's not good." Her eyes went wide but looked at me again.

"She's better than me and I don't even know who I am. So please, tell me how I can find my father."

Her expression smoothed. She blinked. Her eyes shone with tears before she walked upstairs. I followed as far as the landing and waited, finding it hard not to focus on the fact I was wearing my shoes on the carpet. A big no-no growing up.

When she returned, Mom gave me an envelope. "Your father sent this after I made him leave."

"M-made him leave?"

"He was a horrible man. I see you have inherited his traits and I'm willing to bet your girlfriend has a similar set of her own."

Her words confirmed Sophie's assumptions. "You knew?" My gut roiled when her rigid stare answered me. "You knew he had power and didn't reach out to get me out of the sleeping curse?"

Again, no answer. Not even a flinch at calling it a curse and not a coma.

She crossed her arms. "You think I don't know what those rings mean? You think I don't know who has you twisted into someone I can't recognize? My own son." She shook her head. "If you choose this path, with her, with them, you are never welcome in this house again."

Knowing she hid so much from me, that she knew about these powers, that she left me in that park for years to suffer without seeking help, I rushed out of the house satisfied not to look back.

Driven by a hurt and fueled by a fierce anger, I walked down my old street and pulled out the twenty-plus-year-old letter from my father with shaky hands. Rain darkened the page, so I folded it up and jogged to a nearby Tim Hortons, hiding my father's words from the rain in my pocket. With a pop and a glazed donut in front of me to give me the chance to sit and read, I opened the letter, craving to devour my father's words more than the sugar.

My Love,

Now that you know about me, about our sons, about the world I belong in, you need to know I had every intention of telling you. If I only had the chance, I would have divulged the information years ago so you could have

made an informed decision in marrying me. I was terrified by your reaction and feared your scrutiny. I was right in assuming you are incapable of handling such knowledge.

No matter how much you hate me, know that Caine is innocent. I know he will show the most promise, but if either of our boys begins to show signs of emerging abilities, you need to allow them to contact me. I'll never be far. They may be scared and even volatile due to no fault of their own. Exiling me will not hide these gifts forever. It will only create confusion and alienation. They need to understand they're not alone. Prepare yourself to look at the situation clearly. They may choose to turn their backs on me and whatever ability they inherit as soon as they learn the truth, but it needs to be their choice.

Please tell them I love them, no matter what your story is for my absence, and know that throwing me away could never stifle my love for you. Reach out to me at Eli's day or night. I beg you, Joyce. You will be able to see when they change. Do not force them to walk around Blind. You have your eyes open to us now. You need to give them the knowledge of the choice when the time comes.

Never living a day without you and our boys consuming my thoughts,

Danny Berisford

I read and re-read the letter, the paper's deep creases probably from a time my mother sat and did the same.

Danny Berisford. My father's name. Or maybe Daniel. Whatever

I was expecting, it wasn't Danny.

Hours passed. I didn't know how many, but the sun was up. The morning breakfast rush in full swing. I wondered if Sophie was awake, and then pushed the thought aside.

After re-reading the letter again, I called the operator who found an E. and B. Berisford residing at 62141 Mud St. E., in Tweedside, near Stoney Creek. The 'E' had to stand for Eli. Eli and Danny were family.

Equipped with only the flimsiest of information, I lingered in my seat, contemplating what I might be walking into. I had so many questions. How did my mother find out about the power? Or the rings? And how could he walk away from his family? Divorced couples managed to operate with civility for their kids. Danny had power. My mother couldn't have *made* him leave. Maybe she ran away, but then how'd he know where to send the letter?

Leaving my donut uneaten, I called an illegal cab company that had been around since I was in high school. Cheaper considering I had a ways to go.

I contemplated calling Sophie. In the reverse situation, I would want her to tell me so I could be there for her. Like when she included me when meeting Olive. But the last thing I wanted to do was make things more dangerous for her. Since I didn't know these people and had refused Ranlyn's guards, I couldn't risk bringing her into this. I put my phone away and put her out of my mind.

A dented white car rolled up beside me at the coffee shop curb. "You goin' ta Tweedside?" The burly man's stomach touched the steering wheel, but looked harmless enough.

The man drove above the speed limit without stopping for stop signs when he could get away with it, getting the most out of his flat rate. Silent for the most part, a man doing his job, until he asked me what I was doing up in Tweedside.

"Visiting family," I answered.

The man chuckled. "You dunna' sound happy 'bout it," he said with a lethargic Eastern Canadian accent.

"You know how family is." Most people had family they dreaded, but they are blood so you love them regardless. This wasn't the case for me yet was all the answer I had.

My comment was all it took for the driver to prattle off about his sister-in-law and her four brats. Then bleed on about being unable to complain or his wife would kick him to the couch. I hmm'd and ahh'd at the appropriate moments, listening enough to hear him pause for a response. The bulk of my mind recalled parts of the letter already memorized. My father had a name and now I knew what it was. Why would my mom keep Danny's surname?

Hatred bubbled for Danny letting my mother take us kids away. A part of me wanted to know the man, to confront him, and make him answer my questions. An inner struggle that wouldn't quit until I met Danny face to face and heard his side of the story.

The cabby missed the address and had to turn around. In farm country, the houses were few and far between, so it took longer and the driver was getting sweaty and more annoyed with every minute.

He left me standing at the end of a long driveway to a traditional farmhouse. I took a moment to look over the blue siding and small front porch before going up the wooden stairs and knocking on the door. Hours had passed and here I stood, zero concept of what to say to whoever answered.

Shit. I should have called first.

A young boy of maybe six or seven answered and looked up at me through the screen door.

"Hey bud." I attempted a non-threatening expression. "Um, is one of your parent's home or grandparents maybe?"

The boy stared a moment and then slammed the door shut, leaving me to wonder if he'd return with someone, or if I would have to knock again. After another minute, the door opened. This time a woman my mother's age answered, her jaw dropping, her hand grabbing the frame of the door for support.

Her gasp echoed in the silence of farm country and a moment

passed before her shocked features morphed to confusion and then wonder. "Caine?"

"Yeah. Yes, I'm Caine. You know me?"

Her answer came in the form of her opening up the screen door for me.

Conflict clouded her tone as she told me to "Take a seat," motioning to the living room couch. She left me alone on the worn brown floral fabric, my ass on the edge and picking at my nails while I waited for what came next.

The smack of another screen door and hurried steps echoed from the back of the house could have meant anything. Did I waltz into a trap? Was she headed off to curse me? Fuck, I should have told Sophie where I was going.

A tabby cat roamed the room and rubbed itself against my legs, welcoming me with more affection than the woman. Family photos hung from the walls, but I was too freaked to check them out to see if I could find a man who might look like me.

The squeal of a back door and heavy boots were audible from the direction the woman disappeared. A man came around the corner with the woman behind him. I stood up thinking I may need to defend myself or that I may be looking at my father, though the latter seemed unlikely. I looked nothing like the much shorter towheaded man.

"Holy shit." The man looked me over a moment and cleared his throat. "You weren't kidding, Bernie."

I said nothing.

"Hey there, Caine." The man extended his hand. "I'm Eli. This is my wife Bernadine. The kid is my daughter's son Andy."

I didn't even see the boy watching me from a small hall off the living room.

"Nice to meet you all." Since he didn't attack me immediately, I felt safe enough to shake his rough hand. "Sorry for disrupting your morning. I should have called. My, umm, my mom gave me a letter from my father, and it brought me to this address as a place where I might find him."

Eli hesitated and took a seat on the lazy-boy chair next to the couch. I sat down as well.

"How much do you know about Danny?" he asked me.

"Nothing. Today was the first time I learned his name." They nodded and gave me nothing more. "As I said, my mother gave me a letter he wrote. Here...." I produced the letter as evidence. "This is everything I know."

Eli read the letter, as did Bernadine, sitting on the arm of his chair and looking over his shoulder. Shaking his head with a sadness I didn't understand, Eli handed me back the letter. "Do you understand what he means when he talks about abilities?"

This made me laugh. "I do but haven't been able to use them yet. My girlfriend introduced me to a coven. I joined recently. A lot of crazy things have happened in the last few years, so it's important to me to find out about my abilities and some basic ancestry. Figured I'd start with family since I'm told the powers are sometimes genetic."

Eli looked to his wife who smiled for the first time. "Well, Caine, as far as family goes you can start right here. I'm Danny's brother, your uncle." He spoke with shadowed pride. "Sorry for the run around. Even though the letter and those eyes prove who you are, we have to be cautious. You understand."

"Of course." My eyes. That explains both their reactions upon seeing me. "Believe me, I know all about discretion. I can't tell you how much I appreciate anything you can tell me."

Eli laughed. "Don't worry about it. It's good to hear your blood's strong. Does your brother have any abilities?"

The question cut a little. "Cole didn't get the chance to find out. He died a few years ago."

Grief overshadowed their expressions as I explained the accident with a disconnected neutrality. I sounded more engaged when I got to how Sophie changed everything. "Once I was awake, it was natural to jump into the magic stuff and our Coven Leader suggested finding my lineage."

With the visit going so well I held off on questions about the Berisford name and what Donovan could know about it.

"You have to make sure we meet this girl some time." Bernadine sounded friendly, a nice change from her earlier, silent, shocked greeting. "Who's your Coven Leader?"

"I don't know her full name. We call her Aunt Lacey, though she's obviously not my aunt." I laughed, knowing I was sitting in front of the only aunt I've ever known.

Again, their faces dropped.

"You know her?" I guessed.

Eli rubbed his hands together. "We've met. In passing and not for some time, but yes, we know her. Has she spoken about her past at all?"

Caine smirked. "At my Initiation, yes. About her son."

"What about him?" Bernadine pressed.

"He and his wife gave themselves to the Witchburners and they passed on their powers to find new vessels. My girlfriend and I. Apparently." I showed them the ring and watched as their eyes narrowed. I twisted it. Wearing jewelry was weird to get used to.

"You're Gareth?" Eli clarified pointing to me. I shrugged in chagrin. "Well, holy shit!" He laughed a belly laugh filling the family room walls. His laugh was so achingly familiar. It took me a moment to realize it was my brother's.

"So, you and your girlfriend are carrying around their power and you haven't even learned to use it yet?"

I nodded, embarrassed now that he put it that way.

Eli laughed so loud I laughed in surprise. "You had no chance, did you? In your blood or invasion by suicidal Magics, no way you were getting away from the power." He wiped tears of laughter from his eyes.

The laughter died, and Eli became serious. "That's amazing, but I think the reason Bernie asked about her past is because Aunt Lacey, as you called her now, knew your father a long time ago, so I think you're in good hands."

"What? Wait a second. She knew my father?"

"Sure did. Helped him refine his abilities before they lost touch." Bernadine's slight squeeze of her husband's shoulder had Eli looking up at her. "Come on Bernie, the kid should know."

"You sure about that?"

They stared at each other a moment.

"Please," I interrupted on the edge of my seat. "I need you to tell me everything."

Both sat back an inch.

"Feel that Bernie?" He looked up at his wife. "That's why."

"Feel what?" I asked.

"You don't know what you did?" Bernie asked me.

"I didn't do anything."

Eli smiled. "You tried to persuade us."

"Persuade? I didn't do anything."

"Wow, kid. No one will be able to resist you when you're at your full capabilities."

"But, I didn't—"

"Oh, it's fine," Eli assured. "Believe me, it's perfectly fine."

Nothing about this was fine. I tried to persuade them? How many people have I done that to? My thoughts zeroed in on Sophie and her decision to try out a relationship with me. Then Ranlyn letting me leave and even my mother. Did I persuade them too?

Eli went on. "Now, your father knew Aunt Lacey once upon a time. We knew her as Elsa but had heard she changed it," he paused. "Your father went into a nasty state when your mother left. It wasn't Joyce's fault. Danny gambled, like so many do, that the Blind will stick around once they've found out the truth. He lost. Changed. Started following less than honourable practices."

Less than honourable? "My father's not fightin' with the good guys anymore, is he?"

Bernadine's head tilted with sympathy.

"We tried," Eli said. "But once he let the darkness take over," he paused, rubbing his hands together again, "I couldn't bring him back." He eased back in his chair, the movement stiff and painful looking.

"Power has a tendency to turn people into shadows of themselves. Taken over by a dark power which has them forgetting about humanity as if they're elevated above its laws. We Berisfords have a famous past littered with deplorable behaviour. Danny and I gave our word to each other never to lose ourselves like our father did. Unfortunately, Danny shut us out."

Well, that explained what had Donovan so freaked out. He knew what the Berisford name meant, knew what I came from, what I could become.

"We tried so hard, but he stopped listening." The pained regret in Bernadine's voice said more than her words.

"I'm sure you did."

A sense of loss grew within me. On the way to the farmhouse, I attempted to prevent myself from knocking on the door with high expectations. I let the truth of my father's nature wash over me and the realization that Aunt Lacey knew all along. Anger for this fact was greater than for my father's betrayal of his promise to Eli.

My family was evil. My father was evil. A part of me was evil.

13

CREATING CHANGE

"I have no idea where the fuck he is and it's pissing me off," I ranted to Kim. "Caine's cell is off, and Ranlyn won't tell me a damn thing, except, 'He's got it.'" I mocked Ranlyn's tone. "When I ask, 'Got what?' Ranlyn repeated, 'He's got it,' like some Bro-Code you need a pair of walnuts floating in cheese cloth to understand."

Kim snickered.

"I'm trying my best not to play the crazy girlfriend right now. I don't think he's out dicking chicks, though even if he was, I can't police his dick."

"What? Damn right you can."

"I wouldn't want to. Whatever. I don't like the disappearing act. He knows better."

"Better than what?"

"I'm just worried." I redirected since Kim didn't know about my dickhole ex. I was shocked I had even tried to draw a parallel between Caine and my ex. "Plus, I haven't heard anything from Serena about Olive either. We should've stayed and watched my grandmother reverse the Binding. But nooo, I had to get pissy and storm out instead."

"Hindsight, doll. If it helps, I was convinced she'd follow through. It could've taken her a while to work the spell since your grandmother doesn't practice like she did back when she bound Olive to The Royal. You can't turn it on like a faucet."

"Fine. You're probably right."

"And if Ranlyn's not concerned about Caine, then chances are Loring isn't a factor," Kim reasoned. "They'll call, and you'll feel like an idiot. You have bigger things to worry about, like training a new kid behind the bar tonight."

Oh, right, my actual job. My sack-tugger boss Drew had called to tell me to come to work early to train someone.

"Yeah. You're right."

"Hmm. Maybe I can amp up your tip quotient."

"You can do that?"

"I can try."

"How?'

"Target something. Something most people eat or drink. Martini olives?"

"*Pfft.* The Lush doesn't bring in martini drinkers. Aim lower."

"Beers?"

"Hmm. Not everyone drinks beer either. Maybe ice?"

"Too diluted." She thought a moment. "Oh, I know! The coasters. Everyone who gets a drink, even non-alcoholic, gets a coaster. They're paper, originally trees. Oh yeah, I've got some ingredients to work with."

I sat back into my couch. "You know, you're a bit scary sometimes."

She straightened. "Damn right I am."

I arrived at The Lush in an acidic mood after a ride in from Ranlyn.

He parked and slipped under a cover spell and followed me inside. I hoped Kim could make good on her threat, er, promise to amp up my tips because feigning a genuine smile was already exhausting.

I wasn't even in the door, and already I was on the clock. First, I held the door open as Drew was booting out a rowdy customer who had too many. Considering he had never curbed customers before, something bad must have went down.

"Get in here!" he barked at me. The bar was overcapacity. He pointed at a young woman in a short skirt and talked above the din of voices. "This is the new girl."

"Taryn." The frightened newbie had her hands shoved into her jean skirt pockets. She peered over the bar at the room teeming with people like she already regretted accepting the position.

I ignored her. "What the fuck, Drew. What's with all the people? You giving out free booze?"

"Nothing's ever free. Eddie's on the floor playing runner. You two are back here. Make her useful." After giving these bold instructions, Drew tucked tail and scurried off into the back office and shut the door.

Wonderful.

"You have any experience?"

Taryn blinked at me and hesitated. Yup. Total newbie. The best I could manage was to set her up doing basic barback duties: popping caps, pouring beers, and replenishing garnish, while I dealt with customers who expected every bartender to be a mixology expert.

I repeated an order to Taryn again. Then, I noticed her ears were a blazing red and she was starting to dart back and forth from the counter to the fridges doing nothing but moving her feet.

"Don't lose it on me yet." I plunged a glass in the ice basin.

"I've been here before. I've never seen it this busy," she said.

Come to think of it, neither had I.

Was this Kim? I didn't want six times the tips if it meant six times the work. Geez.

In the middle of all this, I looked up and saw Caine.

He was all smiles. Mr. Disappearing Act graced me with his presence ten hours too late. He would have to wait.

"Busier than a free celebrity hooker here, Caine." I scowled as I mixed three drinks at once.

"I can hang out."

"Order something or go home. I can't have you staring at me all night while I'm working my bag off."

Ranlyn appeared at his side. It was so busy, no one noticed he popped up out of nowhere. "One of the guys can bring him to your place, Sophie," he offered as he glared at Caine. I didn't know what that was about and was too busy to ask questions.

"Whatever." Easier to dog him out at my place. I'd be too exhausted to head to his place and doing so over the phone was unsatisfying.

Caine didn't address him, instead he yelled above the noise, "No way I'm sleeping tonight and I have huge news to tell you."

"Sure. If I don't lock myself in the bathroom to contemplate self-harm first." I'd chastised myself for joking about self-harm later. Right then, I didn't give a shit about anything but surviving my shift. The underboob sweat alone was chaffing my nerves. When Taryn dropped and shattered another glass, I heard a pin drop in the bucket of fucks I had left to give.

Caine reached over the counter and gave my arm a light squeeze. His thumb stroked along my skin. He looked at me with such intensity it took me away from Taryn's muttered apologies. Guilt and confusion overwhelmed me as he left. I sent him daggers and he gave me a moment of peace in the midst of chaos. Unfair when I was so desperate to be angry.

Ranlyn ordered a scotch. "The good stuff."

"Call Kim," I snapped.

"Can't talk on the phone when I'm parched."

I picked up the handheld drink dispenser and sprayed him in the face with a jet of soda water. The crowd whooped like it was the beginning of a wet t-shirt contest.

"Hey!" Ranlyn scrubbed his face with his hands.

"What gave you the impression I'm in the mood to take your bull-shit today? Was it the vein in my neck? No? How 'bout the one in my forehead? And if you tell me I'm overreacting, I swear on every pair of frat boy blue balls in this room I'll hold you down and use this as a sinus cleanser." I held the dispenser out like a gun.

The sight of a dripping, disheveled Ranlyn suddenly made all things better in my world. The bubble of laughter that escaped was evidence I was done with my tantrum. "Here." I passed him a hand towel. "Now, call Kim and get her to reverse whatever Kitchen Witch shit she pulled while I get your scotch."

"What did she do?"

"Just tell her I value my sanity more than I do my tips."

———

As soon as the chaos subsided, Taryn took a bathroom break and disappeared. She left without bothering to collect her night's wages or tips, which left me with her cut. If my pockets weren't full of two months' worth of tips and my feet weren't so swollen, I'd have kicked Kim's ass.

Ranlyn wanted to drive me home, but I wanted to walk. Even with my feet killing me, I was too restless, forcing him to follow me like a creeper down the street.

When the rain hit, I welcomed the gloom of the downpour, uncaring that the rain soaked through my clothes. Instead, I wanted to dance my way home. I was disappointed when Caine showed up with an oversized umbrella.

"Ranlyn called. What are you doing? You wanna get sick?"

I turned to Ranlyn and gave him the stank eye. I flipped him the bird for good measure.

"It's water, not Ebola-snot falling from the sky," I told Caine. "If it rained rum you would have found me lying in the middle of the road with my jaw fused open." I raked my fingers through my wet hair. Caine laughed at me while I tilted my head back, my mouth open to the sky like I couldn't get enough, even if it wasn't rum.

———

Leaning against the door frame of the bathroom as I towel dried my hair, Caine's grey eyes shone as bright as his soul glow.

"Why are you staring at me like you want to wear my skin?" I asked him.

"Aunt Lacey trained my dad."

I waited for the punchline as I headed back to the living room. "Are you their love child? Or is Gareth and that's why you're his vessel. Eww, you'd have your half-brother inside you."

"He wishes," Ranlyn muttered and took a sip of water in the kitchen.

"Does he? Something you need to tell me?" I asked Caine with mock seriousness.

"Shit no," he scoffed. "Why would I want to be related to Aunt Lacey?"

"I meant your father," Ranlyn said.

"Your father is related to Aunt Lacey?" I questioned Caine.

"What? No."

"I'm so lost." I took the offered water from Ranlyn enjoying screwing with Caine.

Caine signed. "Wait? You know my dad?" he asked Ranlyn.

"Heard of him. You've inherited his gifts. Use them on me again and you'll be skirting Loring on your own."

"What'd you do to him?" Then I mock whispered, "Teach me and you've earned a dozen free blowies. No expiration date."

Caine stood slack-jawed as if weighing out the chances of me following through.

I made a sound like a game show buzzer. "Times up. Now tell me what you did to Ranlyn and what was so important that you took off all day on someone with disappearing ex issues." Ranlyn could hear everything in my head anyway, so I didn't bother to hide it.

He sucked air.

"Oh, you finally got it?"

"I'm sorry. I got busy with farming and training."

"Farming? I don't even know what to say to that."

"These arms are useful for more than cuddling."

Ranlyn groaned.

I crossed my arms. "You're not allowed to be cute right now. I'm still mad at you."

His smile disappeared.

"Persuasion is a serious gift," Ranlyn said. "Get a hold of it and quick or you'll be locked down until you do."

"Persuasion?" I didn't like the sound of that.

"That's what I've been trying to tell you. It's a family trait. My family taught me to control it, so I don't use it accidently anymore."

"Accidently? You've been persuading people? To do what?"

"Not you, Sophie," he said quickly.

"You don't know that," Ranlyn corrected him.

Caine's expression showed he didn't.

Fuck. I tried to think of past conversations with Caine. Did he persuade me? How would I have known? What if he orchestrated all of this?

"Sophie...." he tried but I was already a few steps away from him. "Okay fine, I don't know for sure, but it won't happen again. I found my uncle Eli and his family, and they taught me how to control my powers and explained the persuasion trait."

"What do you know about them?" Ranlyn asked in an interrogating tone.

Caine glared at Ranlyn. "I know they're all I have after my mom disowned me for trying to find them. I trust them."

"He can persuade you," I said. "How do you know you can trust anything he said?"

"Because I can. He knows things about my parents."

"What about your father?" Ranlyn asked.

"He wasn't there."

"Doesn't mean they're not in contact."

"They're not. And it's none of your business if they were."

Ranlyn took a step towards Caine. "Do you understand the security risk you posed, not only to others, but to Sophie? Your place is ransacked, you persuade me to let you leave—"

"Accidently persuaded."

"...and then you spend the day out of contact with Magics we have no insight into."

"Your place was broken into?" I tried.

"Not by Eli."

"Someone connected to Cole did or his box of stuff wouldn't be missing."

"Was there a brick of gold I missed?" I asked. "The jersey couldn't have been worth a B and E."

"You don't know who or why someone broke into my place and I'm not doing your job for you, Ranlyn."

"Rude much?" I muttered.

He stared at Ranlyn. "I would never put Sophie in danger. We both know she's your main concern."

"My orders include the both of you, but if I find this new family of yours poses a threat, I have no qualms with kicking your newfound family's front door in to ensure my orders are upheld. You understand?"

"I got it."

"Good. Now what do you want to tell me about them?"

"Nothing."

"Nothing. You sure about that?"

"Yeah, I'm sure."

A note of tension thrummed between them.

"Fine," Ranlyn said and turned to me.

I didn't need to read his mind to see he was done with Caine and wanted to be sure I was fine with Ranlyn leaving me alone with him. I nodded, indicating I was, but a part of me was terrified.

Ranlyn left and locked my deadbolt with a spell, presumably taking up standing in my hallway.

"I didn't choose to be a Persuader any more than you chose to be a Soul Seer, Sophie."

"I know," I said in a weak voice. "You said Aunt Lacey trained your dad? Is she a Persuader too?"

"No, but she helped him figure out the control aspect of it. Her name wasn't even Lacey back then. Eli called her Elsa."

"She's old. Probably changes it when people see she's not aging."

"I guess."

I sat on the couch. "How does your Persuasion power work? I don't want a live demonstration, just tell me the mechanics of it."

He sat next to me, and I tensed.

"I can't hurt you any more now than before I knew about it. "

"You hurt me worse by refusing to pick up your phone and then shutting it off even though you know what kind of danger we're in with Loring, plus my personal issues, but right now, I need to know about you power and how it works. Explain it to me."

"Okay." He paused. "When my power is enacted, I can focus it through my eyes to catch someone's will. Then I can persuade them to do what I want."

"You catch people's will, their free will, with your eyes, and just have at it? All doors opened, all consent given, just anything?"

He nodded.

I shot to my feet. "Holy fuck, Caine." I paced a few steps. When I looked at him again he was still on the couch, his grey eyes staring at me.

Those grey eyes.

I looked away from him. "How would I know if you did it?"

"You wouldn't. Not unless I wanted you to or didn't cover my tracks."

"Wow." I didn't have a clever or creative response. While there was an array of advantages a power like that could give someone, mostly diabolical ones came to mind, I was mostly concerned with myself. If I didn't know when he was persuading me, how could I trust him?

I felt his hands grip my arms as he stood behind me and, again, I tensed. He didn't let go, he just stood there a moment before wrapping his arms around me and holding me to him.

"Please don't be afraid." His voice was sad. "Today was an amazing day for me. I know I fucked up with you, I should've called. You didn't deserve to be left in the dark."

"No, I didn't."

"I know. I'm sorry."

"I don't know what to do with this."

"Nothing's changed."

"For me, everything's changed."

He let go of me and I regretted losing his warmth.

He walked past me and went down the hall.

I didn't know what he was doing and followed him, curious, yet suspicious.

I found him looking in my closet. I watched as he pulled out a thin scarf and handed it to me. "You always said you loved my eyes. Now they're a weapon."

"You can't walk around blindfolded the rest of your life."

"No, but I can tonight."

He kept his eyes looking down instead of meeting mine.

"Or I can leave. I know you're not comfortable with this, but I need your trust and I understand why it'll be hard to get."

I didn't know what I wanted. Fear ruled me for a long time, though so did a manipulative prick, and while Caine wasn't a prick, he held the ability to manipulate me far worse.

Caine waited. Keeping his eyes down. He was making a point and all I needed was to decide. The man was far too understanding.

I took the scarf and covered the most beautiful eyes I'd ever seen.

While Caine could hurt me in many ways, I didn't believe he would persuade me for the purpose of taking advantage of me.

"Emotions play havoc with our control." I tied the scarf over Caine's long hair. "You've only had one day with your uncle." A smile teased the edges of his lips. "We've still got some ways to go in the trust department, but that's not all your fault."

"It's okay. I get it."

I believed he did.

"I've spent all night serving a bar of spelled dickholes so you'll be doing the heavy lifting."

"Spelled?"

"Mhmm. My day doesn't standstill just because you ignore me."

"I can make up for it."

"Yes, you can," I told him and reached for his belt.

"Mmm," he moaned and picked me up off my feet. I wrapped my legs around his waist and my back was pressed against the wall. "Like I said, these arms are for more than cuddling."

———

My body moved against my will. Shaking, convulsing. Pounding muffled in the distance. Indecipherable talking. I gasped awake expecting the worst.

"Shit!" Caine jumped at my reaction. "Someone's at your door." Water from his wet hair dripped down his neck onto his wet dappled chest, a towel hung loose around his hips.

I stood too fast, fighting my tilting equilibrium while failing to hide my flushed reaction to a tasty looking Caine. He gave a sly grin as I stumbled down the hall to find my peephole blackened. Serena's telltale sign. I expected my cousin. My mother, I did not.

Serena pushed her way in with an edgy smile, my mom's expression far less cryptic. This smile was one she pulled on before the yelling began. Before she started, the shower turned off in a blast of water, indicating I wasn't alone. My eyes widened, Serena laughed, and my mom shook her head.

"Dropping by to say hi?" I deflected.

Bosco came down the hall and started barking at our company. Serena scooped him up as he whined through a big yawn.

My mom paused before saying, "Aunt Olive, huh?" I looked at Serena who said nothing. "I told you not to play hero, Sophie Olivia. You're sticking your nose in ancient history you don't understand."

"I understand more than you. Olive doesn't deserve this regardless of what Grandma says."

"Serena said the same thing." She sneered at both of us. "I'd like to believe she's sane, Sophie, I really do, but mental illness is no guesswork. Do you understand the repercussions of having Olive released when she could potentially be of harm to herself or others? People could get hurt. Olive could be arrested or institutionalized somewhere much rougher than The Royal. She's been in there a long time. She's not going to walk out the doors and be cured after all those years. You need to be realistic about the ramifications of Olive being injected back into the world."

She had me hanging my head like a reprimanded child.

"There's good news," Serena said.

"Depends on how you look at it." My mom glared at Serena.

Serena shrugged. "Olive will be happy."

"What happened?" I asked.

"Olive is being released," my mom said without a hint of happiness.

"No shit. Really?"

"Sophie Olivia." My mom's attempts to scold me went ignored as Serena explained.

"Yesterday's evaluation cleared her. They decided to release Olive on an out-patient basis. Mr. Kleinfeld will visit and assess her adjustment. They'd only release her in the care of a responsible party and nearly pissed themselves laughing when I suggested myself.

Aunt Lu works with the courts and has more to lose if Olive kills a fourth grader or guts someone's Yorkie."

I looked to my mother. "Are you?"

"I am."

I exhaled in relief.

Mom stuck her finger in my face. "I'm warning you right now, Sophie, if I think for a *second* that something's wrong, I'll ship Olive back to The Royal without a hint of remorse."

"When can we get her?"

"Sophie, I'm serious," my mom reiterated.

"I get it, but Olive's already lost critical years to that place. We need to do it now."

"Cool down, tiger," Serena said. "Official release time is three o'clock. Get your shit together first." Serena stopped me before I made it down the hall. "Olive has to stay here."

"Here?" Serena nodded.

I looked at my mom.

She raised her hands. "Signing her out is as far as I can go and I'm still contemplating on backing out. Besides, you've got an extra room."

"I have an office. I doubt Olive sleeps sitting up and the cushion of my computer chair is so thin I get bolt prints on my ass."

My mom made a sound of disgust and that was the end of that. If I wanted Olive out, I was going to have to figure out the logistics. If only the estate was in better shape.

Instead of arguing I headed to my room to get ready. Caine was doing the same.

"Olive's getting out?" he asked me.

"Yup. And living here, apparently."

"Ranlyn will love that."

"Since he gives a shit about my happiness, I think he will." I opened the closet in search of a shirt.

Caine made a sound of disbelief. "Not so sure happiness is part of his orders."

"Sulking about his distrust with your long-lost family isn't going to make you happy, is it?"

"No."

"Then stop doing it."

"I'm not sulking."

"You are." I pulled a shirt off the hanger and turned to him. "Find something to do that makes you happy. Today is a good for me and a great day for Olive. I'm not about to let anything ruin it."

"I want to figure out who robbed me."

"Good place to start. Include Ranlyn. He's knows more than he's saying because he doesn't have all the answers yet, but he's good at what he does. Aunt Lacey trusts him, so should you."

Caine nodded and gave me a kiss before he left, hopefully to find Ranlyn. I was happy he didn't bring up the previous night and I had to admit I still found it difficult to look him in the eye without fear of what might happen. That couldn't last.

When I went back out to the living room, Mom was sitting on the couch with Bosco. A mix of anger and anxiety layered her expression. Knowing my mother's analytical mind as I did, I expected a barrage of questions about Olive and what Serena and I knew. She asked none and requested a cup of tea instead.

The quiet of my mother's car was painful as the hour and half we wasted at my apartment before leaving.

We reached the institution by 2:30pm giving ample time to sign paperwork. Mom and Serena sat with the Administration Officer and Mr. Kleinfeld getting everything signed while I found Olive in her room. She sat on a stripped-down mattress, surrounded by two small suitcases and clutching the quilt her aunts had made.

"Ready to blow this pop stand?" I joked. Olive's smile was strained. I sat next to her. "You okay?"

Olive swallowed several times before answering. "I should be running naked out the doors flipping everyone the bird along the way, but I-I can't make myself stand." She held my hands. "The Royal was never my choice, but over the years it became my home. Don't get me wrong, Firefly, resuming my life is a dream-come-true, but this place is all I know."

"I can't imagine how hard this is. Do whatever you're comfortable with, and we'll help the best we can."

"I haven't been outside of these walls since the seventies. Everything I once knew is lost or has moved on." She sighed. "You know, I was adventurous in my time. Always into something or going somewhere, surrounded by people of all kinds. Now, all I want is to see my home again."

I cringed. "Olive, no one's lived in the estate since you did. It's not in the best shape. We'll get it back to its former glory, but it'll take time."

She dashed away a tear with a trembling hand. "Where am I supposed to go?"

"For now, you're staying with me, if that's okay with you." She didn't really have another option, but it was important to start giving her choices.

Olive agreed after I insisted she wouldn't be a burden. I helped her to her feet, and called the orderly waiting outside her door to help with her suitcases.

Before meeting my mom and Serena at the front, I reminded Olive that Mom didn't know anything about our family magic or the estate. Olive hated keeping the secret, always had, but agreed to hold back for now.

After a tearful goodbye from Mr. Kleinfeld and a few of the nurses, Olive was ready to leave her homey prison. Pausing before she crossed the threshold, we waited as Olive made the final step, bracing for an episode from my grandmother's Binding. The sun couldn't have been brighter than her smile when nothing happened.

The Royal City Wellness Centre became a house of solace for Olive. Although imposed, over time it nurtured her. I couldn't fault it for being the place my grandmother chose to stow her.

The drive back to my place was as quiet as the drive in.

We lugged Olive's suitcases and several cartons of plants up the six flights of stairs in my building. The one and only elevator was on hold for a new tenant moving in. Olive plonked onto the couch. Bosco introduced himself to our new roommate by jumping in her lap before she caught her breath.

"Aren't you a rascally little fella?" Olive ringed at his enthusiasm. "The Royal brought in therapy dogs." She grinned at the memory. "None as happy as you!" She scratched Bosco's back and played with his tail. He absorbed the attention as if starved for it.

Once Bosco calmed, the excited ambience followed. Insecurity loitered, everyone too afraid to spill the Magic beans. To our surprise, my mom cut the silence by inviting Olive to the fast-approaching family reunion. Regardless of her sister's sinuous nature, if Olive planned to reintegrate into the family, dealing with her sister was unavoidable.

Olive then stood and walked over to where her plants were on the floor. "Well, what do you think, Joshua? Is it time to visit Elizabeth?" She picked up a potted ivy so lush the vines draped over its basket, and sat it on the thick windowsill. "It has been many, many years, Topper," she continued her conversation with the fuchsia bromeliads I carried home on my lap and placed him on the sill next to Joshua.

"Olive...." Serena started but didn't seem to know where she was going with it.

"I've spent decades of my life away from my family, my sister included, with no one but my plants to care for. One's like Lily here," she picked up a purple hydrangea and carefully added her to the sill, "and Jean," a walking iris. "How many do you expect to attend the reunion?"

My mom's expression was tight as she answered, "About sixty."

Olive nodded, walked slowly back to her seat. She looked at my mother with a beaming grin and said, "I would love to see what has become of my family."

"All right, then," my mother replied.

The tightness in my chest released. I knew what Olive wanted to discover, thankful she didn't spell it out in front of my mother.

Serena deflected by explaining what usually happened at the reunions. Olive listened intently as I watched my mother. She never relaxed enough to join in the conversation and left soon after. While I understood why she took off, I was afraid she would send Olive back to The Royal for talking to her plants and hoped she boiled it down to Olive being eccentric and not insane.

Soon after, Caine and Kim came over. Olive greeted them with tight hugs. She pulled back from Caine with an exuberant smile. "You're shining brighter today. I see someone's discovered their gift."

Caine's grey eyes beamed. "I have." I didn't notice the difference until Olive pointed it out. He told the story I had already heard about Eli and his family. "I couldn't bring out my power before. Now I can. By the end of the session, I could influence my Aunt Bernie to give the chickens back massages if I wanted."

"Lucky birds," Olive said and smiled.

He continued with exuberance. "After the persuasion stuff, we worked on fighting skills and Telekinesis, which is technically another form of influence."

"Holy shit, Caine," Serena said. "After one day you've surpassed Sophie's weed growing."

I gave her the finger.

"Well, Firefly, you could always work with Caine's family. They must be a strong coven to produce such immediate results."

"I'd have to meet them first," I mumbled and regretted the dig.

"You'll meet them," Caine assured me. "They want to meet you." He looked at Olive, "I just found out they existed. And they *are* powerful, but not in a coven. I don't have a crazy past life story like Sophie, but they can definitely train me."

"Past life?" Olive looked at me.

I glared at Caine.

"Yeah." Caine continued. "Meeting your past life husband is kind of a big deal. Especially since he can see you in a frock every time he touches you."

"Husband." Serena scoffed and mock gagged.

"Wait. Psychometry?" Kim blurted. "Donovan uses psychometry for his palm reading, doesn't he? That little shit."

"Impressive skills in a lover, Firefly."

"He's not my lo—"

"Why would any version of you marry that asshole?" Serena interrupted.

I envisioned myself intricately carving Caine's tongue out with a melon baller and feeding it to snapping turtles.

"How long ago was this past life?" Olive interrupted me.

"I don't—"

"Olive," Kim interjected. "The room still needs to be set up for you. I've got extra sheets and stuff at my place." She looked at Serena. "Why don't you help?"

The gracious offer saved me. I couldn't talk about Donovan with them. Not about our past. It created a sense of discomfort close to betrayal.

"I'll take the couch," Olive said.

"No, I can take the couch tonight. Tomorrow I'll move my computer out of your room."

"Not a chance, Firefly. I won't kick you and Caine out of your bed for no reason."

I looked at Caine. After he told them about Donovan, I didn't want him around. I would rather pull his nails out with rusty tweezers than snuggle, but I also didn't want to make things uncomfortable for Olive her first night out.

Serena and Kim left to get some things for Olive from Kim's apartment. Since I was too busy simmering in anger to notice things got quiet, I was surprised when Caine called my name.

"What?"

"Olive wants a demonstration."

"Of what?"

"Of his newfound telekinetic prowess," Olive said. "I haven't seen a show of power, besides you growing my lovelies back at the greenhouse, in many many years. Plus, look at him, he's twitching to show someone."

Caine laughed and then shot to his feet and ran to stick his head out of the door. Ranlyn followed him back in.

"Figured I'd include him so he didn't get freaked about the power use," Caine said.

"I don't get freaked out," Ranlyn said and sat on my cedar chest.

"Sure you don't, Jeeves."

He shot me a playful scowl and Caine got on with the demonstration.

Energy built and spilled out into the room as Caine closed his eyes. His power rolled over my skin. Olive shifting in her seat and fussing with her skirt confirmed she experienced the same.

Caine reached for Bosco's squeaky rabbit on the floor, but didn't touch it. Half a second later, the rabbit shook and looked alive enough to hop away on its own. Bosco sat remarkably still as his cuddle buddy began to shift.

Like heat rising from pavement on a scorching day, a colourless wave surrounded Caine. I had to stop myself from gliding my fingers through it, even though I was desperately curious if it was tangible to the touch.

Caine elevated the toy to eye level and let it hover. A sly, victorious smile teased his lips as he flicked a finger, sending the rabbit bouncing down the hallway, Bosco on its tail. Olive clapped, and the wavering energy around Caine dissipated.

"Fucking awesome!" Serena exclaimed as she and Kim had returned. "You could see the power all over you!"

I spun to her. "You saw that?"

"Everyone can." Kim chuckled. "It happens when you expend a lot of energy. It'll lessen as his power becomes easier to use."

"Why haven't I ever seen it before?"

Kim shrugged. "The people you've seen use have had more practice."

"You have immense ability, Caine." Olive was clearly delighted. "You'll be valuable when you learn the meat of it."

I agreed. "Did you guys feel it when he levitated the rabbit?"

Serena and Kim hadn't, but Olive's lifted eyebrows signified how much she sensed.

"Is that normal?" Serena wanted to know more.

"Yes," Ranlyn confirmed. "Anyone with the power can sense another using their own within the vicinity. Helpful in avoiding a coming attack and to gauge what you're up against."

Olive fidgeted with her skirt hem again. "I can attest to that. On several occasions, it was unavoidable. One easiest to explain was a time the power didn't so much help, but rather should have warned of an incoming attack.

"As with working a family business, it isn't always smart to form a coven with family either." She looked to her nieces. "Jilted by the decision to name me heir, Elizabeth forged a small, yet significant, attack during a gathering near the Port Dalhousie pavilion. Everyone used magic whether surrounded by the Blind or not, but it remained inconspicuous.

"A thrum of power danced over the grounds, too strong for public use without the Blind noticing. By the time anyone could intervene, my sister used her power to knock me down. I appeared clumsy to someone who didn't know the difference." Olive fidgeted with her hands in her lap but kept her chin strong. "Once I dusted myself off, I assaulted her physically instead of using my powers because I didn't want the Blind seeing me use magic. We'd already gained their attention when I fell.

"Our gifts should be common knowledge and she was well aware of my take on the subject. Hiding what we are from Blind society grates on my tolerance, even more back then, but I never used magic in front of the Blind because I knew what kind of trouble it could bring down on my family. After attacking my sister and screaming at her for using the way she had, my outburst became evidence to sway other Blind family members to testify my mental stability had deteriorated, and I was a danger to others.

"Because I persisted in trying to convince them of the existence of our abilities in the process of fighting my case, I am responsible for my defeat. For not shutting my mouth and allowing the ability-born family to handle the situation. Or flee the city, another option I refused. Once Elizabeth made me a target, I sought to spread the truth to those who couldn't possibly listen."

"It's a goddamned house!" Serena spat, pacing angrily. "This is insane."

"Not a house. It is an estate and a title," Olive corrected. "Being heir means control of the family purse-strings. Elizabeth craved status. I wasn't one for flamboyant use of my power, so my sister never saw the full expanse of my talents." She sighed and shook her head. "I would have shared it all."

"At least you can use the money to get the estate back in order quickly."

"At the cost of my family," Olive said. "Your ancestors would be appalled."

I had a feeling they would be. I was appalled. How could things get so bad and no one stood up for Olive?

Talking our throats dry until our eyes drooped, everyone left late. With Olive situated on the couch under the family quilt for the night and Bosco as a bed buddy, Caine and I went to bed.

"Sorry for bringing up Donovan," Caine said as I changed into pyjamas. "I didn't realize it would be such a big deal."

"Spare me. You knew what it meant."

"It was more for the fact you knew about one of your past lives. How many people can say that?"

"It's hard enough for *me* to deal with and now Kim knows too. He's gonna figure that out."

"Why would that matter?" Caine sat on the corner of my bed.

"Because it hurts Donovan to see us together, and everyone doesn't need to know why."

"Sorry if I can't bring myself to feel bad for him."

I sat with my legs curled beneath me. "Apologizing with sarcasm is worse than not apologizing at all. How would you react in his position?"

"I would've done anything for you, but I'd also expect a fight. I won't stand down, now or a thousand years from now."

"So, you get him better than you think." My sarcasm was thick.

"Okay, fine."

I was happy Caine understood and tried not to fixate on how he spoke of me as a possession to be won. "I can't stand you two fighting like a pair of high school dick-wads with raging hormones. Right now, it's passive, and I do appreciate your restraint." Caine nodded as if it was an arduous task. "But, why can't you both be happy without me being the one thing that makes the difference?"

Caine leaned down onto an elbow, looked up at me, grinned with intense smoky eyes, and squeezed my hands in my lap. "Sophie, you are the *only* thing that makes the difference. Imagining my life without you is miserable at best. I know I've tried to explain my all-consuming affection for you, but I still don't think you grasp how serious I am. I can't say whether it has anything to do with some universal magic pull, a Nya and Gareth thing, or plain ol' love, but the moment I saw you, you become someone special to me. Losing you would be unbearable, so hell yeah, I'm going to do what I can to avoid getting booted to the curb over some dude who makes everyone want to punch him simply by existing."

My words failed me as I sat there like a jackass moron, staring at one of the most beautiful men I'd ever seen and fighting to convince myself he was magnifying a feeling I didn't think possible—about the "L" word and his distaste for Donovan.

"I feel the same."

Fuckballsoup. So much for resisting. I couldn't believe I had said that.

He looked genuinely shocked by my words. "What?"

"I...I feel the same." Breaking my habitual repression of frank emotions hurt, literally. The muscle or vein or whatever the fuck was in my neck pulled and ached as I swallowed hard. "I felt something the moment I saw you in the park. After we bypassed the spooky 'what if he's a cannibal and wants to eat me stage,' seeing you every time I went to bed filled me with an unknown sense of comfort and stupid-little-girl excitement."

"Cannibal?"

"Serious consideration went into that theory. Ask Kim." A nervous laughed escaped me. "I haven't shared my life with anyone in a long time, and I can't seem to stop myself from sharing my heart with you."

The romance was a tad gag-worthy, but it was the truth. I rushed on, needing to get it out before I puked.

"It wasn't a case of not finding someone else, more I didn't think I could survive the disappointment if it turned out as horrendous as the last time. I don't know if it's some type of magic pull either. This power is scary as hell. All I can do is allow it to grow and change me. Being with you is the same. Caring about you changes me. Even saying all this gushy shit scares the unholy-bejesus outta me."

"Here I thought you were still on the fence."

"My luck is more like a shiny penny got stuck in my shoe and I'm chasing it in circles because I'm too freaked to think rationally and take off the fucking shoe, because removing the shoe makes me lesser in some way. I don't have room for lesser." I shrugged. "I didn't want me speaking all that aloud to somehow flush our progress down the shitter."

Caine jumped at me, both falling back onto the pillows, my arms tucked tight against his chest as his weight pressed into me.

"I'll help you take off your shoe." He pecked my lips. "I love you to the shitter and back, Sophie."

"I love you to the shitter and back too, weirdo," I said with a truth that scared the hell out of me.

14

———

THE OTHER ONE

I opened my eyes to find Caine's smiling face, he kissing me with breathtaking intensity. Being awake was worth it. Until he told me about the conversation he had with my father.

"Tell me I'm dreaming."

"What? He's nice." He propped himself up on his elbow as I blinked through sleepiness. "Someone must have told him about me because he wasn't surprised I answered the phone."

"My father's never been nice to any of my boyfriends." Not even Brock, and everyone loved him.

My paranoia peaked while my stomach knotted.

He shrugged. "We're going to his place for dinner tonight. I got the impression saying no wasn't an option."

"Sounds like dad." The invitation stunk of ulterior motives.

Serena came over to hang out with Olive and soaked up some of Olive's old stories and help her get situated more. When Serena got there, I asked her, "Did you tell my dad about Caine?"

She tried to hide her culpability and failed.

"Narc! What'd you say to him?" I was frantic.

"Nothing bad."

"*Pfft.* That's relative."

She huffed. "Uncle Thom was chillin' with my dad watching some NASCAR race yesterday, and I was there and...." Her face contorted as she braced for my reaction.

"And?"

Serena raised her hands in surrender. "Relax, it's not like he wasn't going to find out eventually." I hit her with a stern gaze. "Okay, it's no biggy, he asked me how you were doing, and I said, 'Great, especially since you've been seeing Caine'. I figured Adam would've blabbed already. Apparently not. He asked who Caine was. I told him he was a guy you've been seeing and that I thought you guys were serious because you're always together and he spends a lot of nights at your house."

I groaned.

"It's not *that* bad."

What she said outweighed the issue of my dad hearing it second-hand. Granted, that was my fault, but I could see my father's face as Serena revealed aspects of his daughter's life. Rightfully hurt and determined to find out for himself.

Of course, to Serena, he would seem to handle this without affect. My father and I shared that quality. The calm, collective way that made others assume we cared about nothing, when we cared too much. Having others see our inner reflections was too personal. My anxiousness has bled out for the world to see too often lately, but until the dreams, I locked down everything.

Unless something sent us over the edge, which was usually when no one expected. Then the other side of our personality kicked in, the side that could debate a point until the other gave up in pure exhaustion or evoked a torrent of anger or sadness. Not always the most attractive.

My father's happy reception over the phone was a guise. If Caine had turned down the invitation, my father would have been on my doorstep while I was still snoring.

"Are you going to pull some witchy thing and curse me with a yeast infection or something?" Serena asked.

I snort-laughed. "You deserve some itching and burning. He invited us to dinner tonight."

"Ouch. I might deserve that infection after all."

"He spoke to Caine while I was still asleep and sounded 'nice'."

"Well, suck it up, bitch." Serena landed a heavy hand on my shoulder. "Unless you want daddy popping by for a visit with your recently non-crazy great-aunt, have fun and bring chips."

———

Out of sight, but on guard, Ranlyn was in the wings somewhere. Before we got out of the car Ranlyn let Caine drive so we could pretend it was his vehicle. Also, Caine and I had a necessary conversation outlining off-limit topics. Anything magic related, including Aunt Lacey and Donovan, which should have been obvious, but I needed to be sure. My father was a perceptive man. One slip and he'd sink me into a pit of lies I'd never crawl out of, both of us knowing it without calling the other out.

Caine leaned in to kiss me. "You're unbelievably adorable."

"Fierce," I called after him as we got out of the car. "I'm fierce. So, watch your ass, buster."

We knocked and heard my father bellow from inside for us to come in. Before we could, Ben opened the door.

"Hey Ben, how's it going?" I said to my twelve-year-old half-brother.

"Good," he responded with a nervy gaze behind thick glasses up at Caine.

Caine introduced himself with an extended hand. "Hey Ben, I'm Caine." Straightening himself, Ben extended his hand and shook Caine's with verve, all shyness faded.

We reached the living room after passing through a hall lined with school photos and family shots of my nanny and dad's seven older brothers, each shorter than the first until my father—the shortest at an intimidating five foot five.

My dad stood from his recliner outfitted with remotes, magazines, snacks, and anything else so getting up was unnecessary during a favorite show. He fixed the waist of his jeans and walked towards us.

"Hey dad." Projectile vomiting *Exorcist*-style was a possibility by this point. "This is Caine." I tried not to look nervous, unable to utter 'boyfriend' in my father's presence.

"Hey sweetie." He held his gaze on Caine. "Hey there, Caine, how're ya?"

"Good sir, it's nice to meet you."

"Anything else is better than sir."

They shook hands.

"Sure, cupcake."

I wanted to die.

Dad chuckled and went back to his recliner. I gave Caine a death stare, but he smiled, happy about the comment.

Ben sat in front of the TV trying to pretend Caine didn't intrigue him.

"What'cha been up to lately, kid?" Dad asked.

"Not too much, working and stuff." I hated lying. So many life-altering events occurred since I saw him last and not one thing was a safe topic.

"That's good. Where you working at, Caine?"

My heart dropped out of my ass. No matter how he answered, if it didn't consist of a job title, Caine would seem lazy and sucking off his daughter's hard-earned money.

"I'm not right now. Need to get things figured out first, but I'll get something soon. I hate feeling useless."

"That's good, don't want to get stagnant." Dad fixed his glasses and I could see my father's thoughts like a text bubble above his head, hoping Caine wasn't one of those men always *about* to do something. Ones who never get around to it.

Dialogue was arid. I didn't know what to say and knew my father would stray from anything too personal unless I offered it up. We sat and watched the news until my dad announced he had to start the barbecue.

Ben, who was still pretending to watch the news with the rest of us, turned to Caine. "You wanna play Latch and Key?"

Caine looked to me. "Is that a video game?"

Ben's forehead creased in astonishment of Caine's lack of gaming knowledge. He was willing to teach, so Caine followed him into his room to become the pro Ben was after hours of accumulated play time.

With Caine entertained, I followed Dad out to the back deck he built with a little help from me, giving him the chance he was itching for to say whatever was on his mind. As he scrubbed the grill I sat in one of the outdoor chairs under the stripped roll away awning and waited.

After two solid minutes of silence and a sparkling grill, Dad spoke. "So, he doesn't know what Latch and Key is?"

Not the ice breaker I expected. "Ah, nope. I guess he doesn't."

"Every guy his age has heard of it whether they're a gamer or not. Where's he been hiding? Or is he one of those new-aged guys against TV?"

"No, he's this-age. He hasn't been hiding, not on purpose anyway." He looked at me confused. "He's been in a coma." Why not be honest about the few things I could talk about?

Dad looked through his specs at me with disbelief. "I didn't expect something so serious. Serving overseas would have been a good answer, but I suppose a coma's a good excuse for being out of the loop on gaming culture."

"Serena left that part out."

"Yeah, she did." His eyes stayed on the grill. "For how long?"

"Almost four years."

His eyebrows perked up, he adding his shabby whistle. "Good excuse for unemployment."

"I think so," I said looking out at the classroom special bird feeder Ben made teeming with life.

"Had to be pretty rough if he was under so long."

I was happy he showed some interest and had no problem explaining the situation. To a degree.

He whistled again when I finished. "That *is* rough. Has he been awake long?"

"Month or so."

He looked at me with suspicion while laying burger patties on the grill. "And you've been dating how long?"

I smirked. "Month or so."

He gave a deep chuckle. "Geez girl, did you at least wait until they removed the catheter?"

I laughed, remembering thinking about the catheter situation at one point.

"Is he all right? In the head, I mean. Like, he's not damaged, is he?"

I sputtered a laugh. Nobody asked me that one yet. "His head's all right. No lasting damage."

He nodded and looked back at the grill.

I stood to lean into the banister and soak in some sun. He became quiet in a way I recognized. A telltale sign the worst was yet to come.

"Sophie...." he started as I gnawed on the inside of my cheek in anticipation, "you're into this guy, and I feel horrible about the whole coma thing and his brother, but the way Serena described it, you two are moving pretty fast."

I picked at my nails. "It's hard to explain."

"It's weird for me to even say, but you've been doing good with work and your schooling, which is great." He paused. "I don't want to see you get hurt again."

My defenses roared, feeling his dangerous direction.

He went on. "Caine seems nice, but so soon after he's been through a traumatic event doesn't seem smart. You can't fix everyone, darlin', and I know you're still touchy about Brock." I cringed at the name, my teeth clamped down, throat constricted. "Rushing into anything won't erase him from your past. I know you know all this, but who knows what Caine's thinking."

"Dad, I realize you're doing your fatherly duty here, but there's too much I can't really explain. I'm trying to move on."

I had no idea he'd be thinking of Brock when I stepped through the door. I didn't want to hear about my past and future relationship failures.

"I'm not saying this stuff to be mean, kid. I wish you'd protect yourself. Think realistically."

"Believe me, I get it." In that moment, it became clear I also inherited my father's views on matters of the heart.

My eyes burned. My power creeping up and tingling my skin as I fought to keep control. I was on the cusp of losing it. I grasped control of my power, but my tears rebelled when my dad wrapped an awkward arm around my shoulders and pulled me close, the barbecue flipper still in one hand.

"Didn't mean to make you cry, kid."

I laughed cheerlessly. "I'm fine."

"Tears don't equal fine."

He rubbed my shoulder with a square palm, but even with his apology, his words stung. "I didn't say Caine was the one, Dad, but let's not talk about the other one." My laugh more natural this time.

"Okay, I promise I won't bring up the other one again," he mocked. "But if Caine's not the one, at least you got some fancy jewellery out of the deal. Though extravagant man-rings are odd. Are they supposed to mean something?"

Back to adjusting the grill temperature, he missed it when my jaw hit my shoe and rolled across the deck. I spaced on the rings, and of course my father was observant enough to notice both of them.

"Oh...um...well...."

My father never gave a fuzzy squirrel shit about gemstones. Fear of an engagement loomed in his discomfort, so I focused on the fact they were smoky quartz but claimed ignorance of their meaning.

Thankful he didn't press for more, I mentally whipped myself. A dual existence needed better ass coverage.

"Come now, Firefly. We both know what those rings represent."

"Firefly? Did I mention that name? I don't remember—"

"Do you prefer Salix?" Dad looked up from the grill and smiled a smile I'd never seen before.

"Dad?"

"*That's not your dad, Sophie,*" I heard Ranlyn's voice in my head.

"What the fuck?"

Not-dad swung the barbecue flipper around with casual intimidation and shook his head at me, donning that same smile.

"Loring?"

He gave a whoop of a laughter from my father's lips so loud every part of me cringed. Then turned the burners down and flipped the patties like he'd done it a million times.

"No need to fret, Firefly. Your father is blissfully ignorant within this burger-loving physique, as is the grey-eyed vessel busy impressing your father's offspring to in turn bank greater hours within your sheets."

"*Find out what he wants,*" Ranlyn directed me.

"Get to it, Loring," I said, feigning confidence while I freaked out that pissing him off meant him making an example of my dad. "You don't hijack someone's body for no reason. Whatever important message couldn't wait for a face to face has to be pretty big."

"Hmm, yes, I suppose we should conduct business before the meat dries out. Such poor quality these are. Where does your father procure his selection? The corner store?"

My fists clenched. "Pop out of his skin and I'll ask him."

Loring laughed. That noise grated every bone in my spine. "You can imagine the damage caused if I were to pop out of him, as you described it." He laughed again.

"Loring!" My outburst gained his attention. "You mentioned business?"

He adjusted the temperature again, closed the barbecue lid,

placed the flipper down, and turned to me, each movement slow and considered.

"Everyone you know is in danger," he told me. "Every acquaintance, neighbour, friend, lover...every road travelled followed, every decision observed, every weakness scouted. Those you've laid trust in have failed you. The security detail surrounding your building and following you between the layers of reality, all a well-orchestrated waste of resources."

"Then why haven't you nabbed me yet?"

He shrugged my father's shoulders and clasped his hands in front on him. "Elements needed to be in place. While I gather these, my flock has made efforts in my stead. Unsuccessful as of yet, though...."

"A well-orchestrated waste of resources," I finished.

He smiled and pointed at me. "Precisely. Not without gaining invaluable information in the process, however."

"So, I'm vulnerable."

"That you are, Firefly." He using Olive's nickname for me pissed me off more and more. How much more of my life could he steal?

"Get him back on point," Ranlyn cut in with sideline commentary.

"Yes," Loring said, "is it quite an annoyance, is it not? Why not join the conversation, chap?"

Fuck. Loring could hear everything in my head. Vulnerable was right.

Ranlyn appeared at my side. "If your show of tactical intelligence is over, Sophie would like to return to her family."

"Over?" Loring pursed his lips and took a step toward us. "Over would be an inaccurate characterization of this conversation, Ranlyn. I understand your dear Soul Seer requires her father back in a role you would be ill-equipped to fulfill regardless of the hours you dote on her. You played and failed at that game as well, did you not?" Ranlyn didn't answer and I realized I never spoke to Ranlyn about his family before, or lack of, if what Loring was saying was true.

"Now," Loring turned his back to us in a show of confidence as he returned to the barbecue, opened the lid, and began flipping burgers again, "this conversation is missing a nugget of flair, but since you insist on pressing the timeline, I will acquiesce."

He put the burgers on the warm shelf and closed the lid again.

"I've known of another Soul Seer, many years ago. She was unworthy of the power she wielded. You are fresh and mouldable and it pains me to see you fall in with the lot you have. Until you make the suitable decision to join me, you too will be unworthy of such gifts. Olive would be a suitable substitute. Not as appealing to gander at, but possesses the same skills. If you prefer, I could shift my attention—"

"Keep fishing. She's off limits as much as I am."

"Pity. Others within the outfit securing your life have already opened their eyes to the losing fight and have proved their worth by enlisting in my ranks, saving their family the pain of knowing them, of being related to a Magic with so little respect for their lives they lie to their faces and put them in danger to preserve such lies. As long as you seek to hibernate within your deceptions, they will be at my disposal."

What could I say? The answer was already in my mind which was open for Loring to read. I'd rather my family knew about my powers than join Loring or let him get anywhere near Olive. I couldn't see his black soul while he was squatting inside my dad, but I knew it existed, and I couldn't do that to myself.

"All right then," he said, opening the barbecue lid and put my father's hand on the hot grill.

"Don't!" I screamed. Ranlyn grabbed my arm.

Loring pulled my father's hand off the grill and lifted it, blackened stripes charred his skin. He took in a deep breath and smelled my father's burnt flesh.

"No?" he then said to me.

"Stop it. Hurting him doesn't solve anything."

Loring nodded and then put my father's other hand on the grill and left it there. I heard the skin sizzle while Loring started at me through my father's eyes without a twitch of pain.

When he pulled away his hand this time, the charring went deeper, the damage greater.

"This game can continue until no skin remains, you do understand this, yes?"

I looked at Ranlyn in panic of what to do, I didn't have the magical know-how to overpower Loring.

"Fine," Loring said then took off my father's glasses with blood dripping and blistering fingers and started to bend over to place my father's face on the grill.

Before I could scream, Ranlyn's power lashed out and shoved my father's body into a chair. Ranlyn rushed forward and pinned him down by force, spouting a spell.

I rushed forward and grabbed my father's hands, but I couldn't heal. I couldn't do anything.

"You can't hide from me, Seer," Loring seethed. I looked up to see the strain in Loring's borrowed features, a sign Ranlyn was winning. "Remind your precious Elders of that."

With a grunt, my father's body went limp, and Loring was gone.

"He'll wake in a moment," Ranlyn told me. "Get him to the hospital. I'll be there, undercover. I can't heal him, but we'll make sure he doesn't suffer."

"What if he remembers what happened?"

"He won't."

I wrapped my arms around him, thanking him with a thick voice of gratitude. He held me back for a quick moment before reminding me he needed to go back under a cover spell before my father opened his eyes.

"Can you let Caine know so he can shield my brother as much as possible?"

"I will. The Elders too, as well as reinforcing security on—"

"Who? Everyone I know?"

"Yes, if needed."

A groan behind me signalled my father waking up. Ranlyn disappeared under a spell as my father was opening his eyes and started swearing.

Caine drove Ranlyn's car as my father cradled his hands against his chest. Ben sat chewing the neck of his shirt, his eyes too wide as Caine rushed through traffic. When we got to the hospital, I told the triage nurse it looked like Dad passed out and grabbed the grill reactively. It meant a barrage of tests he didn't need, but at least he didn't remember anything.

"Sorry about dinner, kid. You want to grab something from the cafeteria?"

"I'm fine, dad. I'll make sure Ben eats something. Can I get you anything?"

He held up his bandaged hands. "A pretty nurse to hold it while I pee?"

I laughed. "Looks like you're sitting down lady-style for the next while, pops." Since he would need assistance with his jeans, I flagged a nurse and sent them my dad's way. He would have to manage at home on his own and opt for sweatpants until he healed a bit.

Ranlyn rushed to Aunt Lacey's for an herbal mixture, the one she dosed me with to better heal from the stabbing, so I slipped it into Dad's black coffee and added a straw. He didn't complain about the taste. The pain killers had kicked in and he wasn't complaining about anything.

Everything was set up close to my dad's chair so he could pass out for a few hours. I made sure to add an herb mixture into the jar of my dad's instant coffee, putting Ben in charge of making them for dad. Since he only needed to add hot water, he was good to go and felt useful instead of scared. I had a feeling my dad would have more than enough coffee for days while off work healing up.

Since the wounds weren't as deep as my stabbing, I was promised the mixture would numb his pain and get him through the worst of it within a couple of days without interacting with the medication he was prescribed. He would think it odd to heal so fast, but healing him immediately would have been more suspicious. Not that I could. Again, growing flowers did fuck all for my father right now. I needed to get a handle on my powers and quick.

Once Ranlyn confirmed safeguards were in place for my father and brother, we left with another handshake exchange between Caine and Ben and a promise of a Latch and Key rematch. I promised to check in, knowing it may not be in person. Returning when things were dangerous was irresponsible. All I could hope for was Loring having played out the Dad card and has moved back his attention to me.

As I said goodbye, my dad gave me a look of gratitude that filled me with guilt. He may have still questioned what happened in those few minutes he lost or worried about what it meant, but he would never know how close to evil he was or that it was all my fault.

15

FELINE FRENZY

"You need to check out your apartment," Caine told me before my eyes were open.

I flung off the covers. "Why? Was there a flood again?"

"Hold up," Caine stopped me. "No flood. Rearranging is all."

"Rearranging? Olive?"

He nodded. "I think she's bored."

Since Olive got out of The Royal, she was glued to the TV, primarily designer shows, and taking notes. Redecorating my apartment satisfied her itch. Taking over my second room was one thing, I was happy to offer it, but she was getting out of hand.

I stormed down the hall bypassing new paintings I didn't even look at. Fixated on the monstrous piece of furniture at the entrance where I caught my dishevelled reflection in the mirror inlaid into the combination bench and coat rack. The carving was intricate and stained a deep chocolate lacquer I had to run my fingers over.

"Oh good, you're awake."

I turned to Olive's high-pitched excitement and gasped as I saw the rest of the living room.

"Not your style?"

"Holy shitpickles." Everywhere I looked, my eyes hit pieces of furniture I never bought. "Olive. What. The. Tits?"

She hugged me. "Your consequence for refusing room and board. And I don't recommend eating shitpickles, Firefly."

"That money's yours, Olive."

She waved me off on her way to the kitchen while I was distracted by a painting of an artist I loved, having no recollection of sharing that with Olive. This one was a female figure with over-sized green eyes that pierced through the bubbles of water and lily pads she drifted in.

Beautiful.

The entire apartment, from the deep grey sectional, black book-shelf/TV stand combo, flat screen, and art pieces, was perfect. It was as if the woman crawled inside my head and took my thoughts to a designer.

"Waffle?" she asked me.

In my shock, the smell of food escaped me. The waffle iron and plates she served them on were also brand new, black and sleek. I loved them.

"Damn, you're titsgold."

Olive laughed. "And you are the soundest sleeper I've ever met. Think you would've heard Caine and Jeeves cussing up a storm bringing the hall tree in."

I mouthed the words "hall tree" to Caine who motioned towards the piece with the mirror I was admiring.

"Stop worrying, Firefly." Olive put a plate of food in my hands, guiding me to a new dinette set. "As heir, you need to get used to such things."

"Olive...."

"Pish posh, my darling. You're it, confirmed or not. Now I'm off and taking this little man with me." Bosco's leash hung from the hall tree. He jumped onto the bench and sat like a gentleman while she put it on. Somehow, she found time to train him.

"Where are you going?"

"To get a money order for the contractor. The man refuses to deal with personal checks, though the inspector, exterminators, and the cleaning crews didn't complain. He'll be by this afternoon so I must skedaddle." She kissed me on the cheek and she and Bosco were gone.

According to Olive, the hydro company account for the estate was active and paid direct through the heir's account. A flip of a switch would've saved on wasted cell phone battery and maybe I could have caught a glimpse at whatever caused me the odd sensation, though I didn't know if it was something anyone could physically see.

Caine plunked his dish in the sink. "Not hungry?"

"I think I have whiplash."

He used strong hands to knead the knots from my tense shoulders. A moan vibrated in my chest. "You know," he said breathy in my ear, "Olive will be gone long enough for us to christen the new couch."

"Mmmm. You do have a lot to make up for."

His hands stopped. "I do?"

I looked up at him. "For not waking me up before Martha Stewart took over. Damn skippy."

"Well then, I best get started." He gripped my t-shirt and pulled it over my head, exposing my breasts.

I laughed as my hair fell around my face. By the time I could see, Caine was at my side on his knees with syrup on his finger he then circled my nipple before bringing it into his mouth. Sensation rocketed between my thighs. I gasped and held his head closer to my body. He lifted me off the chair while his tongue made lazy circles, his mouth still attached to me as he laid me out on the sectional and knelt beside me.

His fingers reached beneath the edge of my pyjama shorts and teased me without mercy. I didn't miss my old couch at all. Not one bit.

Since our relationship benchmark was no longer a secret, anytime Kim witnessed an extra-long kiss or lingering embrace, we were subject to her giddy squealing.

"You two never get old," she said after Caine opened Ranlyn's car door for me.

"Shut it, Kim. You've watched too many rom-coms."

"Can't help being a hopeless romantic. You guys are adorable."

"Some would call it nauseating." Ranlyn piped up from the driver's seat.

I got it. I'd be happy when the honeymoon period was over so we could delve into a lower maintenance level of comfort. Being in love was exhausting.

Between reintegrating Olive into the world, checking in on my dad including a home visit where I kept waiting for Loring to speak to me through my dad's lips again, working at the bar, and getting school work done, Caine took up my remaining time when he wasn't helping Eli on the farm. I still couldn't picture Caine driving a tractor, and when I tried, it turned into cowboy porn.

Caine's soul brightened a little each day as farm work always ended with practice and, again, I wished I could see my own soul colour. I got the impression Caine's glow superseded mine, but Olive wouldn't confirm either way.

We arrived at Aunt Lacey's first, besides Donovan who was on his usual bar stool at the kitchen island. An instant reaction to shrink away from Caine to ease Donovan's discomfort hit me. Resisting took effort.

The meeting was normal compared to others. No Initiations, impending deaths, or rituals. Danger always loomed, but since Loring's possession trick, he had been quiet. Ranlyn didn't like it. No way Loring tucked-tail. He had been coming at us and other Mother Coven members with unrelenting force. No. He was gearing up for something big.

The Sect split into groups to work on their skills while I was still stuck in sunglasses. I felt like a pretentious princess wearing them. Olive found it difficult to teach something she controlled as a child, but she was trying her best to explain it to me. Denise took every opportunity to make Corey Hart references. After finding myself humming the song while I reached for toilet paper, I vowed to get a handle on my gift even if only to say a big "Fuck you, you twatfuck discharge" to the Coven mean girl.

At the back table, we updated Aunt Lacey on the unravelling of our family histories, she not at all put off by Caine's Uncle Eli helping Caine with his powers. I expressed concern for not excelling quicker since I hadn't much time to practice. Aunt Lacey validated my concerns, but again, told me to keep doing what I was doing and create time when I could. She was right, but I didn't like it.

"Now that you can influence inert objects, Leith, you need to work with matters in motion," Aunt Lacey told Caine.

Before he could question the directive, she telekinetically rose a four-inch, porcelain, black cat figurine off the table, said "catch", and flung it towards Coveners chatting on the couch.

Kim and I gasped as Caine reached out as if to snatch someone before they fell. Instead of a person, he nabbed the black cat in mid-air and suspended it a few feet from Louise and Jared who flinched when they noticed the figurine spinning in lazy circles in front of them.

"Bring it to me," Aunt Lacey commanded.

Caine took a deep breath to intensify his power, which also intensified its effect on the whole room while the bubble of energy covered his body, delivering Aunt Lacey the dollar store object. Once the figurine landed safely on the table, the Coveners erupted in applause. Every face had a wide congratulatory smile. Every face but one.

Donovan was on the floor against the wall at my back, furthest from the table, surrounded by his usual fan club. When our gazes met, I squirmed beneath the weight as the rage within his dark eyes roamed free. Though Donovan claimed to be a solitary being who still enjoyed public interest, this was always on his terms. He hid the full range of his abilities and Caine performed his to an audience like some magic show at a bratty kid's birthday party.

His smouldering anger trapped me until a din interrupted the room's celebration. Kim freaking out broke Donovan's stare as I watched it morph into horror as he sprang to his feet. Aunt Lacey's expression now shone with the same fierce anger, directing it over my shoulder at Donovan.

Pain lanced my arm. Fingers grabbed at me. Blood. Lots of it.

Something attached to my skin. Not attached. Inside. The black cat.

Caine fingers were a vice around my arm. He went to rip the piece of porcelain out of me, until Aunt Lacey yelled at him to leave it.

"Bring her to the kitchen." Aunt Lacey's deadpan command was as unsettling as the thing sticking out of me.

Pain grew, pulling me out of my fog of shock as they whisked me up the stairs away from Donovan's guilt-laden mask. Did he make the thing explode? He *was* looking at me when it happened.

Blood pooled and overflowed into Caine's cupped hands beneath my wound, leaving a blood trail as Kim pushed us towards the sink.

Caine shoved my arm under the rushing water inflicting the first real shock of pain. A raucous scream thrashed my throat as I caught myself from collapsing by bracing my body into the counter. He wretched my arm away from the water, letting go of me all together. My arm fell limp at my side. His apologies warped in my ears as throbbing coursed through my arm and up and down my whole body as I slinked to the tile.

Aunt Lacey pushed through the swarm of Coveners and bent in front of me. "Salix, please listen through the pain. Concentrate on my voice." I bit down on my lip and tried. "The porcelain is deep," she told me. "It can be removed, but then you must decide what to do."

"Take it out!" Caine screamed.

Aunt Lacey ignored him. "You can go to the hospital or you can heal yourself."

"Jesus-fuck, you know I can't!" I wanted to slap her.

"Bypass the pain and concentrate on closing the wound. You are strong enough to do this, Salix."

I squinted through tear-soaked eyes pleading for Aunt Lacey to get it over with. I knew Aunt Lacey could hear my mental appeal I was too proud to say in front of the others. Then I remembered how helpless I felt at the hospital with my dad. If only I could have healed him before he woke up and saved him the pain. Aunt Lacey was right. I needed to try.

"How?" Damn it all to Hell, this is going to suck donkey balls.

Before I could chicken out, Aunt Lacey had them help me into the backyard. The crisp air punched into my lungs. Blood seeped around the porcelain, dripping down my arm, and off the fingertips of my useless limb. The porcelain severed something because I couldn't move it on my own.

Caine and Kim braced my fall as I sat loose legged in the grass, woozy, breathing too fast. The Coveners remained inside, rubber-necking behind the glass doors, as Donovan and Ranlyn came out with us.

"Lie down and be still," Aunt Lacey told me.

A flush of sweat rolled over me like a blanket, my fingers cold, pain refusing to subside. Guided by Caine and Kim, I knew their tenderness didn't matter when I was about to endure a fuck-tonne of pain.

"Wiccum, take off her sunglasses and hold her down." Aunt Lacey motioned to my left shoulder. "Leith, I need you to persuade her."

"How?"

"Gain her focus. Influence her to concentrate on you. Make her forget the pain."

He moved to my right side and clutched my hand, looking down at me through a tear-glassed gaze devoid of confidence in the task.

"It's fine," I told him. I thought his ability to influence me was the worst possible gift. Right now, I didn't give a fuck as long as he hurried the fuck up.

"Wend," Aunt Lacey continued with her instruction, "remove it."

"I can do it," Ranlyn volunteered.

"No," Aunt Lacey told him. "Wend. Get in position."

Donovan took his place at my side.

"No!" Caine revolted. "He won't be able to see anything if he touches her."

"Concentrate on your task, Leith," Aunt Lacey commanded and then shot Donovan a look that made him cringe.

Donovan and Caine exchanged a set of intense glares.

"Do your job right and she won't feel a thing," Donovan hissed.

"Leith," Aunt Lacey interrupted any further squabbling, "Now."

A bead of sweat dripped down my forehead, and across my earlobe. My whole body trembled in pain and blood loss as Caine hesitated.

"Try." My voice shook as I prepared to feel everything.

Caine closed his eyes an instant before his power grew. He forced his calm as the energy spread into the yard. When he spoke, Caine's voice resonated through me, the compulsion to listen inescapable while his voice echoed in my head.

"Sophie, look at my eyes, block all other sounds but my voice. There is no pain. Your body is numb. The only thing you feel is my hand holding yours." He reiterated this directive in different sequences, always the same concise words.

Background noise existed, but I didn't care. I was content to lay out and listen to every word. I wanted to talk, to beg Caine to tell me more, to never stop saying my name.

"Pieceofshitmotherfuckingasshole!"

Caine blinked and I recognized the other voice. Donovan. Abrasive. Desperate. Everything I didn't want.

The strength of Caine's pull began to fall away when my other arm dropped. Donovan. He had let go. Caine looked away from me.

"Don't," I heard myself say. A plea with zero embarrassment. Caine squeezed my hand and looked back down at me. Then the euphoria of Caine's voice encapsulated me again. All tension released from my body as I sunk into the soft cadence of his voice.

Worry meant nothing. What was there to worry about? No pain. No one else. Just me and Caine.

Time meant nothing until Caine looked away again and dread poisoned my calm.

"She's shaking again!"

Kim?

I was shaking. Why was I shaking?

Pressure in my left arm made me flinch.

Caine was looking away. I waited for the calm, it pulling away from me instead of pulling me towards it.

"Leith, stay with Salix!" Aunt Lacey yelled.

His voice returned, but my curiosity to look and see what was happening started to war with Caine's words. I could check it out and Caine could have me back, right?

I turned. The amount of blood was shocking. Donovan's fingers were knuckle deep inside my arm, something wrapped around them as he dug into my muscle. I gasped and flinched. An audible crack punctuated my fear as a piece broke off.

Caine grabbed hold of my face and was talking again.

"It broke off," I said.

"It's okay. Look at me, Sophie. You can't feel anything...."

He went on. But I could, I could feel.

A spike of pain zinged up my shoulder and down into my finger-tips. I cried out. More yelling happened around me while Caine's influence lost all hold. He resorted to helping Kim press me into the grass to keep me from thrashing around.

Donovan kept fighting with the piece of cat, more now since it broke, and blood covered his fingers. Worse yet, his visions were getting in the way, and he had difficulty concentrating on me.

Screaming didn't help, but I couldn't stay quiet when Donovan's fingers dug into the jagged mouth in my arm and strummed every nerve with nauseating agony.

"Wend, you need to hurry," Aunt Lacey called out to Donovan in desperation.

"No kidding," he growled back.

While my muffled screams warped in my ears above the low mewling of the onlookers, I suddenly felt nothing. Air rushed into my lungs, shock ran through me. I opened my eyes to new surroundings. I was walking in long grass. A sunny day scene splashed before me.

Dark night and pain stole the smell of flowers away and dragged me back into Aunt Lacey's backyard driving searing pain through to my toes.

What the fuck was that?

More yelling around me faded by the hum of my blood pumping too hard.

Sunlight stole me away again. Tight arms held me. A bright, dimpled smile exuded joy. I know that face.

Snapped back into the backyard, angst and torment replaced Donovan's expression of bliss as he dug into my flesh.

A sparkle of contentment stole me away again. A dream, a vision, an escape to—

A grunt of relief and Donovan fell back onto the grass of Aunt Lacey's backyard. Pain and whatever the vision was left me shaking, but nothing as excruciating as Donovan's fingers digging into my arm. If I could have passed out, it would have been easier for all of us.

Heavy breaths raked my throat, my tongue cotton-dry as the wound throbbed. It wasn't over. A gaping hole still spewed blood where the cat once nestled.

Jared barrelled through the crowd with his wide shoulders, handing over a towel and returning to the other intrigued spectators.

"This would have come in handy earlier," Donovan griped as he wrapped my arm, his hands and forearms streaking blood art across the cotton.

They helped me sit up. Dizziness, spotting my eyesight. I wilted against Caine's chest, trying to blink the spots away.

"She may be too weak to heal herself," Donovan said.

When I opened my eyes the spots were gone and Aunt Lacey crouched in front of me. "You should be brighter," I told her. The fact Aunt Lacey's soul was muted was a troubling sign of how weak I was.

"I know, Salix. I can heal you and, if this takes too long, I promise I will. Nonetheless, I truly believe this is an opportunity to prove how powerful you are, if only to yourself."

I wanted to believe her, but I swore a sumo-wrestler was perched on my shoulders. Caine's nullifying influence, and then enduring the intense pain in its absence, hollowed me out. Plus, whatever the fuck those visions were.

Perfecting my healing skills could save my family or friends. I needed to do this.

"Let's give it a whirl," I huffed.

Aunt Lacey gave a proud smile. With help, I straightened away from Caine, my arm hung listless in my lap.

Aunt Lacey told the Coveners to come outside but keep their distance. Many looked grateful to sit down instead of cramming themselves at the glass sliding doors. Though Denise and her taga-long friend, Jamie, looked bored and glared at me as if I was inconveniencing their night.

"In order for this to be pure, I cannot touch you." I hadn't realized Aunt Lacey's intentional distance throughout the ordeal until now. "If you require help Wend will focus you." Aunt Lacey looked to Donovan, not asking his permission, but he was staring at me, waiting for some type of reaction.

I expected the cockiness that was Donovan, surprised by his apprehension. Possibly from the glimpse of the visions, he looked different. Compared to him back then, he was miserable, and I hated the fact the shining smile in the visions hadn't followed him into this life.

"Evoke your power, Salix. This time direct it to your arm. Envision your wound mending and knitting together. Envision the state of your skin before and keep your power focused on the injury site. The point is generating enough power to accelerate your body's natural defence system. The power takes your instinctual need to heal and amplifies it."

"I get it. I've watched enough medical dramas. I'm sure I'll manage," I joked, then winced as I tried to shift my arm.

Aunt Lacey smile was laced with worry.

"Do I have to put my hand over it?" I asked to clarify the mechanics.

"No. However, you will need to remove the towel or it will obstruct the skin from reconnecting."

"Of course, wouldn't want the towel to make a mess of things."

The attempt to unwrap the towel made me want to create a whole new word for fuck. I didn't let a sound escape as Donovan and Caine sprung to help. Donovan was closer, handing my makeshift dressing to Kim who threw it aside, disgusted.

Ranlyn chose to stand, arms crossed, and tense. "You should begin before you become too weak to proceed."

Closed eyes, a few deep breaths to focus on bringing forth my power, and I overshot, losing control and having to backpedal. I heard the intake of breaths of those around me as it affected them. The energy crawling across my skin caused a vibration which made the wound ache. An ache so deep it felt as if the cat had shotgun blasted a hole right through me, leaving nothing but ragged skin and shattered bone like childhood cartoons when extreme violence with your cereal was still socially acceptable.

"Concentrate on the power, not the pain," Aunt Lacey spurred me on.

I attempted to push the power to my left arm, as with the stem of a flower, trying to envision it healing itself. All I could think of was bloody torn flesh. This time I cried out as my power throbbed with a kick of pain of steel-toe boots and a biker's attitude.

Someone's hands grabbed mine. I felt him hesitate, knowing it was Donovan before looking at him. When I did, his eyes were soft, too soft for this. He wasn't seeing me, not the me in front of him. As he held tighter, I slipped into the vision I had while he was removing the piece of cat from my arm. A serene moment. For half a second, all pain disappeared before I was vaulted back into the present to his voice guiding me, somehow seeing beyond his own visions.

"Work with your heartbeat to slowly draw the power into the wound. Think of the blood receding with the pain and your flesh closing around it." Donovan talked in circles while I was a rundown car battery squeezing every volt of juice I could to sustain my power's stability.

Flashes of an unknown rendition of us kept blocking his thick voice. Concentrating as hard as I could, I fought to force out the vision and think of the gaping wound crying for attention.

Time plodded in a creeping pace, my exhaustion mounting.

Donovan grew quiet. I figured he gave up, until I opened my eyes. Instead of expected disappointment, I found a satisfied smile dimple his cheeks.

"You did it, babe." He gave one last squeeze of my hands before letting go.

I swiped away lingering blood and found nothing. No gash, no colour of death, nothing. "It worked!"

The Coveners clapped and celebrated for me.

"Thank you!" I wrapped Donovan up in a big hug and pulled away apologizing when I realized I assaulted him with visions.

"Call me your cheerleader," he said humbly.

"Those pom-poms did more than cheer. I couldn't have done it without you. Thank you so much, Donovan."

"It will become easier, Salix." Again, Aunt Lacey was all too confident in abilities I had not yet demonstrated, but even I had to admit this was huge. I had a hole torn through my skin big enough to plant flowers and the only evidence it existed was a pinkish puckering that looked like it would heal and disappear in little time.

Albeit excruciating, I was happy Aunt Lacey talked me into

trying. It was an accomplishment I couldn't have received by enduring a needle and stitches, no matter how many I sat through.

Everyone's soul glows had me squinting again. Kim handed over my sunglasses, and I put them back on and gave her a tight, rocking hug.

"That was incredible to watch, Soph."

"You naughty voyeur." It felt good to laugh.

Caine was behind us waiting his turn. "I'm so sorry, Sophie," he said quietly holding me so close I grew uncomfortable with the audience.

"It's not your fault, Caine. I'm fine." I couldn't tell him I suspected Donovan was the true culprit. As far as I was concerned, Donovan also fixed the problem.

"If I was stronger, maybe you wouldn't have felt anything."

I pulled away, moved his hair from his face with my hand lingering at his jaw. "You made it as painless as possible."

I hoped he forgave himself soon.

Pieces of the porcelain cat and trails of blood were everywhere.

As I picked up one of the bigger chunks of cat, I cut my finger. Nothing big, the size of an actual paper cut this time. I forced a dose of power into my finger, pressure pulsed like I wrapped a rubber band around it, and I watched as the cut closed itself shut like a zipper. It amazed me how easy it was. Small cuts at work or playing with Bosco would be enough to get in some practice.

Caine was nearby helping with the clean up and felt the sudden usage of power. "Are you all right?" I told him about the small cut. "Remind me to come to you instead of reaching for a bandage next time." He kissed the top of my head before we continued tackling the mess.

At the end of the meeting, Aunt Lacey reminded everyone again about the Lughnasadh celebration we kept hearing about.

Caine used the bathroom before we were set to leave, so I took the moment to speak to Donovan alone. I found him talking to a short young woman in her mid to late twenties with sandy hair. I thought her name was Christina or Christy though couldn't remember. Christina or Christy was speaking *to* him, not *with* him, and when Donovan saw me walking towards him, he left the woman to talk to herself as he met me part way.

"That was rude." I gave Christina or Christy an apologetic glace.

"Please, she was talking about modern harvesting on corn crops across Canada. I wanted to pull my teeth out."

"Obviously, she wanted to talk to *you*, not about crops or whatever. Be nice, she likes you." Christina or Christy probably searched for conversation relating to the Lughnasadh harvest celebration and turned it into something wholly uninteresting.

"Next time she'll have to make a play so I can reject her quickly."

"You're such a dick. She could've been planning her speech all night."

"Then she needs a ghost writer."

I made a throaty sound calling him a dick again.

"Something you want to talk about?" he asked.

I led him to the back table where all important conversations took place fumbling on where to start. A few deep breaths and I was still unsure, so I jumped to it. "I wore a long white and blue faded patterned dress..." His expression dropped. "My hair was halfway down my back and wavy, a lighter brown. You were wearing brown pants with suspenders—"

"How do you know that?" His interruption was abrupt.

"I-I think you showed me."

Tension pricked the air between us as he remained unreadable.

"While you were pulling the cat-thing out of my arm, I got flashes of us together. Not of us now. You're not the suspenders type." I laughed, he didn't. "I, um, figured it's what you must *see*, but without any addition of Caine or other stuff from this time."

His eyes dropped to the table. Embarrassed? Ashamed? Troubled? I couldn't tell. After a silent moment, he said, "Now you know."

I nodded. "You were so happy then."

He cracked a wry smile. "So were you."

He was right. I glowed and not in a brightened soul kind of way. Uncontainable happiness exuded from me as much as it did him.

As we looked at each other across the table, a host of questions lingered. Questions I couldn't bring myself to ask. Why make him relive it when I had no intention of learning who I was back then? That person wasn't me, neither was he, and Donovan and I couldn't be the people we were to each other back then.

One other thing needed to be said. "I know it wasn't Caine that made the cat shatter." His expression along with his body stiffened. "I'm not mad. I know everyone assumes Caine's power went wonky. I saw your face before it happened, you were angry, then you looked so...guilty. It wasn't Caine."

"I didn't know that would happen."

"It's fine, I'm fine. I guess I wanted to be sure. Not that it matters. You helped me. In a way, Aunt Lacey helped all of us tonight."

"How so?"

"Well, she helped me heal, something I've never done on purpose. She helped Caine use his persuasion in a new way, and then you helped me by getting that thing out of my arm. And the visions helped me understand different things tonight. I'm glad she talked me into it."

"Me too," Donovan admitted. "Now you know I wasn't lying about seeing us together, 'cuz I know you did," he gave a hollow laugh as I smiled. "And I think the experiment helped me deal with the visions. It's difficult with you, more than with others, especially as you grow stronger. But as long as you don't surprise me, I think I can control them better when we touch. Not that it happens often."

I understood what he meant. "It took a lot for me to fight through them. When you helped with the healing they kept interrupting me. It was distracting."

"And how's that feel?"

"Fuckin' sucks dead frogs."

He laughed. "Yes, it does."

A mutual understanding of his psychometry did help. The

visions were intoxicating. A dream you never had need to wake from. No wonder he looked at me the way he did.

He leaned closer to me over the table. "They're not the only reason I want to be with you, I hope you realize that."

I shrugged.

"Babe, believe me. I've separated my feelings from then and now and although the past seems stronger," he paused searching through those emotions, "it's because I had you then. In this life, I don't know what that reality feels like."

I didn't know what to say but he had no problem going on.

"Look, I don't want to be your dingle-berry bestie following you around. I don't want to pretend like I'm fine with you and Caine because I never will be. Ever. I can't pretend. This is no high school crush or pub crawl conquest. This is real."

He stopped as if expecting me to bolt or argue. Instead, I sat and processed as he went on.

"You *are* special, I've said it before, but it's not because you're a magical being, it's that you're special to me. The person you are now, today in this time. I'm not the man I was back then, nor do I expect you to be the woman you were." He sat back in his chair and crossed his arms. "I wish you had the opportunity to get to know me. Not the jackass that comes out when you're here since you're usually with *him*. I think I'd surprise you."

Again, I didn't know what to say. His explanation made sense. He wanted me to know where his heart stood, with me in the here and now. I believed him. He was right in saying I didn't know him. I had no inkling of the person he was aside from his antagonizing Caine and everyone drooling over him at every meeting.

Swaying from Donovan's deep eyes, I saw Caine come down searching for me. He sat on the couch and waited when he noticed who I was talking to.

Noticing my attention flicker, Donovan turned to see what I was looking at. "I guess you have to go."

"Not because he's beckoning me." I didn't like his implication.

"Ranlyn's driving. Also, I left Bosco with my Aunt. She hasn't been alone much since she was released from the institution."

"Institution?"

I nodded.

"Guess I don't know much about you either."

I smiled and stood to leave. Before I did, I needed him to know. "I'm not going to tell him it was you."

He surprised me by placing a warm hand over mine that lingered on the table with a hint of a flinch. He returned a tender, dimpled smirk. "It doesn't matter, but thanks."

As I walked away, I realized Donovan would get pleasure out of Caine blaming himself for the cat shattering. I thought again about whom I was protecting and why, and had no clue what the fuck I was doing.

16

LOFTY SECRETS

Since all communication between Olive and those working on the estate was over the phone, I insisted we make a trip to view their progress and ensure no one was messing around on the job. Money was no object. Whatever estimates rolled in, Olive paid without question. Wasteful or excited to spend it, I wasn't sure, but it was time for her to see her home again.

Raccoons accessed a broken window and nested their furry butts and their family's furry butts in a closet. Though the Exterminators were more horror-struck at the few decades old spider infestation. Both the eight-legged squatters and the long-tailed variety of pest a high priority for eviction.

Under the canopy of trees blocking an otherwise unencumbered sun, the re-painted butter cream trim shone. We stepped out onto the stone steps to gaze upon the estate's transformation. I was in love before the makeover, in the daylight and with the greenery tamed, I was school-girl level crushing.

Olive stared up at the estate with adoration glittering in her eyes. I could only guess at what she must be thinking after decades of distance between them and wondered if her memories matched reality.

When she was ready, Olive inhaled and switch gears, surveying the grounds with a critical eye instead of that of the young woman who dreamt of returning one day. She stopped at a few pots of colourful flowers staged for the next days' planting and then stepped through the arched double doors with hesitant footsteps as Serena, Kim, and I followed, leaving Ranlyn under a cover spell outside where Olive asked him to remain.

He didn't argue.

The interior was steal-your-breath enchanting. The intricate chandelier now polished to a diamond-like sparkle that shone down on the waxed, dark wood plank floors. The front parlour teemed with life. Every piece of furniture, decor accent, and portrait gave the room a consciousness as if no time had passed at all.

A stuttered inhale stuck in my throat as the odd sensation returned. No timid brush of my skin this time, skipping right to the confident touch on my chest like an intricate handshake, seeping into some place deep within me.

"That's how I know you're heir," Olive said looking to me with teary happiness. Her hand was in the same position as mine, pressed into her breastbone.

"What is it?" I asked.

"The estate, welcoming us home." She smiled as if this was the most natural thing.

"How does it know?"

Tears fell on her cheeks, a small head shake telling me more than words. She may not know for sure, but Olive trusted this place and whatever power it held.

My great-aunt put her arm around my elbow and held tight as the sensation dissipated as if going about its day. "It's so much more than I remembered, Firefly. So much more."

Guiding Olive to one of the red and gold velvet claw-footed love seats, where she let go of a few more tears. Serena and Kim wandered, checking out each trinket and embellishment they missed during the first visit. Everything down to the spiralled spindles on the staircase and the telephone niche held character impossible to duplicate in an apartment built within the last fifty years.

"The estate belongs to no one," Olive told me. "Retains independence, standing after all these years, strong to the foundation. It will stand long after we're gone. Though maybe not you, Firefly. I see you around for a while."

I nudged her shoulder. "You don't want to live forever?"

"Ha. No. No, I don't."

"Why not?"

Olive's gaze was sympathetic. "Humans aren't meant to live forever. We're born, we live, we die, and then who knows. A long time has passed since any in our bloodline chose that path, though I could be wrong since I'm oblivious to the state of the family these days." She patted my hand. "If a prolonged life is what you want, at least you won't have to spend it alone." Her implication was I'd have Caine at my side.

I didn't comment.

"Answers will surface as you adapt to this life and this house may be the first piece. Everything around you is saturated in centuries of memory from the Magics who dwelled within it. It has its own story to tell. At one time, I believed I would be a part of those stories. And while the estate remembers me," she placed her hand on her chest where the sensation had grown, "we are strangers."

"The estate wouldn't have greeted you if it was ready to let you go. You're still the heir."

Olive smiled and patted my hand. "I do love this place, but I'm merely a placeholder."

Contemplating my future had me thinking of the past. With a left turn in topics, I asked, "What do you know about past lives?"

"Well, rarely do you find a virgin soul but there's strong proof they exist."

I nodded. "I think I saw mine, but I don't know if I can trust what I saw."

"This is what Caine mentioned when I was released from The Royal? A past life with your coven-mate?"

I nodded, thankful Caine stayed home today. "Donovan."

"You saw this past-life with Donovan?"

"Saw it, felt it."

"Do you have a memory of ever doing whatever it was you saw?"

"Fuck no." I winced. "Sorry, but no. Plus, I looked different. Peasant dresses aren't my thing."

"Sounds like you know your answer."

"Okay, but if a Magic is skilled at imagining this backdrop starring me as a historical romance movie extra, and I somehow channelled that fantasy, how could I tell the difference?"

"I'm not sure you could, Firefly. What does your gut tell you?"

Donovan may have been desperate to be with me, but I doubted he was so creative or creepy. His reactions to touching me were genuine, and I realized it was my own baggage pre-judging his motives.

"I guess it's real," I admitted mostly to myself.

"You don't look happy about this revelation."

"One more thing on my list of convoluted shit to sift through when I'm already elbow deep."

Olive laughed. "It seems unfair but with true happiness comes pain. The world's way of balance. You need to decide which are worth the price."

What a true and torturing thought. Figuring out which things to feel happy about, without knowing the price you would pay for allowing yourself to feel them, was impossible.

"Don't fret, Firefly." She squeezed my hand and I realized was clutching hers too tight. "You have plenty of time to wrap your head around whatever it is you want in this life." She stood, wrapping her arm around my shoulder, and walked to join the others.

Each room was as gorgeous as the next in its own way. The

estate's study had packed shelves of books. Built-in shelves showed wear on the lowest shelf from being scaled for books out of reach, yet not far enough to use the sliding ladder. Pulling myself away from it was only possible knowing I'd be back to spend many hours curled up in the deep leather couches.

Modern kitchen appliances were ordered special, taking on the appearance of the past century, until you examined them closer. Olive opened one of the cabinets to examine the contents within; their doors decorated with stained glass inlays in earthy colours matching the rich green of the walls. In the center of the room stood a thick butcher block worn with use and I felt the compulsion to run my hand along the grain.

A six-foot-wide wooden staircase covered with deep burgundy pattered carpet creaked beneath our feet as we climbed to the second floor. Long hallways branched to either side with half a dozen or more rooms with as many baths or half-baths.

The master bedroom was larger than my entire apartment, the deep chairs in front of the brick fireplace the perfect cozy nook to relax in. The bed had a monster-sized headboard and hand-carved posts thicker than my waist.

I ran my fingers over every bump and ridge of a scene carved into the headboard. Cherubic angels bracketed one corner. The other, cherubic demons. Each with a set of wings from their chubby bodies. Their smiles contained opposing intent, keeping watch of a scene ensconced with elements of both if you looked hard enough. Early settlers danced, others read or cooked, while some congregated outside a church.

A young man and woman frolicked amongst the thick trees, separate from the others. I was reminded of the vision of Donovan and me. My past life drenched with overpowering love for the man he was.

Woven into the scene was adults and children tied to trees, held captive on their knees, or strung to wooden pyres engulfed with fire. The artist captured tortured faces in a realistic depiction of the

Witch Burnings. Hidden amongst such captivating images you lost the impact of horror unless you focused in on the torment.

Is that what happened to us? Did we die together in the Witch Burnings?

"A scramble of conflict, carved in rosewood." Olive was next to the bed and smiled when I jumped. "The smell still permeates the room and will for years more. A gift from someone important though I can't recall who from or for." I smelled it without realizing it came from the headboard. "It's an honest piece and but a small part of Magics history tainted by hatred."

"But most of the real Magics escaped persecution, right?"

Olive's head tilted. "Yes, but some never admitted the existence of their abilities to anyone, not even family. If they ran, they would be left to their own resources. A single person traveling was suspicious, especially a woman. Most burned were innocents, but some ability-born fell too early. Bloodlines were lost. The true gruesome acts of the Witch Wars never made it onto the pages."

"Witch Wars? Like a Witch civil war? They fought each other?"

She nodded. "Both sides were guilty of ugly acts while fighting their prospective allies. Either they were doing their best to keep it under the radar or, in times when witchcraft was not looked down upon, there wasn't a need to document it. Not everything gets passed on."

I had experienced witch-on-witch conflict already, but the scope she implied sounded far broader than Loring's attacks.

"What were they over? Did our family have anything to do with them?"

Giggling, Olive pulled my arms to get me off the bed. "Not today, Firefly. Today we revel in the fact we're still here, this house still stands, and you, my darling, are fit to carry our family into the future."

Leading me out of the room, I itched with questions.

Olive reached a door at the end of the hall and called everyone over. The others exited from different rooms. "The cleaning crews never made it passed *this* door." Olive's smile brightened. "However, entering will be a bit difficult with my telekinesis being rusty. Think you can help?" She asked me. "See the corners of the door frame, how they form squares?" I nodded. "Pull them out."

I struggled to pull out the left corner square and had to use both hands. A metal post was connected to the square, jutting into the wall, stopping when I had pulled it out about five inches. The second one was stiffer, causing a squeal that pierced our eardrums.

"We'll need oil next time." Olive swatted dust away from her face. "All right, Firefly, spin the first square counter-clockwise until it stops, then the other, and then push them back in, in that order."

I followed her instructions. When I pushed the last square back into place, a series of clicking noises and scraping metal came from inside the wall. The door slid into a pocket in the wall with a banging stop when the doorknob jarred the frame. Everyone but Olive shrieked.

We shuffled inside, scanning the room as Olive slid the pocket door shut behind us to the sound of more mechanical clicking noises, presumably locking us in.

In a room smaller than the others, I anticipated something remarkable. I looked around and wasn't impressed. The wood panelled walls were green washed with crown moulding to match the rest of the house. An old sewing machine sat on a wooden desk to the left side. To the right was a shelving unit with baskets of yarn, sewing essentials, and reference books on sewing and fashion construction.

"Seems like a lot to go through to protect a sewing machine," Serena's said.

"Actually, yes, it is precisely constructed to protect a sewing machine." Olive went to an old metal light switch and pressed the top metal button, causing the bottom one to pop out. Nothing happened but Olive didn't look worried. Instead, she sat in front of the sewing machine and fidgeted with excitement.

"This sewing machine is a paw-foot style of Ketchum's Patent.

Means nothing to any of you, but it's an antique from the mid-1860s and was a big deal the day the then heir, Geo Ballard, installed it."

She pointed to the faded patent dated on the needle plate. As faded as the ornate white and yellow flowers and gold filigree design.

I'd never heard the name Geo Ballard and wondered how many heirs there have been.

"Others have sat here, none so exquisite. More important is this particular machine works much like the locks to this room."

Without further explanation, she spun the wooden handled metal crank towards her a few times, switched direction, then cranked it more times. Repeating this a few times in different sequences. More mechanical crackling followed, but nothing happened once they stopped.

Olive walked over to the shelves, grabbed hold, and heaved.

Nothing.

She grunted and threw what little weight she had to throw around.

"Can I help you *not* throw your back out?" Kim asked.

Exhaling in defeat, Olive straightened her cardigan. "Would you be a dear?"

Kim switched places with her. "I just pull?"

"That's the idea."

Kim grabbed hold of the shelf, paused, and gave a bracing pull. A cough of dust escaped from a seam behind the shelf, covering her.

I burst into laughter as she pulled the shelf open as far as it would go, revealing a darkened doorway. Kim shook herself like a dog and smoothed her hair back.

Olive led the way inside. I lightly touched Kim's shoulder and she jumped, thinking it was a creepy crawler of some sort and then swatted at me and raced into the dark entry before me.

A filigreed metal staircase spiralled skyward, difficult to ascend for someone with long legs, as our knees hit the stair above. Two large metal doors capped the top of the stairs like we were exiting a tornado escape hatch, landing us in the middle of an enormous room.

"Holyfuckballs!"

The estates attic stretched the span of the house. A layer of dust covered everything including the stale air heavy in my lungs. The vaulted ceiling pitched with thick beams running parallel to the rise of the roof and then across the space. You could wield a foil against a grungy pirate, leaping to the clash of metal from the beams to the hanging chandeliers. Long shelves held more than books. The walls featured portraits of strangers and strange places I had never travelled.

Kim held her hands behind her back as if afraid to break something while she explored. Serena touched everything she set her eyes on.

Olive reached a desk and turned, her words a splash of sound, throwing her voice around in echoes. "This space is where we come to speak about anything and everything involving our history, to strengthen our abilities, and discuss strategic manoeuvres." She pointed as she spoke. "The walls are magically sound-proofed, as well as enemy-proofed. There's an area for practice, potion creation, reading, and meditation. We have resource tomes, crystals, herbs, talismans, runes, spirit and curse boxes, tarot cards, angel cards, and so much more I haven't the time to list. All collected over the duration of the Ballard family's existence. Gathered since it was a mere hut in the 1600s when some of the first settlers migrated from Europe, then eastern Canada, and changed hands over and over again." She gave a melancholy shake of her head as she looked at the wall of strange faces. "Our ancestors would be appalled at our current state." She took a deep breath and found her smile. "But that *will* change."

Thick dust filtered through my lungs and danced in the light from circular stained-glass windows high above my head. Everything from my power, Caine's awakening, my past-life with Donovan, Nya and Gareth, Aunt Lacey's Coven, and Olive standing free from The Royal, all boiled into a collective mass I struggled to wrestle.

The room swayed. I caught myself by collapsing into an old chair. A hot flash raced up my back and had me fighting not to pass out.

The odd sensation in my chest from when I entered the estate returned, a pressure I met with a deep breath as the estate or whatever magic kept watch within it flushed me a needed chill to douse the heat and allowed me to regain my composure. Whatever the fuck it was, it was vigilant to my needs.

"Come look!" Olive called from across the room.

She blew dust off an old gramophone before setting the needle and filling the rafters with soft music as I made my way to her and sent out a silent "thank you" to estate for helping me.

Olive picked up a large book. "This is the Ballard Family Tome." A crest was stitched into the leather cover; a black sable with a griffin surrounded by red and white plumes headed by an elaborate helmet. "Each heir to take temporary possession of the estate has faithfully added to our history." She smiled, but Olive's tone soured. "My hope is to add to it before you take up the mantle, Firefly."

"Aunt Lacey has one too," I deflected. "She said it was a family heirloom. I guess it's normal in families." This was a statement and question in one. I had no clue. "Though she went by Elsa before, so I don't know if she catalogues the name changes."

"Elsa?" Kim asked with confusion.

I nodded. "Caine's family knew her as Elsa."

"Elsa's your Coven Leader?" Olive asked.

"Yes," Kim said. "Do you know her?"

"I've heard of her. In those Witch Wars I referred to," she said to me, "Elsa led the charge. Commander and frontline infantry, fighting alongside her flock in the trenches. Always landing on top. She's one of the oldest Magics I've heard of still creeping through time. If you're conflicted on working toward immortality, Firefly, Elsa's the expert."

"Definitely," Kim agreed.

"Hold up a sec, people!" Serena interrupted and pointed at me. "You're telling me that *you* could live forever?"

Oops. I forgot I left that part out.

———

We dropped Olive and Serena off at my building and waited in the small front parking lot of my building for Kim to get her stuff for the coven meeting as well as grab Bosco for me. Coveners were getting used to the Coven mascot and it was the safest place for my furbaby. Caine was already waiting when we pulled up and jumped in as Ranlyn popped out to speak to one of the guards stationed in the hallway. Something about a guard's personal issue and being present for a quick shift change.

Ranlyn turned to me in the passenger seat and Caine in the back. "Undercovers are around the perimeter. Tinted windows won't save you from giving them a free show, so behave." He jumped out and, after a quick look around, disappeared under a cover spell without breaking stride.

"I need to learn how to do that." I was in awe of his seamless talent.

Caine unclipped his belt and leaned between the seats to pull me in for a deep kiss, Ranlyn's warning be damned. His lips left me overheated and drowning in regret to end the "free show" for whichever guards were gawking or rolling their eyes from the invisible sidelines.

"This would be much more fun in my own vehicle," Caine said evoking a giggle from me.

"Won't stop Ranlyn from tagging along, so unless you're all about witnesses...."

"Yeeeaahh, no thanks. Though, it does give me an idea."

"Maybe you should kiss me more often."

A lusty smile narrowed his smoky eyes. "Come here. I need some inspiration."

My fingers scraped down his stubbled cheeks, a fond memory from that morning's escapades gifting me tingles.

"Any ideas?" I asked as I pulled away.

"I'll surprise you."

"Hmm, not sure I approve."

He smiled and sat back in his seat. "Too bad, darlin'."

"Oh really?" I unclipped my belt and was in the backseat and on his lap so quick he raised his hands as if to ward off an attack. When my lusty intentions became clear, he wrapped them around me as I pulled him on top on me to lay us out in the back seat to enjoy his lips longer.

A voice had my eyes pop open, my lips stopping as I listened a moment longer.

"What's wrong?" Caine asked, but my focus was outside the vehicle.

Can't be. I shot up and looked towards my building. A sledgehammer to the solar plexus had me choking on air and grabbing hold of my curling stomach.

Caine grabbed the hand. "What? What happened?"

A full-body wrench of pain mixed with warring numbness. The taste of bile hit my tongue. Pain in the back of my skull branched out and polka-dotted my eyesight.

"How?" I heard myself say.

"How what?" Caine asked.

His voice snapped me out of my fog.

"Move!" I forced him back against the door.

"What? Sophie, what are you doing?"

I squatted on the seat in front of him with my back to the windshield, shielding his view.

In an anxious sweat, I forced myself to turn back to the building. Caine tried to look around me. I shoved him back into the seat.

"Don't!" I yelled and clutched onto his shoulder so hard my nails bit into his skin, for the first time feeling my power buzz with my panic as he cried out in pain.

Caine grabbed my wrist to try and pry my fingers loose. He grunted as my power surged to keep him in place while I stared him down through blurred sight.

"What the fuck's going on?" He asked through gritted teeth.

I couldn't say it. It couldn't be true.

He grabbed my shoulders and spun me to the side, making a go for the door handle.

"No!" I reached out for him to stop, the car door locks punched into place, spell locking us both in.

Shock rounded his eyes, but I couldn't focus on using my words. My thoughts drew my attention inward. I saw everything yet nothing at all.

Caine brought me to the surface by grabbing my face. "Sophie, calm down and breathe normally." Power washed over me. His power. Counteracting my own like a balm. Snapping the rigidness from my limbs like a broken elastic band. "Tell me what's wrong."

"Jack's back." My robotic voice trembled.

Caine sat back and let his control go. "Who's Jack?"

As the feeling of his influence dissipated it took a few seconds to answer. "Promise you won't go out there."

"You locked the doors. I can't if I wanted to."

Tears escaped. I ran shaking hands over my thighs and through my hair. The scale of vulnerability so raw my body felt foreign.

The piece of shit stood, laughing with his wife, both finishing a smoke as if it were a normal day. He was dressed up like a church-going family man. Theresa may have forgiven him. She may have forgotten how many of her bones he'd broken and how many bruises his fists had left, but I still saw the cowardice beneath his button-down façade.

"He's the one who stabbed me."

The leather of the seat moaned as Caine shifted. I tried to talk but he raised his hand and closed his eyes, stopping me in some type of warning. When his power surged, it became clear. His anger had caught up to mine and he was working to control his ability, losing the battle.

His energy became so potent, I felt painful waves of pure rage radiating from him. I couldn't leave since I locked us in and didn't know how to reverse it. I called his name, gripped his shoulder, all while his power took over and gained in strength. Yelling was useless. The persuasion power was his specialty, not mine. His power consumed me, driving my own power to the surface to protect me. Energy bloated the small space and suffocated me. I curled my knees up in front of my chest in a feeble attempt to gain distance.

Caine clutched his seat with one hand. The other tore into the headrest in front of him. A half-second later, a burst of energy pounded against my body and sucked the oxygen from my lungs.

Gasping with a ragged breath in, my eyesight spotted and waned before filtering back to a pair of red eyes inches from my face. I jerked backwards and smacked my skull on the window.

"Shit. Sophie, are you okay?" It was Caine, the blood vessels in his eyes all broken and turning the whites bright red.

Was I knocked out?

"Besides feeling like a crash-test dummy? Peachy. You?" Thirsting for oxygen, thinking that type of detonation should have torn him apart, my ribs ached with every breath.

A face filled the vacant slice of window behind Caine where half the glass was missing, the rest hung in a thousand small pieces. "Fah!" I yelled in a half-baked version of "fuck" as my hand shot up. The energy still bouncing around inside of me shot out towards the man who screamed out in pain, grabbed his face, and fell to the ground.

Yelling came from all directions until a white film wrapped around the car and we couldn't see or hear anything.

"What the tits is happening? Is it Loring?"

"No idea," Caine mumbled as we tried to focus to see through the film.

An arm reached through the film into the glassless window. I freaked and slammed my foot square into the hand before it could grab the door handle.

A curse cried out. "*Sophie, it's me,*" I heard Ranlyn's voice in my head.

"Shitballs."

Ranlyn reached in with his other hand, opened the door, and stuck his body through the white film. "You broke my hand."

"Good, dickhole. You don't get grabby when I can't see your face. Feel lucky you're not like the other guy."

"That other guy was one of the guards checking on you Seedlings bent on announcing your presence to Loring's goons. You compromised his cover."

"Oops."

"Yeah, oops. Thankfully, he can be healed." He looked at Caine. "You mind explaining why you Hulked out in my vehicle?"

I was so proud of the reference I couldn't contain my palm raising for a high-five that went unappreciated.

After a moment, Ranlyn jumped into the front, swiping off the fallen glass from the seat, as Caine explained. "Once it was happening, I couldn't rein it in. That man...." he stopped, and his power tickled the atmosphere again. "I thought he was a vegetable."

"What man?" Ranlyn asked.

"He's supposed to be." I looked at the spider-veined windshield where I had seen Jack, but the white film was still in place.

"What man?" Ranlyn asked again, his tone clipped.

"Jack." I told him.

"Jack?" After a confused moment and, I'm pretty sure, checking my thoughts for clarification, he understood.

"Why is he here?" I needed to know. "Aunt Lacey said he'd spend the rest of his life a drooling idiot."

"Sophie, I'm so sorry." Ranlyn's expression was apologetic.

"Don't be sorry. Call her and get me answers."

Ranlyn got on the phone. I looked back at Caine, his eyes still blood red and painful looking.

"I could've hurt you," he said.

"You saw someone who tried to kill me. If I wasn't so freaked, I would've Hulked out too." I attempted a smile but lost it. "And so, there's no questioning it, that's your only pass on the influencing thing. I'll admit it was effective and one of the coolest abilities I've seen so far. Don't do it to *me* again."

His lips twitched in a ghost of a smile. "I figured as much."

Ranlyn said goodbye and ended his call. "Aunt Lacey will look into it. For now, you need to get to work. Fix my windows and we'll get going."

"Wha—? Fix them?"

"Your damage, your clean-up. Let's go. We can't drop the screen until they're fixed."

"The screen?" Caine asked.

Ranlyn motioned to the white film.

"I realize I'm a Magic and have an all-powerful witchy family and such, but I've got nothing that'll fix your windows unless you want me to get Olive's craft glue. I'm tits-gold at puzzles but this is a tad outside my skillset."

Ranlyn wasn't letting me out of it and was using the moment as a lesson. He added a reminder that Kim and Bosco were waiting for me outside the screen, and we still had a coven meeting to get to.

I managed to surface my power by thinking of crossing Jack in the hallway, wondering if he remembered trying to end me. Anger, or more likely fear, had my energy springing forward and out far enough to encapsulate the vehicle and whatever glass dotted the pavement.

Caine and Ranlyn inhaled in response to my power crowding the small space. With some direction and encouragement from Ranlyn, I put my hand on the door next to me and envisioned the empty spaces filling with spotless glass. Power heated my palm. Curious to see if it was working, I opened my eyes and watched cracks melt away and glass confetti rise from the ground to find its place. First, closest to my hand and then creeping along until the cracks disappeared, re-establishing the glass's rigidness until every window was factory new.

"I have the most amazing girlfriend!" Caine wrapped his arms around me and planted a hard kiss on my cheek.

Ranlyn didn't say anything, leaving me with a proud smile before starting up the car. A few seconds later, the screen fell, and Kim was jumping into the passenger's seat with Bosco in her arms demanding to know what the fuck happened.

Before my power dissipated, and before Kim passed Bosco of to me, I turned to Caine, he thought for a kiss, but my fingers bracketed his temples and held him still. His eyes fluttered and his face scrunched as my energy built, he resisting my hold as he tried to pull away. When I finished, I had him move his eyes around and confirmed I healed the broken blood vessels.

I pecked him on his lips. "Now no one will mistake you for a zombie."

"Wow," Kim said as Bosco jumped through the seats onto my lap and hit me with a barrage of kisses.

"I'll let the boss lady deal with my broken hand, thanks," Ranlyn complained as we took off.

"Perfect. I'll let her know you called her that." He narrowed his dark blue eyes at me in the rear-view mirror and I narrowed mine back in jest.

———

"What happened?" Donovan demanded, coming at Caine as he was the first in the door.

Ranlyn grabbed Caine's arm as if to propel himself between them, ready for a brawl. Aunt Lacey gave a command for Donovan to sit and for the rest of us to eat up.

Donovan's tension remained, but we focused on the homey aroma of stew coming from the kitchen. Last thing I needed was for Caine and Donovan to get into it.

Broth with stew wasn't a part of my palate. I separated the potatoes and vegetables and mashed them together with butter, salt, and pepper, and took a seat at the table with everyone. Donovan's jaw was set so tight I didn't know how he managed to eat. He was simmering hotter than the stew and refusing to engage with anyone.

"You massacred it!" Kim laughed at the amalgamation of food.

"Means more broth for me," Ranlyn said with a face full of steam from his bowl. His hand looked like it would bruise but I doubted it was broken.

To deflect from Kim's judgey-ness I posed a good question. "So, Aunt Lacey, did Jack's true love kiss him and wake him up? Or is this not how his fairy tale was supposed to end? 'Cuz I tell ya, I was told a different version. One where he's actually the super evil bad dude and he gets his just desserts."

The hard clank of Donovan's spoon hit his empty bowl, making me jump. "You should've let me kill him," he sneered at Aunt Lacey and shot up from his chair with a loud scuff on the floor, his bowl in his hands as he took it the sink and plunked it in with another loud crash.

Momentary guilt flittered in Aunt Lacey's eyes, but she recovered quickly and put down her spoon. "Wend, your love for Salix does not justify murder. You know why."

Awkward much? I stopped myself from looking at Caine, but Kim's stiff expression said everything I needed to.

Donovan leaned onto the table next to Aunt Lacey with fierce intensity, but she didn't wilt beneath his stare. "So now this sociopath gets to terrorize her by existing? How the hell is that justice?"

"He didn't see her, right?" Kim questioned.

"I don't give a shit!" Donovan snarled at her before I could answer. "How is she supposed to keep this shit in the rear-view when he could show up at her door or hitch a ride to the lobby in the same elevator?" He turned back to Aunt Lacey in low voice. "Do something or I promise I will."

Donovan's reaction impressed me. As did the ripple of enraged energy rolling off the guy.

"I agree," Caine said, surprising the shit out of the rest of us including Donovan who stood stalk straight, looking down at him. "You won't quit your job," he said to me, "but even if Jack never steps in the bar again, he lives down the hall. I can't bear knowing you have to go day in and day out dreading the asshole might cross your path. I stopped myself from going after him, but only because you accidently used your power to lock me in the car. Next time I might not be locked down."

I didn't know how to respond. A part of me wanted him to take care of Jack, but my first instinct was to stop him from learning who Jack was.

"Thoughts like that won't lead you down the right path, Leith," Aunt Lacey said evoking a confusing reaction from Caine who glanced at me and then away and down at his bowl.

Donovan moved quick and touched Aunt Lacey's forearm. To gain her attention? I didn't know. But she pulled away and glared at him. Could his power work on even her? What did he see? Was it about Caine?

"I've already got people allocated to him now," Ranlyn said.

Donovan straightened and crossed his arms. "They can't watch the perimeter, the building, Kim's and Sophie's apartments. Your resources are stretched. Maybe you'll spend days on end without sleep to watch her, but unless you can replicate yourself, your people have to take over, and they're not good enough."

"My people are Elite," Ranlyn argued.

"Sure they are." Donovan concentrated back on Aunt Lacey. "Do whatever you need to. Jack can't live like nothing happened."

"This is what is going to happen." Aunt Lacey paused and looked at all of us and then at Donovan. "No one is going to do anything. Salix is strong, she can handle this man on her own if need be." She continued above Donovan's arguments. "If there is a need, I will return Jack to his previous state. Doing so now would draw needless attention to this man. I refuse to give him, or whoever broke my spell, the attention they seek, nor will I stand idle and watch any of you two make ill-minded decisions."

Ranlyn nodded in response and looked at me in a show of confidence. He was already on top of protecting us and wasn't backing off anytime soon. While Jack might never get another chance to attack me with Ranlyn and his guards around, that didn't mean it wouldn't hurt me every time I saw him. Ranlyn couldn't protect me from that, even if I knew he would try.

"What I do want to try," Aunt Lacey continued, "is a Falaichte spell."

"You think that's necessary?" Ranlyn asked.

"I do," she answered. "While devoid of my sight as it pertains to the Lughnasadh celebration and under consistent threat from Loring, it may be the only way."

"But we'd be hidden from everyone, even you?" Kim added.

"Like ghosts?" I jumped in. "Can I haunt people? I've got a list."

Donovan sat again and asked Aunt Lacey, "Did you see something?"

"Nothing, which is precisely the catalyst for the Falaichte spell."

"Am I a ghost already?" I mumbled as everyone ignored me.

"Can the spell be affixed to an object?" Ranlyn asked.

"I swear they deserve it," I kept on.

Kim giggled and I mouthed Denise's name. She nodded animatedly.

"No haunting people, Salix," Aunt Lacey acknowledged me as I pouted. "Yes, I believe it can be. A talisman would be ideal and removable when in need."

"Do we get to know what this is first?" Caine asked. "I don't want to be a ghost."

Donovan huffed. "No one's a fucking ghost."

"Well, some people are," Kim joined in on my thread of annoyance.

"That they are," Aunt Lacey said, and Kim beamed a smile at Donovan's scowl. I had to laugh. "A Falaichte spell hasn't the power to pass an individual to the spirit world, though it will hide any essence from even the spirits themselves. Not physically, though I believe such a spell will hinder Loring and other devotees from finding you via location beacon or the like."

"My team can use this as a ploy in moving them around. False convoys, changing up personnel...keep Loring guessing with a shell game."

Aunt Lacey nodded. "If crafted with a backup plan in the case of a successful kidnapping."

Ranlyn looked down at this, the impact of shame too great to hide. So far, he'd saved my ass, but not everyone's.

"Give me Nya's ring." Aunt Lacey reached out to me, and I found myself hesitating to remove it. "You'll get it back," she promised, then looked a Caine, he understanding she needed Gareth's ring.

"Can you use my earrings?" Kim asked. "I don't usually take them off." Since I met Kim, her diamond studs in her second earring holes were firmly in place.

"Yes, they'll work."

She looked at Donovan.

He put his arm out across the table. "It doesn't come off," he said indicating the braided, leather bracelet with a small metal charm hanging from it.

She stared at him, he stared back. In true Donovan fashion, he had to be difficult.

"I'll make due," she compromised.

We all got up to head to the basement.

"Did you bring her cards?" Donovan asked Kim.

"Yeah." She pulled out my tarot cards from her bag and handed them to Donovan.

"Hey! How'd you get those?" I protested.

She huffed. "I knew you didn't need them."

"I didn't say she did," Donovan said. He looked at me. "Just wanted to see if you could use them."

"I could've saved you the subterfuge. They're crap and I'm crap-tacular at using them."

"You were craptacular at growing things at one point, too, weren't you?"

He had me there.

"How'd you know where to find them?" I asked Kim as we descended the stairs.

"I've been in your room," Donovan answered before her. "Nice feather pillow by the way."

"Stalker level creepy, dude."

Donovan gave a small laugh. I didn't dare look at Caine to see what he thought about it.

As we went to sit on the basement carpet to work on my tarot skills, Aunt Lacey touched Caine's shoulder, calling for him first to work on his talisman. He huffed before he left with her. I didn't get why.

"Think of what you want to know," Donovan said.

I shifted my attention, noticing that Aunt Lacey sat in a different spot at the table than normal. "Seriously, Donovan, a pasture of maggot-ridden cow paddies could predict the future better than me. I can't remember what the cards mean, normal or reversed. What about consecrating them? Denise said it helps."

Donovan snorted. "First of all, file any sentence that includes 'Denise says...' in your memory bank under 'bullshit the dumbest bitch in the world thinks she knows'." Kim agreed. "As adorable as you are when you pout, you're getting half-assed results because you're half-assing it."

I stuck my tongue out at him and he returned a sly, one-dimpled, smirk.

Kim uncrossed her legs, stood, and smoothed her jeans. "Your power will help its effectiveness, but you need to practice. Gwen's getting better every week. By the time I get back with my tea, you could bother to memorize at least one."

"Please. At this point, palm reading would be easier," I joked at Donovan's expense and earned myself the middle finger as Kim giggled all the way up the stairs.

"Palm reading's hard work," he told me.

"I can see how getting visions to fill the gaps of their past could work up a sweat." I laid the sarcasm on thick. "Especially when they don't know you can do it."

"At least I'm accurate. The book I gave you is good. You should read it. Besides the fact I'm literate, the psychometry makes me more precise."

"Yeah. Sure." I snatched the tarot cards from his hands and grazed skin. His eyelids fluttered, his whole body tensed. "Holy shit. My bad."

He blinked and inhaled. "All good. Only a flash of you. No complaints."

Hoping to divert the conversation and dial down the look he was drawing me into, I remembered his diversionary tactics. "So, you think Loring let Jack out of the spell?"

"I'd put money on it. The Falaichte spell should give us a leg up. Loring's too lazy for gumshoe work."

"Ranlyn won't let anything happen to me." He hadn't followed us downstairs, and I felt the need to stand up for him.

"Never said he would let it happen. Can't say the same for his people. I don't know them, so I don't trust them. Not with your life."

The intensity of his stare was as reassuring as it was off-putting.

"And having Kim steal my tarot cards?"

He one-shoulder shrugged. "I wanted to see if you could use them."

"Weak and you know it."

"Fine," he paused. "I see you once a week, maybe twice when shit hits the fan. You're always with him." He chinned in Caine's direction. I looked over and saw him wearing a more intense expression in reaction to whatever Aunt Lacey was saying. Donovan touched my socked foot to regain my attention. "How can we get to know each other better if we never do anything together?"

His honesty was jarring. "I guess that makes sense."

He straightened. "And since you haven't taken off to Kim or Ranlyn, I'll take it as a sign you're okay with quality time."

"You can delude yourself into thinking anything you want." I went to grab the cards and hit his skin again. This time, the vision was stronger as I watched his pupils dilate. Instead of pulling away, I held the contact a moment. I didn't know why, but I did.

Kim and Ranlyn's footsteps descending the stairs made me pull away.

Donovan blinked and said in a soft voice, "Sometimes the delusion is all I have."

DESPERATE MEN

Caine

Before I could sit with the others in Donovan's favorite spot to see Sophie tarot read, Aunt Lacey touched my shoulder.

"Why don't we start with you, Leith," she said and headed towards the back table.

If I was the paranoid type, I'd think there was a conspiracy to get me away from Sophie every time Donovan was around.

Sophie gave me a small smile as I followed our Coven Leader. Leaving was like losing a small battle, but last thing I needed was Donovan knowing how much he got to me.

Aunt Lacey tripped me up by sitting on the opposite side of the table as she usually would.

"I thought this would make you at ease," she said, and I realized I could see the small group over Aunt Lacey's shoulder. Wonderful. Hopefully Donovan didn't recognize her tactic. "Seeing them together sets your nerves on end, Leith, but you need to trust her instincts."

Donovan couldn't get away with anything without Sophie's say-so. While she may be more careful these days, far less managed to manipulate her.

"It is a shame she is subject to this predicament," Aunt Lacey said. "Two men of power universally connected to her in extraordinary ways. You have no concept or comparison to understand what this does to her."

I felt like a shmuck. Sophie had no more control over this then I did.

"It's not because she feels the need to choose between the two of you," Aunt Lacey continued, "although either one of you is *well* suited. She's drawn to both of you, her emotions tethered to two souls in ways she's too novice to separate." I waited for her to keep going. There had to be more. "There is," she confirmed, hearing my thoughts. "For Salix, seeing either one of you hurt or in mental distress causes her sorrow, though with Donovan, it's making itself more known in the form of a direct emotional connection."

I fidgeted, uncomfortable with the topic and wishing I knew a way to get rid of it.

"This tether is not part of her gifts, something to control or suppress through practice," she went on even though I'd already heard enough. "No, it's part of her soul, because at one time or another she pledged it to both of you, through Gareth, who is still a part of you, and to Donovan's past self. This will never fade, never subside, even a death would cause a part of her to parish. I suspect the connection will gain in its potency as she becomes stronger, and her strength grows every day."

"Tell *him* that," I said hearing anger simmer in my voice, hating that he evoked this in me. Seeing the way he looked at Sophie as she looked down at the cards in front of her re-enforced my fury.

"I have." Aunt Lacey slid a hand forward refocusing my attention. "I am doing my best to work with Wend. He knows they once shared a life together and knows that *if* she so chooses, he will relive that happiness and believes a part of her also loves him in this time. I can't fault him his efforts."

I took a harsh breath in, and a zing of pain shot through my jaw as I clenched my teeth. Thinking back at any time I had seen them together, even in the first meeting where she overcompensated by desperately ignoring him, the fact the prick might be right pissed me off more.

"Are you familiar with the phrase 'Never tempt a desperate man', Leith? A common phrase, though ignored too often to the perils of those who discount it. Wend is this desperate man. Make no mistake, as you look to him in disgust, you glimpse within the mirror."

If she was trying to make me feel better, her pep talk sucked. I'm nothing like Donovan and could care less about how desperate or misunderstood the asshole felt.

"If you find yourself without her, you will be him. And don't for one moment take the fact that she loves you for granted. She has a lot of mending of her own still to accomplish. Any love received at this point is a gift. She may not be capable of more, Leith. You need to accept her as is."

"You can't know that."

Aunt Lacey raised an eyebrow in challenge. "Wend *would* accept her as is without expectation and would find himself fulfilled. Don't let hopes for change be your downfall."

"Why is wanting Sophie to be happier a bad thing?"

"Because expectations to be something you're not, to feel something you don't, evokes a weight of failure greater than love can best. Your expectations speak of yourself and, while valid to your needs, hinder this exercise she agreed to knowing she would suffer."

"Suffer?"

"As I said, mental anguish against either of you saddens her, and in this situation, you or Donovan get what you want, not both. So, she suffers."

If she was going to suffer anyway, I'd rather Sophie suffer at my side than Donovan's. A part of me wondered if this was how other Berisfords justified hurting the people they loved.

"Why haven't you told her about Daniel?"

That one I deserved and didn't know how to answer.

"Sophie makes a point to share things she needn't have to, before you even awoke from your sleeping curse." I understood she meant Sophie and Donovan's kiss. I wonder who else knew about it.

"I know."

"Then why?"

"As you've pointed out, I'm in a neck and neck race with Donovan. If she knows about Daniel and the rest of the Berisfords, it could shift things in Donovan's advantage."

She was shaking her head before I finished. "Lying will shift things to his advantage and is not the real reason you deceive her."

"It's not the fact that my father is evil, it's that *so* many others in my family have been. I don't need her worrying I'll follow in the same footsteps."

"This uncertainty is yours alone, Leith. You need to make the decision to be a good person and to use your abilities with positive intent. You chose by being here after knowing the truth."

I adjusted in my seat and leaned forward to speak lower. "And is the truth about Berisfords killing Ballards in the Witch Wars supposed to help win her over?"

Aunt Lacey leaned forward. "Unless you plan to slit her throat in her sleep or cut her down in battle, you will have nothing in common with your ancestors. Disregard for another's life is not genetic." I crossed my arms again. "Trust her and trust yourself." She leaned back in her chair. "You Seedlings make things more difficult than they need be."

I cracked a wry smile, but I felt more discouraged than ever. "What about the spell?"

"I don't need you for the spell. Join the others while I ready your talisman."

———

I chewed over the image of Sophie's reaction to Jack while she was busy with Gwen getting some tarot card reading tips. The orange-haired reader was quickly becoming a pro and Aunt Lacey swore she was the one to go to if Sophie wanted to pursue tarot reading. Since Donovan was hanging out with them as well, as an extension of their earlier attempts before other Coveners arrived, I was hanging back. Or trying to.

"It was truly traumatic," Ranlyn said having overheard my thoughts as I sat on the end of the couch. I looked up to see him standing with a coffee cup in hand

"Oh, I know, but her reaction to Jack..." I struggled to keep my anger in check as my power surfaced on impulse. "It was like she was reliving the attack in front of my eyes. I guess I hoped it wasn't so life-threatening."

"I wasn't present for the healing, but from what Aunt Lacey described, if Sophie wasn't found in time, she would be dead."

My power boiled.

"She said she thought Donovan helped too. With the healing." I saw the faint scar from the stab wound but the psychological damage wasn't so faded.

Ranlyn took the corner before answering. "He did. Even pulled the knife out of her. I'm unsure how much of the details Sophie knows. Maybe remind yourself of his part in saving her life next time you want to skin him alive. Even if it's deserved."

"And it usually is."

"Indeed."

At least one person understood.

I exhaled in frustration, running my hands through my too long hair and flexed my fingers to try and lessen my power. "Never met someone who makes it so freakin' difficult to hate in my whole life." I thought of him healing her and his teachings to control her power, the guy was always available as her caretaker.

"Oh, Donovan's easy to hate." Ranlyn took a seat next to me. "But you can't make her hate him, no matter how much he messes with her head."

"Don't I know it," I muttered.

I tried not to watch them and found myself unable to stop myself. "When we got here," I said to Ranlyn and paused, trying to work out what to say, "Donovan felt what Sophie felt, didn't he? Aunt Lacey might have told him what happened with Jack after you called her, but he already knew firsthand."

Ranlyn took a sip from his cup. "Seems so."

Fuck.

"You're going to tell her about the connection," Ranlyn told me.

"I am?"

His coffee cup stopped half-way to his mouth. "Unless you want me to." The look he gave me told me he wouldn't be coy about me already knowing.

"I will." I may be on Ranlyn's security details, but he protected Sophie in more ways than one.

Denise came around with expansive itineraries for everyone for the Lughnasadh celebration, all events optional. The gathering itself was at a place called 'Diluculo'. I never heard of it, but it was near a beach as a few others talked about the clear water.

From the accounts of others, I expected a lot of alcohol, as well as pranks created with magic and ingenuity. If it was anything like my college days—and it sounded like it was—you don't volunteer without a serious imagination. Blake pulled a big one on Jared the last trip. One he stopped Blake from repeating with a beefy headlock.

Instead, Blake gushed about the return of the 'Ghost Vacuum'. A prank where someone places a vacuum in random places: under their sheets, in the shower, linen closets, for them to happen across. Thus, giving that person a turn to hide the vacuum in a weird version of tag. I didn't get why it was so funny, but Jared promised once you fell victim to the 'Ghost Vacuum' you would relish the chance to pass along the joke.

Donovan left to go upstairs and I saw a window of opportunity.

"You fight and you hitchhike home. We clear?" Ranlyn said.

I didn't respond and followed Donovan. By the time I caught up, Donovan had gone into the bathroom after Kim.

I stood near the living room away from everyone. Kim saw me and gave me a side-eye. "What's up?" she asked.

I shrugged. "Just waiting."

Her eyes narrowed. "Really?"

I nodded.

She looked toward the bathroom and back at me. "Oh, Caine, he's not worth it."

"I just need to talk to him."

"Caine...."

"I'd like nothing more than to kick his ass, but hurting him hurts her so I can't. You're welcome to stay. It might actually help." Kim was a tyrant when she had to be. The shake of her head told me wasn't looking forward to this.

"Am I interrupting something?" Donovan said as he came out of the bathroom and saw Kim and I standing together.

Ignoring his implications, I spoke smooth and deliberate. "I need your word that you'll back the fuck off." Kim tensed and Donovan pulled a face. "Of me, Donovan. Of trying to weasel your way in and purposefully pissing me off or coming after me like you did when we first got here today."

"You want me to be sorry I was pissed you couldn't handle your shit and put her in danger? Not fucking likely."

"I know you know about the connection."

Donovan exhaled and looked away from me.

"What connection?" Kim asked.

"You're a jealous little fuck, Caine."

"What the hell's the matter with you?"

Kim tensed at my reaction. "Guys, come on."

"This is ALL about her!" My voice cranked, causing Kim to take a step towards me as I had stepped towards Donovan.

"Cool your jets, turbo." Donovan flashed a conniving smile. "Got a thing with anger management I see."

"Stop goading him, Donovan," Kim tried, but the guy didn't even look at her.

"How can you justify acting like you do knowing hurting me hurts her?" Donovan didn't respond. "Have we not had this conversation before? Man, I'd love to duke it out and move on. But I'd do anything to keep her safe, even if that means walking away from your bullshit."

"Easy for you to *act* like the good guy all the time, isn't it? In front of her at least." Donovan's expression twisted. "You and I both know what's inside of you...Berisford...itching to escape." I looked at him, daring him to say it out loud in front of Kim, yet praying he wouldn't.

Donovan lifted a hand and waggled his fingers. "Not even Aunt Lacey can keep me out."

When we were at the table discussing Jack's future, Donovan's brief touch absorbed the conversation when she warned me of the dangers of my thought process. Now he knew I feared my evil side, as any Berisford should, and also knew Sophie had no idea it existed. It was the emotional cannon fodder Donovan needed to bring me down. A lie big enough to fracture our fairy tale.

"Are you blackmailing him?" Kim asked receiving no answer. "What is it with you two?"

"You prove my point every time you open your stupid mouth," I said. *"It. Hurts. Her."* Donovan pursed his lips, narrowing his eyes as Kim looked toward the kitchen. I didn't care if others overheard. "Fighting for her is one thing, I know how worthy she is." Kim groaned at this. "These games you play are cruel and do one thing and that's not making her love you. I'm asking you, for her sake, let it the fuck go. Do what you need to try and sway her decision, I'm up for the challenge. If it doesn't cause her pain, I couldn't care less. But let go of this need to break me down. Not all of Sophie's heart belongs to me and I'm coming to terms with the fact I can do shit-all about it. We're all planning a long life here. I don't want this back-and-forth bullshit to be the extent of our futures."

I left Donovan to soak in my words, heading for the bathroom to

18

REUNION

Climbing into the back of my mom's van, Serena looked as enthusiastic for the reunion as I felt. I looked her over. "Were you skull-fucked by a cactus?"

"Ugh. Thanks for pointing it out, bitch. Of course, Gilda went psycho on me before people took hundreds of pictures and splashed them all over social media. Make-up made it look crusty." Gilda was Serena's calico cat who was famous for her cantankerous attitude, ironically much like Serena's. "Maybe a bird will shit on me and round out my day." She joked but it happened an uncanny amount of times.

"Come here." I moved closer to her.

"Dude, we're not those kinds of cousins."

"Shut your crusty hole." After an uncomfortable moment, I healed Serena's scratches. "You'll have to contend with the birds."

"No fuckin' way!" Serena looked into a make-up mirror from her purse. "Christonacracker."

"What?" my mom called from the front seat.

I waved her off. "Nothing. Can you turn the a/c up?" She did, then went back to chatting with Olive, who had given me a quick look, sensing the power I now let subside.

Mom fought against Kim tagging along. Serena argued she wanted Kim there since I would be 'busy' with Caine, and Adam and Hunter found excuses not to attend at all. Since I didn't know what to expect from my grandmother, I wanted as many magic-capable allies possible.

Ranlyn and some guards would be around, but I asked him to remain off the property and keep a look out. I didn't see them when we arrived.

"You sure you're ready for the ambush?" I asked Olive.

My great-aunt smiled. "Thrilled."

If my grandmother knew Olive was coming, she'd throw a shit-fit. Olive is family. If we didn't let people go because we didn't like them, I'd boot my grandmother from her own house.

While Olive agreed an ambush was our best option, my mom argued herself into a rage. Everyone eventually agreed my grandmother wouldn't kick Olive out if she showed up, so we won and everyone would be forced to play nice.

I didn't know my great-aunt well enough yet to identify her smile's intent. Malicious, conniving, or an expression of excitement? I braced for a scene.

As we entered the kitchen, Serena's mother, Karen, the oldest sister Bethany—who also lived in town—and our grandmother were busy splitting up a batch of my grandmother's famous coleslaw into large, blue glass serving bowls.

Serena greeting her mom gained our grandmother's attention who looked up to see her sister standing in her kitchen. Her expression transformed from delight to bleak in a flash, her arms limp with shock. The bowl she held listed forward dumping handfuls of coleslaw to the linoleum. Bethany jumped out of the way as Karen scolded their mother with a nagging 'Ma!' and snatched the bowl.

"Hello, sister. Aren't you looking bright today," Olive greeted with a sly smile.

"Sister?" Karen looked up from the coleslaw splattered floor from her mother to the rest of us.

Olive meant it literally. My grandmother *was* brighter. Not the drowning, suppressed soul glow I saw before, but not too far from it.

"Can you girls take these out for me please?" my grandmother asked her daughters.

Karen seemed suspicious, and stared daggers at my mother as they brought out the bowls, exiting through the back door. When the closed door quieted the rise in voices, the tension grew as we waited for who would speak first.

I decided to start. "Is the change in your soul glow because you quit drinking the Jesus juice or necessary to release Olive from The Royal?"

With a stubborn chin held high, my grandmother said, "I will never give my soul over to the Devil."

"Still drinking the Jesus juice," Serena muttered.

"You inch closer to the Devil than I, sister." Olive spoke with sweetness. "What you did was inexcusable, though since you are blood, I am willing to forgive your selfishness."

Insulted, my grandmother's features contorted.

Olive continued. "I know you believed you were deserving of heir and acted out of envy. Know that I don't wish your soul the torture you've forced it to endure when imprisoning me for your own gains. Gains you refused to take control of because of your guilt."

Elizabeth's eyes squinted in anger. "The day they gave you the lineage I knew it was nothing but lies. A false position to fight for when they had chosen a successor before the battle begun. I knew the true one to give my heart to did not come from within us. These tricks, these acts of devilish piety, are against His will and only He can save my soul from perdition. I know where I'll go when this life is over, do you?"

"I do, sister," Olive responded with confidence. "And if we meet again in His Kingdom, will you denounce Him as well?"

Elizabeth scowled with immeasurable malice. "How dare you

mock Him! You will burn screaming for redemption, seething at the demons who made you a fool by befriending you with their charms. Charred flesh will rip without an ounce of remorse, and I will garner no sympathy."

My grandmother's hatred for the blood that empowered our family was no secret, but the string of obscene remarks shocked me.

"Conviction in every word you spew is unmistakable, sister. As is your power breaking through the fractures in your rationality."

Until she said it, the power thrumming the air went unnoticed, but it nibbled at me as my grandmother did her best to convert or condemn us all.

"No matter how much hate you preach you cannot erase the power. You need it to spread your poison, and that is something you cannot hide from us. Even now your power pollutes the air and chills the bone with its sickened malevolence. My heart aches for the sister I knew, yet love regardless of how blind you are."

My grandmother was about to rebuke when backyard noise spilled in from the back room. By the time my mom reached the kitchen, a staredown had ensued. From the lack of conversation or the hostility choking the room, mom spoke with caution.

"Everything okay in here?" The underlying unease in my mom's voice was distinct.

"Catching up, dear." My grandmother's Stepford smile brightened as she recruited her daughter and the other smiling masks of her opposition to help bring out more food platters.

The charade was on.

We placed our homemade goodies with others on a long table covered with an olive-green linen tablecloth under a large neutral dining tent. I wanted to turn and check out the guests, hoping to see a sun-filled backyard full of enlightened bodies of Magics. My anticipation and dread had me fussing with trays on the table instead of turning.

"Come on Lite-Brit, you're killing me," Serena pushed. "Which one of these hick townies are rockin' the special blood?" She could have asked Olive, but she was chatting with Karen and Bethany for the first time.

Holding my breath, I spun to check out the crowd. When I spotted our cousin Liana, it sparked an idea. Seated at a picnic table with our cousins Tasha, David, and Jacqueline, Liana had slopped potato salad over the edge of her bowl onto her lap, leaving the others in hysterics.

"Liana...." I said with embellished astonishment.

"No! Liana?"

"Yeah!" I ramped up the pretense before letting it fade. "She'll never get the stain out." The insidious grin my cousin's way revealed the joke and earned me a solid punch to the meat of my bicep for my poor taste of humour.

I winced and rubbed the spot trying to make the pain dissipate. The hit surprised Kim and Caine, but they laughed once they realized they didn't have to break up a fight.

"You deserved that." Serena wasn't ashamed one bit.

I shook out my dead arm. "You're too easy."

"Come on, Soph, before I give up and find the booze cart," Serena whined.

"Calm your vag, girl."

A few bodies gave off a glimmer, not unlike Kim's, so they could be practicing or could be naturals without a clue, but it was less than I wanted and everything I expected.

I pointed to my average sized cousin with long, light-brown hair and skater gear. "Ronny. He glows a bit, but too low to know about it.

"Aunt Gloria, the sixties-something woman fanning herself like freakin' British royalty, and Aunt Iris, her sister with the weird feathery, scarf thingy are glowing far too much to be unaware of their power. Olive said they were active members in the previous Ballard Family Coven, so I expected the soul glow.

"Uncle Dwayne, the non-cowboy in the cowboy hat and boots is a bit brighter than Ronny. There are too many normal people in my way."

"The Blind," Kim corrected.

"All right, folks, it's mingling time." I looked up at Caine who was as nervous as I was.

Past years I kept close to those in my life on a daily basis, so mingling was awkward. What I was going to do with the information, I was unsure, but I needed to know. If I could get inside their heads like Aunt Lacey, I would feel better about approaching them on the subject of the family coven, but telepathy was among other abilities I had no had clue about.

With the excuse to introduce Caine, I managed to take a peek at everyone, he staying barnacle close and glad-handing for my benefit. The bright sun made it difficult to spot a glimmer from good skin or a trick of the light, so he followed my lead and played his role.

We ripped ourselves away from Uncle Roger, promising a return visit for his R rated jokes that had Caine howling. On the opposite side of the long yard, the kids played soccer, staying clear of my grandmother's garden. I noticed my cousin Mason leaning against the fence watching the others play, his soul glow haloing his body. Dim but present. He had no clue how special he was.

"What'cha up to, Mason?"

"Watchin'." He kept his eyes on the ball.

"Do you like soccer?"

He nodded.

"Why aren't you playing?"

He shrugged, giving me nothing to work with.

"Are they being jerks and not letting you?"

"Didn't ask."

"Do you want me to ask for you?" He shook his head showing he wasn't interested in me doing anything for him.

I was a shy kid too, but had fearless cousins like Serena to follow around. When the ball came closer, followed by another young kid, I took a chance.

"Hey James, need another player? Mason can play."

"No!" Mason looked at me for the first time. "I suck."

I bent down to him. "Kid, they all suck."

"Sure," James said as he ran to catch up with the game.

"Try and suck less than them," I sort-of encouraged. He looked mortified but joined in.

I felt lighter for the small deed for a kid who I hoped would never again sit around waiting for an invitation.

Caine wrapped his arms around me and kissed my crown. "That was sweet. You're gonna make a great mother one day."

I snorted. "Keep your voice down, my uterus might hear you and pitch a revolt. I don't have the provisions to deal with my period today."

He laughed, leaving me to hope he realized that role was off the table.

A helpful distraction from the vagina-ripping topic was asking Caine for a favour.

"Cheat? You movin' to the dark side there, Sophie?"

"*Pfft*. No one will see. Parents are doing everything to ignore their kids."

The kids scurried around like cattle, so Caine had his power engaged and readied, which was a lesson in of itself. Energy thrummed as he struggled to keep his power steady.

Fifteen minutes later Mason booted the ball towards the net made of discarded coats. Leland, the goalie chosen for his girth and none too happy about it—kids can be so mean—got as low as he could. With his hand hidden between our bodies, Caine shifted the ball's trajectory. Leland tried to maul it and missed.

"Fuck yeah! Oops." I laughed and bounced in place as Mason and his team celebrated. He had help, but the scheme boosted Mason's confidence.

"Practicing, are we?"

I jumped and turned to find Olive with her arms crossed.

"Oh, I wasn't—"

"It's fine," Olive waving it off. "Power thrummed across the yard.

Took me a bit to shake off Karen to investigate. You held steady. Nice job, Caine."

Caine beamed. "Thanks."

"Mason needed a little advantage." I pointed him out.

"Looks like Mason has his own advantage though, doesn't he?"

I wondered what Mason would be capable of, hoping to be involved in the discovery.

"There aren't many others."

"I know, Firefly. Seems the lines died out quicker than anticipated. You have no idea how much their darkness saddens me." She sighed. "We used to be a family to praise. Revered. A people of infinite power and possibility. Now the only gloating over there is pie recipes and maxing out their undead mages. Took me a moment to realize they were talking about a video game." She shook her head and muttered, "Nonsense", as Caine and I laughed.

Until a solid plan existed, we were stuck with hints of glowing souls. The catch twenty-two was that we had to ask people, and rejection posed a greater threat if they wouldn't keep the secret.

Through the sunny day and balmy night, we settled into the familiar crowd as years before. Minus my grandmother who found herself too busy to sit at all. The backyard was lit by tall bamboo and paper lanterns, a soft luminosity lighting faces with warmth, plus, the benefits of fighting off mosquitoes.

Serena made good on her promise to the girls and snapped a candid photo of Caine and I on her phone. We didn't get the chance to pose or demand a do-over before Serena texted it to our friends.

"Stop bitchin', I'll send you a copy," Serena promised with a sneer.

Picking up a soiled paper napkin and winging it at my cousin, I caught a glimpse of my mother's face. Disappointment.

"You did a great job, mom. Everything looks perfect."

"Thanks, Dolly." She smiled but looked past me to Olive across the table. "Is whatever happened between you two so bad you can't sit at the same table together?"

No one had to ask who my mother meant, but her question had the rest of us steeling before the answer.

"Well, darling," Olive began, her hands folded on the tabletop, "it is a difference in minds, in beliefs, but as you see I hold no rancour for my sister. I was held against my will, directly caused by my sister's actions, and still I contain the capacity for civility for the sake of the family."

This wasn't enough for my mother.

"Still, thirty-five years ago, something more had to have happened. I was present for the altercation that led to you going into The Royal. Granted, I was under ten, but I saw nothing except two sisters fighting."

"No, you wouldn't have," Olive replied as a matter of fact.

This infuriated my mom. "Why do you insist on keeping this a mystery after all this time?"

Olive looked at me. I understood the silent question in her stare, she was asking for my permission to tell my mother about our family's powers. My mom wasn't capable of knowing. She would keep the secret, but it would eat at her from the inside out. Her world was fact-based. Something of this magnitude would cause her too many sleepless nights.

The silent exchange between Olive and I lasted a fraction of a second, though not unnoticed by my mom who sat back in her chair as if harmed.

Olive turned to my mom. "I understand our evasiveness is difficult to comprehend, nonetheless, I assure you it's necessary. In this case, time does not determine worth."

My mother's glare slid my way. Everything in me screamed to wilt and give in, but I held strong, hoping my mom saw the apology deep behind the stone that helped me keep the secret.

Defeat echoed in my mom's exhale, her shoulders straightened as she stood with control. This was her courtroom face and I hated seeing the disconnect speared my way. "Fine. Guard your secrets. I'll leave you to discuss them."

I dropped my head onto the picnic table. Caine rubbed my back, but my anger wanted to shrug him off. Instead, I let the comfort perforate my self-loathing.

"Do you know that man?" Olive asked.

"It's a reunion, Olive. Chances are you're related," I said without lifting my head.

"He's not one of us," Serena said. "Unless someone brought their shady dealer as a date. He's mowing down the sweets."

With a Styrofoam plate balanced in one hand and a camera in the other, his blond head dipped to the plate to take a whole date square into his lips and then chomping with his mouth open. No one paid him any attention as he moved through the crowd snapping a few pictures.

"Nasty soul glow about him," Olive said.

"Shady porn director lookin' dude's a Magic and I'm not? Bullshit." Serena pouted.

"He's Tainted." The haze of his soul glow was difficult to miss.

"Tainted?" Serena asked.

"Evil," I answered.

"Touched by evil, but he's not all gone," Olive added. "He *was* at some point good-natured."

As if he felt us staring, the Tainted photographer looked straight at us between passing family members. He stopped and lifted his blocky camera to snap a few shots.

Mom would have mentioned hiring a professional photographer. With cellphone technology, why bother putting up the money? And the Tainted photographer's camera was old, not antique or trendy. Even more disconcerting, the man tucked-tail and ran back through the crowd once he took the pictures.

"Why would he take our picture?" Kim asked.

"Let's ask him." I shot up from the table and tore across the yard after him.

Caine called after me, but my attention was on the Tainted guy who moved with surprising agility. Around tables and people, all the way to the end where the kids still played soccer by flashlight, and then over the fence.

I grabbed the fence. A yank had me stumbling back. "What the tits, cocksmack? What are you doing?" I yelled at Caine.

"What are *you* doing?"

"I want that camera. Some creepier takes pictures of us and runs off? I don't think so."

A deep grunt caught our attention. We popped up onto the ten-foot fence and found the Tainted man on the ground at the feet of my great-uncle Lewis whose bright white and green soul glow surprised the shit out of me. He reached a wide palm towards the man, a force of energy extending from his palm and hitting the man square in the chest, throwing him back down on the ground.

"Get the camera!" I yelled and noticed the kids were clamoring to get up the fence. I shooed them down before looking back to Lewis who was now staring at me and Caine. His hesitation was enough for the Tainted photographer to take off running.

Up and over the fence, I had to force myself to look away from my uncle, who had a soul brighter than Olive's, to chase after the man. Caine's long legs had him passing me in seconds and rounded the corner long before I did.

My lungs burned. Each breath of fire was evidence of how out of shape I was, as I forced my body into forward motion. Caine stood on the sidewalk of Dunnville's Central Park. People and children sat in lawn chairs and on blankets for a late-night viewing of the movie Sandlot set up in the huge, cement bandshell. The smell of hot dogs and popcorn wafted on the summer night air as the Blind were oblivious to the Tainted man hiding somewhere among them.

"There's too many people," I heard Ranlyn say as he materialized next to us.

"Did he still have the camera?" I asked and coughed, fighting to catch my breath.

"Yeah," Caine said.

"Can you see any souls, Sophie?" Ranlyn asked.

"No."

"I can," Lewis said as he approached behind us, my great-uncle wheezing worse them me as he pulled at the waistband of his slacks weighed down by his large belly, he covered in a sheen of sweat. "Bastards are cover spelled, but they're there. Though I see you've got your own people here as well."

"I seriously need to learn how to do that," I mumbled in envy.

Ranlyn watched Lewis as his gaze swept the crowd. They shared a silent moment before Ranlyn said, "Got it," and took off behind the huge cement bandshell.

"You've got talented friends, Sophie," Lewis said as he wiped his brow.

"And family, apparently," I responded before we followed my mind reading guardian.

A few steps toward cover and I went down hard. My chin bounced off the grass, teeth bit through my lip with a splash of dirty pennies on my tongue. The movie screen sparkled and wavered in my spotted eyesight. Before I could gain any sense of what happened, I was being dragged away. I tried to call out and my voice was strangled.

An unseen trap held my legs and stopped me from kicking free. No one to fight off, no one I could see. I flailed for the wading pool devoid of kids too busy enjoying the show. The powder-blue cement hole filled with water thrashed my palm as whoever had a hold of me didn't let up an inch and ripped me further away from the safety of the crowd.

I looked back down at my feet and didn't understand what I saw. Before I could work it out, I was hauled into an open manhole and hit free-fall speeds long enough for my stomach to hit my sinuses before a jarring stop and splash rocked my bones. Blinding pain shot through my hip and up my spine. Moments passed of desperate, shallow breathing before I could fill my lungs. When I did, I regretted it.

Slow-moving water, less than a foot deep, splashed over my legs screaming with pins and needles. My nose was assaulted with something close to the rot and decay of a swamp. The echo of water and my labored breathing surrounded me in the pitch dark. Panic hit when my night vision had nothing to work with and left me dangling in fear.

Who dragged me down here? Where were they? Could they see me? Could they hear my thoughts? I put my hands out around me and felt smooth cement to my left. I braced myself against a curved wall and stood in case I needed to run. Run where? I had no fucking clue. The ceiling stopped me from standing fully up, my neck at an awkward angle if I tried.

"Whoever you are, how 'bout you stop playing with your dick and make a move already."

Nothing but quiet. Whoever was after me might not have had a dick, but they were getting off on seeing me helpless and struggling in the dark.

Fine. If they weren't coming after me, then I was going to busy myself with finding a way out. I reached above me and couldn't grab onto a ladder or anything else to get me out of the sewer or storm drain or wherever. I wasn't leaving the way I came.

With a hand out front of me and the other still on the wall, I inched forward. I thought of Ranlyn and the others aboveground. Were they fighting? Did they know I was missing? Were they looking for me?

Shit. The Falaichte spell, it hid me from everyone.

I pulled on Nya's ring. Before I could slip it off, a flash of light stole my attention and rocked my entire body with snapping electricity.

Muscles clenched to the edge of ripping.

Eyes rolled.

Jaw forced shut.

Grunts of agony.

Veins straining.

Relief.

Hitting the ground like a ragdoll came with no extra pain. I had no control of the moans that escaped, of the twitching, of the rolling into the fetal position. I couldn't think.

A mouthful of swampish water had me rolling onto my back. I was not going to die in inches of water.

"Asshole," I said in barely a whisper. "That you Loring? If not, you're a fucking coward. Collect me yourself."

I reached for Nya's ring again and was hit with another dose of electricity. This time, the lights went out completely. When I came to, someone was jostling me, grabbing at my arms. No, my hand. I fought back best I could, jerking partially numb limbs to make whatever they were trying to do more difficult.

"Be still," a deep voice demanded. I screeched when he cranked my fingers backwards, flipped me on my stomach, and wretched my arm up until my shoulder protested.

"Fuck a goat," I grit through a shaky voice full of anger trying to keep my head above water. I failed when he cranked my arm higher behind me and dunked my face until my cheek ground against the cement.

Thrashing around did little to get them to let go, but I didn't stop, instead, making sure my Converse connected with their shins and anything else I could catch.

Power surged through me for the first time. Instinctual. Beyond my control.

Whoever had a hold of me cried out. A familiar noise. The man who tried to kidnap me from my apartment.

He let go. I flipped over and scrambled to my feet as fast as I could. Gaining oxygen and cradling my left arm. A flutter of words filled the small space and dim light emanated from the man a few feet from me, illuminating his face enough to confirm my enemy was Loring's devotee from my building. He was staring down at his hands held in loose fists in front of him.

They were black.

They changed back to his skin colour before my eyes. He healed himself.

Panic stole my breath as I braced for impact, be it an electric ass-whooping or something worse, when splashing came from behind me.

"Sophie!"

Holy fuck, Ranlyn.

My guardian's mumbling preceded a light that filled the tunnel.

"Never tire of being Loring's errand boy, do you?" Ranlyn said to the man. I looked and saw what I had back in my apartment. Grey eyes filled with a lust for something. Vengeance maybe.

"Never tire of playing the hero, do you?" The man responded. "Don't forget, you haven't saved everyone."

Rage sliced through Ranlyn's expression as he sunk down in a defensive stance. His war cry matched the man's as Ranlyn rushed past me in a blur and charged at the man who burst into a cloud of smoke on impact, both men disappearing.

"Fuck. Ranlyn?" I called, but nothing but the sound of water and my voice called back.

The light spell Ranlyn did still held, so I use it to head back to where I was dragged in and looked up to the manhole to see a face I didn't recognize, but didn't care because the soul glow surrounding it was light and untainted.

"Where's Ranlyn?" The woman with severe features asked.

"Wherever the dude he went after is."

"Fucking Christ," she mumbled and said, "Reach up."

I did, though my left shoulder wasn't happy about it. Instead of being thrown a rope I couldn't hoist myself out with anyway, the woman telekinetically lifted me with the ease of snatching a chip.

When I got onto asphalt, I collapsed back on the road. Caine was on me immediately, asking if I was okay. Lewis stood behind him, hinged at the waist looking me over.

I stood up and stopped Caine from fussing over me. I didn't want to talk about it yet. I looked around and saw the place I was dragged from. The movie on the bandshell screen was still running, but no one was left watching. "Where is everyone?"

"Fighting spilled over," Caine said. "People ran."

"Fuck."

"No Blind were hurt, but Ranlyn's team are working the damage control angle. As is Lewis."

"How?" I asked my great-uncle.

"Sometimes it pays to have people on the police force. And the paper." When you were knee deep in politics in a small town like Lewis was, the advantages were far reaching.

I nodded. This would be something the town wouldn't soon forget. Unless erasing memories was a part of Ranlyn's teams 'damage control' procedure. I had no clue if they could.

Lewis clapped his large hands together. "Make a habit of running after the Tainted, Sophie?"

"Nope." I swallowed hard, fighting back the flood of emotion catching up with me, and swiped at my wet hair. "First one. You?"

He gave a deep chuckle and a sympathetic gaze. "Only one that's got away."

I took a deep breath and found myself on the edge of breaking down. Uncontrollable tremors took over with my adrenaline dump.

I was given clothing from the woman who pulled me out of the hole: black yoga pants, black zip-up sweater. She didn't look happy to give them up, but I needed to get back to the reunion. I used the mirror of one of their SUVs and a wet napkin from someone's dinner to wash away the blood, dirty water, and black streaks of make-up all over my face and then another to clean the rest of me the best I could.

I looked dishevelled, but it was the best I could do.

Seated in the passenger side of the SUV, I looked at my hand and saw a few missing layers of skin on my middle finger where I wore Nya's ring. I had tried to remove it to counteract the Falaichte spell. I must have been able to get it off before I was hit with the second dose of electricity. The man had shoved it back onto my finger to try and hide us.

I had got it off long enough Ranlyn found me. It made me nauseous to think of what would have happened if I hadn't got it off in time.

Other scrapes and bruises were visible as well, my shoulder was still a mess. I calmed myself enough to evoke some power and get to healing. Took a few times, but I managed enough to swing a baseball bat if I had to, but it didn't stop me from falling into a fog of thoughts of what happened, what could have happened, and what I would do without Ranlyn around. I needed him more than I wanted to.

Lewis got his car and drove us back to the house to rejoin the reunion. It wasn't until I was seated at a picnic table with those I showed up with—minus my mother and plus Lewis and his wife Priscilla—that the fog lifted, and I asked about the camera.

"Did anyone get it?" I asked.

The others at the table all looked at me and then each other. I missed something. Olive was holding my hand. When did she do that?

"Sophie...." Lewis started, he was seated next to Olive—his sister —someone he wasn't given the heads up on her release either.

"*Sophie?*"

I gasped when I heard Ranlyn's voice in my head.

Instead of letting Lewis continue, I bolted through the yard to outside searching for Ranlyn. He popped up by a line of parked cars when I called his name. I ran for him and wrapped my arms around him, elated he was okay. I had no chance in stopping the tears and he moved us behind a tall pick-up truck where people couldn't see if they came out to their vehicle.

"You okay?" he asked me though he had dried mud and blood darkening his face and blond hair and looked worse off.

I nodded and wiped my tears. "I don't understand what happened. Did you get the camera?"

"The camera was a ruse. One to get you to follow the bait. The storm drain was a holding place meant to keep you until they got Caine and anyone else they could."

I made a throaty noise. "And I delivered myself and put everyone else at risk. Of course I did."

"No one saw this, but we were ready and you're a survivor. You getting Nya's ring off helped."

"Oh good," I said with heavy sarcasm. "I only paid for it by being electrocuted twice, nearly drowned, and my shoulder ripped off. Fun times." My voice cracked and I had to fight to collect myself.

Ranlyn sighed. "I'm sorry, Sophie."

I shook my head, feeling the blame for getting him into whatever trouble followed me down into the storm drain.

He hugged me again, holding tight, no doubt hearing my thoughts and having no words. I rejoined the others after Ranlyn promised he was okay and that he would continue to thwart Loring and his devotees plans. I wanted to believe him. To a point, I did, but I couldn't live like this forever.

19

BOUND TO BLEED

Working my lady berries off on minimal sleep at the bar and at the computer on assignments, was the zombie-inducing price I paid to attend the Lughnasadh celebration. No choice if I wanted to return with my stupid, yet unfortunately needed, job and grades intact. Also helped with keeping my mind off the incident at the reunion. "The incident" was how I addressed it these days. I didn't need to express details, I memorized them, dreamt about them enough. Donovan wasn't happy I refused to talk to him about it the next day, but I couldn't make myself. I was okay now and I had work to do.

Caine thought it was a gross show of opportunism on Drew's part to work me day and night, but I wasn't in the position to complain. Threats to go to the labour board or the police on him for his dodgy dealings at the bar only got me so far, and I wanted to hold onto the chit for a more desperate occasion. Until I made something of the degree I was still working on, job security was a joke.

Silver lining of being at the bar all the time was staying clear of Jack and Theresa. By the looks of Jack when I saw him, and according to Kim, he was living the straight and narrow and Theresa never looked happier. The honeymoon period punctuated with rambunctious sex Kim had the joys of hearing from across the hall.

Either he was sober or hid his drinking well because he hadn't walked into the bar. He could also be staying clear of the crime scene. I wondered how long it would last before he went back to treating Theresa as an outlet for his anger and continued the cycle of abuse. Old behaviours were a few short-fused arguments away, though for Theresa's sake I hoped I was wrong.

I managed to evade Jack, until tonight when I went to meet Ranlyn outside and had to pass the building office. Jack was inside with the super talking about plumbing issues and saw me pass by. Neither of us spoke to each other, but Jack froze as I scurried off and got into Ranlyn's car. While I kept my shit together and acted like nothing happened, keeping my thoughts elsewhere so Ranlyn wouldn't catch on, an hour passed before my heart found a natural pace.

Lack of sleep was getting to me, and I was ecstatic when customers cleared out early. The smell of lemon-fresh cleaner I used to wipe down the tables tickled my sinuses. When I turned to get away from the overpowering smell, Jack was standing inside the bar staring at me.

It was my turn to freeze.

"How's it possible?" Jack whispered.

He needed to leave before I flipped out. From the camera's point of view an assault on his button-down, khaki wearing, sober ass would look unprovoked.

"We're closed, Jack. Please leave." My jaw clenched so hard my words contorted. My power began to simmer. A prickling presence on my skin like crawling bugs agitated from their nest. Rising close to the point of no return, my energy hovered as if too scared shitless to take the leap. A power burst on camera would be worse. Impotent anger, choking fear, and heart-rending misery boiled inside me at dangerous levels threatening to undue everything I worked for.

Jack positioned himself in front of the exit and my chances to tip off Ranlyn's guy outside. Jack had nothing about him to indicate he was anything more than another patron looking for a pint. In this case, Jack didn't need to be a Magic to hurt me.

"That night's a little fuzzy for me." His unblinking eyes were intense. "But I do know *you* should be dead."

He disgusted me. No evidence existed regardless. It infuriated me he remembered and was happy to live on pretending nothing happened.

I repeated myself, attempting strength and demanding confidence. I held the aerosol can of chemicals ready as a weapon if necessary. I was pretty sure it would blind him, if not I could throw it at him, but I couldn't use my power on him even if I found a nugget of control.

He took a step closer, making me jump back, my power lashing out and throwing a bowl of snack mix at him from the bar to his left.

Fuck. So much for control. Get it together, Sophie.

Jack flinched as the bowl hit him and peanuts and pretzels scattered across the hardwood. Aching to be free, my power rose to cloud my ears and hammered in my gut. If he wanted me dead, he was going to have to fight harder than last time. Granted, he had sobriety on his side, but I was ready.

Tension grew to an insufferable level as he stood in silence, making no comment on the snack mix projectile. Did he know about Magics now? My eyes burned from being open too long in fear Jack would take the smallest opportunity to attack.

I had to say something. "If you try it again, my friends won't be so lenient." Jaw still clenched while my power fought to overtake me, I stared him down, set to move if my body needed to.

This threat was the only weapon greater than lemon-fresh cleaner. The security cameras were not equipped with sound. If we were overheard, my warning would be cryptic enough to confuse the sharpest cop without jeopardizing my job, yet enough for the rest of the Coven to know what happened.

Of course, explaining the flying snack bowl wasn't so easy, but Jack was closer to it then I was.

Jack's face morphed into a mess of thoughts as the stalemate continued. I couldn't read his mind and wished I had the ability to crawl inside his head and find out his plan.

Too restless waiting for Jack to make a move, my muscles screamed in protest, seeking action or relief, so I made my own.

"You left me for dead." This caught his attention. "I could have ruined you, but you're too fucking pathetic to make the effort." My chin quivered with my adrenaline, weakening my speech, but I kept talking. "Promise to never step foot on this property again, leave Theresa, and fuck off somewhere I don't have to look at your grimy teeth ever again, and I'll stop my friends from turning you back into a drooling freakshow." He didn't move. "Your choice, Jack. I suggest you take the deal. I'm not a game show host, there's no door number two, and you don't get to finger-fuck the hostess in the green room."

No words shrouded in mystery this time.

Heartbeats pounded before he broke. His brow dipping as he surged forward.

"Don't!" I yelled and reacted, my hands flying up to brace for his attack.

Instinct took over, my power's instinct, not mine. A rush of energy from my hands found their target, blasting Jack in the chest and throwing him backwards into a wall. A neon beer sign shattered and crushed a single table, sending the bar stool flying.

Jack sprawled on the ground surrounded by neon glass and dust floating around him. If he didn't wake up in two seconds I was fucked. My mind raced. What if someone walked in? I hadn't locked the door yet because we were still technically open.

While my mind spouted a few faces of who could help me hide a body, Jack began to stir. Relief soared through me and tingled my toes. His eyes opened, capturing me as anticipation trapped me. He stood up and wobbled, bracing himself against the wall and grabbing his head. His fingers came away bloody.

"You cunt." His voice was weak but sounded so much like the old Jack it bolstered my hatred for the piece of shit. He stumbled forward, still bent on coming after me.

I flinched at his threat and a couple of chairs staked on the table near me flew out, landing in front of me to block Jack's path. He was too unsteady to hop over the chairs and come after me with any verve.

It occurred to me that I had questions.

"Who woke you up?"

Jack leaned forward, one hand on the back of a chair, the other on the back of his head.

"Why are you here?"

Jack shook his head and smiled. "Such a dumb bitch. Always someone stronger, always someone bigger to take you out."

"Who?"

"He said you'd know who." Jack found this hilarious. That laugh sparked memories of the attack that happened where we stood not long ago. Fuck the questions. He needed to leave.

Sick of cowering beneath his threats and being a victim by those stronger than me, I made a conscious decision to give the chair a tele-kinetic push, one that sent Jack stumbling backwards again. This didn't stop him from laughing, so I used my power to push him back further towards the door. He raised his hands in defeat, laughing another moment, until cradling his head again and walking out.

Once the door shut behind him, I froze in place for a full minute. When my body allowed it, I hopped over the chairs, ran to the door, fumbled with the keys, and locked up. I went back behind the bar and shoved my hand in the sink full of ice and then ran a handful of cubes on the back of my neck. The cool burn forced my power to take a back seat.

Post-traumatic stress was a fucked-up thing.

Facing Jack, confronting him with truth, and standing strong when every fibre within me screamed to cut ship and run, took every-thing I had. I hoped my threat was enough to keep him away from the bar, from Theresa, and—my biggest concern right now—myself, since I topped his shit list. The constant state of hyper-vigilance was trying on my nerves, and I couldn't handle the possibility of him being around the corner anymore.

Eyes squeezed shut and breathing in a way that could ease child-birth, I was mentally and physically exhausted, quivering as if stripped naked and left in the cold. The phone ringing had bile shooting up to the back of my tongue. Hoping it was Ranlyn's guard deciding to do his job, I answered with as much calm as I could muster.

"You'd think for a bar the number would be easier to find! Are you all right?"

I recognized the voice, but couldn't place it.

"Hello? Sophie, are you there?"

"Yeah...yes, I'm here. Sorry, who am I speaking to?"

Pause. "Donovan."

"Shit." Relief poured through me. "I'm sorry."

"Are you okay?"

"I'm fine."

"Bullshit. Something's wrong. Tell me what."

"How did you—?"

"The connection, remember? I felt your distress. Something big happened. Now tell me what before I drive down there to make sure no one's holding you at gunpoint."

"The connection?" Couldn't be. I knew it existed, and that he felt the emotional rollercoaster I rode while down in the storm drain, but I never knew what triggered it or how intense the emotion had to be to be detected. He was far more sensitive to it than I was. Or at least more aware. "What did you feel?" I rested my head against a free hand with an exhausted elbow digging into the bar.

"You. In trouble. Please, babe, tell me what happened. You're freaking me out." I couldn't find my voice. "Look, I know you don't trust me. I *will* fix that, but please, tell me what's happening."

"Donovan, it's not a trust thing. I'm fine. Rattled, but fine. Jack was here. He's gone now. I doubt he'll come back." Or at least hoped he wouldn't.

"That son of a bitch!" There was a collective rush of creative cursing and a smash of something in the background, his fist through the wall? I couldn't tell, but he was pissed, and I didn't need the connection to point that out.

"Donovan," I yelled to refocus him. "It was the first time he saw me since Loring woke him up. Or he said I would know who woke him and I assume it's Loring. Still, he was surprised I was alive. I handled it."

"You're not telling me everything."

"You're right, I'm not. I'm a tad freaked, and my powers went all funky and I'm lucky I didn't kill him." I told him about the man in the storm drain, but not how I accidently turned his hands black or how much it freaked my shit that I might hurt someone else by accident. It reminded me of the flower from the 'Make it Grow' test and I had no idea how I did it. Jack was a spotted prick, but I couldn't kill him.

"What do you mean your powers went funky?"

"Donovan, please. I can't do this now. I have a mess to clean up. Things are locked up here, Jack is gone, and I don't have the energy to spend all night reassuring you I'm fine, but I am safe now."

"Where the fuck is Ranlyn's guy?"

"Outside counting his taint hairs. Who the fuck knows?"

"I'll talk to Ranlyn."

"No. I'll talk to Ranlyn."

He was silent a moment. "I know what I feel and I can tell you believe you're safe, but don't delude yourself into thinking you're fine. You're not. Not even close."

"Regardless, thank you for checking on me. I do appreciate it." This was genuine. "I need a moment to gather my brain and work on damage control."

"I'm always here for you, babe, never doubt that. If you ever need me, whether I can feel something brewing or not, find me. Consider me on-call. Especially tonight if Jack returns or if you see him at home. Please, please, Sophie, let me know. I'll be up late anyway and my ass can be there in a hot minute, I shit you not."

Since he rarely used my name, hearing him say it somehow brought up the level of seriousness.

"I will."

"Promise?"

"I promise."

Caine was the closer option, being less than ten minutes away, but I'd call Ranlyn if it came down to it. As much as it would be nice to see Jack go down, I was damn proud I handled him on my own.

After talking with Donovan, I looked at the mess I had to clean up and was happy for the distraction. The neon sign was a goner until I remembered I could fix it. Since my power was still buzzing with my adrenaline, a few quick minutes was all it took to get it back in working order, but I'd never look at it the same.

Finished with the mess, I went outside and found myself alone on the street. Ranlyn's guy was MIA. Another missing guard couldn't be a coincidence. A ten-minute walk would get me home instead of calling someone and waiting longer, so I decided I'd keep my head down and race home.

A horn honked behind me, I ignored it and kept walking. The honk came again, this time the car in my peripherals.

"Pussy's not for sale, asshole," I said without looking.

"You sure? I hear I'm a good lay."

Looking to the asshole, Caine's bright smile shone brighter than the headlights of the gleaming dark blue car he drove.

"Jump in," he said.

I went to the passenger side of the two-door beauty and leaned down to look at him. "You didn't have to car-jack someone to get laid, you know."

"Sure did. Wanna gun it to the Grand Canyon?" He wagged his eyebrows, making me sputter a laugh. "Get in already."

This was the most expensive car I had ever set foot in. Immediately struck with that new car smell, I was afraid to put my alcohol sticky shoes on the spotless floor mats.

Caine's expression turned serious. "Donovan called me."

"Was he the one who said you were a great lay?"

"Sophie."

"Caine."

"He called because he wanted to make sure I was doing what I could to protect you."

"Caveman," I muttered.

"Do you want to tell me what happened?"

"Want to? No. I want to get home and hope I don't cross Jack on the way there, then sleep like a rockstar in a pool of drool."

He nodded, but I saw his look and he meant to push me about it after a minute or so. "Where's the guard?"

I shrugged.

"He left?"

"I don't know. Ranlyn doesn't equip them with ankle bracelets."

"Sophie."

"Are we saying each other's names again? Because we already did this."

He grunted, his impatience colouring his cheeks as he pulled out his phone. "Call Ranlyn."

"Now who's the caveman?"

"I'm driving and Ranlyn needs to search for his man. Call him. Please."

Before I could remind him of my tendency for motion sickness, the car leaped from the curb, pushing my body into the black leather seats. A red light stopped us and gave me a chance to breathe.

"Are you going to call Ranlyn?" he asked me.

"Are you going to enter a NASCAR race? No? Then maybe slow your roll so I don't replace your new car smell with half-digested deep-fried pickles."

"Sorry." He clutched my hand and kissed its back, his lips causing my breath to shudder as his piercing grey eyes smouldered.

As the light changed his gaze turned back to the road as I regained my composure in a sleepy state of incitation.

"What do you think of her? Amazing, right?"

I didn't share Caine's enthusiasm, though he looked delicious and windswept. I would have thought him tantalizing if I wasn't focused on keeping my stomach settled.

"It's something, Diesel," I replied with sarcasm. "Where'd you get it?"

"I bought it. Low mileage and I got an amazing deal on upgrades."

"Please tell me you have a licence."

"Of course. While you were working so much this week, I figured it out. Turns out I was good to go. Had to have my doctor fax over my medical records stating I wouldn't be a menace on the streets and that was it," he said with a laugh. "I knew I had to jump at this baby before someone else did. I'm lucky you're working so much. I don't think I could have kept it a secret any longer."

In my parking lot, I jumped out of the car, happy my feet were on the ground.

"You okay?" he asked as he got out.

"Yeah." I slammed my door shut. Caine's face looked like I insulted his dead brother. "Sorry. I'm used to shitboxes."

"You're forgiven." He kissed my crown and put his arm around my shoulders.

"I used my power to attack Jack. Like, on purpose." I surprised myself by saying this out of the blue. I kept talking before he asked questions, telling him what happened, it coming out of me in a flood.

"I...I'm glad you're okay." He managed, but he had a mouthful more and I couldn't tell what he was swallowing back. Anger? Worry? He seemed to be having trouble saying what he wanted.

"Can you call me next time?" he asked.

"I can promise that now, but I doubt this'll happen again. The bar is my job, and I don't want my two worlds colliding. I already obliterated that boundary. If someone checks out the tapes, now or five years from now, they'll see me attacking Jack, plus, doing it without touching him. I bet that's a big no-no and I don't know how to erase the footage."

"Aunt Lacey does since someone had to before." 'Before' meaning the last time Jack attacked me, but he refrained from saying so.

He pulled me into a hug, one I needed and for some reason feared I wouldn't get. I think I thought he would be mad at me. As it was, I couldn't believe Donovan called him. This surprised me more than my magic taking over. Had that happened before? Donovan calling Caine? The devil must be wearing snowshoes.

"What is it?" I asked Caine looking to the car and searching for a change in topic.

This was a jumping off point for Caine as he knew everything about what I learned was an Infiniti Q60. He rambled non-stop about engine size and horsepower, all I would have found interesting if not so tired.

I adopted a love for the classic muscle car from my mother's ex-husband. Never something I could picture myself behind the wheel based on price alone, but if you want power and sex appeal on wheels, a 1960s Pontiac GTO sure did the trick.

Beautiful car or not, I cared of nothing but seeing Bosco to snuggle under my sheets with for the next ten hours. Everything else far away from my mind as I felt the exhaustion of fighting with Jack winning.

While we were fine out in my parking lot, Ranlyn's guards were all around us even if we couldn't see them. One of our own guards was already missing, so we went inside.

From the entrance to my door, we never saw a single person. Time would tell if Jack would ever resurface.

———

The day before the Lughnasadh harvest celebration I woke up groggy after sleeping most of the day. When I dragged my ass out of bed and threw it into a shower, I hoped to feel more awake. Not a chance. The grogginess clutched onto me like it had separation anxiety. Of course, my luck to get sick before a trip.

I slumped down next to Caine on the couch, who was flipping through channels as I leaned against him. "I think I'm getting sick."

He put his arm around me and kissed the top of my head. "Well, whatever you have, so do I. I'm feeling run down."

"Sorry. Hazards of working in customer service. The people we service are too tanked to mind their germ holes."

He leaned over and kissed my forehead. "You don't have a fever, but you do look kind of sick."

"Thanks Dr. Berisford. You're not looking so—" I gasped.

"What?"

Before answering I looked him over again. "Your soul, it's not glowing. Not at all. You look normal. You're not supposed to look normal!"

"Maybe you can't see soul glows when you're sick."

"Then why would you feel weird?"

"I'm sick too, Sophie. Maybe my abilities don't work either."

A mere cold could counteract innate abilities?

"Do something," I demanded.

Caine gave a sleepy chuckle. "We can play doctor if it'll make you feel better—"

"No. Dick is not a cure. This isn't porn."

"Could be," he mumbled.

"Make something move. Use your power so we can see if it works."

Caine huffed and sat forward to target a set of square, black candle holders on the coffee table, his hand outstretched. Nothing happened. He tried again with the same result. "I can't feel anything. There's nothing to work with. It's like I'm at square one again."

"Where's Olive?"

"Aquafit."

Olive was at the gym more than I had been my whole life, admirable, but I could have used her expertise right now.

An idea struck. I raced to the kitchen and pulled out a drawer making it recoil on its stoppers and grabbed a steak knife. Digging the tip into my skin and dragging it down the length of my forearm stung less than I thought it would, the pain delayed.

"Sophie!" Caine snatched the knife, but I had already done what I needed to. "What the hell are you doing?" He turned the tap on and grabbed a cloth.

"Wait. I want to see if I can heal."

"Don't you think you could've done something less drastic?" He left the kitchen in a hurry.

The bathroom fan turned on as I put my hand over my wound and closed my eyes, willing my power to erase the jagged slice. I concentrated with all my mental fortitude to rally my ability, shaking as I dug for it within me. No internal stir responded. No butterflies in my stomach, no rush of energy, vibrations, or bug crawl across my skin. No power arrived to snub out the persistent sting of my arm.

"Fuckshitdammit!"

Caine grabbed my arm and thrust it under the running water, adjusting its strength as I cried out. The cut wasn't as deep as the porcelain cat, but it wasn't pretty.

"Why would you do that?"

"Extreme incentive might have worked better than something small like tossing around my décor. It needed to be urgent."

He shook his head. "What if you did serious damage? That was so stupid."

After a moment of shaking off the word "stupid", I had to remind myself he meant what I did was stupid and not me. It *was* stupid. Now that the water turned red and my arm sported a ghastly smile I didn't need, I realized how impulsive the experiment was.

Caine pressed the towel onto the gash and held it tight for a long time as neither of us spoke. With no gauze to cover the wound, he took packing tape and adhered the small hand towel to my arm.

"I'm not sure how effective that'll be, but it'll do until we get to Aunt Lacey's." He started pulling his shoes on.

"I'm not even dressed."

"Then hurry up."

Okay, this pissed me off and had me rebelling against rushing at his command. A part of me knew this was the definition of stupid. I was bleeding and needed medical attention and here I was focusing on my baggage instead of addressing it and getting clothes on. I wasn't there yet, and I was in pain and fuck him, that's what.

Caine knocked on my bedroom door, again, trying to hurry me along. I yanked it open. "My arm's not going to fall off, Caine, so cool your fucking jets turbo."

The look on Caine's face baffled me. Concern was understandable, the attitude was a ridiculous overreaction that pissed me off more.

Ready, but still rushed, I stumbled out the door as my sandal wasn't on right and tripped me. Caine reached out to steady me with Bosco cradled in his other arm.

Ranlyn appeared, breaking his cover while guarding the hallway. "What happened? You okay?"

"No. Apparently, I'm a crazy cutter with wet hair," I answered without addressing his confused expression flashed at Caine and grabbed the keys off the hook to lock the door.

"I'll meet you at Aunt Lacey's once I get another guard up here," he told us as I punched the elevator call button with unneeded force.

We burst in the door at Aunt Lacey's and found her and Donovan at the kitchen table. "Do you live here?" I blurted, wondering why he would hang out with an old lady all the time.

His brow creased as he shot to his feet.

"What's the matter?" Aunt Lacey asked in a tone I had never heard from her self-assured voice.

"Our powers are gone." I let go of Bosco's leash and he trotted over to his water bowl. "We woke up feeling odd and now we can't do anything. It's gone."

Donovan looked me over. "What's wrong with your arm? Why's your hair wet?"

"'Cuz showers are created to get wet." Donovan popped an eyebrow in intrigue. "And the arm was a stupid experiment."

"Sophie—" I cut off Caine's apology and told Donovan and Aunt Lacey what I did.

"Your I.Q. is terrifying," Donovan said. "You could've at least waited until someone fit to handle the repercussions was supervising." He motioned to Aunt Lacey. "Or she could have told you what was going on without the need to harm yourself."

"It's already done," Caine said and then asked Aunt Lacey. "Have you seen this before?"

"I didn't see you travelling here." Her voice in a bit of a daze. "Nor did I see you cut your arm."

Aunt Lacey's second sight had been faulty and now we were another blind spot.

"I didn't feel your panic either," Donovan added.

We knew what that implied, and I didn't want to see Caine's reaction to the reality of our emotional link's growing strength. Seemed as I grew stronger, so did the connection, but right now, the tether was cut.

"Let's start with the arm." Aunt Lacey removed the towel and looked at me with a comedic grimace.

I shrugged. "Seemed like a good idea at the time."

While the cat figurine protruded from my arm, Aunt Lacey refrained from touching me so she wouldn't begin the healing process with her potent touch. In comparison, this flesh wound did nothing in response to her contact as she cleaned the wound.

"I see we're going to have to do this the traditional way," Aunt Lacey admitted what I suspected.

We made our way down to the basement after putting Bosco out to play and Donovan retrieved a first aid kit. He opted to stand beside me while Aunt Lacey worked.

The kit was no ordinary pool-side provision. This one contained a multitude of herbs, linen stripes, and sewing essentials. Old-world ideas. Aunt Lacey lathered me up with different salves made of ingredients she muddled into a paste. Worry crept through her expression as her hands stayed busy.

When she pulled out the needle and thread, I thought I was going to pass out, but she promised the salves would absorb the majority of my pain.

"You got this," Donovan encouraged. Having him and Caine in my space had me struggling to focus on my breathing.

The salves worked. I still felt the pressure of the needle puncture my skin and the thread drag through the hole to pull my wound together. I could have had Caine work his influencing powers, but I didn't want to add the pressure of the possibility he may fail again. I could deal with the pain.

When done, Aunt Lacey closed the kit and folded her arms on the table. "This is rather unsettling for me. I'm blocked from both your minds. I see you in front of me and yet you're absent. Can you see our souls, Salix?"

"Nope. That's how I knew something was wrong. You have no idea how weird it is." I gave a sober laugh. "I never thought I'd miss it. I can do without the strain, but it's so wrong."

Caine put a hand on my back in comfort. Successful though awkward while flanked by Donovan looking to me with identical airs of pity. I had to get up and pace.

Aunt Lacey sighed. "Someone has bound you both in an attempt to thwart your abilities."

"Loring?" I guessed.

"Maybe," Aunt Lacey responded.

"Probably," Donovan corrected. "Though why them? The Mother Coven is wide-spread and far more talented."

Aunt Lacey's eyebrows rose. "The only thing that makes a lick of sense is some connection to the Lughnasadh celebration. For weeks, someone has blocked myself and the Elders from seeing the gathering. Whatever plan Loring or others have cooked up, you two are pawns."

"Could this be my grandmother? I don't know if she's strong enough, but she's pretty pissed." I only saw her in passing after we arrived at the reunion with Olive.

Aunt Lacey shook her head. "Too many loose ends."

Donovan took the seat beside her. "Why not bind you instead?"

"Granted, Wend, I am much older and practiced. Therein lays your answer. A Binding needs to be cast by another equally as strong to encumber my abilities, which is no easy feat. It takes time. Personal effects from your target. With guards missing and with questionable loyalties, they could have procured the ingredients from either of your places."

"Can we reverse it?" I asked.

"Loosen enough to give you a measure of your Soul Seeing back, yes."

When I called Kim, and told her we needed her for a spell, she jumped at the opportunity without knowing what it was or what for, further confused on how we got to Aunt Lacey's in the first place.

While we waited on Kim, Aunt Lacey and Donovan ran around gathering ingredients. Aunt Lacey returned with the grimoire and asked for Caine's cell phone. He handed it over.

"Would you mind picking up Salix's Aunt Olive at the gym before her bus arrives?" she said to whomever answered.

"Aunt Lacey, I don't want Olive involved."

She hung up and kept gathering needed ingredients as she spoke. "Salix, I have not recruited Olive because I am aware her coven, and consequently your family, fell to pieces. She is, however, immensely powerful. More important, she is your family, and you're facing a crisis."

I gave her the win, still uncomfortable having Olive and my Coven Leader in the same house, especially on Aunt Lacey's turf.

Kim arrived, Olive and Ranlyn moments later, and met us in the basement. Olive gasped when she saw me.

"Are you okay?" Kim put a hand on Olive's shoulder.

Olive looked me up and down and then at Caine.

"I can't *see* you." I understood what Olive meant.

I hugged my great-aunt. "I can't *see* you either."

I introduced Olive to Aunt Lacey, and they nodded across the room at each other, Aunt Lacey wasting no time in explaining.

"Every bit of power will help unshackle these Seedlings of whatever evil has woven itself around them. Until now, I had not invited you to coven dealings for I knew you were less than thrilled at your own coven's dispersal. I assure you, it was not with intentional disregard, but a mere understanding of your position on the matter."

"I appreciate your understanding," Olive returned. "Not to say being one of your flock wouldn't be an honour, but with determination, the Ballard Family Coven will be strong once again."

Aunt Lacey nodded. While both women were at an understanding, I felt guilty. Olive wanted me in the family coven, but to have it stated in front of my current Coven Leader seemed intentional.

Olive looked over the large bandage making a tsking sound. Kim's face contorted at the dried blood outside the bandage.

"It's nothing," I told them.

"It was stupid," Donovan corrected from the open closet he reached into.

"Can it, dillhole," I bit back. "You want a better story, how about I tell you how my powers went wonky and I threw Jack around the bar like a baby squirrel?"

20

THROUGH THE VEIL

"You know what freaks me out?" Donovan asked me as I sat on the floor.

"Long toenails?"

He paused as he placed a small bowl in front of me. "What?"

"Ooh, I bet it's spiders. Tough guys are always afraid of spiders."

"Sophie."

"Fack. I get the full name treatment. You must be terrified of them."

This got me both dimpled cheeks. "Can I finish what I was saying?"

"I suppose."

"At first, I hated our connection because I can feel your emotions, but can't do anything about them. Now, I want it back. No matter the complications it creates, I'd rather it exist than miss out on anything like this again. Seeing you walk through the door, tore up, and having no clue? That's far worse than feeling useless across town."

Damn. "I'm not sure what to say to that, but I think I get it. It was nice to know someone knew what happened with Jack even if it only got me a phone call."

"And a skulk outside your work until Caine picked you up. And then your building all night watching for Jack."

"You did not!" I laughed.

"I wish." He laughed. "Boring as hell and my phone ran out of juice."

I pouted. "You poor thing."

He sprinkled some ingredient into the bowl. "Worth it."

Set up and ready to go, Caine and I sat on our bent knees while the others circled around. Aunt Lacey in front of us, Donovan to my left, Kim to Caine's right, and Olive at our backs. Ranlyn sat about ten feet away, acting as a channel so we could siphon more power if needed. Donovan handed Aunt Lacey two large black bowls, each with a black candle in its center. Water filled the bowls halfway up the candle's length. He placed another in front of me, the one he had been working on, another like it in front of Caine. Aunt Lacey lit a long wooden match. The stink of sulfur stung my nostrils as she handed it to me and then another to Caine and motioned for us to light our candles.

"Picture the candle as the vessel for the power binding you," Aunt Lacey explained in the dim lit basement. "As it burns away, so does the evil against you. Once the wick reaches the water and drowns, it takes under with it, its bonds."

The concept was straight forward yet clear we would be sitting for a while.

In the smaller black bowls was, what I thought, a black rock, but became clear was charcoal. Donovan and Kim lit them and the other ingredients already in the bowl. Olive took a pair of scissors and began searching the back of my hair.

I pulled away. "You best be checking for lice."

"I won't make it noticeable, Firefly."

I reluctantly let Olive cut off a piece of my hair.

As the scissors closed and the strands passed to Donovan, I couldn't help but look at how much she chopped. Caine lost strands as well. If he hadn't kept the style long he would have a bald spot.

That begged the question of what they would've done if he was bald. Did pubic or armpit hair count? I stopped myself from asking.

Donovan and Kim put the fresh cut locks into the bowls with the flaming charcoal. The hair curled and smoked, the smell not as corrosive as I imagined, the other herbs masking its harshness. Aunt Lacey pulled out a set of straight pins, long enough to make me nervous, and handed one to Donovan and Kim. Each held one over the flame until blackened.

Aunt Lacey instructed, "Prick your fingers and add within the same crockery three droplets of blood. Your blood and hair represents the embodiment of yourselves needed for the spell to identify you as the affected."

Jabbing a sharpened piece of metal through layers of skin was not an everyday recreational activity, though it would be the second time for me today.

"Get it over with," Donovan said perhaps gauging the apprehension on my face.

I swallowed the light gasp as I punctured my skin then added blood to my bowl. The candles within the water continued to burn down, leaving globs of wax floating along the surface like tar. I noticed they burned quicker than normal, though still would take some time.

"Now, Salix, Leith, close your eyes and repeat after me."

"Blood, coal, and earthly elements times three,
no longer permitting this treachery.
Sight given and breathing free,
as flame destroys aspects of thee.
Evil who doth attempt despair,
binding light with sightless air.
Darkness spread from those in harm,
shall never again ensnare my soul within its arms."

Aunt Lacey waited the appropriate intervals between lines. Repeated again, and then again. She instructed Donovan and Kim to continue while Caine and I now mimicked them. Aunt Lacey and Olive spouted off another incantation. This one in another language spoken softer to allow us the ability to hear Donovan and Kim repeating the original spell.

Power of the others cradled me. Encapsulated my body in a cocoon of soothing energy as they went on. Their voices fell into the background as my limbs felt so light I swore I was floating. I did my best to focus on the incantation, wanting to lose myself in the weightlessness.

This lasted a long time. Hazy smoke indicating the ending of the spell. The candles extinguished moments from each other and my body regained its sense of gravity.

The easiest way for me to confirm its success would be to peek through my squeezed lids to see the other's souls, but I was afraid we failed.

Aunt Lacey sighed. "Much better."

The alleviation in her voice snapped my eyes open. Bombarded by bright souls had me blinking to force them to adjust, the relief as great as the discomfort.

Caine squeezed me tight. My happiness dampened when I saw Kim over his shoulder. Her glow registered low anyway, but carried an unmistakable sheen. Now I saw nothing around her. Reassessing the room while the others spoke around me, I realized everyone shone duller than they should.

My eyes met Aunt Lacey's. I thought, *"Do I sound the same?"*

Aunt Lacey caught my question, which was a start. She looked at Kim and then Caine, who was speaking to Olive. By the time Aunt Lacey answered, Donovan caught on that something was up.

"What's wrong?"

His question made everyone else take notice.

"The unbinding has not eradicated its hold. Sophie sees your soul glow as I can access her thoughts, however, these thoughts are weaker than they should be," Aunt Lacey explained.

"And you're all a little murky." I left comments of Kim's non-existent soul glow to myself. She didn't need the reminder her glow was weak in the first place.

Since my ability was still muddied, the assumption was Caine's would be as well, he opting to forgo testing the theory.

———

A night's sleep made no difference. Our powers were still weakened, and an invisible string-like sensation remained over our bodies like an irritating sweater. We kept stretching as if loosening our muscles or readjusting the spine could break the bindings. Nothing worked, leaving us to face the gathering as we were.

Aunt Lacey suggested we travel in Caine's new Infiniti. Chances were she knew he would opt to travel alone for the opportunity to test his baby out long distance. Enough seats were available for Donovan, yet he drove himself. I offered, but Donovan gave a cheerless laugh and said he'd "rather crab-walk the whole way".

I didn't push it.

After hours of driving, Aunt Lacey instructed Caine to take the next left, but he couldn't see a road. Donovan was long gone so Caine slowed the car to a crawl before spotting the one-lane roadway hidden by overgrowth. Nothing more than a dirt road with grass and sprouting weeds. We drove another fifteen minutes surrounded by tall, thick-trunked trees.

The trees opened into a field full of parked cars. No designated lines broke up the grass into seven by twelve sections, though dozens of skilled drivers parked side by side. Caine found a spot on the outside of the lot where we met the rest of Aunt Lacey's Sect.

Duffels and backpacks littered the ground around the Coveners as they talked in groups. Jared and Blake were already at it, mock wrestling and being obnoxious without concern. Denise and her tag-a-long Jamie sneered at them.

Ranlyn arrived and waited with the rest of us. His people were on guard duty, but he wasn't leaving us anytime soon.

Donovan wore a backpack with a single strap across his chest, in his hands were a stack of clear plastic cups and a tall chrome thermos. Each of us grabbed one of Aunt Lacey's bags, as well as our own, and then shuffled to keep up as Aunt Lacey and Donovan walked into the open grassy field with the Coveners.

Caine carried the heaviest of Aunt Lacey's luggage, an over-sized and over-packed red duffel slung over his shoulder.

The walk felt endless, the stretching field an enormous open area with nothing but sun-beaten grass. A Saskatchewan-like landscape with surrounding forest in the distance. The sun shone too bright, making me realize I forgot my sunglasses. After an exhausting couple of weeks, I had little steam to keep me going.

Kim spoke in a laboured pant. "Sorry to sound like the five-year-old of the group, but are we there yet?" Aunt Lacey giggled but didn't answer. Kim did sound like a kid but to her credit, it *was* the first time she had asked.

Another ten to fifteen minutes of sweaty walking passed before Donovan stopped and dropped his bags. We dropped our bags and stretched out our sore bodies while we had the chance. Some giving up and laying out in a sweaty heap.

Aunt Lacey extended her hand to the ground and brushed dirt from a rounded stone with a crude design carved into it. A design I somewhat remembered.

"You would have seen it on the grimoire, Salix. It's the Coven's symbol." Aunt Lacey must have read my mind. "This stone was laid into the earth at the first mass coven gathering centuries ago, calling to its leaders so all would not lose their way." She lifted her hand, palm up, as those around her leaned over to see what she held.

She wasn't holding anything.

The Coven's symbol illuminated in the center of her hand.

Symbols and ancient lettering moved around the circle and extended down her fingers and her wrist, creeping along the surface.

"It's Theban lettering," Kim recognized.

I remembered it as the lettering in Aunt Lacey's doorway protection spell and the stitching within the hem of the Initiation dresses she wore. The symbol glowed like it was emitting light from within her skin as it pulsed and moved in strong white and metallic silvery tones that caught the light like a brand.

Aunt Lacey reached back down to the stone, this time laying her palm flat. Within an instant of contact, energy hummed around us. A magic everyone felt regardless of their soul glow.

"That's what it feels like?" Kim took in a breath of the power, her hand to her chest. She closed her eyes, revelling in its energy.

Beneath our feet came first a vibration and then a cone of the same silvery shimmer sprouted up from the stone, growing tall above our heads. This cone of energy surrounded Aunt Lacey, spiralled around her, the intense energy causing us to step back. The vibrating ground stilled. As the silver cone pulsated with energy, Aunt Lacey stepped out of it, her body moving through its silvery threads disrupting its shape.

Donovan poured out two to three inches of thermos contents into the clear plastic cups and passed them around. The liquid was thick as a milkshake and orange with coloured chunks floating around in it. Aunt Lacey instructed us to hold off on drinking it.

"That looks like pure vomit." My comparison was spot on, the colour alone causing my throat to clench.

Caine opted to smell it, his face contorting in disgust. "Smells worse than vomit." He pawed at his nose. "What the hell is it?"

Donovan's laugh was smug as he continued to pour out more glasses. Aunt Lacey spoke over him. "Tono di voce," she said with what sounded like an Italian accent. "This concoction is the key that will allow your body to pass through the veil to the meeting site. It will be unpleasant but quick."

"*Pfft,*" Blake huffed. "Unpleasant? Feels more like being sucked through a garden hose lined with glass while being castrated and eviscerated." Aunt Lacey gave him a hard look he shrugged at. Jared gave him an elbow Blake scowled at.

"I'll be the last to go as I have my own key." Aunt Lacey lifted her palm, still showing the pulsating symbol the stone calls from its Coven Leaders. "Leave your things. I'll bring them through with me. Donovan...."

Donovan walked into the silvery cone of light, gave me a devilish look, and raised his glass with a last trite salutation before sucking the liquid back like a shot of whisky. The viscous liquid clung to the cup like it refused to let go.

He doubled over with a deep grunt of crippling pain that shocked the hell out of any of us who hadn't been through it before. The spiraling cone of light spiraled around him, building speed, strobing from metallic tones to every other colour in rapid succession. The colour and symbols surrounded Donovan and moved along his skin like Aunt Lacey's palm, snaking feathery lines of energy along his body.

A spear of pain hit me and dropped me to my knees. On all fours in silent horror, I saw the symbols and colour coursing through my body like scarab beetles as I gripped the grass. Every nerve in me throbbed as I looked up at Donovan, desperate for reprieve. Blake's garden hose description was a closer comparison than I thought possible.

Caine leaned over my shoulders, holding onto me as Ranlyn hovered on my other side. Raucous sounds of pain escaped my throat as the pitch of surprise from the others behind me echoed in the field. I couldn't speak to ask questions, my jaw clenched shut as pain overwhelmed me.

Donovan was less than a body length away from me when the cone closed in on him, hugging his body like a miniature tornado, then dragged him under. Engulfed by the earth, no sign of his dissension in its wake. Then the cone slowed to its initial form of energy and freed me from the pain.

On my knees and panting like a dog, my guts felt twisted with permanent damage. Whispered voices questioned what happened to me, some concerned, others suspicious. Fuck them. The energy to give a shit bled dry the moment Donovan took a swig of that drink. What was even worse than feeling the pain as Donovan moved through the earth, was that I still had to travel through it myself and would be subjecting Donovan to the same excruciating pain.

Aunt Lacey's reaction confused me. She looked as stunned as the rest of them. She knew about the connection, what was with the eyeballing?

Aunt Lacey spoke in a disconnected voice. "Emotionally, not physically."

Of course. I never felt Donovan's pain before physically. The porcelain cat gouging my arm, but not his, made this clear. This was pain in its purest form.

I still felt Donovan's apologetic discomfort and the ghost of pain his body endured. Why the change? Evolution of our bond? Or maybe the place we were going heightened the connection? Aunt Lacey didn't speculate. For someone who knew damn near everything, this being a mystery to her scared the shit out of me.

An answer wouldn't come staring in awe at each other, so Aunt Lacey called for Kim to go next. It took some coaxing and a brave face from me, stating I was more so shocked. She smoothed her hair behind her ears, stepped within the silvery cone, squeezed her nostrils shut, and drank down the concoction.

Her blue-green eyes disappeared as she fell to her knees. Looking as if she would vomit on the spot, the silvery cone changed colours and sucked her down with an echo of a dampened scream. The cone returned to its natural state waiting for the next supernatural tourist.

Caine volunteered to go next giving me more time before enduring it again. He drank down the disgusting concoction, doing everything possible to keep his spasmodic body under control. His lips held together between his teeth, not to let out a sound. It became apparent his pain left me directly unaffected, though I still hated seeing him go through it. Then the cone hugged him, too, in its ephemeral grip before swallowing him whole.

I glared at the cone with hatred at the thought of going through that pain again. With guilt, I was glad my connection to Caine was nothing like with Donovan, or I would have to go through it three-fold.

Aunt Lacey poured me another glass since my cup was busted and spilled all over the ground.

My hands shook. "This is going to hurt him again," I said, imaging Donovan's anticipation on the other side.

"It appears so," Aunt Lacey responded with a sympathetic tone.

I closed my eyes and counted to three. Before I changed my mind, I stepped into the cone thrumming in magic and downed the liquid. What grazed my taste buds tasted like fomented fruit and smelled like fermented fruit that had been shit out by a goat.

Again, my kneecaps hit the ground as I gritted through a scream. The pain racked my body, tearing me apart down to the last molecule. Eviscerated and castrated was how Blake described it. I didn't have a set of balls, but I could imagine his description pretty well hit the mark.

I prayed for the pain to stop, but it dug deeper as the pulsating colours of the cone radiating from my body and obscured my vision. The steady floor of the field disappeared, and I went blind. The pain clamped my eyes shut as they rolled in their sockets. It was like I was strapped to a rollercoaster I never signed a waiver to ride. G-forces threatened to mince every inch of my body, the ancient symbols moving under my skin like burrowed, angry rats.

Grass was beneath me again and the sounds of a man in pain cried out above my own grunts. Firm hands grabbed hold of me and held me while I waited for the ripping to end. As it dissipated, I opened my eyes. Caine looked down at me, concern stitching his brows. Donovan lay on his back in the grass with his hands over his chest.

"I'm sorry," I whispered.

He shook his head and blinked away tears of pain. "No need, babe."

After a moment, we regained the ability to stand, and I took in my first look at where the rollercoaster from Hell landed.

I expected to see a lot of people, a lot of enlightened souls, but this was far too much. My eyes widened at the sight of them, then snapped shut as I had to fight against the shower of light. I turned my back on the section of Magics I could see and towards the few people I could stand and covered watery eyes already tearing down my face like I French-kissed a potent onion.

"Where are your sunglasses?" I heard Caine ask while another Covener popped through the veil gripping their bodies in pain.

"On my dresser. Great time to have the memory of an eighty-year-old. At least I brought headache meds 'cuz this is going to be a bitch of a weekend."

"Here." Donovan shifted his backpack to the front, as he neglected to leave it with Aunt Lacey and pulled out a pair of dark aviator sunglasses. "You'll need them more than I will." I hesitated. "Take them," he insisted, so I did. They were a bit big but would suffice.

Through the dark lenses, Caine's unique grey eyes were near non-existent. The whites and the grey blending together. Creepy.

Aunt Lacey came through with the Sect's luggage surrounding her. The ride apparently left her unaffected, since she wasn't on the ground writhing in pain like the rest of us. Because she didn't need to drink the liquid to cross over, her body already possessing the 'Tono di voce' to enter. She didn't suffer the intensifying surge of horrendous pain from the energy the concoction created to act as our own ill-fitting key.

She checked on everyone, passing through as they recovered and took hold of their bags. She looked to Donovan then to me. "Are you two okay?" We nodded, but the doubt in my gut wasn't all mine.

"All right," she in a delighted tone. "Now that we've all made it through the veil, it's time we get to the party."

Not everyone shared her zest for the upcoming events. Most were still getting over the veil-birthing experience and had the pleasure of shouldering Aunt Lacey's heavy bags.

A sign ahead was like many of the small-town signs, crafted from one immense piece of wood and painted with complimentary colours atop two long stilts high above our heads. In large lettering the sign read, "**WELCOME TO DILUCULO,**" then in smaller cursive underneath, "**For the liberation of the power**."

I laughed. "Diluculo?" I struggled with the pronunciation. "This place has its own name? I thought Diluculo was going to be a town, not...well, wherever we are."

Aunt Lacey spoke with pride while they stood beneath the fifteen-foot sign. "Of course, it has a name. It has everything its own. We created this place."

"Wait, you created it?" Caine asked surprised and fumbled with the luggage.

"Not alone," Aunt Lacey gave a laugh at her questioning. "Many years ago, the Elders and other powers came together to construct a place where we could gather. A haven without the worry of those without the knowledge of our world becoming aware. 'Diluculo' for us represents the dawning of a new time and space. This space, where there is no shame, no disguises, and no fears to speak of. On the outside, we risk persecution and alienation from the Blind less fortunate to either be born with the power or introduced to it. Here you are free to do anything you like without shying away.

"Do not feel the need to withdraw from others invited along, they are much like you, once lost and now burdened with purpose." Then she took in a deep breath and continued walking.

As we passed the sign, I gazed upon all the enlightened souls, amazed by how many there were. Hundreds. All ages and cultural backgrounds, and so many soul colours. Souls shone in different shades of my normal colour wheel of yellows, greens, and blues, plus metallic gold and silvers. Still, I had no idea what any of it meant and wished my family quirk came with a manual. When I got back, I would have to remind myself to talk more about it with Olive and Lewis.

One thing that had to be personal to Diluculo was its smell. Homey and earthy yet filled with undertones of florals and even fruit. The mixture was inviting without being overpowering enough to nauseate. The sky, so clear and brilliant in the most unbelievable blue I had ever seen, was unnatural outside of here, also a Diluculo thing.

Children played with corn dollies and wheels. Our surroundings decorated for the celebration with stocks of corn. The seasonal colour bled into every second person's clothing and little kids wearing orange and yellow ribbons. It looked like many traditional Thanksgiving set-ups yet embellished a thousand times over.

Still walking to our cabin, we saw a group of children tease one other by levitating his ball cap out of his reach. Magical monkey in the middle. I felt the need to step in, but Diluculo overwhelmed me, and I figured they would work it out amongst themselves like other kids on the playground do.

Kim pointed towards a man with a chocolate lab jumping and bouncing into the air beside him and his daughter. The little girl looked maybe four in a pink corduroy dress. Hair tied in an orange bow on the top of her head that bopped as the dog was trying to get the balloon at the end of the string she clutched.

We thought nothing of it until Kim motioned again to the balloon. It wasn't red or blue but clear. And it didn't move like a typical balloon or reflect the light quite right. The dog jumped high enough to catch it within its sharp teeth popping it with a hail of water. The balloon was a bubble. The girl thought it was hilarious especially since her dad created another one by making a goofy face and blowing through his circled thumb and index finger. The daughter jumped, clapping and laughing as they continued, the bubble and the dog bopping up and down with each step.

With the ride on the way in being so excruciating, I wondered how the chocolate lab fared. Animal abuse came to mind. Though many other animals ran and played about the grounds. I would never insist Bosco endure the pain so he could vacation here with me. He would be happier getting spoiled at my mom's.

Aunt Lacey made an off-the-cuff comment that their eyes didn't look so animal-like to her. It was enough for me to doubt the fur and feathered creature's origins while taking more keen scrutiny over them. If my retinas weren't already seared from the light, I would have noticed that all the animals running around possessed yellow soul colours. This brought on a whack of questions Aunt Lacey laughed at and kept walking.

Crowds of people converged in slow moving pockets, giving us time to take in our surroundings. Makeshift kiosks and blankets laid out along the gravel walkway with people selling merchandise. As we stole a quick peek we found herbs, potions, loads of handmade jewellery, quilts and throws, books, and gemstones for sale. About everything you would need to practice the craft and so much more.

Pricing looked reasonable and we even overheard someone haggling for a lower price on a pair of Wicked Witch of the East novelty socks. They were a popular item as many were running around in traditional hokey Witch costumes.

At least they had a sense of humour about Magic's checkered past.

As Kim and I side-eyed each other after passing an actual working maypole—in use no less—it was clear we both experienced a sense of 'what world we were transported to?'.

The cabins were on the far side of the camp in long rows forming a semi-circle so it took us a bit to reach them. They were larger than ones I had been in a few times during childhood summers. Camping mostly consisted of spider-filled tents and rain-soaked sleeping bags. In behind the cabins, others opted to be closer to nature and slept in tents amongst the trees. Maybe it was an easier way for parents to get some alone time, by kicking out the brats for the warm nights.

I realized I worried about the animals first, but the veil-crossing would have been torturous for a child and Aunt Lacey had no explanation for that.

Moving past the first few rows of cabins, where the majority of Coveners would be staying, we continued down a footpath stomped into the grass from overuse. We stopped at the last row of ornate painted cabins, larger than the other rows of bungalows. Aunt Lacey led myself, Donovan, Caine, and Kim to a sage green with white trim cabin and a front porch which held a swing and wooden chair. It looked like a doll house with perfect white shutters and an inviting wicker woven mat on the foot of the threshold.

Aunt Lacey didn't pull out a key or even murmur an incantation, the door opened of its own volition as if welcoming her home. Caine, Kim, and I looked to each other certain the weekend was bound to surprise us at every turn.

Inside, the cabin was also traditional. Medium stained wood panelling covered the walls of the living space to the left of the entrance. Real wood, not the fake stuff, and the furniture was old but sturdy and well taken care of. As in Aunt Lacey's home, photos in different sized eclectic frames spanned the walls, side tables, and fire-place mantel.

Finding them fascinating, I walked over to the collection on the mantel piece of a wood-burning fireplace. It formed the focal point of the room with its white painted bricks, blackened by soot and light marble mantel piece. A painted female figure above found a home amongst the others. It wasn't of Aunt Lacey, maybe a relative, but it was unlike the one in the Victorian room of Aunt Lacey's home.

I shifted the sunglasses to the top of my head to see a familiar face in a small frame. Kim. A candle in front of her illuminated her simple beauty. The flame flickering in her blue-green eyes as she gazed down upon it, her red hair over her shoulders as she sat, captured her peaceful essence.

Near Kim's on a circular wooden side table that held a tall lamp with a pale drum shade, another caught my eye. Since most were closeups of people's faces, it didn't fit to have one so distant from the subject. The black framed photo now in my hand had its subject in the shadow of a tree on a bright day. As I looked closer, I realized the serene figure was Donovan. Back against a tree near a body of water, he sat reading a book, untouched by the bright sun blazing in the background. Nothing like the arrogant guy I sort of knew. He looked content, as if whatever he read was drawing him into its realm, captivating him. For some reason, I wished I could see him look like that. Since we first met, it was all troubled, tortured, and anger in those dark eyes.

A hand snatched the frame. I yelped. "It's illegal to photograph someone without their knowledge. Voyeurism I get, framing the photo for your mantel afterwards is sociopath-level creepy."

"At least it's a good photo." I noticed we were alone when I looked to see if Caine overheard me.

"Aunt Lacey's giving the grand tour. I see you were distracted." A cocky grin caved his dimples.

"Couldn't help it," I said. "Never seen you so content before."

A smile tugged the edges of his lips. "I'm not always miserable, babe. Not a screw in your smile kind of guy."

"Part of your persona?"

He snorted. "Not at all. More comfortable within my own head, I guess." Dammit, I knew how he felt. "Most Magics are only interested in what you can *do* or what you can do for *them*. I don't trust easily."

I sat on the arm of the nearby couch. "A screwed-in smile has its purposes. I wouldn't get a dime behind the bar if I couldn't separate myself from the person that works there."

Donovan nodded. Then his expression changed. I picked up stirring emotions but couldn't identify which ones. This place accelerated the connection, and it was unsettling to feel things I didn't create.

"I want to know you, Sophie."

I raised an eyebrow. "Bold considering you keep evoking my protective nature."

"You don't need to protect him."

"When someone's attacking someone you care about, it happens.

And it works both ways." He looked at me with question. "When he acts like an asshat about you, I get defensive, and I'm sure you could fight your own battles. I don't want there to be a need to. Last time I checked we were all legal drinking age and could tie our own shoes."

His dimples deepened. "You're right, my shoes are expertly tied."

I smiled then looked away from his lascivious stare. Shitbubbles, I did it again. I found it difficult to talk to him without ending up saying something that strengthened his yearning. Too tough to keep the lines from becoming blurred or obliterated all together.

"I know I've said it before, that I'd *try* and be civil. I feel what it does to you." He huffed. "I'll say I'll try again, but honestly it just feels like lying."

I looked up into the dark pools of his eyes, understanding I was asking too much, but it didn't stop me from wanting to donkey kick both of them.

"Every time he makes you laugh or does something to make you happy, I feel that too. All it does is remind me of what I'm missing out on. Nothing makes that better."

Now I felt cruddy, dirt-in-every-crevice-down-into-my-core type cruddy.

Thinking again about Caine, I thought more about that for a moment. If Donovan could emotionally funnel my happiness, and now physically in Diluculo, then if Caine and I...shit. I didn't even want to think it.

Before I could stop myself, I said aloud. "You haven't had sex since all this started have you?"

"What?" He laughed, rocking back on his heels.

"I would have felt it if you did. Not physically since that's new, but strong emotions are easier to read. I haven't picked up sex emotions from you."

"True. Can't say the same for you."

"Oops."

He nodded. "The last couple of times at least since the connections become stronger."

"Huh, that's ridiculously awkward."

"Not as awkward as realizing what was happening halfway home with some half-naked ugmo in my passenger seat. I faked an allergic reaction to her peach lip gloss to get her out of my car." I burst into a laugh drawing him in. "I may give it out for free, and more often than some, but I'm particular about who I whore around with."

The thought of him kicking out that chick gave me belly laughs.

"The point was for me to play nice-nice with Caine, right?"

I snapped my fingers. "That'd be swell, yes."

"Okay, well, you two *not* having sex would be swell for me."

"*Pshaw*, I bet."

"The best I can do," he clucked his tongue, "is promise no snide comments while he's around. I'll keep my trap shut and try my damndest to be genial." He pointed a finger in my face. "But I'm not promising it'll last past the first conversational experiment."

"More than enough," I said satisfied with his conditions. I hugged him with enthusiasm as I felt his arms grapple my ribcage with the feeling of elation I wasn't sure from who it originated.

"It's for her, you know?" Caine turned the corner, his voice deadpanned as he leaned his hands onto the back of chair.

"Were you eavesdropping?" Nothing pissed me off more.

"I came down in time to hear his promise. I was going to go back upstairs but..." He didn't finish and focused on Donovan. "I don't know you. All I know is what she tells me and your behaviour in front of me. So, as far as I'm concerned, and for as long as you can keep it up, I have no problem with your presence in her life, which also happens to be my life."

Caine was treading on the line of understanding boyfriend and possessive jerk.

Donovan didn't respond. He stayed quiet to keep his promise for more than five minutes. I nudged Donovan's hand with my own. He held onto my two end fingers for a moment before I squeezed his then pulled away before that too caused a fight, knowing he would be seeing my formal-self in our former life.

"I'll try my best as long as you do the same." Donovan ended up sounding more like a computer program for the vocally impaired.

Caine nodded and turned to leave the room. "Come see our room, we get our own bathroom."

"'Kay," I said irked he was throwing it in Donovan's face that we were sharing a room, though I was never asked if it was okay.

Once Caine's footsteps disappeared upstairs, I turned back to Donovan.

"Don't say anything." It was obvious he was trying not to crack a smile.

"Oh, come on." I dug a playful elbow in his side and laughed. "You did good."

He pulled me in for another hug, we both holding each other. This time I felt him flinch as our skin connected, then still with his arm around my shoulder we walked towards the staircase. "Oh babe. If you weren't you...."

"I know." I wasn't expecting anything but was hopeful to survive the weekend without them killing each other.

21

FANFANATIC

Our room was nice. A quaint set-up wrapped in toile wallpaper in a neutral scenic design. I sat on the plush queen bed and smoothed the beige blankets, soft beneath my fingers, as Caine put away the small amount of stuff he brought into an off-white dresser.

Forming the words to explain the connection cock-block was ten times harder than expected and one hundred times harder waiting for Caine's response.

"Well." He sighed and took another moment of thinking while I wished I could tunnel into his skull for his thoughts. "I can't mind-bend a solution here." He gave a hollow laugh that bloomed guilt in my gut. "I don't particularly like that you were talking about sex with Donovan at all, but it's better we know. Are you wanting...? I'm mean, what do you want to do?"

"I don't want to break up."

"Oh, good."

"Sorry, that's not what I was gunning for. You needed to know why I was freezing you out. Believe me, giving up your dick and all you do with it is not something I would do without good reason. And you can still entertain yourself. I don't even have that option."

He laughed again, this time with more ease. "I guess Kim can use the condoms I brought. Someone should get lucky."

"I'll let her know we've got her uterus covered."

We sat, holding each other's hands, stuck in thought, until Caine broke the silence. "I get you're trying to protect him, but at some point—"

"I know, I know."

"Plus, whenever it does happen, you're not going to be thinking about him." He kissed my forehead.

Cocky regarding his skill level or not, he was right. Donovan would be an afterthought. For our time Diluculo at least, I could survive the weekend without it, right?

We joined the others out back. To the left was a glistening beach. White sand kissed the edge of crystal clear water. A Witch-made oasis as perfect as they could invent. Formidable fresh water waves for surfers without worry of teeth or tentacles, a fishing pier, and a spell against drowning. Something to do with buoyancy. We wanted to jump in, but Aunt Lacey insisted we glad-hand with important Magics first.

Eddies of dread filtered from Donovan. He gave me a hard look of annoyance I laughed at.

We moved too slow, like ducklings on the tail of their mother. And not because Aunt Lacey enjoyed an unhurried pace, but because so many people stopped us to say hello or make quick introductions to our Coven Leader all nervous and bowing. No one back home bowed. I half-expected them to pull out a tit or ass cheek to autograph. Aunt Lacey was a big cat in this jungle and others gawked at us with envious stares craving to be a part of the entourage.

Now I understood why Donovan was so grouchy. After an hour of shuffling beneath the hot sun, my patience was waning.

We stepped into a store called 'The Witch Hunt'. The shelves overflowed with toiletries, magazines, books, and candy. Everything you couldn't get at the merchants outside.

I stuck Donovan's glasses back on the top of my head. Taking on an exposure therapy approach with the few brightened souls in my company.

"Is she here?" Aunt Lacey asked a young woman behind the counter with long, black hair and yellow-blonde streaks peeking from the bottom layer as well as a thick helping of eyeliner. Though the lip ring gave her an edge.

Skater-girl tore her blue eyes away from Donovan long enough to answer Aunt Lacey and then disappeared through a cloth draped door and returned a moment later. "Be out in a minute," she relayed.

While Donovan had plenty of admirers, this one had no compunction in making it noticeable. Shame sparked as Donovan busied himself at a magazine rack. I grabbed a random magazine, a *Men's Health* mag with Josh Duhamel featured as an avid fisherman, figuring this was what Donovan did. Unless he wanted to know `How to get the most luscious lashes`.

His eyes stayed fixed on the magazine now comparing bikini styles. "Her name is Nicole. We met last time I was here and spent one I-wish-I-could-forget night together."

"And now you're ignoring her," I said in a monotone as I flipped the page to a protein drink debate.

"Like she has lizard toes. After, having her follow me around like I deflowered her, I don't want to get fixed into talking to her again."

"Maybe you did deflower her. She looks verrrrry young." I exaggerated for my own amusement. "I thought you were choosy with your women, Donny-boy. Your compass become a little skewed?"

"Ha ha. Don't call me Donny-boy. When we get together you can scream my name in different languages, but Donny-boy is off limits." I giggled and ignored his assumption of us "getting together". "Alcohol was involved. And yes, she's legal drinking age."

"Must have been her birthday." I laughed a little too loud and he shushed me.

Caine walked over. "Can I get in on the joke or am I part of it?"

Both Donovan and I said "No". Caine turned to leave when I grabbed his arm to stay.

"Oh, come on," I said to Donovan, and he waved it off.

I explained in a melodic voice for effect. "Donovan here shared one lovely drunken evening with Nicole the cashier-slash-skater-girl and now she's part of his stalker fan club."

Adam got himself into this same situation time and time again. I watched as chicks showed up to my brother's shows and he would do his bastard's best to find creative ways to be anywhere else.

"You should be used to it by now," was Caine's reaction. "Half the Sect's in your fan club."

"Yeah, well, no one in the Sect has seen me naked," Donavan said leaving us both shocked. "Aunt Lacey made me promise," he added, making us laugh again. That made much more sense. He plunked the magazine back onto the rack, out of place, and upside down.

When Nitsa and the other Coven Elders attended a Coven gathering at Aunt Lacey's, Donovan had commented that they acted like schoolgirls every time they saw each other and today was no different. Nitsa wrapped Kim up in a Nitsa-brand hug before the Elder turned her attention towards us three at the magazine rack.

I shoved the magazine onto the rack and scrambled as it fell. Donovan caught it before it hit the floor and added it to the rack himself.

"Salix!" Her husky voice rang through the store. Nitsa hugged me before I could say anything. She stepped back while still holding onto my shoulders. "A little Binding can't hold down the Coven's resident Soul Seer, now can it?" Nitsa leaned closer and hushed her voice to say, "How does Nicole's soul fare?"

I thought about what Donovan said. That people always want something from you or want to use what you do. I didn't much care about this instance and made an honest assessment. "Not even a nightlight," I answered.

Nitsa threw her head back and laughed. "She's not too bright a conversationalist either. Oh, but you would know, wouldn't you Donovan?" She was chiding him, but he refused to engage.

Aunt Lacey introduced Caine. Nitsa was present for his sleeping curse awakening, but had left town before he attended a coven meeting.

He extended a hand she didn't take, instead, she stood back and accessed him. "Oh, Leith, you are a strapping young man, aren't you? And powerful to boot. You have one formidable body and mind for a Berisford." Caine's mouth opened but nothing came out. "We've figured out our one too many soulmate issues then?" She gave a small gasp and focused on Caine. "Your persuasion gift must give you a leg up, yes? I have said it before, you are one lucky girl, Salix."

Caine and I attempted smiles for the sake of respect. With what was brewing inside of Donovan, he impressed me by not flipping her off and trashing the store.

"This Loring business has caused quite a stir as well." She turned over my arm to reveal the jagged scar of my forearm since I couldn't get it fully healed once the Binding was loosened.

I took my arm back. "Amazing that you've been alive for a millennium without developing a keen sense of social cues, Nitsa."

She smiled and crossed her arms.

"Unless you enjoy watching others squirm," I added.

"A little." Nitsa laughed. "Nicole," she called over her shoulder, "you should be taking notes from Salix here on how to conduct a challenging conversation while remaining fascinating."

I shook my head, but couldn't help being drawn in. The woman had her charms.

As with Aunt Lacey, the same song and dance of awed and bowing Coveners slowed us down on the way to the other Coven Elders who Caine met for the first time. He thanked them for their part in the Awakening Ritual and then they talked some about Loring's kidnapping attempts and general threat increase.

The entire experience was exhausting.

———

We gathered around a main bonfire at sunset. Sweaters and long pants were unnecessary as the night was as warm as the day. Mosquitoes weren't invited to the Diluculo-making process, though I missed the sound of cicadas in the trees.

With the Mother Coven congregated in one place, my eyes were in a chlorine-saturated haze like after a day at the pool. Until he wiped away a set of tears, I didn't realize how much it affected Donovan. Then I remembered them looking like that at Aunt Lacey's Coven gathering when I attended bar for her.

Could the connection have been strong back then? I tried to think of other examples. The night I woke up at Caine's on a rollercoaster of confusion, rage, and hopelessness came to mind. Could that have been Donovan? If so, he wrestled with a toxic mix of emotion that night. When he looked at me with a questioning look, I turned back to the bonfire instead, concentrating on the flames to ease my mind.

Enormous tree trunks made the bonfire a beast in what looked like a pyre. No witches were burning tonight. This was all celebratory.

Nitsa commanded the Coven's attention. Our Sect stood at the front of the heaping pile of wood beside Aunt Lacy who was now sitting in a tall wooden chair. Next to her, in chairs much like her own, were the other Coven Elders: Hallden and Roon. Only now did I realize how important to the Coven Aunt Lacey was. She was their Elder. My Elder. The Leader of the Mother Coven itself. No wonder everyone bowed to her.

Nitsa's chair was empty as she spoke to the flock in an empowered voice, circling the fire to speak to everyone. Periodic cheers broke between her sentences.

The moment Nitsa's voice flooded our ears with her conviction and veracity, I realized why Nitsa was the Coven's spokesperson.

"We, this Coven, have been a collective strength for many a century." Everyone cheered, then eerie silence took over while waiting for whatever came next. "Many worthy brothers and sisters have fallen victim over such time, while we Magics, Pagans, Norse Magics, Mages, Warlocks, Alchemists, Elementals, Druids, Enchanters, Transmutators, Witch Doctors, Kitchen Witches, all us heretics, hid. We hid beneath the underbelly of humanity, forced to roam the world as the Blind, ignorant of its boundless potential.

"My fellow mystics, as each of the last one hundred years passed, and the world grew to open its eyes, we triumphed in spreading the word of the true existence of the power to the blood-born and Blind alike, more than in any century before it!"

Hundreds of cheering voices bounced off the trees and buildings around us as Nitsa's charismatic speech. Her unyielding pride for her coven alive in the atmosphere as a vibrating power rushed through me.

"For those new the fold, Lughnasadh is the celebration of the harvest. An important Sabbath. As we worship the earth, to strengthen us, to do our biding in the name of all that is pure, making the decision to wield the power for good over evil, it repays us with its bounty and keeps us strong-willed and whole at heart. Remember flock, when you are out in the world, cherish Earth's gifts as you cherish your own."

Another roar of triumph ensued.

"Now," she looked more solemn as she walked the fire's edge, "there are whispers of evil chatter among us." Worried murmurs filled the air. Nitsa took a moment to quiet everyone down. "Whispers, mere whispers." She paused and smoothed her hair. "Bindings on the strong and influential, slayings of the weak, and Tainting of virtuous souls with lies masked as assurances, all tricks of the desperate. Do not be the fool. Engage your intuition. No matter how strong your ability you *will* sense the presence of evil. If anything, *anything*, calls to your instincts as a potential threat while within or outside our sanctum, seek out an Elder or your Sect Leader.

"During this year's celebration, do not venture into the wood alone or in small groups. We are safe here, but in the infinitesimal likelihood this creeping evil has infiltrated Diluculo, I would rather see you gather in herds than die a lonely sheep cut down by the wolf."

Her warning left its mark on the jovial faces of the Coveners. With the deaths of some and attacks and bindings on others, I wondered why they held the celebration at all? Angst, curiosity, and suspicion filtered from Donovan. As I saw he and Aunt Lacey exchange a tense look, this didn't make me feel any better.

"Now," Nitsa said, clapping then sanding her hands together, "we are more than ever standing strong. We are no house of building blocks struck down by the child. So, without worry, without allowing evil to scar our time within our most trusted of all Creations, let us rejoice and relish the company of our kin. For it is Lughnasadh, and we are celebrating!"

The pyre burst into flames as she lifted her arms, the blaze higher than the surrounding trees. I jumped back into Caine and Donovan on either side of me and grasp onto whatever I could. It wasn't the most flawless segue from Nitsa's fierce warning to rejoining the night's objective, but it did the trick getting everyone amped and ready to party. Everyone began a wild dance, beating at drums, and playing an instrument or two or running off to do their own version of celebrating.

Donovan laughed at me. I slugged him in the shoulder and then felt it jar my bones, and he laughed harder because of it.

Our small group retreated to our cabin with the Elders, we four mortals took a seat while our immortal Elders paced the floors.

Roon, a Hoodoo Priest in African tribal dress for the celebration, sported a shaggy greying beard and carried a carved walking cane. He looked as wise as Hallden looked prestigious. The Warlock with platinum hair down the back of his tailored suit was as cold as his ice blue eyes.

Besides the Caine's Awakening Ritual, I didn't know them well enough to read their personalities. Was Hallden always so cold? He and Roon always ready for an argument? Too hard to tell.

And they weren't even talking. Not with words anyway.

The collection of old colleagues paced the small space in mimed conversation, carrying on a telepathic conversation. All hand movements and head shakes punctuated by sneers and malicious laughter from Nitsa as she smoked her lungs raw from a long-stemmed cigarette holder.

Having some time to check the immortals out, my eyes adjusted to see through their too bright soul glows and found a silvery metallic glint others lacked. A glint like the silvery key of symbols giving us entry through the veil.

Patience at its end, I sensed it before Donovan erupted. "Can someone *please* tell us what the fuck's going on?"

Hallden, Roon, and Nitsa looked to him with disgust, but Aunt Lacey took point.

"As you well know, clarity regarding the events of our celebration have eluded us all for far too long. Loring has taken credit for the majority of acts against the Mother Coven. No surprise. And yet, we cannot see how this unfolds within Diluculo or how Loring plans to carry out whatever plan he has hatched."

"Binding a pair of Seedlings makes less sense than his conversion of Mother Coven members," Hallden added in his Germanic accent. "Treason is damnable, even in Loring's cursed values system. Why trouble with the efforts when he gains no beneficial members?"

Nitsa stamped out another cigarette and exhaled the excess into the air. "He'll break us down member by member if need be. Spill his Tainted energy all over our Coven and its sanctuary."

"We don't know that he's infiltrated the veil," Aunt Lacey argued to which Nitsa waved her off as if Aunt Lacey was being naïve.

"This place fills with the Duppies. I feel them!" Roon flailed his cane as he talked.

Hallden made a sound portraying his exhaustion with the topic. "No Duppies or ghosts or anything the like exist within the Creation, Roon. You're as mad as a March hare to think it." Roon huffed as he was ready with a retort. Hallden continued with a waving fist. "A length of red fabric will not save this Coven from its enemies! You need to proffer tangible resolutions before we die by the hands of an enemy in front of us, not beyond the veil." He added a "My word" under his breath as Roon seethed and stroked his long beard with ivory carved rings on his fingers.

The Duppies thing confused me and how red fabric would conquer them, so I moved on to something I could comprehend. "People have already died, right?" I moved my glasses to my head, hating the glare but unable to stand them on my nose any longer.

"Yes," Hallden answered. "Deaths and disappearances."

"Like Ranlyn's guards?" I added. "Too many of them have gone missing. They can't all have defected."

Nitsa laughed her usual throaty laugh. "Of course, not. For a member of Ranlyn's guard to have gone undetected as one of Loring's flock? Absurd."

Hallden scoffed. "Ranlyn is no omnipotent creature to which no one can deceive. Be realistic, Nitsa."

"I am," she argued, "Plus, Salix would have identified a Tainted soul if one parked outside her door," she said than muttered, "Realistic indeed."

"Actually no," I countered her. "I rarely saw any guards, but Ranlyn. Most were under cover spells or outside. I can't see souls under cover spells yet."

Caine leaned forward in his seat. "Kidnappings, bindings, possessing Sophie's dad, all a little passive for someone who's supposed to be all scary and stuff, don't you think?"

"Yes!" Hallden agreed as if Caine had sided with him.

"Absolutely," Aunt Lacey agreed. "However, if we follow through with ill-conceived plans of war, we'll find ourselves lost while Loring enacts his plan. None of us enjoys the guilt of lives lost on our conscious."

"So many already," Roon said with quiet despair, leaning on the back of a chair.

"It's not assumptions," Kim chimed in. "Loring walked into Aunt

Lacey's, took credit, then killed someone. He wants the Mother Coven dead. Seems pretty clear to me."

Hallden flashed a smug smile. "One would think crystal clear."

I remembered Olive mentioning the Witch Wars that occurred during the Ballard family's existence. She was never involved, but even Olive understood what a war would mean.

"It's much worse than she described," Aunt Lacey answered my memory. I nodded, remembering Olive mentioning Aunt Lacey as fighting in the trenches.

A pre-emptive attack held the possibility of far more deaths than they were willing to sacrifice. So, we left the Elders to their thoughts with no greater reason for why our powers were bound.

———

In our bathroom, Kim and I had some girl talk while we got water-resistant for the beach.

"Wow, I should'a dyed my hair before we left," I said checking out my roots.

"Stop nit-picking. But, yeah, hold on." Kim scooted out and returned as quick with a large candle and wooden matches.

Kim lit the candle and turned off the bathroom light.

"If you're trying to get cozy with me, sorry, it's gonna take more than candles."

"You wish. Here." Kim flipped through pages of a small booklet and handed it to me, open to a page with the heading: Spell to Change Hair Colour in Kim's writing. "You've watched The Craft too many times."

"Don't knock it, that movie rocks. Yes, it's corny, but they were on the right track. Probably had a Kitchen Witch on the writing staff. *This* spell works. I know 'cuz I wrote it." She flipped her gorgeous hair to one side.

"This is your secret?"

"What can I say, my hair is my vice." She gave a shameless shrug.

"You can do anything you want with a good spell and honest intent. With your power, it's a no-brainer. Unlike in the movie, this one doesn't shake out. So, when you're thinking of the hair colour you want, make sure you're focused or it could get ugly. I speak from experience."

I was beyond skeptical but had nothing to lose and a head of hair like Kim's to gain. After summoning my power, feeling it simmer with a hum that tickled my skin, I formed a clear vision of what I wanted and recited the spell out loud, trying not to laugh and spoil it.

> *"My will of beauty, my will to be said,*
> *to change the colour upon my head.*
> *See my vision, allow it to hold true,*
> *without vanity at heart, to bring thought to view.*
> *Infuse my locks to grow strong and thick,*
> *to make this change, I will it, quick."*

After the last corny line was cast, I closed my eyes again and focused even harder on the colour I wanted.

"All done." Kim's voice gave no indication of success or failure.

When I opened my eyes and Kim turned on the light, I found my hair darker than my natural brown, close to black, but softer, more chestnut than asphalt, with impeccable shine.

"Holy fairy farts!" I leaned closer to the mirror and ran my fingers through my hair.

"Is that what you wanted?"

"Kim, you're a fucking genius. You've earned a trip to second base after all." I moved my part checking the continuity, amazed by how silky the strands felt with no split-ends in sight.

"You won't have to do it as much as you would at a salon because it grows with your hair. Eventually it'll dull and grows a bit faster than normal, but it stays until you change it."

How could anyone look plain with such a spell? I couldn't stop touching my new hair.

"Caine won't be able to keep his hands off of you, you sultry beast. When you christen that comfy looking bed tonight remember the rest of us and keep it down. Oooh, on second thought, I have a spell for that too."

Moving past my excitement at sound-proofing my room for rambunctious sex, I explained the parameters of the emotional/physical cluster-fuck with Donovan. Kim didn't have a spell to counteract that kind of bond.

"Hopefully it'll cool out when we get back across the veil."

"They're sexy as hell. You can have both and you're not touching either one of them, how fair is that?"

"Even if I could have both, I don't play games like that."

"You think they care? I bet their plum sacks that if you were with both, they'd forgive you and ask for more."

"Dude!" I nudged her shoulder making the lip gloss she was applying smudge across her cheek. "Do I look like the tag-teaming type to you?"

"Oh, come on." She wiped her face. "I didn't mean at the same time, though that could be deliciously interesting. Good idea."

I shook my head. "That wasn't my idea, gutter princess. With where your mind's at you're going to need all the condoms we can't use."

"Nah, I'll leave them for the three of you."

"Shut your face."

"See? You know it," Kim said with mischief as I failed to suppress my smile.

We emerged from the bathroom to find Caine on the edge of the bed and Donovan leaning against the doorframe. Both wore awkward grins.

"We should have used your sex sound-proofing trick on the bath-room," I mock-whispered.

"Plum sacks?" Caine said with a raised eyebrow and Kim and I laughed until we were out of the cabin on our way to the beach.

22

CIRCLE OF EVIL

Bonfires lit up the shore all the way down the sand and we longed to check them out. The first bonfire we passed included skater-girl Nicole. Donovan pushed us passed as Nicole stared at him and chewed at her lip ring. Passing another group made of guys dressed in their swim trunks carrying their towels on their way back to the cabins, one caught Kim's eye.

"Mmmmm...nice bum, where ya from?" she said to herself. I giggled and looked back to see a blond eyeing Kim until he turned back to his friends.

"He looked like Frog," I said making the connection of Kim's type and surprised since Donovan looked nothing like them and I knew she had a crush on him at one point.

"He did," Kim said with an exaggerated pout. She wrapped her arm around mine. "Sucks he can't be here. He'd have a blast."

Since Caine's moving-in party, the two had spent some time together and chatting and texting whenever they could. Too bad she would need to keep this part of her life a secret.

The fourth fire-pit lit up the familiar faces of our Sect members. Rachel and Deidra, an adorable young couple always attached at the hip, looked cozy in their own little world amongst the others. This included the tanked and burly Jared holding a three-quarter finished bottle of spiced rum and arguing with a usually quieter member, Matt. Matt stole the bottle from Jared mid-argument about a basketball player. Jared knocked off Matt's hat making him choke on the alcohol and earning him a tongue-lashing for wasting "good booze". Blake, our Coven storm chaser, was shirtless and cozy with a petite brunette from a different Sect. He was teaching her the perfect way to roast a marshmallow while she was content in pretending she didn't already know how.

"Livin' the high life in the 'big cabins' I see," Denise slurred and staggered drunk into Donovan. She draped her arms over his shoulders standing close enough to kiss before he turned his head to the side.

"Easy, girl." With some finesse, he handed her over to her friend, a short, tanned girl with long dark hair someone called Winter. She was no less-in-the-bag and stumbled in the sand.

We could still hear Denise's complaints as we moved closer to the water. She didn't understand why Donovan didn't want her and her friends were being supportive by telling her he wasn't worth it. Though their attempts were half-hearted as they paid more attention to their drinks and throwing marshmallows at each other.

"See," Caine said with nonchalance. "Fan club." Donovan didn't think it was so funny, but I did, explaining it to Kim since she missed the conversation back in The Witch Hunt.

Kim and I pulled off our shorts and tank-tops. As I was adjusting the straps of my bikini, a rush of desire hit me between the thighs so strong I took in a ragged breath. I looked around and found Donovan who was close by to witness me undressing.

He tried to turn away, his embarrassment flooding me for his accidental voyeurism. His guilt was unmistakable, yet not enough to drown out the yearning.

With Donovan's lust pulsing through me, I found myself unable to look away from his body. Chiselled, yet not as broad as Caine's, both shoulders tattooed though I couldn't concentrate on the art. He looked like a Calvin Klein underwear model. His swim trunks hung low on his hips to show off a delicious v-ab. A dark treasure trail of hair led down from his bellybutton accenting his hard stomach stirring my imagination of what it led to.

Donovan's overwhelming emotion enveloped me like broken waves. Drawn together without the knowledge of whose emotions made the choice, our senses overtaken. We stood staring at each other, hit over and over by the visceral need to run and fuck each other right on the beach.

"Whoa, girl." Kim grabbed my arm, breaking my fixation when she spun me in her direction.

Did I move towards him? I was a few feet from my clothes, so I must have. We were still more than five or so feet from each other, but what if Kim hadn't stopped us?

A shiver ran through my whole body like an aftershock. I closed my eyes and fought to regain my self-control, heart still racing, breath too heavy.

"You okay?" Kim asked.

Undiluted lust meant words didn't exist.

Once I could shake it off, my next thought was of Caine. I looked around and saw him wading out in the water on his back. "Holy-fucking-shit, did Caine see that?"

I looked again and saw Donovan dive into the first break of waves. Seeing this caused a resurgence of hunger for him and I had to turn away.

"No, but I did." Kim lowered her voice. "What the hell? I *was* serious about what I said before, but I don't think Caine would be so forgiving if you *screwed* Donovan in front of a hundred people."

"I don't know what happened. He saw me...I felt...I don't think we could have got away from it. Can you imagine what would have happened?" What if Caine wasn't so enthusiastic about getting into the water? What if he were where Kim was standing? Monumental disaster.

"Stop freaking out. Caine didn't see anything. I'll make sure if I'm around that it doesn't happen again. Don't look at him."

I was grateful for Kim's devoted friendship, but "don't look at him" was piss-poor advice. Especially when he looked so delicious.

The warm water was a helpful distraction, but sexual tension returned when Donovan stood above the water or if he caught a glimpse of me and his lust overtook mine.

We swam for about an hour, wanting to return in the day when we could see the bottom of the clear water. Donovan stayed much to himself but remained nearby. Though, I swore he was doing things to set me off on purpose. Brushing back the water from his hair, making his biceps flex, or the way he would fix his swim trunks, first lowering them an inch. Every time he knew it worked, feeling the result boiling in my blood. I put in a few digs of my own to get back at him, making the situation worse. I stopped after Kim had to step in front of me and remind me of where I was. Again.

Around the fire, eating flame-scorched hot dogs and marshmallows, we talked about different Magics and abilities people had over beer and red-cupped alcohol concoctions. Also, Blake brought up how he got Jared good with the resurrection of the 'Ghost Vacuum', placing it outside the bathroom door so he tripped over it, landing hard, and knocking the vacuum and a coat rack down with him. This got the crowd roaring.

It was a fresh change from the last few weeks of constant hypervigilance. I didn't know where Ranlyn was, but I hoped he was having a break and some fun. He earned it.

As I finished my second rum and coke and Jared insisted on a refill, we attempted to explain the invisible hair-like spider webs wrapped around us because of the binding. Most were half-listening and inebriated to some degree anyway.

Caine moved my hair over my shoulder and ran his fingers down my arm, causing a shiver that affected Donovan in the middle of eating his fourth fire-scorched marshmallow. When I looked back to the fire, Denise was giving me a hard stare over the flames. One I looked away from in favour of conversation with Kim, when Denise tried to make another try for Donovan. Donovan set her aside, but not with enough finesse to ease the hit to her pride.

Denise glared at me with alcohol-glazed eyes. "So, how's it feel to be the coven slut, So-phie?"

Others around us gasped and Kim, Caine, and Donovan jumped to defend me.

"Hold up," I tried to motion for everyone to relax. Kim was like a guard dog, her hackles on end. I could handle drunkards, usually quiet well.

Denise came over to my side of the bonfire where I sat on my towel. "You think we can't all see it?" Her arms waved around her motioning to the other Coveners. "You and your 'power'. Some creepy past thing and whatever's' goin' on with you and Caine. You've enslaved them."

I stood and did my best to talk to Denise on an equal level, even using her coven name as she always corrected people to do. "You've been there for the rituals. You saw the whole shit-slinging monkey circus that is my life. It's not a weekend at the spa, I promise you." Denise was beyond reason. If she was at The Lush she would have been bounced, but I had nowhere to bounce her from.

Denise's eyes narrowed in their fury as her power rose, a slight influx like it too was half-in-the-bag. My power reacted on instinct, as if readying itself in case I needed it. I didn't want that. Last time, with the man in the storm drain and then with Jack, I used when I didn't want to. Hurting Denise wouldn't help this situation.

As Denise continued to tell me what type of person she thought I was, words from her mind, not from her lips, spoke louder than whatever she rambled about. Denise had a recent break with a guy she worked with who had then humiliated her in some way in front of their co-workers. Psychologically, I understood her struggle, but embarrassing me wouldn't wipe the memory of her crying in front of her co-workers. People from other bonfires were prairie-dogging it, gunning for something juicy.

Anything I said, Denise twisted into some evil agenda including me making up the Loring threat to get myself close to Ranlyn and his guards. She implying his crew guarded me in a carnal way.

I didn't even know how to respond to that.

While I tried to shift to an alternate tactic, Denise got bored of listening. Her negative thoughts escalated her anger as she closed the gap between us. She reminded me of Jack's contorted expression as she charged to strike me down.

Instead of hair pulling or whatever she planned to do, I used her momentum, grabbed her by the shoulders and swung her around. Sweeping her legs with one swift movement, I landed Denise on her back in the sand with a huff of alcohol-drenched breath. Everything began and ended so fast even Kim didn't have the chance to react. The move surprised everyone, even me, as the voices around us reared up and then fell silent.

Still clutching Denise, I fought not to let my power seep out and disintegrate her skin. The ache of my energy ready to find a target was so great I was afraid to move.

"I'm not Craig," I hissed. Whispers rose around us. "Whatever people think about me isn't my fault, nor do I give a shit, so get the fuck over it. I'm not looking to make enemies and I'm not getting paid for this catfight bullshit, so I'm done."

Instead of fighting or screaming, Denise turned her head and vomited in the sand. I shot up and away as my stomach lurched as the putrid smell of Denise's soured orange coolers hit me. We got out of there, leaving Denise mewling in her self-pity, returning to the cabin.

Kim bounced in excitement when we reached the cabin kitchen. "The snobby bitch deserved more than she got. And who's Craig? Whoever it is, you freaked Denise right out by talking about him."

I shrugged. "She was drowning her sorrows, I guess," I added once I finished telling them what I heard.

They all stared at me, Donovan leaving the fridge ajar.

"Oh, come on. Don't look at me like I'm a freak. I'm in the

kitchen of a cabin in a pocket of magic beyond the veil and you're looking at me like I'm the weirdest thing you've heard about all day."

Donovan leaned on the open fridge door. "Damn right you're a freak, babe. You're nothing like the boring asshats around that fire."

"You heard her?" Caine brought us back to topic with a hand on the small of my back.

I was still wearing shorts and my bathing suit top so his large hand soft on my skin sent a shudder through my spine as it had around the bonfire. Donovan closed the fridge door with force at my response.

I sat in the high stool around the kitchen island to get some distance as my senses were on edge from drinking and slipped my tank top back on.

"I think I did. It was weird."

"Soph, that's amazing. Hate Loring all you want, but all this danger around every corner has forced you to get stronger." Kim was red-cheeked on an alcohol driven ride of never-ending excitement.

"I'll remember to thank him."

"Just saying...."

"Yeah, well, Denise was pissed. Maybe her thoughts invaded mine. She has more power than I do."

Kim and Donovan argued this until Kim left to shower off the sand and change and then she wanted to do some late-night shopping with the merchants. She was betting on them being easier to haggle with. Caine decided on a shower as well and kissed my crown before leaving. I was up for the shopping adventure, but was heady from drinking and needed something non-alcoholic.

Donovan poured us both a glass of lemonade. As I took a gulp, he asked, "What's the guilt about?"

"Hmm?" I still had a mouthful.

"I feel guilty and don't know why. I figured it's a borrowed emotion."

I grunted and put my head down on the cool countertop.

"What's the matter?"

"Everything."

Donovan laughed. "Anything less dramatic?" He took a long drink of his lemonade, looking too damn sexy without Kim around to save me. I looked away. He laughed.

"Are you doing it on purpose?"

He shrugged with a sly dimpled smile as he licked a drop of lemonade from his lip. I was about to start screaming when he did something he hadn't done before. He closed his eyes, and with dark lashes haloing his lids, he breathed in and out, and dusted my bitchiness, using his own emotions to temper mine.

"Cool, huh?" he said once I was stable.

"So, you realized what else you can do to fuck with me, and you pull that shit out on the beach? What if Kim hadn't been there or if Caine was? I could strangle you."

"If Caine was, it would have been that much more interesting." He took another sip of his drink. I went to start again and he added, "I had no control then. That surprised the hell out of me. Right now, I was testing a theory. I can't remember how it started or how it stopped, but I do remember you chastising yourself for it afterwards."

Shit. "I'm not ashamed, or it wasn't because it was you. If Caine saw us, or if things got heavier—"

"Believe me," he leaned across the counter to wrap his hands around mine hugging my glass with a concentrated gaze strained through a wince from his visions, "if something's going to happen between us, I want it to be real. I want you to choose to be with me because it's what *you* want, not because we're tied up in some emotional hamster wheel we can't escape." He removed his hands from mine and blinked while he took another drink as if holding his visions at arm's length was more taxing than normal.

"Agreed," I said once I found my voice.

Feeling how genuine he was through the connection, made me feel better regarding his motives.

"Do you love him?" Donovan asked looking me straight in the eyes.

"Yes," I answered immediately, knowing he knew the answer already.

"Do you love me?"

My chin began to quiver. "Yes," I chirped, knowing it was true, feeling an ache as I said it. Water rushed to my eyes, but I blinked the tears away before they fell. I couldn't believe I said it aloud.

"Oh, babe, I'm sorry." He rounded the kitchen island, but I couldn't let him embrace me like I knew he wanted.

"I tried not to."

"You don't need to explain."

"I don't want to hurt either of you," I said, engulfed by my duplicity. Not everyone could appreciate what was beneath Donovan's playboy exterior and quarrelsome attitude, but something about him I couldn't help but love. I knew it wasn't influenced by the borrowed feelings of our past-life. It was something about *this* Donovan I cared for.

"It was selfish of me to ask knowing you'd either say it or lie about it, in which case I'd still know. I guess I needed to hear it."

I wiped my eyes. "Fuck, you're a masochist."

He laughed. "Too true. A masochist with impeccable patience." He leaned forward and pecked my forehead, a flicker of a vision hit him. "The important thing is that I *am* committed. For now, I can live with knowing you love me, even if you're with him. For now," he said with restored cockiness.

I couldn't help but smile as he blanketed me with comfort without physical contact, an ease I craved to sink into. I squirrelled away the sensation into my memory for when I needed it. Donovan wasn't the only masochist.

We set out to score some deals. The alcohol had diluted a little and I felt clearer headed, but the guilt refused to subside. I hung on to Kim and tried to channel her high energy, but the avoidance could only last so long. I would be alone with Caine before bed and needed to say a few things he wasn't going to like.

A vendor claimed to have a true quahog pearl in his possession.

We were skeptical and moved on. I picked up sunglasses for myself so Donovan could have his back, and a ring for Serena, white gold with a sapphire gem, her birthstone. Adding to the sales pitch, the seller explained the sapphire held properties of protection and wisdom. Kim nodded in confirmation. It was an absolute steal, especially after Donovan bartered it down by half. Kim was right, perfect time to haggle. Donovan happened to be a pro, though left me to wonder why.

Caine and I were looking over my buys as Kim was still shopping. A necklace with a dark amulet caught her eye. "What do you mean?" I heard her say. What I saw wasn't a cordial exchange. She was tense. Something wasn't right.

"Kim?" She didn't respond to me.

I approached her as she was putting on the necklace, then the merchant she was talking to collapsed and so did the one next to them. Everyone else followed. No screams, no commotion, just hundreds of Magics walking the grounds of Diluculo and sitting around the pyre enjoying their night, fell where they stood. Silence reigned. The crackle of the fire the only activity within earshot.

"What the fuck happened?" Donovan demanded as he ran over to us.

I knelt to feel for a pulse on the sweaty neck of the merchant Kim was talking to and found a steady, normal beat. "I think he's just passed out."

"He said to find him." Kim pulled the necklace off.

"Find who?" Donovan demanded.

"What do you mean?" Caine asked.

"The guy!" She frantically motioned at the unconscious merchant.

I knew something wasn't right. "It's okay. What'd he say?"

She stammered and I had to stop myself from shaking it out of her as Donovan raged.

"I liked the necklace." She held it in her fist, away from her as if she didn't want to touch it at all. "He was telling me about the properties, though I already knew, and then he said that he found us, and we needed to find him."

"Did he say who?" I asked.

She shook her head no. "But he said the necklace would bring me there." Her voice rose. "I didn't even want to put it on. He pulled some mind shit and made me."

"We have to assume it's Loring," Donovan said. "We need to find Aunt Lacey."

"How?" Caine said. "Search every passed-out body in Diluculo? She could be anywhere."

"No, but we can check a few," Donovan bit back. "If it is Loring, he's waiting for us, which means we have control of the timeline. Rushing to find him leaves us vulnerable. We can search a bit, get prepared, and then find out who did this. Play it smart."

Donovan was right. Either he's great in a crisis or he's done this before.

We stayed together and ran to The Witch Hunt close by. Nicole was laid out in one of the aisles with a couple of bags of marshmallows around her, a small amount of blood coming from her head. Donovan raced behind the curtain to search for Aunt Lacey while I healed cashier-slash-skater-girl's wound. I couldn't help everyone, but I could stop for her.

Aunt Lacey wasn't there. She wasn't in our cabin or in the other Elder's cabins either. We found Ranlyn outside of a smaller cabin with a bunch of others. He looked fine, but was also unconscious.

"Fuck!" Donovan was furious and nothing I said made it better. Didn't help I was emoting along with him. "Wait, I know a place she might be."

We passed the beach. I couldn't look. Too afraid to look. Until I remembered the buoyancy spell and was relieved there wouldn't be a bunch of dead bodies face down in the water.

A twenty-minute walk through dark, dense forest brought us to a ritual site. The place was empty, and we were left standing on the edge of a large pentagram created with boulders distinguishing its points with smaller stones.

"I don't know where else to search," Donovan said in defeat. "Next step is to get ready for—"

The ritual bowls at each point of the pentagram ignited in flames, jolting us in surprise. A man wearing dark clothing stood opposite us on the ritual circle. Fear stuck in my throat.

The man with grey eyes spoke in a deep, well-controlled voice. "Continue to search, but you will not find your precious Coven Leader, son."

Panic rose in gasps as I started to lose it. No one except Ranlyn saw the man the times he attacked me. They didn't know how dangerous he was. I grabbed Caine's arm, but I couldn't talk. I couldn't warn them. The heightened connection multiplied Donovan's confusion mixed with my panic had locked me in spot.

"Who's your son?" Kim asked.

The man smiled.

"What are you doing here, Daniel?" Caine asked with no love in his voice.

The eyes. Of course, the eyes. If I wasn't already near incapacitated, I would have blurted a "How the fuck do you know him?" How could he know?

By this point I was shaking. Donovan moved closer to me as at some point as I let go of Caine, leaning into Donovan to keep my knees from buckling.

"I've come for you, Caine," Daniel answered in a way I interpreted as a threat, though Caine didn't.

"You've got shitty timing. Twenty years ago would've been nice. A birthday call, spam email, anything." Caine's apathy was foreign to me as he mimicked his father's listless tone. "You had chances to involve yourself in my life. Why now? Why here?"

"I knew you would be here."

"Fine. I'm here. What do you want? And what did you do to everyone?"

"We needed to rid the possibility of interruptions and gave you the map to find what you seek. Why you would choose to associate with a Ballard after how many Berisfords cut them down, is beyond me, but only solidifies my decision." When his slate eyes slid to me, I wanted to vomit as a thousand questions attacked my brain.

His family killed mine? How?

"Who's we? Interruptions from what?" Caine asked without commenting about Berisfords and Ballards. Did he already know?

"Follow the necklace," Daniel concluded before disappearing. No running away, no smoke and mirrors. Gone. I didn't think he was here at all. Another illusion. Another lie.

I sank to the ground no longer able to hold myself up, Donovan falling with me. "What's the matter with you?" Donovan's voice shook as he pleaded with arms around me. "Say something."

Instead of gripping tighter to my reality, I fell deeper into myself. The questions and impact of what I saw too much to verbalize. Intense thoughts were scattered, too intense, theories fighting with each other as I over-analyzed each. A voice brought me through the haze and I found myself looking in Caine's eyes. They were the last thing I wanted to see. They were too close to Daniel's. Too cold.

"Sophie, calm down," Caine said and a wash of relief extinguished my panic and I could only focus on him. "Tell me what's the matter."

"Daniel's your father. Daniel's evil. He tried to take me." I heard myself say.

I snapped out of my dissociation to find Caine and Kim kneeling in front of me. Had Caine used his power on me? How long had I been sitting here? Donovan's hand touched my shoulder and shifted to get a better look at me as he too cleared the fog as we sat together, me between his legs and leaning back into him on the grass. I don't know what cleared my brain goo, but when I reconnected with my environment, I looked to the place I last saw Daniel.

I looked up at Caine. "When did you find out your father was evil?"

A beat passed. "When I met my Uncle Eli and his family."

"And about what Berisfords did to the Ballards?"

He nodded.

"I can't...." I was unable to vocalize more.

"He left when I was a baby! How was I supposed to know he'd show up here of all goddamned places?"

"Don't get defensive with me." I stood up, Donovan scrambling to help me. "You could have told me. About my family, about your dad. Or at least told Aunt Lacey so she could put two and two together."

"I knew you would do this," he muttered.

"Do what?"

"Aunt Lacey already knew," he deflected. "It's not like you can keep a secret from her."

"You should have told me," I said with slow consideration.

"I couldn't."

"Bullshit," Donovan hissed, channelling my sinking dread. "After all your preaching of doing good by her and then you do this?"

"So what? You thought I'd hate you for what your family is? For what they did?" My eyesight blurred, my blood pumping against my temples.

"For fearing what I might become," Caine answered.

Kim spoke before I could. "Don't you think having her understand your history, that with her gift she'd be able to see it if your soul became Tainted and, I don't know, help?"

"No, I didn't, actually. Regardless, even you admitted to turning a blind eye when it involved the person you loved."

"Wow. Scummy, epic, low-blow, Caine. Good job." My heart wrenched at the thought of my ex pulling the wool over my eyes and how I was strong enough to tell Caine about it. Now it was the excuse used for him to lie to me? No fucking way. Dizzy with information overload and pissed at my gathering tears, I fought my vertigo. As Caine's words slithered within me, I knew Donovan experienced every wave of unmentionable misery. "Put the necklace on, let's get this the fuck over with." Kim looked at me. I stared back in clear communication that I was done talking to Caine until she slipped the long necklace of her head.

"Wow," she said and pointed, "This way."

I followed, happy to head toward whatever awaited us.

23

NO REAL DAMAGE

Caine

Donovan lingered as Sophie and Kim left. I ran my hands through my hair, hating myself for breaking my promise again by causing her pain. I didn't know what the hell I was doing. Maybe this was the beginning of my decline.

Donovan got up close and said, "The thought of Sophie upset, and I'm here feeling her betrayal and embarrassment without being able to do anything about it, makes me as useless as tits on a watermelon. So, tell me, what are you going to do now?"

I shook my head. This wasn't enough for me and nowhere close enough for Donovan who went on without waiting for me to get my shit together.

"I don't care about your guilt," he said, "or your self-hatred, or your daddy issues, because I don't give a shit about you. I shouldn't even be trying to help, except for the fact that Sophie doesn't hate you enough to move on yet. How one person can feel this much pain and still walk away from the person who inflicted it, I'll never understand, but she did. If we get through whatever the Hell your father is setting us up for, your first move better be to fix this."

"Do you know about her ex?" I asked him.

Donovan exhaled and shook his head.

"They were engaged. Some abusive junkie prick right under her nose, until he disappeared. She knew what he was and never left him, all because she loved him."

"What's your point?"

"It took a crowbar for her to open up to me. I'd rather it end now before she gets too involved. None of my family thought they'd be evil, but they are, my father included."

"If you can't fight me, the guy who's been doing my damndest to dick your girlfriend, then how are you going to turn evil? Believe me, man, you don't have the stomach."

"You don't know me."

Donovan laughed. "Never tell her I agreed with her, but Sophie was right about one thing. You and I are too much alike."

"Don't make this about you."

"I'm not. It's very much about Sophie and her difficulties with distinguishing differences between us. The part she doesn't know, though I'd have told her if in your shoes, is that I came from a family of corrupt sons of bitches too. The difference? The evil fuckers raised me. I was witness and subjected to horrific shit. Forced to participate and tortured in the name of it. People like them think as long as you can heal, there's no real damage. The scars are on the inside."

For some reason, I knew Donovan wasn't lying.

"Now," Donovan went on, "we need to catch up with them and I need to figure out a way to stop this emotional loop shit from coming between whatever we might find wherever the necklace leads. Aunt Lacey might be there, and you'll never be more important to me than her. Fuck this up with your issues and I won't be so nice anymore."

"This is you being nice?"

"Yes. It is," he said and walked towards where we last saw Sophie and Kim.

Again, I believed him.

24

HOW STRONG CAN ONE PERSON BE?

As much as I wanted to bad mouth Caine to Kim, I didn't have it in me. Lies are one part of the equation. I can forgive someone if forgiveness is sought, but the way it happened didn't work for me. And I had to endure this as Donovan emoted along with me.

And more important than our drama, Daddy-dearest with the hell-seeping soul was wondering around somewhere, leading us to an obvious trap we had no choice but to walk into. Everyone else was unconscious and leaving Diluculo wasn't an option I was willing to take.

Footsteps snapped branches behind us. "Just us," Donovan said as we spun to the sound in the darkness.

We resumed walking, following what Kim described was a silvery thread marking a path through the foliage. It was so dark. Moonlight filtered through the trees enough to create deep shadows. It could be taking us in circles, and we wouldn't know the difference.

Instead of listening to inner dialogue I couldn't run away from, I asked Caine to tell us everything he knew about Daniel. Shame was toxic, and his voice was littered with it as he repeated what he learned from his Uncle Eli.

"He possessed the merchant and then influenced me to put on the necklace, didn't he?" Kim asked.

"No idea," Caine said. "But if Aunt Lacey helped him perfect his power, then chances are he's mastered far more than I have. Maybe Aunt Lacey and the Elders are outside Diluculo and that's why we can't find them."

"She wouldn't leave without telling me." Donovan was resolved in that fact and wasn't about to explain why.

"Maybe he does have her and he's trying to get back at her for ditching him when he went dark?" Kim thought.

"That doesn't make sense," Donovan said. "His motives run deeper. Or they're not his motives at all."

"You're thinking Loring?" I guessed.

"Daniel's a devotee. Devotees don't do anything their Masters don't allow."

"I have no clue what devotees do," I said, "But maybe he went rogue and is here for Caine."

"Can't be about me," Caine said. "I have nothing to offer him."

"Come on, Caine," I stepped around a tree I almost walked into. "You're biological kryptonite. Same unique powers, virtually untrained, and baby-fresh loyalty to his enemy. I can't see the silvery glow other immortals have because his soul is so Tainted, but he barely looks older than you. He has all the time in the world and a legacy to uphold. Aunt Lacey said you were going to need to make a big choice. One that if chosen wrong would leave you better off in the sleeping curse. This fits the glass slipper."

Caine didn't have anything to say to that and Donovan and Kim declined to comment. Either way, I couldn't blame him for not wanting it to be true. To live your whole life without a father only to have them appear now, under these circumstances, was bizarre and cruel.

Even though Caine was a triple-decker-douche today, I wished I could get a taste for his emotional cornucopia. He was headed to see his estranged father who was most likely responsible for kidnapping the Elders. One of those people being the woman who brought him into the world of magic and facilitated his acceptance of the gifts he possessed. Even taking myself out of the current conflict, it was unfair for Caine to have to go through all this after all the horrible things he had already endured.

How strong can one person be?

As far as a plan, we had no low-risk strategies. Staging an intricate and courageous coup involving a double-cross with impressive weaponry would be nice, but we didn't have the accessories or the know-how to pull it off. Since we didn't know what Daniel wanted, anticipating what to expect was impossible.

Our plan-less expedition against an immortally evil and truant sperm donor brought us deeper and deeper into the forest. A range of emotions hit me as we shuffled through heavy brush to the sounds of crackling branches and our tense silence as no one talked.

What became clear, was that the atmosphere had transformed. The forest adopted a chill in the air and a buzz of activity living in the trees. The sound of fluttering wings and chattering teeth like the wildlife came out of hiding. Diluculo was a witch-made paradise. There were no bugs. These woods were everything the world was outside of Diluculo, but we hadn't crossed back over the veil. No way would we have missed that.

Burrs scratched my bare legs, branches whipped me in my face, my calves ached in a reminder that hiking wasn't an every weekend activity.

Daniel appeared beyond a few thick trees.

A splash of heat hit the back of my neck and enveloped my chest. Shit, I'm already losing it. Desperate to counteract my building freak-out, I grabbed Donovan's hand, hoping to strengthen our connection and keep calm.

Why it was a shock to see Daniel again, I had no clue, but as soon as the man came into full view, my eyes snapped shut, my control slipping like it took a final step off the ledge with a "fuck it, I'm done" attitude.

My feet stopped, the swirl of panic seizing my muscles as I swallowed hard. Tranquilizing peace rolled over my entire body, flushing away the urgent sense of terror. A squeeze around my fingers told me Donovan was seeing a vision of us. When I let go and opened my eyes to Donovan next to me, his expression was serene, a smile filled with hubris adding to the mix of emotions amalgamating in my skull. Then a sweep of calm rushed over me as he furthermore controlled our emotional flow.

For a quick-tempered personality like Donovan's, I was impressed.

Out of the dense section of forest tapering off to a clearing up ahead, I watched Caine tense like a poised snake. I worried what he would do, his stare was one I had never seen Caine wear, his anger so thick his features turned to stone.

Whatever he wanted to do, he held back, and followed as his father turned his back on us and led us across a field.

Wooden cabins were built in the same semi-circular arrangement as the other cabins we stayed, all in rows. Several out-buildings were peppered around untamed land, bigger than any of the stores of Diluculo, the space smaller than where we travelled from. The largest buildings looked more akin to Aboriginal long houses kids learn about in grade school, two stories high and as long as a football field constructed of tree trunks so thick it made the logs from the bonfire Nitsa welcomed, captivated, and warmed the Coveners, look like toothpicks in comparison.

Unlike the Diluculo behind the buffering of forest, this place was a shithole. Ruins were once cabins, now burnt matchstick houses ready to fall apart with the force of a strong breeze. Gaping holes yawned where walls once held strong.

Daniel led us to one of those cabins. Out in the open space of the field the unhindered winds beat against us. The building towered over us as each step brought us closer. What also grew was the sound of voices escaping the ragged building, at least two. More alarming were the dark figures of two men standing outside of the entrance, flanking the doors like steroid infused security guards. These guards weren't carrying weapons on their hips like cops. The assumption was that *they* were the weapons capable of more damage than a slug or taser.

Convenient bookends equipped with blackened souls and matching stares indicative of lifelong soldiers. I caught their Tainted souls as their inner darkness escaped them, even in the night, swirling around them like a nebulous of evil. Twin sources of darkness in every form, right down to the identical ginger mutton chops.

Identical twins.

And we've seen them before. Outside Aunt Lacey's when Loring killed a man and tried to take me the first time.

The doppelgangers dark eyes shifted in unison to evaluate us like targets, their inert expressions unchanged as we got closer. Daniel stopped about twenty feet away from the opening.

Without command, the men pushed the wooden doors inwards, the flickering orange glow of a controlled fire spilling out into the darkness before the guards resumed their positions. From where we stood outside, the guarded doors were our only exit. I couldn't see the back of the building, but my gut told me this one was chosen for a reason.

Once we got inside, the building was daunting. We stepped onto pressed red dirt, the floors demolished for firewood now burning in a pit in the middle of the room, creating shadows on once Royal blue papered walls. From the look of ragged edges of a floor above, a loft was all that was left of a second floor.

Perched near the fire on a large wine barrel, sporting a grin full of crocodile teeth, was Loring. His legs hung over the edge of the barrel, feet above the ground while retaining an air of dapper fierceness. Pushing off the barrel, red floor dust billowed from his leather shoes as he landed. He fixed his deep purple button-up that revealed dark curls on his chest, an extreme contrast against pale skin.

"Harkin, Earc," Loring called looking past our small group to The Reds who pushed the doors shut and stood in front of them inside the building, trapping us inside.

The shot of "we're fucked" from Donovan was as equally strong as his acceptance, as if he hadn't expected anything less.

Daniel's soul was damn near angelic compared to Loring's. The dark haired, devilish grinned, psychopath in front of us was saturated in undiluted evil. Darkness consumed the space around him. His soul acidic.

I shrugged on my finest poker face, breathing away incapacitating panic Donovan fought to manage remotely, my veneer threatening to crack any moment.

Daniel stood to the side, hands folded in front of him, back straight, feet shoulder length apart, reminiscent of the guarding Reds. Heart of a soldier. A woman stood near him with long-fingernailed hands on lean, scantily clad hips, a sculpted self-righteous brow sizing us up while her Tainted soul had issues making up its mind. As I saw it, her Tainted soul had one foot in the pit of evil, while the rest still tread in the light.

A cur.

The term applied to mixed breeds of dogs, one I learned while searching for Bosco, but also applied to cowardice. This chick was either fresh to her sinister path or too much of a coward to make the defining choice.

Comfortable with her beauty, her piercing blue eyes were cocky as she strode her five-inch heeled boots over to Loring. He wrapped his arm around the waist of her lace bodice and black velvet trench without addressing her as if she was expected to come to him, flipping her bleached-blonde hair over her shoulder as if proud to be called upon.

"Finally, Salix, we meet again, in person. How's your father?" Loring spoke with his smooth old-world accent with a pompous rasp devoid of any true remorse. His smile creased the age lines of his face while still managing to be silver-screen handsome.

"You corralled us here for a reason," Caine said. "I'm not up for reunions, so spell it out."

Daniel and Loring exchanged a look around the chick. Daniel shrugged and Loring gave a stout laugh that made me cringe. "I preferred Cole, much easier to impress."

Loring shoved his free hand into his pants pocket, while I looked at Caine to see if he knew what Loring meant. Judging by the whites of his eyes, he was clueless.

"This boy of yours is something else though, Daniel." He looked back at Caine, tilting his head back with his eyes closed as if taking in the atmosphere. "Much more powerful."

Tensed and looking like he may lose his shit, Caine was breathing too hard, blinking too often, as his power came alive and prickled my skin.

"Easy there, son," Daniel warned and stepped forward with an outstretched hand.

"Don't you dare call me son!"

Caine's outburst made me flinch, but Daniel's warning sounded genuine. Something Caine didn't seem to notice while his cheeks turned red and his fists shook. The man's motives confused me, but he seemed to be scared his son might be in danger if he lost control.

"What do you know about Cole?" Caine pressed.

Loring gave an obnoxious belly laugh in his scratchy booming voice with a loud clap of his hands. "Right there is why I gotta love you, Caine." Then he turned back to Daniel with expressive motions as he yelled, "Kid's got spunk! You, my boy, are a gift to future generations. A man of power!" He fisted the air as if playing to an invisible crowd. "I feel it. The Persuasion!" His tongue grazed his bottom lip like a snake. "You require work. Fine tuning." He waved a finger, then settled his hands in his pockets again. "Yet already such promise."

"You two can play later. I'm not interested in your bullshit agenda," Donovan snapped. "What did you do to everyone? And where are the Elders?"

Loring's dark eyes panned over to Donovan and he tsked him a few times. "You, a Sorrel, speaks with all the clout of your ancestors yet partakes in this fancy of do-gooders you call Elders. Pathetic. You should be at my side instead of challenging me. You and Caine have more in common than the woman you flank."

Kim and I looked at Donovan, but the impact of Daniel's words never touched Donovan's features. Apparently, 'Sorrel' was Donovan's last name, though I hadn't heard it before. Kim looked equally surprised.

"Save your disappointment and skip the foreplay. You got us here, play your hand already."

Loring's laugh came as a sinister giggle his cur girlfriend shared. The man clasped his hands under his chin and turned to Daniel. "Do you desire the honour?" He waggled thick eyebrows as if he was passing on a great privilege to his underling.

Looking to his right, to a green, weather-beaten tarp, a quick hand movement, and Daniel flung the tarp away without ever touching it, revealing stacked, bloodied, and naked bodies of the missing Elders, some missing guards, including a few others I didn't recognize, one face too obliterated to identify.

I recoiled at the sight of flayed skin hanging like shredded meat, revealing dark layers of muscle and blood-soaked yellow fat pockets. Skin still intact had been torn, maybe by small blades, the tissue too bruised to see, some so swollen they looked like they may burst any moment.

They were probably alive when they were tortured. The evil laughing bastard would never find fun in mutilating them after death. No. Each of them endured unimaginable pain until Loring was satisfied and allowed them to die.

Kim gasped the loudest, but no one was untouched by the brutality. As the Elder's bodies were revealed, Loring's immense whoop of laughter and his piece of ass cackle made the horror much more severe. The disconnect between that laugh and what we were looking at was too divided to comprehend. A product of such evil and a side of his fake dicktip-duster, all I could think was I wanted to take the cur bitch looking for street cred down before we joined the pile.

"All of them?" Kim lashed out. "For what?"

Donovan grabbed Kim by the arm to prevent her from getting any closer. He wasn't nice about it, but she didn't complain, too focused on Loring.

Blondie gave an incredulous leer while Loring's insidious grin widened. He enjoyed the spectacle as if it somehow gave credence to his efforts. No part of this piece of shit understood remorse for snubbing out the lives of the old souls. No moral compunction existed in that smile.

Baffled by what I never expected seeing walking into this place, I tried not to look at the heap of bodies, my brain working to discount them as real. I was standing in a bombed-out barn inside a witch-made bubble between worlds with a psycho on a killing spree.

What the fuck happens now?

25

ENLIGHTENING BRUTALITY

My reasoning kicked in as I struggled to make sense of everything, desperate to be distracted from the horror flickering in the fire light.

This freak loves an audience. He wanted us to find this scene. Why here?

"Sharp as a tack, Soul Seer!" Loring answered my thoughts with enthusiasm. "While I do enjoy the extolment of others, this arena was a necessary element." Every sentence was spoken with immense verve as he paced, brimming with passion. "This place was once the glory of Creations. Pario!" He screamed its name. "We gave birth to this Creation before they watered-down the world and named it Diluculo." He sneered at the name. "Pario was the quintessential specimen of the power it professes to be. Our essence is tethered to this world, is it not?" No one answered though he eyed us as if we should have. He scraped his hands along the floor coming up with fistfuls of the reddish dirt he let sieve through his fingers. "The raw dirt and grime that sprouts pure beauty and may even be responsible for mankind itself, in which case, all of us would be the fruits of its labour. Fakes," he pointed to the pile of bodies, "driven by nothing more than their avarice need for perfection and self-serving omnipotence!" He threw down the remaining dirt as he stared at us, pausing his tirade, yet not his fuming rage.

I didn't want his self-righteous attention on me, but his ranting was something to keep my eyes from gliding over to the heap of mutilated bodies still seeping bodily fluids to the floor. Nitsa's ribs were slashes of exposed bone, her green eyes open and staring as if she died in the grips of fear. Hallden's long pale hair, loose and tangled with chunks of tissue and clotted blood, covered his face. Roon was a pretzel, a tangle of broken limbs crippled beyond recognition, his fingers gnarled strips of bone broken and dislocated in gory angles.

One relieving aspect hit me when I focused enough to realize Aunt Lacey was missing from the bloody grouping. Is she still alive?

"Again!" Loring yelled in a tone akin to a five-year old's vibrancy, making me jump. He held a manicured finger to his temple. "So, astute!" Fuck. This mind-reading thing was getting old. "You are correct, Firefly." I cringed at hearing Olive's nickname for me. "Your beloved Aunt Lacey has not yet succumbed to her deserving end."

"You tortured them for a reason." I feigned confidence. "All fun and games or are you making a point?" He smiled a fiendish smile but continued with the game by remaining silent. "Where's Aunt Lacey? She in one of these buildings or a different Creation full of assholes like you?" His smile widened, wrinkling his face further. "Nah. She's here. Psychopaths like you keep their toys close." If he wanted to talk to me, he was going to have to deal with the attitude.

Loring looked to the ground, with a sarcastic shrug of his lips, then peered up at Daniel. "This conversation requires a visual aid, don't you agree Daniel?" Daniel didn't move, his eyes still locked on his son as they had been the whole time. "Retrieve our guest of honour."

Daniel gave an obedient nod, and with one long leap, bound to the loft that used to be the second floor. A moan of agony, and something heavy dragged against the beaten wooden floors above us.

Daniel telekinetically dragged something to the jagged edge. Every eye locked in rapt anticipation.

When Daniel heaved a six-foot tall wooden, oblong shape with barbed wire wrapped around it an immeasurable number of times, to the edge, I didn't know what to think.

Without touching the strange piece of wood, Daniel spun it around. The wood base screeched our eardrums as it revealed Aunt Lacey strapped by the barbed wire to the wood plank, naked, her dignity disposable to Loring as the barbed wire ripped into her flesh, cutting across the right side of her face, down her chin, and around her throat. Her eyes were open, conscious through the pain. She didn't speak, but her eyes prayed for relief.

When Daniel made the reveal, the air in the room gushed with offensive powers, each of us unable to douse our energies against the visual shock, flaring in fury at the sight of our Leader, our teacher, our confidant, enduring such cruel torture.

Things happened fast, but too slow to stop Donavan from hurdling to attack Daniel. I sprung forward. Caine grabbed my shoulders. All I managed was a gargled "Ahk!" and an outstretched hand to snatch the back of Donovan's shirt, catching nothing. A few feet off the ground flying up at Caine's father, Loring looked in Donovan's direction and sent him careening backward, laying him out in the dirt sucking air that flew out of his chest like a scattered flock of pigeons. I was hit by the same breathless shove and fall. Oxygen disappeared from my lungs, both of us writhing in the dirt floor, grabbing at our chests. The veins in my neck strained, close to bursting as Donovan's regret surged along our connection.

Loring made an intrigued sound and mumbled tritely, "Fabulous. Two birds...."

The Reds each raised a hand and sent a shot of energy to both Caine and Kim's legs, taking them down to their knees, trapping them in place by invisible shackles.

A long time passed before my oxygen returned, doubled over and wheezing as Caine watched me with crumpled features from where

The Reds crippled him. Loring's booming laughter made it worse, as did his bimbo cur jumping up and down like his personal cheerleader.

"I find your interpretation a most fitting epithet, Soul Seer," Loring said in response to my cursing thoughts. "A cur." Loring smiled and held his cheerleader close with a hand outlined on her jaw as he stared into her eyes. "She is, isn't she? Not quite committed." The cur looked warily from Loring to me, unaware of what he was talking about. "Don't worry, love, you'll prove your worth soon enough." She looked no less uncomfortable but smiled without it erasing the slim panic in her eyes.

"Why don't you and Elsa join us, comrade?" Loring called to Daniel with a lingering stare at his half-breed arm candy.

Daniel raised a hand to make the wooden contraption hover, then stepped off the side of the loft landing with the grace of a ballerina. He let Aunt Lacey, still strapped by cutting wire, to land so hard her eyes rolled backward as a moan fell from slack lips. The strand across her cheek scraped down her jaw and now cut into her jugular as blood flowed and dripped off her painted pale pink toes.

Something in Donovan crumbled at seeing Aunt Lacey in pain. His breath was restored, but his hesitance meant he wasn't moving to save her again even if The Reds weren't holding us all down now.

Loring strode behind Aunt Lacey and craned his neck to draw his thin lips close to her ear. "Nothing the all-mighty Elder cannot endure, right?" He wretched on the loosened wire from the fall and tightened it around her throat causing horrendous choking and gurgling noises as her windpipe compressed. "You pray for such fortune," he hissed and let the wire go.

Composing his mask of pure hate to something more waxed, Loring circled in front of Aunt Lacey towards us. The Reds telekinetically flipped both me and Donovan over onto our backs, pinning us in submissive positions as Loring looked over him.

"I'll fucking kill you!" Donovan spat, his fists so tight my hands ached.

"Ahh, such moxie, Sorrel. Do you know who you champion for?" Loring motioned to our remaining Elder. "This woman is not the personification of virtue she dares to clothe herself in."

He went back to put a hand on either side of Aunt Lacey's head against the wood structure she was strapped to, his face less than six inches away. Our hold loosened, allowing Donovan and I to shift to our knees. A move Donovan took greedily before his leash hit its end.

"You've killed. You've tortured. In numbers as great as mine," Loring yelled while Aunt Lacey's bleary eyes continued to roll, his heavy breath moving her sweat and blood-soaked hair, "yet you live amongst the sycophants. Idolized. Worshiped." He reached a hand above him. "Held on an iconic pedestal as one of the great Elders when you are no more virtuous than I." He paused. "When you find your place in the pile with the rest of your pitiable Mother Coven Elders, then you will have found your rightful throne."

Pulling himself away from her as if it was a great feat to continue to permit her to live, Loring turned to his fiendish cling-on. "Malina, another treatment, my pet."

"Yes, Master!" she exclaimed like using the title gave her a cheap thrill that perked her nipples.

Without the silky movements of Daniel, Malina ran to the east wall and scaled it like a panther. Her hurried footsteps ran across the loft floor and when she returned at its edge, she held in hand a large, galvanized bucket. With minimal fumbling she grabbed the thin handle and poured its contents over Aunt Lacey's body on the first floor below her.

A shrill noise came from Aunt Lacey the instant the liquid hit her and splashed the surplus to the ground around her, darkening a patch of red dirt as we fought to jump back and create distance. Since our bodies were permitted small movements we didn't get far, turning our faces bracing for some type of burning reaction.

Nothing happened.

Not to us.

A moment passed before the seemingly benign liquid defused

light from Aunt Lacey's soul. Usually her brilliance pained my eyes, now the light around her was faded and sickly. I was too freaked out to notice how diminished her soul glow was when we showed up.

Aunt Lacey's cries thrummed my heartstrings, unable to compose herself against the damage Loring inflicted.

"What is that? What are you doing to her?" Kim shouted at Malina, who laughed like a hyena and lobbed the bucket at Kim's head. Kim recoiled. The bucket missed and bounded with a ping off the ground behind her.

Malina jumped down to join her Master, her trench floated like a cape around her. She planted a sensuous kiss on the man, hugging him with her hips, pressing them against him like she would wrap her legs around him at any moment with a clear invitation. The pair had no aversion to the display in front of a handful of onlookers, next to the mangled woman, plus, the pile of disfigured and rotting corpses. No doubt got off on the show.

"A special treat I requisitioned from an old friend," Loring explained with feigned apathy once he pulled himself away. "Goofer dust, black-ram's head, knotweed with the added bonus of corn oil. After all, this is the celebration of the harvest." He laughed. "Furthermore, some good ol' vinegar for a boost of fun. Perfect." You would think he was describing his famous prize-winning chicken recipe, but after another pompous glorifying moment, he spun to Kim pantomiming a Bob Barker microphone and said, "And what does that equal, Kitchen Witch?"

Kim flinched as he spun expecting a coming blow, then stammered. "Umm, knotweed binds. Goofer dust—"

"Oooh, times up, Kitchen Witch," he said retaining his game show host persona. "Yes, knotweed binds, but my special friend made some especially damning adjustments. What we have here folks is one seriously ill-fated witch." He let loose with another echoing laugh while Malina joined in with her own hideous cackle, all the while Daniel stood tense, keeping watch like The Reds.

"It's keeping her weak." My eyes welled with tears as Aunt Lacey looked to me with an expression that confirmed my Soul Seeing assessment. "I can barely *see* her."

Aunt Lacey was now no more effective than the mortal Blind.

"I'm so happy you're all here to witness the beauty of her fall," Loring said. "Give up, Elsa. Even Gareth and Nya knew when enough was enough." His statement brought Aunt Lacey's eyes wide to study him as he spoke about her son and his wife, the reaction pleasing Malina who bit on her lips hiding a giggle.

"I'm ecstatic after all these years I can still surprise you, my old friend." He circled her barbed trap making her move her head to try and keep her sight on him as the barbs dug deeper and spilled more blood. "Nya was always conflicted over the prospect of forever." He accentuated "forever" with a wave of his hand. "Convincing her to give herself to the Witchburners took a mere nudge." Aunt Lacey mouth slacked without words. "Of course, Gareth would never abandon his love, so even though he was against it, he followed loyal-ly." Concluding his wandering to stand face to face with his victim, he continued as fresh tears streamed through the blood and wetness of the concoction on Aunt Lacey's sallow cheeks.

"You were present that afternoon." He continued. "Watched the blaze devour them. The stench of smouldering tissue filled the square while they spilled their excrement when the pain became too great. Gareth was steadfast in the decision to perish beside his beloved and chose to leave you bereaved." He shrugged as if his part in the killing of her family was minuscule, torture for his recollection inflicted in such depths in Aunt Lacey she risked harming herself more by shifting around in her trap with nowhere to escape his words. "But of course, not without sending a part of them into the future," he added with a hint of disapproval and sneered at both Caine and I.

Aunt Lacey's eyes filled with rage, now thrashing in her restraints as barbs chewed into her bones.

"Eternal life isn't for everyone, children." Loring spoke like a teacher as if he had any right to advise anyone, then turned back to Aunt Lacey. "Since you and your now deceased and neatly stacked friends would have known if I were to have struck Gareth and Nya down myself, I was forced to use less exciting means to achieve certain ends. Nothing unlike the brutality that ensued, right here, on Pario soil. This land I helped *you* create once upon a time. The same land you and your friends destroyed when *you* started the war!" Taking a step closer to gloat in her face again. "You should have known I'd find a way in."

All that escaped Aunt Lacey's lips were indecipherable words strained in a hoarse whisper.

"Deny as you need, oh my teacher," he wagged a finger at her, "you know you are at fault. For the coven and I you sought to destroy were doing nothing but what we were born to do. The powerful should never cower to the unenlightened and, since they were given the prestigious opportunity to join, I don't see it as our fault some refused the invitation."

I pictured the terrified people he claimed to have given a choice to either join or die. Many Blind must have refused the offer and were slaughtered for the Elders to feel a war was necessary.

Loring turned to us four Seedlings, a nefarious grin replaced his previous snarl. "So, I extend to you, my potential pets." Our answers hung off the edge of our tongues before he concluded his pitch, but he raised his hands to thwart a quick dismissal and our mouths were sealed shut. "Let me finish." He bit at his lip, then when satisfied his little spell had shut us up, said, "I've seen those rings before. I know what they mean. Elsa here has been waiting for you two for centuries."

He patted the wood above Aunt Lacey's head. "With the addition to your already powerful inherited bloodlines, I see no reason for either of you to decline. Even the Kitchen Witch here is useful." Kim did not look impressed. "Oh, and of course, Sophie, I wouldn't forget about your true love Donovan," he looked to the subject of his pitch. "Especially knowing you were birthed of the Sorrel flock. It should be no challenge to shed this noble defiance you're carrying."

Donovan and I looked at each other. Not that Loring's word was trustworthy, it was still weird to hear him refer to us as true loves and I wondered why he thought so.

Now Loring addressed Donovan. "They fought beside me and conquered many. Your psychometry alone is underutilized within the Mother Coven. Though most of your skills have been neglected, thrown aside at your request." Loring shook his head and placed a condescending hand over his chest as he looked down at Donovan still held subservient on his knees. "I would be honoured to have you."

Permitted to speak, Donovan declined in a much less than courteous fashion which involved him standing to his feet, bracing his stance, and squaring his shoulders to say, "I'll join. When you floss your teeth with my taint hair and gargle my balls."

This had Loring laughing. As part of the game, the offer giving him justified cannon fodder to state "he tried his best" before we ended up strapped to a plank and thrown in the body pile when he was finished. Since Donovan stood, the rest of us did too. Loring, confident in dismissing us as a viable threat, waved off The Reds.

"I must admit, I am a little surprised at your unenthusiastic reaction, Caine. The pathetic gathering of Sophie's family cannot satisfy your need for a solid familial foundation. Yet the chance to reconnect with your father," he looked to Daniel whose gaze was affixed to his son with an awakened yearning that surprised me, "your brother jumped at the chance."

"What do you know about Cole?" Caine asked, bringing us full circle.

"Oh Cole, he had promise. He did. Your father's need to seek his boys out perplexed me to the highest, but he insisted children of his loins would grow to be powerful men, and since Cole showed promise and you had not, there was no need to recruit you."

"You're lying."

"Do not dismiss it as falsehood so hastily. Suspend your disbelief, Caine, as it seems you never knew your brother quite as well as you thought. For I assure you when he was approached, he welcomed it *all* to be by your father's side and was devoted to the cause."

Loring's account of what had transpired was overshadowed as Daniel bowed his head in some type of lamentable manner. This caught Loring's attention, though Daniel was attempting to collect himself the instant his grief became observable.

"Oh Daniel, do not allow the memory of Cole to intrude on such a momentous occasion. His death was unavoidable."

Caine's eyes widened. "You killed him? He joined you and you..." His anger built with a prickle of power. "The accident?"

"Nope." Loring gave a smug waggled finger in the air. "Not an accident, but a means of disposal. Cole was too eager to cause dissention in the ranks and sabotage my plans once daddy here, let it slip we were attempting to re-enter Pario." He looked at Daniel with disapproval. "Cole thought it would start a war." Loring shrugged. "Knowing what that would mean and, in his zeal, to please his father, he threatened to notify our Coven Master and stole a rather important item needed to get into the Creation. Unforgivable."

Cole's stolen stuff from Caine's. Whatever Cole stole must have been in the boxes.

Why Loring insisted on telling us everything if he was going to kill us anyway was annoying, but I couldn't help but listen and wonder at Caine's memory of the accident. He never mentioned anything different about Cole. He couldn't have known.

"A coven friend with the power to Transmutate made the choice of his favourite animal. A coyote, if I recall," Loring said with indifference. "A step onto an opportunistic curve in the road and all was set. Try as he might, Cole could not save himself and a sleeping curse kept you sedated. Far from dead, but enough. Until you connected with your vessels other half incarnate. Your son *was* a strong one, I'll give you that," Loring granted Aunt Lacey, as if she should have thanked him for the compliment and then looked to me. "Nya's power kept you strong enough to prevent the inebriate Jack from ending you." His voice dropped. "He earned his freedom for braving the attempt."

Another swell of power surged from Donovan, and now from me, as Loring admitted his interference, it taking everything in me not to attack, knowing I would be dead like a swatted fly and would bring Donovan down with me.

Loring paced towards Aunt Lacey to look over his work. I glanced at Caine and saw those smoky eyes focused inwards on his thoughts instead of the room.

A coyote? How could he not notice a coyote? In rural Ontario they were common, but not in downtown St. Catharines. Even in the rain he could mistake it for a dog, but he said he didn't remember anything.

"The weather, too?" Caine asked. "It wasn't normal." Loring shrugged, taking it as a compliment having influenced earthly elements. "And you knew?" he asked Daniel who didn't respond. "Eli will be interested to hear how far you've fallen from your pact."

Daniel's expression hardened. "You knew too much."

"Knew what? Cole's plan? I didn't even know you contacted him or about these powers. How the fuck could I know?"

The light bulb turned on, morphing Daniel's expression to one of disbelief when he realized Caine was telling the truth. He looked to his Master. "You didn't..." He stopped mid-sentence and betrayal walked across his stormy eyes.

"Semantics, Daniel. Either way, you agreed their deaths were best." Loring then busied his attention to the ever-needy Malina pawing at him.

Tension clutched the atmosphere. We watched as Daniel's thoughts drew him in at this revelation of Loring's plans to dispatch both of his children. In a flash and a wail of a raucous battle cry, the tension broke on the end of Daniel's power bloating the air, making us take an automatic step back in an instinctual defensive crouch. Loring flew up off his feet and was slammed into the ground by Daniel's telekinetic attack. Dust billowed from underneath Loring as

Malina screeched when her Master was snatched from her groping hands.

Daniel tossed Loring against the ragged west wall behind him before Loring could find his feet, hanging his Master upside down now facing the group with a snarl of anger.

Donovan spun in a whirl from the corner of my eye, his arms outstretched with a pulse of energy propelled into Harkin and Earc before they could take an interceding step to save their Master. The energy was impressive, it coursing through me, trembling within my hands. Kim and I spun in time to witness Donovan's power hit The Reds mid-stride. His attack knocked them backward through the battered wooden doors, forcing them to crank open and blow outward, and sending the twins and the splintered doors off their hinges out into the darkness.

While Donovan skillfully took care of The Reds, Malina ran to help her suspended lover, letting out a shrill scream and releasing a wave of wind that hurled itself against Daniel in a feeble attempt to blind him with crimson dust from the floor. It paled to Daniel's, or even Donovan's, attack. Caine's father retaining his grip on Loring who moved wildly like a trapped cat against the rough wood. Caine used Malina's weak distraction, experiencing no difficulty mimicking Donovan's efforts, and sent the cur bitch flying. She collided with the dwindling fire, then skidded across the floor into a broken dividing wall. This knocked her out cold while her boots smouldered from the flames.

The dust from Malina's attack coated the air and distracted Daniel enough to release a flailing Loring. Daniel dropped him head-first into the stacked pile of ravished bodies below, their blood smearing across his face and clothing. Loring bounced back into fighting form, looking more savage now in the blood of his victims.

My mind wasn't shifting into attack mode like the others. I was stunned as I watched bodies flying, consumed by power that reverberated through my body from the Magics in the room and the bond shared with Donovan.

Kim grabbed my arm and dragged me to where the wooden doors once hung. "Be my look-out!"

"Look-out for what? What are you doing?" I glanced back at the others after hearing Loring's boisterous laugh and watched as Caine was catapulted across the room, landing with a huff in the dirt. I went to run to his aid since Loring was entertained by the Seedlings attempt to fight him, treating it like a game, until Kim stopped me in another strong grip.

"Those gingers will be back! Give me a heads-up if you see them so they don't cut me off at the neck while my head's down!"

I looked Caine's way again, now getting to his feet, holding his side in pain, and wincing like he broke some ribs. I refocused, peering out into the darkness over Kim now bent in the dirt drawing a line from one end of the doorsill to the other before writing in the Theban Alphabet and reciting an incantation.

As I searched the darkness for blazing red hair, I heard Caine's father scream, "No!" then I was struck with blinding pain in my skull and along my right side deep in my hip. Disoriented, my body was thrown into the doorframe before the ground slammed into my side.

Kim's incantation was now inaudible in my shell-shocked ears. When the haziness cleared, Donovan was staggering in the dirt, blood flowing from a cut on the side of his head, down into his eye. He reached up to wipe it away with his forearm, the cut disappearing along with it so fast I thought the blood was someone else's, until I felt something drip down my forehead. As I reached up with shaking fingers, they came away bright red.

"He's gonna die whether you want him to or not!" Caine yelled to his father after I saw him make another try for Loring.

Daniel attacked both Donovan and Caine while defending and attacking Loring as well.

The scribble and incantation discontinued and, once she was done, Kim helped me to my feet then poked a finger at where the doors used to be. A warbled effect rippled like water, a shield invisible until tested.

Kim looked at me with a sober stare, satisfaction within her bright blue-green eyes. "That should hold them for a bit, but they could get in another way if there's another entrance."

I was impressed and reminded myself to practice more as Kim held no magic within her blood and was far more capable than me.

As far as we could tell, it was Loring for himself against the guys, since Malina was still sprawled in the corner unconscious. Loring had no trouble evading either Donovan or Caine's attacks. Every time Donovan was hit he looked at me to gauge the damage, but Loring wasn't seriously wounding any of us. Daniel was thwarting every effort to kill Loring, pitting himself in the middle of everyone while Loring had his fun.

Kim and I looked further into the building beyond the fire and Malina was beginning to stir.

"I have the perfect thing for her. Find me a bug." Kim ran for the nearest corner when I stood like an idiot feeling the ache of every hit Donovan had taken. Kim returned with something in her hand. "Watch." She closed her eyes and murmured a spell. I watched an odd look cross Malina's face before she started screaming and scampering around, swiping at her arms and body.

Kim laughed with a hint of wickedness and released a handful of floor dust and a cricket and watched as it hopped outside the building, the shield on the door only keeping things from getting in. "I'll keep my eyes on Jiminy's bitch and check for exit options. You can help them better than I can."

"After that?" I said as Malina was still freaking out at the invisible bugs on her body. "If sarcastic insults could kill I'd be an assassin."

Kim laughed and scuttled close to the walls, her red hair splayed around her shoulders, in search of weak spots in the structure.

I ran for Aunt Lacey, who at some point had been knocked over, still fastened to the wooden plank by the ravenous wire, unconscious. I bent down to her level to get her to open her eyes.

"Come on, look at me," I pled, bracing Aunt Lacey's head on my knees. Blood oozed from wounds everywhere, every inch lacerated to some degree, her nakedness still a slash of indignity that for some reason hit me most.

"Why can't you heal?" I searched for the end to the madness of wire.

Aunt Lacey's voice was difficult to hear. "The mixture...I can't."

"I need to get you out of here." I continued to look for a way to excise Aunt Lacey from the barbed wire. I couldn't see a beginning or an end to it. My search became frantic as another body-blow flung me to the ground, something Donovan endured first-hand. I recovered quicker this time though my spine was tweaked and throbbing.

Cradling Aunt Lacey's head again, I still couldn't find the end of the wire. As I pulled, I not only punctured and tore the skin of my hands and wrists, but I made it worse for Aunt Lacey, moaning in agony from my efforts.

"No. No, Salix." I ignored Aunt Lacey's defeat. "Too deep. Help them. Please."

Torn again, I left Aunt Lacey to help the others while she struggled to keep her head up. Until this point, I had contributed nothing to the fight.

Before I reached them, Daniel had thrust his son against the wall, magically pinning him in place. Caine was elevated but unharmed, twenty feet off the ground, unable to fight back.

Satisfied Caine was out of the way, Daniel directed his power to grab Donovan telekinetically and drag him by the throat to his awaiting claws, intending to strangle him. The immediate loss of air crushed my windpipe, the veins in my forehead pulsing and collapsing with the lack of blood flow until Daniel tossed Donovan like a dirty towel into the air onto the second floor, which in turn vaulted my body right along behind him. Both of us landed on old, flowered carpeting, breaking my right arm in multiple places and dislocating my shoulder with a hollow '*pop*' as I shrieked in sudden unfathomable pain.

Over the overwhelming agony, I heard Daniel make a plea to Loring as he still held his son out of reach. "Please, Master! We came here to obtain retribution, you've got it. I say we get the Hell out of here and deliver the flock the good news."

Loring laughed. "You expect me to leave you breathing after your subversive behaviour? You're more of a fool than I credited you for. Your sacrilege can not be left with impunity!"

"I'll gladly take my reprimand in demonstration of loyalty. I've earned it, Master."

In my line of sight off the second floor, Caine's lips were snarled in disgust at his father. I couldn't believe he was begging for forgiveness from the guy who killed his son and tried to kill the other.

Unable to focus beyond the pain to see more, I heard Donovan's muffled grunts as my bones ground against each other under my skin and twanged every nerve they could. I suppressed the urge to vomit as my arm lay limp while I fought to sit up. I swallowed it back with the impulse to scream Fuckfuckfuck over and over.

Donovan ran to me, his lifeless arm at his side. Sprigs of pain pinged with his every step as his bones ground against each other, triggering an agonizing consequence across our connection. When he grabbed my arm, the cry I suppressed found my lips and echoed in my skull before all pain in my arm disappeared and went numb. Donovan healed me.

He inhaled while still looking pained before saying, "Not done yet."

"What?" I said but when he moved my arm, I realized it was healed, but the shoulder was still dislocated. Before giving me a chance to tense, a quick movement reset my shoulder to the chorus of another handful of "fucks." Once the anguish subsided, his dimples caved in exhausted relief.

Under us was a blood and flesh covered floor with other pieces of discarded wood like the one Aunt Lacey was strapped to, along with old furniture. Before I could take in where Daniel ejected us to, Donovan grabbed me by the skull, pressed his lips to mine with a fleshy smack, and ran over to a bundle of barbed wire and back to the edge where the floor had collapsed to create the loft.

I stared in surprise and watched him throw the coil of wire over the edge, telekinetically holding one end of the wire in the air while the rest uncoiled until it reached Loring below and snatched the bastard around the neck.

Donovan spun Loring to wrap him up tight like a boa constrictor, digging in the barbed wire with its teeth and holding him off the ground from the ceiling like a thrashing, well-dressed stalactite. Stunned, Loring struggled to free himself of the wire, but his arms were pinned to his body. Donovan made sure the wire also wrapped around Loring's eyes and between his lips like a gag to prevent a look or incantation from taking us out. With the free end of the wire, Donovan secured it around a thick exposed ceiling beam and left him to hang there.

I was astonished by Donovan's creativity. All he needed was a sparkly bow and Loring would be the best and quickest wrapped present anyone could ever ask for.

26

A FOREIGN HUSK

With Loring gift wrapped in the same grotesque wire used to murder the others, we had a foothold in the fight. The Reds, Malina, and Kim were still M.I.A.

Donovan jumped to the first floor landing hard, shooting needling pain through my ankles into my kneecaps. I opted to scale the wall like a jungle-gym, looking more like an uncoordinated child than a Parkour Pro. With my body in adrenalized shock my feet slipped as I moved faster than my mind could synchronize with my shaky limbs.

Daniel let out a howl of outrage at Donovan's persistent attempt to rid him of his Master, and after a gripped man-handle, threw him to the ground at his feet giving Donovan a hard-fast blow to the head with a thick fist.

Still clinging to the wall like a drunken monkey, I was propelled into the ground and slid shoulder first in the dirt past both men. For Daniel to beat down Donovan he had to release Caine from his suspension, dropping his son. Caine landed awkward, his leg folding under him, causing a throat-thrashing scream and mewling cries.

Vision-fucked, the walls spun, my shoulder and side sand

thrashed making me hyper-aware I couldn't take over the connection and somehow save Donovan as he had saved me. With the head wound boggling my brain I struggled to access my strength to bring theory to life as Daniel was headed to Donovan and grabbed him, my past-life lover on the brink of receiving another brain banger.

A hammered fist with a dose of magic to Donovan's left cheek laid us out and blinded me.

The room blinked with waning consciousness as Donovan took hit after enraged hit from Daniel who stood over him, Donovan's arms in front of his body doing nothing to protect us.

"Do something!" I begged in a bloody slur as I held my broken face. Every time I managed to hold myself up on numb shaking bones, I was knocked down again. Any chance I had at taking control of the connection to save us both was impossible when reality was beaten out of us.

Adrenaline or urgency must have blocked out Caine's pain as we locked eyes across the room, he in a haze through blood stinging my blotchy sight. He stood up, crippled and hobbling on one leg as he dragged the other to pick up a broken piece of floorboard. Between blows, I watched Caine limp towards Daniel and smash his asshole sperm donor across the back of the skull with the force of a home run swing.

Maybe because he was an immortal it didn't knock Daniel out, I didn't know, but it did faze the fucker enough to make him forgot about Donovan and grab at his rattled brain. Relief soared through me from Donovan who was now choking and looking for me from an unrecognizable face.

My worry switched to Caine. Daniel had turned on his attacker with unmatched ferocity, hesitating when he realized who it was. In Caine's hands was now the remnant of the floorboard that had shattered into splinters, creating a jagged new weapon Caine used to plunge through his father's chest, making damn sure not to miss his putrid heart.

Donovan crawled to me and cradled me in the bloodied dirt.

Shock paralyzed Daniel's retaliation, all anger drained from his expression. Caine held the wood in place. His eyes widened in surprise when his father's hands grabbed onto the wood protruding from his chest.

We watched Caine and Daniel waiting for the next coming action. Caine refused to let go of the wood. Their matching grey eyes met, and everything paused. Daniel had to be in immense pain, but he kept his eyes locked to his son's as the moment hung.

This man was no father to Caine, yet I can't say I wouldn't have hesitated if I were in Caine's place. Killing the man ruined chances of answers to all the questions Caine had, but Daniel was the reason Cole was dead and Caine spent years in a sleeping curse. This Magic in the grip of death was the collective product of selfishness and greed, a man desiring nothing more than serving his Master and cared not of who died in the process of obtaining his immortality.

Expression drenched in a swath of relief I never envisioned on Daniel's face, I heard him say, "You deserved to be the one. I won't chase death away."

He then clutched Caine's shirt, hands covered in blood, to keep Caine's hands in place to drive home his resolve to let himself die. Daniel's legs gave out. Caine poised above his father lying in the dirt, his grip on the floorboard never loosening.

As Daniel's heart squeezed its last laboured beat, my soul-seeing eyes watched the darkness of his soul dissipate, growing weaker with every skipped-beat, then gave a small burst of lasting energy that hovered about his body, before settling on the ground and fading away like car exhaust.

Caine would have been close enough to see Daniel's pupils dilate at the moment of death. Hovering over the still and breathless body of his father, he stayed there as if waiting for something else to happen. Half-hooded, Daniel's eyes were still open, unfocused, all angst and hardness removed and replaced by his death mask. Another moment passed before Caine snapped out of his fog and let the floorboard go.

Again, I wished I could get inside his head. His face adopted an emotionless layer as he hobbled backward, hitting the wall before slipping to the ground to resettle where he sat before ending his father's life, staring at nothing.

Loring's hysterical laugh filled the silent barn, though he couldn't see, and his mouth was partially covered. *"You did me a favour boy!"* We heard his voice in our heads, laughing, while he still hung like a bat, entangled in the barbs.

We sat dazed, Donovan still wrapped around me, our bodies aching yet healed. He soothed my pain, rubbing my back and smoothing my blood-soaked hair. He looked like he wanted to say something.

"They're coming through the wall!" Kim sprinted full force into the room with her hands, face, and body smeared with blood. Before we could register what she was screaming about, wallboards were flying at us like tornado debris.

Thwarted by Kim's skilled efforts at every turn, The Reds decided on the most direct way inside and created a cavernous hole in the east wall. Moving at blurring speeds, I found myself on my belly under the solid boot of a twin while he, with his brother's help, grabbed hold of Donovan's arm forcing him to his knees. His head bobbed on his neck after a brutal hit that put him in a state between awake and unconsciousness. My vision swayed along with his as Donovan fought against it, The Reds holding firm, waiting for the kill command from their Master.

Loring's feral laugh swelled once he realized he regained his back-up. The laugh morphed from jovial enthrallment into a sadistic cackle before evolving into a long winded, deep-chested yell while the barbs sliced into the outer edges of his mouth. Still captive on my stomach, I turned my head to the side to see him better, my head still swimming along with Donovan's as dirt clogged my ear and eye. Loring screamed a battle cry like an old-world soldier laying siege against an enemy stronghold. Dime-sized pieces of metal from the barbed wire rained to the floor in plumes of dust as power saturated the air, freeing his body. He landed on his feet as if his frame held no weight.

The bloody holes and tears across every inch of Loring's exposed skin were healed in seconds. All the while, Loring laughed. Endless laughter.

Loring's attention shifted Caine's way, still in some dark corner of his mind. He needed to snap the fuck out of it or I was going to watch him die. Dread rose as Loring drew closer to him.

I started screaming Caine's name, not giving a shit that the boot in my back was compressing my spine and lungs making me strain and cough in the dirt. No matter my volume, Caine wasn't responding.

In order for Kim to reach him, she would have to pass by Loring. No way would he allow that and I didn't know if Kim was capable of taking him on. Instead, she went to Aunt Lacey. Kim couldn't help Aunt Lacey any more than I could, but they had been closer, and fear and grief and hopelessness skittered across her blue-green eyes. I couldn't force my focus on the bloody saliva drooling from Aunt Lacey's lips. Fixing my eyes on Loring gearing up for his next move was better than watching Aunt Lacey and Kim suffer.

Before reaching his target, Loring grabbed and pulled out the jagged piece of wood jutting out from Daniel's chest with a retch-inducing sound of crackling bone and ripping sinews. Blood poured off the crude weapon as Loring took slow, deliberate steps toward Caine and batted him over the head with it, splitting the skin on the left side of his face clean open, leaking blood down his square jaw.

I was screaming, clawing at the ground to escape the boot on my back. Caine fell limp to the floor on his side. Loring gave a righteous hoot like he won an over-sized panda at the fair. Again, I screamed Caine's name, screamed for him to get up and fight. He fluttered his eyes as he lay crumpled.

"Fitting you should perish by the same means as your father," Loring's voice rang, landing another blow, this time a body shot that caused a huff of air to escape Caine's lungs and then drag in a moment later with a desperate rasp.

"Please, Caine, get the fuck up!" I screamed again and again from beneath the foothold of one of The Reds while Donovan was trapped in their hands.

Donovan was lucky they hadn't ripped his arms from the sockets as soon as they got a hold of him, though it didn't stop him from struggling as they held him on his knees. I couldn't think straight enough to make my power work. I didn't know if this was from The Reds or something else.

Loring continued to pummel Caine with the piece of discarded flooring, enjoying it. Caine's face was in the dirt, blood escaping his lips, his ears, and several open wounds. His eyes suddenly opened and met with mine as I cried out. Tears collected on the ground beneath me, unable to tell if he was truly seeing me or not.

Loring switched-up his tactic. Caine lay helpless on the ground, broken and static, as Loring held the floorboard above his head, ready to use it to end Caine like Caine ended Daniel, when I screamed my loudest in desperation and reached out to him.

The whole time I was underfoot of The Reds my power was distant. Maybe they did something, but I was useless. Now, a collective energy of my despair at watching Caine being beaten caught up to me and overrode whatever had stopped me. Intense power filled the breathing space around me as I let out an unrelenting force of energy. It felt as if all my power had exploded from my body in a purging torrent. Not as it did in the beginning, out of control and ineffectual, this was an explosion more than anything I had ever endured.

Thrown back onto her hands with her ass in the dirt, I ignored Kim's horrified awe as unbridled energy streamed out of me and hammered against Loring, forcing him away from Caine and up against the west wall. He dropped his weapon, mouth open, flabbergasted as horrendous sounds of discomfort and then pain thrashed his vocal cords.

I saw the twins drop Donovan in my peripheral, and he fell to the ground with a hard crack of his head that seemed to wake him up and cripple him all in the same blow before he curled into the fetal position.

Without the hindrance of the booted foot in my spine, I paused for a transitory moment, long enough to push my body up from the dirt floor. I vaguely heard agonizing screams from The Reds behind me figuring Donovan gained the upper hand, but his moan came from the ground, and I couldn't concentrate on him long enough to figure out what was happening.

Flooded with a confidence my attack afforded, I continued the onslaught. The force of my power grew as it became more familiar to me and oscillated in colours that pained my eyes while I watched Loring's desperate attempts to escape fail. As I kept at it, Loring's tar-black soul changed, sinking into its darkness then straining as his soul glow lightened.

Like with Denise, I caught tenuous inner dialogue. Feeling the sudden energy within his dominant immortal body snake into the deepest core of him. Loring was distressed I was doing something he had never encountered before, and the unknown scared the shit out of him. He felt torn in a struggle he wasn't controlling. His body fought to regain footing he kept losing and it was beginning to break him apart. Even when I stopped for half a breath, he couldn't find himself fast enough to retaliate before I was on him again, my power tearing at him, changing him from the inside.

Hearing all of this, I used it as fuel to keep going. Even though my body was a foreign husk to me, I could worry later about that, right now my concentration was on one person and the sounds of his inner resistance as it did nothing to save me from ending him.

He was unable to escape me, unable to access his own arsenal of abilities to fashion an attack against this "unskilled Seedling" that held more power than his reconnaissance uncovered. Loring, in one last spout of rage and shredding agony, fell into a last resort option. Holding himself together as the creases of his face deepened, his expression twisted as he doubled over, grabbed something from around his neck, and disappeared. My power hit the wall, scorching the wood until I broke through with a loud crack.

Motherfucker.

I ran to Caine who was now struggling to move, his eyes swelling shut. Blood poured from lacerations on his face and body, the skin of his cheek peeled back like apple skin.

"Don't move! Loring's gone. It's okay," I told him so he would know danger had passed, not wanting to touch him and cause more pain. If he could hear me, he was being stubborn by not listening and fought to right himself.

Since he insisted on getting up, I grabbed his shoulders to move his heavy body. Seeing him straight on, I wouldn't have recognized him had I not seen what Loring did to him firsthand. Tears blurred my vision as I fought to hold them back so he wouldn't see the horror reflected at what I was seeing.

Touching any part of him caused him to wince. He grunted. His lips falling open in a blood-drooling gasp, but I held on, hoping the healing process would be quick.

His head swayed, lashes a flutter as if his sight was failing him. Every second bringing sounds of pain as his legs kicked out in wrong angles, his knee a rip and pop before it straightened and he cried out. I wanted to let go. Tears fell as my doubt grew, even more so when he grabbed my wrist with bruising pressure, a silent plea he couldn't take anymore. A plea I ignored.

When the slice of skin on his face knitted and he took in full dragging breaths, it spurred me to keep going, even as his eyes rolled, and shudders racked his body. Unlike with Loring, I wasn't getting anything from his mind, but the closing of the gruesome gash across the bridge of his nose and drying blood in his beard stubble, told me all I needed to know.

When Caine's grip on my wrist softened and his smoky eyes connected with mine, soft breaths moving his chest, I knew it was over.

"I'm fine," he said with promise. "I think if I had cavities, they're all gone now."

I actually laughed. Nothing akin to Loring's sinister amusement, but a release of tension that had him smiling and pressing his lips to mine. Lingering blood zinged my taste buds with metallic sweetness as excess energy from the attack on Loring still buzzed in my veins, but the power itself had dissipated from wherever it came from. I had never been so grateful for this power. Whatever it was, allowed me to chase off Loring. For now, I was settled in the rapture of surviving.

When I pulled back, we looked to each other in beaming exhaustion as he tangled his fingers in my red dusted hair. I leaned in for another kiss then hesitated and leaned back onto my heels.

"Sophie?" he questioned but I couldn't answer.

Atrocious confusion, gut-wrenching and devastating sadness I had never encountered iced my core. My eyes stung with rising tears I didn't evoke before I understood what was happening. I searched behind me for Donovan. He and Kim were leaning over Aunt Lacey who was still on her side on the floor wrapped in the teeth of barbed wire. I left Caine's side to go to him.

Less than thirty feet from them, those steps to find out if Aunt Lacey was alive or not, passed at a snail's pace. Aunt Lacey was hidden by Kim and Donovan's hunched backs, her strapped and bloody legs all I had to go on. Placing a hand on Donovan's shoulder when I made it to him, his head bowed for an inconsolable moment I had no chance of containing for him, our tears falling in unison.

Aunt Lacey was still alive, she and Kim saying their goodbyes.

Kim's cheeks were smeared with blood and tears as she rested Aunt Lacey's head on her knees as Aunt Lacey's tired gaze met Kim's. Aunt Lacey's feeble voice, once strong and confident, kept failing as she strained to relay every lasting sentiment. I gathered doing so telepathically was no longer an option, this notion heartbreaking in of itself.

"Help Donovan," Aunt Lacey said to Kim. "The Sect needs your balance."

"I'm only a Kitchen Witch."

Aunt Lacey's smile told her how much that mattered, and Kim nodded instead, taking on the role I knew she would excel at, if she could handle Donovan. Kim knelt and kissed Aunt Lacey's sallow cheek for the last time, a sob escaping as she then struggled to compose herself before it seemed she lost hope of doing so.

"Wend...."

Donovan's head popped up, but he didn't reach for her. I didn't know if he wanted to, but even if he did, he would be blinded by visions.

She tried to hold her head up more to look at him but as she did, the barbs dug into her throat, more blood for the Earth. Eddies of emotion from him threatened to swallow me as he watched Aunt Lacey's struggle. He contained the majority of his pain, what he kept inside frightening in its intensity. Everything about this was so wrong. And that's what I got from him. This wasn't right. Regret even guilt was present, and I couldn't understand why.

"Wend, do not allow this to fuel your hate," she said to him slowly. "I've lived long enough for hundreds. No matter the clock we run, we all die. Do not let my death be your downfall."

"I don't know how to do it without you." He pushed an answer through clenched teeth and again I wished I understood the underlying meaning behind the words she chose for him. I leaned into his side, wrapped a supportive arm around him, and he reciprocated with strength.

Aunt Lacey's eyes flashed to me. "You'll have help." Donovan looked to me with tormented eyes. "Don't be afraid to take it," Aunt Lacey told him. He nodded as he swallowed hard.

I wasn't holding up any better as I still clung to Donovan and moved a piece of herb matted with oil to Aunt Lacey's forehead and smoothed her hair. It made no difference but there was no other comfort I could give.

"I can't believe we're going to sit here and watch you die. This can't be it." I shook my head unwilling to accept it. "I need you." I fought to keep my voice steady. "I still have so much to learn."

"There's always more." Aunt Lacey smiled. "You'll get it in no time."

"But I owe you so much."

"No, Salix...you have given me the chance...." She inhaled and her eyes fluttered, "...to see my family reach its rightful place. My Gareth and Nya could not have found two more deserving vessels." She looked to Caine standing behind me. "Now you are more tightly joined to my family through Wend."

Confusion tripped me up until a look a Donovan's newly crumpled features made it clear. Of course. Donovan being related to her explained more than I realized, the surprise of this revelation a shock to hear.

Aunt Lacey paused to breathe. "He needs you, Salix."

I gripped Donovan's hand, trying to manipulate the connection to douse the wretched reality of him witnessing a family member die so cruelly, knowing when our skin brushed I was sending him visions that didn't fit the moment. He held the contact for a moment, allowing the visions to soothe him for a quick moment to better deal with Aunt Lacey's suffering.

"Leith," Aunt Lacey called Caine. He moved so Aunt Lacey could see him without straining. "I saw your sacrifice." He looked away. "You had no other choice," she emphasized in a failing voice. "Thank you for being brave enough to follow through."

His voice choked and he had to start again. "You've been braver than any of us."

She attempted a smile, but the cutting barbs made her wince. She coughed, showing blood-stained white teeth. I fought the urge to tear at the restraints again.

She fought waning strength to go on. "You'll all be okay. You have each other." Her voice weakened as her eyelids sagged. "Promise you won't lose sight of each other because of this." We had no trouble promising her anything at this point. "Live for each day, no matter how many you see."

Again, we nodded in agreement, unable to predict how many days that may be.

"Wend," she said without opening her eyes, "everything is under my mattress."

"What?" He sniffled. "What do you mean?"

"It's all there," she said without further explanation, her eyes never opening again.

Aunt Lacey's body became mournfully still, her neck slack on Kim's knees, all breathing stopped as her body found peace. A wave of all-encompassing sadness pierced through me. This woman who had been alive since before civilization made its presence, living through World Wars, Witch Wars, outliving countless others, and teaching us four what she could in the small slice of time we cameoed in her life, would become a painful memory.

My head still lay on Donovan's shoulder while our sorrow doled between our connected hearts as we broke down. Something shone through my raw closed eyelids. Assuming the bonfire grew to engulf the room, I opened up and was shocked. My gasp alarmed the others. I was too captivated by what I was seeing to answer whatever they were asking.

Aunt Lacey's bright, ethereal soul was returning to her sickened pallor. The treatment from Loring dampened her soul glow down to nothing, but now it returned to the same as before Loring snuffed it out. Engulfing Aunt Lacey's entire body it radiated from within her and became brighter and brighter, more than before, like a white-hot metal.

I blinked as the tears fell, unable to look away from the brilliance. The light far surpassed what I believed possible. When I thought it couldn't get any brighter, a burst like controlled fireworks flew out a few yards from her body, showering us even if the others couldn't see it. I jumped back into Caine still behind me and grabbed tighter to Donovan's arm.

"What's the matter?" Caine asked at the same time as Kim. He knelt at my back, but I couldn't articulate what I saw, too in awe to form words.

Donovan asked in a quiet, uneven voice, "Is it her soul?"

I managed a nod as more tears fell. The burst was Aunt Lacey's soul separating from her body. Her vessel. Leaving Aunt Lacey and lingering in front of me, good to the core. After hundreds of years, she died without so much as a blemish on her seasoned soul.

Unlike Daniel's, which disappeared in a puff of dark smoke, Aunt Lacey's soul held its own as it moved, fading and sharpening like watercolours as I watched it move away from her vessel. No physical features I was used to remained, though she couldn't leave without saying, *"Find trust in others and bring hope to their hearts, Salix. You will lead them to the light."* The soul in front of me then dissipated like she had somewhere to be, though I couldn't see where.

Now Aunt Lacey, a true vessel of history, lay empty. Daunted by the enormity of the question of where it was Aunt Lacey's soul went, my shoulders sagged. How could I ever describe witnessing someone I loved die and watching their soul leave their body to anyone?

"She's gone," I told them when I could speak again, my voice sounding aged in my ears. Uncomfortable and dry from holding them open, I forced my stinging eyes shut.

Coupled with this moment was the realization that Aunt Lacey was never immortal. She may have lived for an immeasurable amount of years, survived battles, vengeful enemies, and debilitating family tragedies, but in the end, she still fell on her knees at death's door. Only the soul lives on somewhere in the light of another plane of existence, or to one day be recycled as with my previous life with Donovan. At some point, if I made the jump over the ditch from mortality to agelessness, I would eventually die too. No matter how long I staved off meeting the end, the end was inevitable.

We were at a loss. The Elders were all dead and we couldn't leave their bodies as Loring would have wanted, to rot in the place he blamed them for destroying. They needed to be taken care of respectfully. Kim and I did our best to unwrap Aunt Lacey of the wires, having an easier go at it without the pressure to race against the reaper. In her nudity and an attempt to preserve her vessel's lasting dignity the task was left to us while the guys looked for something to cover her with until others were brought back to do so properly.

The Elders were covered with the tarp after Caine and Donovan moved them and the nameless Coveners into a row instead of mounded in a pile like soiled socks. A sheet on the old furniture in the loft was good enough to cover Aunt Lacey. Daniel was left uncovered and lying where he fell. The bloody carnage and smell of blood and decay was unforgettable.

During clean-up, I saw piles of grey ash, walked by them a few times before I realized what I was looking at. The Reds, their bodies smouldered and extinguished. What happened to them? I thought back to the last time I saw them.

"I've never seen anything like it," Kim said from behind me. "You were attacking Loring with whatever that was, and then they turned black and crumbled without you even touching them. They were freaked. Dropped Donovan, who looked hurt but not like them. They looked at each other like big dumb brutes before falling apart."

Killing them without contact wasn't the case. The one twin *was* touching me; standing on me, to be more accurate. But as I stared at the ashen bodies flaking into the dirt, I couldn't help but remember the dandelion from my first 'Make it Grow' test. Donovan said I had the power to enhance life by making the flower grow, but was capable of producing the contrary. I did the same to Daniel in the storm drain, but this was enough to kill them? Why would it affect the other twin when they weren't touching each other? Could they have been that connected? It disgusted me to think of what I was capable of.

Maybe she saw my revulsion, but Kim directed my attention elsewhere. This wasn't hard to accomplish. We needed to return to the others and hope they were awake. The Elders were gone. A chain of command had to exist. Could their deaths cause the Coven to fall apart? Donovan said it wouldn't. The Coven was so old the Magics within it would fight to keep it alive. Hopefully without fighting amongst themselves while lobbying for the next Elder positions.

Before we left the barn, reluctant to leave the Elders and the nameless others beneath bloodied shrouds, Kim ran back into another part of the building where she had been during the fight. We waited for her in pure physical and emotional exhaustion until she returned carrying the trench coat Malina was last seen wearing.

"Barely any blood. She took if off to fight me," Kim said with a haphazard smile and a rascally wink. "Bitch owes me one." I couldn't help but laugh, still wondering what happened with Kim and the devilish blonde. Once I had time to process the shitstorm we survived, I would ask her.

27

ELEMENTAL

The walk back to Diluculo was agonizing. We moved in morose silence. What now? Who could we go to? How would we seek recourse? Modern justice was out of the scope of this world, no lone gumshoe could handle the truth let alone the creativity needed to uphold a justifiable punishment even if Loring resurfaced.

The decision to be a part of a world where their brand of justice was eye for an eye, was a frightening angle to consider. It was either that or you're bullied by the greater power taking control of the universal playground. No legal absolution while Magics were still under the radar. Retribution for what would be coined the Lughnasadh Massacre was on Donovan's mind, yet this made me no more at ease. With the loss of our commanding Elders, what kind of fight could we bring? I had no clue. I didn't know enough yet, but from the emotions Donovan locked down, I had a feeling vengeance was all he was focused on.

A small dose of relief came as we crossed back into the Diluculo side of the Creation and saw Coveners milling about. Many were confused, but appeared uninjured and fit to return to the festivities, unaware of their loss. Others, ones with more sobriety, knew different and were seeking answers in those around them.

A part of me wanted to delve into a keg, but no amount of alcohol would make me forget what I saw or what I did back in Pario.

No one noticed our red eyes and tear streaked faces full of dirt. They even looked past the blood until Donovan led our dishevelled group to a few Magics, one with a metallic rosy soul glow. Before he saw me, I ran to Ranlyn and held on so tight and fought falling apart.

"Sophie?" He pulled away enough to look down at my face, dark blue eyes wide with worry.

Without saying anything, Ranlyn led us to his cabin close by, a one-story painted in neutral colours inside and out and decorated in a way that looked as if everything grew into itself over years of usage, not quite as put together as Aunt Lacey's. We stood instead of dirtying the furniture by sitting, though blood was already flaking away.

Once the door closed from outside ears, we told Ranlyn everything about the unsanitized version of our paradise and the horror which happened within the barn.

"All of them?" Ranlyn paced, astonished by the Elder's demise. Donovan nodded. "This is unheard of. The Elders expected an all-out war, coven vs. coven, as it usually was since preliminary attacks had already been forged. This was too focused, too personal."

"Loring doesn't care about the fallout," Donovan told him. "He got what he wanted. A war would heighten the fun. I'd expect one."

Ranlyn agreed, lost in thought, processing what we lived firsthand.

"What happens now?" I asked, pulling Ranlyn from his contemplation. "Loring escaped. He didn't decay from my release of power like The Reds, so it's a fair assumption he is alive and pissed off."

"For the moment, the death of the Elders may satiate Loring's retribution enough for him to think twice about returning. By your accounts, the coven Loring belongs to was ignorant of his attack. Daniel's death may give him a scapegoat thwarting any possible blame, so they wouldn't follow suit with a war. Not right away. This also meant Loring might take his time planning any retaliation. All presumptions, but unless we hear anything from back channels, it's all we have to go on."

Ranlyn called in others who were high on the 'Elders Next in Line' list, another man and two women, and us four young Magics were forced to relay the story again and again. We finally sat down, exhausted by the fight, the immense emotional distress, and the recalling of a horrific time we would all relish forgetting, knowing it would be etched into our minds forever. With each perspective Elder that arrived, the chaos in the room grew.

A tall man who spoke in a thick Hungarian accent, Miklos, who worried his thick hair and beard, was obsessed with the recipe Loring used to subdue such powerful Magics, hoping to prevent a repeat with other Magics. They prattled off theories, in the end concluding the goofer dust kept the Elders ill as the knotweed bound their bodies treating their powers like a parasite the knotweed was saving them from. Like their power was a sickness being forced out of their body by an antibiotic. The black-ram's head would take advantage of their bound abilities, killing them slowly through the ripped flesh. The kicker was the unknown proprietary ingredients Loring never mentioned.

Hinapouri, a fierce and beautiful Maori Warrior with long dark hair, tanned skin tattooed with tribal designs covering the left side of her face and trailing down her neck to her left shoulder and torso, was personally insulted Loring broke into Pario and then Diluculo. Her role was security, and their defences had fortified three-fold once whispers of evil circulated. They played with the idea that the significance of the night being the celebration of Lughnasadh, a spiritually powerful day, facilitated Loring's access, coupled with whatever Cole had stolen from Loring. A more daunting thought was a traitor may be amongst their midst. No doubt with the way Hinapouri seethed at the thought, traitors were not dealt with lightly.

A quiet elderly woman of Asian origin sat in a padded chair with clouded unfocused eyes that minutely changed with the nuances of the conversation. She chirped in every so often with an amusing retort, causing Miklos to snap at her using her name, Veata, sharply, telling her she would be better off not speaking if not offering useful theories. She would snicker and sit quietly like she was far beyond the young minds of those whom she shared her company with and thought them below their efforts.

I looked to Kim, surprised Miklos was so disrespectful to someone of age and power as I could tell Veata was the brightest soul of the bunch. Veata assured us in a confident tone and a thin-lipped smile that Miklos's opinion meant more to himself than it did to her.

I liked Veata.

Another hour passed when not even Veata's candour settled our uneasiness. Hinapouri and Miklos planned tactical responses while Ranlyn remained diplomatic and tried to appease their ego's and douse their bloodlust while pushing for peaceful solutions. By this time, Veata stopped talking altogether, possibly sleeping.

Their strong souls were so bright in the small cabin with nothing resulting from their endless chatter but talk of revenge and medieval forms of torturous penalties. It bored and infuriated me. Between their talk of revenge, my soul-scorched eyes, and the surges of hatred and despair from Donovan, I snapped.

"The goddamn Elders are fucking worm food!" Yup, I freaked my shit.

They spun to me shocked, even Veata perked up with a growing smile. I stood for a sense of confidence, terrified by the scowl on Hinapouri's tattooed face.

"There are hundreds of people out there who need to know why they were unconscious, that their Elders are dead, and that regardless of Loring and his devotees that their Coven is still strong. That twat-bucket Loring got what he wanted, so can you please get your shit together, get a group rallied, and retrieve their fucking bodies!" Mention of their bodies put shame in Ranlyn's eyes. "They're still lying in that horrible place gathering flies and you're here bickering about your next move?" Then enunciating each word continued. "There is no war!"

My voice softened with my exhaustion as my skull was thumping. "Call everyone together, reassure them everything is okay. We're going to need it to have some type of funeral or celebration of their lives before you go sticking body armour on every able person around the bonfire."

I hoped they would focus on that aspect, the fact the Elders had been alive for centuries and not the tragedy of their deaths.

"Now," I continued. "I'm going to shower off the blood and body gunk so fashionably dried to every part of me. Have fun figuring this bunk out." According to all their soul glows, they had lived long enough, they could learn to get over my disrespect.

An assembly of Coveners were outside Ranlyn's cabin, all moving back when the door opened. As soon as they saw our bloody conditions, they stared, none making an attempt to ask questions, and none of us bothered to update the looky-loos, not even of our own Sect. We needed a scrub down, hoping to wash away some of the memories of that night.

———

Once squeaky clean, at least on the outside, we donned pyjamas and sat on the couches that faced each other in front of the fireplace and mantel holding frames of nameless faces of those Aunt Lacey loved. Exhausted, yet unable to sleep, I kept thinking over that night, Aunt Lacey's words, Loring's claims of knowing Cole, and what we were supposed to do now, until I passed out where I sat. As did the others.

Nightmares were inevitable, but mine were not my own. I saw myself kneeling before Daniel, taking blow after blow, hearing the bones in my face crunch, tasting the tangy blood running over my tongue down my throat. Suddenly, Daniel's face morphed into another man's with dark hair, his long and straggly, his beard and dark eyes a perfect match. Above the crunch of my bones was the sound of a child's screams, desperate moans as arms that had been slashed a thousand times limply attempted to protect my devastated facial bones. Others circled me in a dark room, chanting loud, their voices vibrating in my ears partially plugged with blood. What they said was important, but all I could focus on was the pain and the deep question of why, why was this happening to me? Did I do something wrong? Was I bad? I can't take anymore, please stop hurting me.

The last crushing blow was not of a fist, something much harder, metal that came from behind, slamming against my skull under my right ear before agony peaked and everything went black.

Waking with a start still on the couch in front of the fireplace, the pain of the beating lingering as my hands rose to protect my face. I heard a deep gasp, more guttural than my own. When I searched the space around me for the source, Donovan was sitting up with his hands in front of him duplicating my defensive posture.

I had been dreaming of him as a young child.

He now attempted to restrain the all-consuming prophetic dream too real to be the product of an over-creative nightmare. A dream so terrifying he awoke in a sweat, his chest heaving in his attempt to reconnect to his reality. When Donovan realized the attacker was a heinous memory and saw I had been subject to the sadistic replay of some childhood trauma I still didn't understand, his expression morphed from one of oppressed panic to relief as his present filtered back.

As an echo of recollection, whatever happened to him was heinous. I didn't know who the man was, why he was hurting Donovan, and why the others were standing around watching, but the dream gave me some understanding into the person Donovan was. A victim of childhood trauma triggered by the day's events, a child I hoped Aunt Lacey saved. I couldn't force him to talk about these horrors, especially with the others asleep on the couches with us.

We looked at each other for a moment as I filtered compassion and understanding through our connection. It seemed to satisfy him as we fell back into our original sleeping positions, Caine and Kim still breathing softly and unaware. After taking a steadying breath, Donovan forced a smile, his usually dark intense eyes remarkably soft. When our eyelids fell, we both drifted off to sleep.

———

An authoritative knock on the cabin door woke me up. The sun was at high-noon, a manifestation of Diluculo's magic, as a tired-eyed Ranlyn stood at the door. Caine let him in. Throughout the remaining night and into the morning, they retrieved the bodies of the Elders plus the few missing Coveners and his guards, and in a few hours a cremation ceremony for the Elders would be held.

All were expected to attend.

As decided by Ranlyn and the new Elders, a version of the events in Pario would be told to the Coveners, important details being left out for reasons Ranlyn didn't fully explain. Since mind reading was still an option for some Magics, it compensated for the lacking details, though rumours already circulated.

Many didn't know about the connection between Caine and Daniel, nor did they know of Donovan's connection to Aunt Lacey or even Aunt Lacey's connection to Daniel or Loring. The deaths of The Reds and Malina were never revealed either. Only the four of us and the new Elders knew the gruesome truth, and we were tired of repeating it.

No one planned on a funeral, so appropriate attire was scarce. Everyone who packed a semblance of black was wearing it, mostly in the form of black t-shirts and dark jeans or skirts. Older Magics among them had no shortage of mourning attire, consisting of long black dresses or cloaks and black lace over bereaved faces.

The bodies of the departed Elders were all wrapped in beautiful cloth stitched with symbols and bright colours like mummies, hiding their heinous injuries. The Coven's crest lay on top of where their faces were, each Elder treated as an equal without distinguishing one from another as they lay on top of a wooden platform with kindling and firewood all around.

Ranlyn, now steward of the Coven, came forth and quieted the crowd as many mourned aloud. We four young Magics were placed near the new Elders, wishing to assimilate with the crowd. Stares were unavoidable as seen through my new dark sunglasses since the last ones were lost in Pario.

Scrutinizing expressions from people ranged from pity to fury and even envy. Some thought we should feel lucky to have fought and used our powers to protect and not in practice. These were the worst ones and we ignored them as much as possible. They didn't know everything about what happened, but the dead and wrapped Elders should have been enough to snuff the thought to the quick.

I didn't want to cry, I didn't want to sit and watch them burn Aunt Lacey's body, nor was I interested in the way the proceedings were held. If I didn't know one of the decedents, I may have paid attention, but all I could think of was trying not to sob and worsen my already rampant emotional hangover, clinging onto what control I could to accomplish that.

Across the connection, I could tell Donovan refused to acknowledge an ounce of grief. Between both our attempts to dampen all the shitty things cramping our emotional dam, we were pleasantly numb.

I was holding onto Caine's hand when a flash of light and the unsettling noises of the jumpy crowd brought me around, but I didn't react as they did. The fire was started. No ordinary fire, the bodies didn't burn as expected. The low fire burned in blues and greens without crackling or popping as wood invariably does, the fire not even throwing off heat. I doubted Donovan and I could block that out and no others stepped back from the pyre to save their eyebrows.

As Aunt Lacey burned in the heatless fire, silent tears ran down my cheeks, though I never felt any sadness. No sobbing, no mewling, only tears and pleasant numbness.

The deceased Elders were ash within a half hour of ignition, another indication of some magic catalyst. I had watched enough forensic TV to know a body takes much longer to break down under greater concentrated heat. The shrouds used as wrappings were also left untouched, pristine, and yet crumpled as the bodies beneath them broke down. With a sudden breeze, the fire went out with a sucking *'whoomph'* and all that was left were sheets full of ash.

Ranlyn stood atop the undamaged platform. His gaze settled on me a moment with watery dark blue eyes and looked over his Coven. "We give these children of nature back to their mother, back to the way they began, to live on, in the earth, the air, the fire, the waters, and to the spirit of this world and the next."

He, with Miklos's help, while Veata and Hinapouri sat in tall backed wooden chairs, gathered ash from each departed Elder and sectioned ash from each Elder into five pieces of cloth.

Ranlyn held up the first cloth made of yellow fabric depicting a grey triangle and dagger. This poultice-like pouch wasn't secured with ash inside. The fabric lay slack in his palm as he faced east.

"Into the wind, they take their journey as one with the *air*, where they shall soar and gaze upon us all with the coming of each morning sun, to guide our thoughts peacefully to endure this unwelcome change." A warm inviting breeze picked up as he spoke, swirling around our bodies, power buzzing around us and in our lungs. Unfolding the bundle, Ranlyn held it high. The breeze caught the ash and it cascaded gracefully away in a blackened haze until it dissipated with the wind. The yellow cloth was handed to the shaking hands of Miklos. Ranlyn offered a consoling hand to his shoulder who then took a moment before handing Ranlyn the next bundle of white fabric.

Another triangular symbol in red bearing a wand through its middle with licking flames surrounding its entirety was stitched in pale cloth. After Miklos tied the fabric with a leather thong, Ranlyn perched it in his palm and faced south, continuing with a strong voice.

"Into the fire, which consumes the vessel to release their spirit from its living bonds, for now with their passion for life and pure essence of divinity, they will become that fire within us all. A fire that will bring forth progress within our Coven, a fire which will drive us into our futures with ambition and purpose."

With a hitch in resonating power, the cloth spontaneously set ablaze in Ranlyn's palm with the same blue-green flame. Another gasp enveloped the crowd. As Ranlyn had put it, the departed Elders had become the flame within us, a cool flame ablaze in our veins. This sensation doubled in me and Donovan causing our heads to bow with an uncomfortable moan as the fire licked from our bellies, smouldered in our lungs, and escaped our esophagus to graze our tongues. I grasped for Donovan's hand, he already grabbing for mine, and pressed the other into my chest to relieve some discomfort. The contact and resulting distraction from Donovan's visions allowed us to douse the intenseness until it became manageable, simmering deep within.

Our reaction didn't go overlooked by interested Coveners, including the new Elders. Once Donovan and I could re-open our eyes, we had more onlookers than ever. We dropped our hands and turned our attention back to Ranlyn, who had continued without the hindrance of the inattention of the crowd and his council.

Light blue cloth shone like iridescent satin in Ranlyn's palm. The depiction an inverted triangle coupled with a cup to represent water, and lay untied in his palm as he faced west. Again, he held it to the sky, his eyes gathering clouds.

"Submerge into the ever-flowing waters in which it cleanses within its pools of our love. Leave us blessed and purified in their passing, free from fear and despair." Drops of rain fell from the oppressing atmosphere, nothing torrential yet enough to cover the attendees in a spiritual chill. "Bring with the universal showers a sense of knowledge, an intuition of self, and the essence of survival, for with it gives us life without these all-knowing souls to guide." The waters continued to fall upon the cloth washing away the ashes of the Elders.

Not everyone enjoyed the change in weather but invited the

sense of calm, a purification as the rain dappled our skin, tension and sadness waning with the water.

The other newly appointed Elders had been sitting with silent strength in their sorrow. Now on their feet they slowly walked away. The ceremony wasn't over and others who attended these proceedings before knew to follow the new Elders, the rest falling in behind.

In a slow uncharacteristic walk, we passed the white sand beach devoid of revelry and stopped at the forest edge of Diluculo. Ranlyn held up a velvet green pouch decorated with a pentacle and yellow square to the north. His voice hitched as if the heaviness of his emotion hit him over again, proceeding thick-voiced.

"Into the ground, we inter their essence beneath the soil where they shall come together as one amongst the Woodland of Energies where our dead meet the earth to grow strong in their demise, as they had undeniably achieved in their long-celebrated lives."

At his feet Ranlyn reached down to a pre-dug hole, as wide as it was deep, and placed the pouch with care. Covering it with soil he patted it down with a strong hand and hesitated before standing, muttering something too low for other's ears, and took a few steps back. An influx of power simmered, making me shiver. After a quiet moment, the packed dirt began to crack as if a small animal was attempting to broach the surface. Instead, a thin green stem emerged. The audience watched, captivated as the stem grew a leaf, then widened and crawled out of the soil, reaching two feet in half as many minutes.

As it grew, I realized the forest we walked through to get to Pario was a graveyard. Each tree represented one or many fallen mystics. The most amazing aspect was that the forest was massive. So many trees, so many departed, with no possible way to calculate how many dead filled the branches.

"The strongest tree will grow in its place," Ranlyn said in a booming voice over the sound of the crowds increasing awe. As the trunk continued to grow, branches reached above our heads causing us to step back to allow its widened girth, "to live and breathe once again as they have become one with the earth. To stand tall and watch over all of Diluculo and their flock. The spirit of these beings will never be lost to those who remember them. Honour what made their existence one of light and virtue. Channel their essences, as they are as inspirationally grand as the tree which grows before us."

Ranlyn was handed the last piece of fabric bearing a symbol of a wheel stitched into more white fabric. Those accustomed to the process fell to their knees, leaving the new Elders the only ones standing, Ranlyn's eyes cast skyward.

"Hear us our departed Elders," he strained. "Grant us your lasting presence. Infuse your flock with your spirit!"

The sky above us brightened, the sun burning. The bright orb reminded me of the sun after Caine left the park. Too hot, too close, filling every spectator with its solar embrace as if it was indeed infused with the Elder's infinite power.

Some swayed in discomfort with the rise in vibration. More experienced Magics welcomed the increase of power, lifting their arms above them. I looked to Kim, her face pale, her hand to her chest as her cheeks pinked with the heat, still in awe though clearly uncomfortable since true magic wasn't her everyday experience.

The sun grew more imposing with each passing moment. Ranlyn spoke on as if it took all his will to manage it. "Please, our Elders, as we have called you forth in this time we regretfully say farewell. Allow your successors to be one amongst the many who led this formidable Coven through centuries of greatness. Grant us as ones apart of those invisible to time itself so we might carry this Coven to success years beyond our given time on this Earth."

The overwhelming buzzing of power in the air, in my veins, in the sun spears themselves, became more and more erratic, reaching back to the uncontrollable days when the power grew without provocation into the runaway fuse that ended in a shockwave of energy. I held onto myself like I might break apart. The sky enveloped us and the space around us, blinding us as the cries of the Coveners filled Diluculo with reverberating echoes.

Someone grabbed my hand with a bone-bending squeeze as if they would die without it. A wave of calm came as Donovan's visions hit him and granted us some peace. He pulled my body in close to his to resist the unfathomable force our connection worsened.

It took a few moments once the power dissipated for anyone to move. We were on the ground in the fetal position until our vision refocused. The new Elders were laying on the grass like the rest of us, no better at withstanding the onslaught of power. Ranlyn helped Veata to her feet and waited for the others to gather themselves.

They were no longer enlightened souls of powerful beings. Silver underlined their bright white soul glows as the previous Elders had before them, Ranlyn losing his pink, frilly soul glow. I was told immortality was gained by years of practice when the body was so saturated with power time had no effect. Apparently becoming an Elder gave you cutsies to the front of the immortal wait line, a bump in status equipped with a superb employment benefit package.

As I searched the silvery souls of the Elders, Ranlyn's eyes caught mine and without words was looking to verify the status of their souls. I nodded in confirmation. Ranlyn's smile broadened, his excitement crawling into his voice as he spoke with restored exuberance.

"They *all* will be remembered. *All* will be celebrated. Let's not allow today to be a day of tragedy. Allow this day to be one of recognition. Recognition of the great beings who touched many lives, for we are all blessed to have had them a part of ours. This Coven will never fall. No matter the century, no matter the calamity we face, we stand as one!"

As he concluded his speech with a raised fist meant to rally his people, the crowd broke into a barrage of yelling and clapping. Tears still fell in a collection of sadness for their fallen members and a showing in confidence in their new leaders knowing no one could ever forget their last ones.

28

INTO THE FUTURE

A great feast was held, still celebrating Lughnasadh through the wreckage Loring caused, and then the anointment of new Elders who sat in their respectful seats around large wooden tables which replaced the pyre. Plate upon plate was served of every thanksgiving food I could think to make. The pig roast looked disgusting yet tasted delicious, as long as you didn't look the head in the eyes and saw beyond the fact it had a metal spike shoved through its ass.

As day drew to night, Diluculo was restored to its original excited cadence, reaching the bottom of many alcohol bottles, recounting happy stories of the Elders, swimming at the beach, and playing games.

Aunt Lacey's untouched room was a harsh reminder of her not making the trip home with us. The members of her Sect, including us, sat on the beach together around a flickering fire. This time, Denise kept her distance and her blood-alcohol level low. The Coveners were afraid the Sect would dissolve, but were assured Donovan and Kim would keep it going. Kim made a point to make sure everyone knew to come to them with any concerns or even ideas as she wanted each person to get the most out of every meeting experience while retaining the traditional aspects of Aunt Lacey's teachings.

Donovan became intolerant with the prospect of sobriety, a bottle in hand at all times, until the effects became too much for me. Because we both needed it, I ignored the run-off of his intoxication, but as the night went on, my head began spinning.

Flopping my head on his shoulder when he cracked open another bottle I said, "You've had enough, kid."

He looked down at me through glazed eyes. "Kid?"

"Yuppers," I straightened. "You got my head doing the tilt-a-whirl and seeing one of you is plenty, thanks."

He snort-laughed. "Sorry, babe." He embraced me in a sloppy apology.

When he didn't pull away immediately, creating space was difficult. Not because he held on tight, though he did, but because he was emoting an extreme desire of keeping me close, and it took a lot for me not to want the same while in my borrowed intoxication. Not to mention, Caine was on the other side of me and we were attracting too much attention, no doubt boosting already rampant rumours.

"It's fine. Lay off before I start puking."

He laughed again, guzzled the whole beer, and mumbled a dig about me being a lightweight. His caved dimples had me elbowing him in the ribs.

To chase away some of run-off from Donovan, Kim and I walked the shoreline. Crystal water lapped our bare feet sinking into the warm white sand. We searched for seashells and colourful rocks, as I attempted to shake off the excess of alcohol. Wavering a moment in my footing and in my thoughts, I asked Kim about Malina. Kim's soul glow shined brighter. She smiled with a hint of blush as I pointed this out.

"As you saw, my cricket spell worked. When it wore off, she was pissed and it came down to hand-to-hand combat, which I tell you I need a *lot* of work in."

"Clearly you won."

She shrugged. "I got to the mirror first."

"Mirror?"

"I think they used it as some type of portal to get into Pario, but I'm not sure. Malina was protecting it and then tried to escape through it, so I figured it was a good idea to smash it into tiny pieces. She wasn't too happy."

I didn't need details of how Kim killed Malina, but Kim simplified the impact. Having to take a life, even in self-defence, was a big deal.

I stopped and hugged her tight, grateful Malina hadn't got to the mirror first, suggesting she mention it to Ranlyn as she hadn't before.

Caine and I had a moment alone as well. I did my best to remain strong as I said, "I don't care about your family or what they did to mine. I'll talk to Olive about that later. I also don't care about your dad. I don't care if he's evil, web-toed, or Episcopalian. This isn't about your Tainted daddy. You lied to me about important shit and used what I told you about Brock as justification to do it."

He nodded and bowed his head.

"It kills me every day to not be able to tell my parents about this world, fearing their inability to accept the new person I am, but you know everything. I need to know the truth, not pieces of what you think I can handle."

"I know." Shame flooded his voice.

"I also told Donovan I love him."

Caine's lips parted in surprise. "You love him?"

"The connection is a great lie detector. I didn't want him to think I was ashamed of my feelings even though I don't understand them or plan on acting on them. He deserved the truth and he deserved to hear me say it. Like you deserve to hear me say it and not have it pop up and sucker punch you in front of other people. We haven't been alone since for me to tell you and then everything with Aunt Lacey..." He understood where I was going.

"What now?" he asked as if fearing my response.

"I'm not one to drop anchor when things get rough, but understand, I won't let you do that again. Of course, you can, that's your choice, but that'll be the last time. You know my past. I may have taken it back then, but now? I'll walk away and move on because I can't do anything else."

Softening of his expression told me he understood.

The embrace was one we needed, though once we rejoined the others, I noticed Caine gave me as much space as I needed while remaining close, showing me he understood I needed it even though I never told him so. Or maybe I thought that's what he needed and gave him space. I couldn't tell.

Afterwards we sat in the grass and watched as the sky was illuminated by fireworks. Blake and Jared and others in a team had a hand in creating the best mixtures of shock and awe: amazing colours, ones that crackled like popcorn, fizzled like sparklers, and even made shapes. Every pair of eyes, kids, adults, and animal alike shone while sparks flew and dissipated into the night.

The cloud that loomed over us persisted the next day. We swam and ate in the afternoon, walked around the merchants again, none as content to haggle as when we first arrived, though many wore ice blue ribbons to honour Hallden as he was the head merchant in charge of their dealings.

Ranlyn met us on the porch of the cabin as we gathered our belongings to leave, his silvery immortal glow reaching me first as he came to say his goodbyes.

He wanted to ensure Aunt Lacey's Sect was continuing and that any and all of the Elders were a phone call away if needed. Donovan thanked him, agreeing to do his best in keeping up the Sect as it was always run by Aunt Lacey and held in high regard.

Ranlyn reassured Diluculo would be reinforced against the infiltration of evil. Kim told him about the mirror and he mulled this over, promising to tell Hinapouri.

"Loring won't stay away long," he said. "You're all loose ends and a challenge to wrap up. Keep your eyes open for any threats and let us know, no matter how small. I'll keep guards on all of you, but, as you know, it might not be enough."

We would never again under-react when gut feelings told us otherwise.

"Are you sure about our souls?" Ranlyn asked me.

"I'm new at this, but I'm not blind. You were all granted immortality as a gift. A light as bright as Aunt Lacey's soul after she died."

"You saw her soul?" His eyes glistened.

"Yup. You and the Elders are now the same. No more pink glittery soul for you, Jeeves." He gave a small laugh. "Now you'll have a long time to figure out how to bring the Coven into the next centuries. No pressure," I added, trying to soften the charged moment.

Ranlyn held my hands as I looked at him with slight nervousness. "To have such a gift..." he said with a shake if his head. Then he wrapped his arms around me as I did him and tears threatened again. He pulled back as I forced my emotion to retreat. "I know Aunt Lacey is proud for you being Nya's power's vessel, but even without her influence, you are precious to the Coven. I am honoured to consider you one within our fold." His words caused a measure of shock as they sunk in. I appreciated him saying so and would miss having him outside my door.

Ranlyn spoke to each of the others as he had with me and then we threw Aunt Lacey's bags over our shoulders to leave behind paradise as well as Hell, forced to leave behind Aunt Lacey in the Woodland of Energies with so many fallen others.

The journey out of Diluculo was as horrendous as it was on the way in and Donovan and I experienced it twice over, equally as painful with each pass. We would miss Diluculo, but it would never hold the same nostalgia as it would for others, and we weren't so quick in craving a return visit if only for the painful trip through the veil.

I knew Donovan was headed back to Aunt Lacey's, to the big empty house to check under the mattress. In a mafia style move, Aunt

Lacey said everything was there, so I had no doubt Donovan was headed there first.

"We're going with you," I told Donovan.

He shut his trunk with force. "No, you're not. You have no reason to." He passed me to get to the driver's side door.

"Donovan, I know you can handle yourself and don't need a shoulder to cry on, that's not what I'm offering…though you know I'd be there for you if you did." His jaw clenched. "I'm not letting you do it alone. Suck it up, we're going with you."

He jumped into the driver's seat and shut the door, sticking his elbow out the open window looking above his aviators. "Seriously, babe—"

I bent to meet him at eye level. "This is where you learn I'm more stubborn than you. We'll meet you there." Feeling his pain as he dealt with whatever he found while in a different city was pointless.

After a thorough inspection by Caine to ensure his car survived the days parked unscathed, we were on the road. I never offered to drive. The drive was Caine's therapy. He needed it and I was too distracted.

"Is that okay?" I asked half-way into the ride.

"Is what okay?" Caine responded confused since nobody was talking.

"Going to Aunt Lacey's to be with Donovan."

"I'll go anywhere you ask me to." He kissed my hand, not willing to argue with me by the looks of it.

"You're coming too, Kim," I called to the back seat.

"Of course, I am. We can't leave him there alone, he'll off himself." A joke, but a scary thought. The dark emotional climate from Donovan was unpredictable. I didn't know what he would find, and it made me nervous to think Kim could be right.

Warm summer wind blew through the open car windows as Caine peered stone-faced out the windshield. Again, I wished I could feel what Caine was going through. I didn't think he regretted killing his father, but it was ludicrous to believe he felt nothing for doing so.

The power that drove Daniel away from his family and drowned him in darkness wasn't present when Caine thrust the crude weapon into his chest. Although he could have accessed it, the power did not save nor defeat Daniel. He allowed Caine to kill him, showing what little humanity he possessed.

Plus, Caine struck Daniel down to save Donovan. Saving Donovan was also saving me, but still, I remembered telling Caine to "do something" and killing Daniel was the result. I couldn't shrug off responsibility for my part in the outcome.

We parked in Aunt Lacey's driveway hating the fact she wouldn't be inside at the kitchen table or in the basement waiting for us. Kim led the way upstairs to Aunt Lacey's bedroom. The connection was already alive, and I worked to understand the emotions filtering through from Donovan.

A pair of French glass doors stood partially opened at the end of the upstairs hall, the glass covered in white lace. All we saw was a white mattress against the wall. Inside was Donovan sitting on the naked box spring toying with an envelope in his hands.

"There's one for all of us," he said as we entered and paused at the sight.

He didn't mean an envelope for the four of us, he meant the Mother Coven in its totality. Each envelope had a name on it. Some were to other Elders, one's that had died with her, others still alive. The ones addressed to Coveners other than her immediate Sect included postal information, stamped and ready to be mailed.

"She knew," Donovan said with anger wading below the surface. "She knew she was going to die...she didn't tell me."

"Is that what your letter says?" Kim asked in a soft tone.

"No, my letter says pretty much what she said." He paused. "And, apparently, the house is mine." He threw up his hands. We were as shocked as he was. "The deed to the house is here, all ownership papers already in my name, the bank accounts...all mine."

Reading how this affected him was hard to decipher. Happiness, intrigue, anger, dreadful confusion, all warring inside him. He turned his head and wiped a fallen tear.

"Are you okay with that?" I asked wiping away the same tear on a different cheek.

He shrugged. "The letter said she feared her life may be ending because of her inability to see her own future. She told us that part, why not the rest?"

"Didn't want to worry us?" It sounded logical but unhelpful. "This was her way of telling us, to make sure you were taken care of when she couldn't do it anymore, and to leave a piece of wisdom behind."

"I guess so," he said though I sensed his disbelief.

The others searched for their envelope in the pile on the box spring and Caine and Kim opened theirs and read them in private. Kim paced out of the room, but Caine stood against the wall to read his over. I couldn't bring myself to open mine. Instead, I sat on the box spring next to Donovan.

"All this is yours now. Think you're up to it?"

"Not a fucking chance. She asked me to continue the Sect, with Kim, and gave me the responsibility of her legacy. How can I turn that down?"

His dark eyes were so sad. "It's a lot for one person. Don't be afraid to ask for help."

He looked at me, smiled and bumped his shoulder into mine. "Thanks," he with sincerity.

"You gotta make this place your own. A painting and redecorating party will have to be soon. Unless you're into white lace."

He laughed. "I'll make sure to give you a call. Though now I have a whole Sect to do my bidding." He gave a menacing, dimpled look and I gave him a stern one back, which made him laugh.

We were laughing when Kim returned with red-rimmed eyes. "Did you open yours?" she asked me as Caine finished his and refolded it to fit back in the envelope.

"Umm, no. Not yet."

"Why not?"

"I don't know."

"It's weird," Caine saved me from explaining, "to read something from someone who wrote it before they died. It's a new one for me."

If only Cole had thought to leave him something. He owed Caine an explanation and all he would have was what Loring told him. Guaranteed something along the way was twisted by the evil fucker.

Still, I couldn't bring myself to open the envelope. To write something, a note for someone containing information for a loved one, words you needed them to read, to know they cared when they knew death was coming for them, was bizarre. I pictured Aunt Lacey with a pile of papers, thinking of the perfect message to leave, pouring her heart out in the case of her death.

Heartbreaking.

"We heard her last words firsthand," I said to the others. "She wants us to work together for the Coven. This letter can't tell me anything more important than that."

They agreed, though I still hadn't shared the lasting words Aunt Lacey said as her soul left her vessel. More words I couldn't handle at the moment.

At my insistence, we camped out for the night, setting up blankets and pillows on the basement floor, except Donovan who called the couch "since it was *his* house now". They agreed because I wouldn't budge, even with a dozen rooms upstairs to choose from.

Laying on the thick carpeting with the others close by, I couldn't help reminiscing about other times I found myself on the basement floor: My first meeting feeling out of place, Initiation night, getting my coven name, saving Caine, the unbinding, and although I don't remember it, the night of the stabbing where they healed me, releasing my power being the most significant since the others were impossible without it.

This basement brought me so many amazing things in such a short amount of time, and connected me to such genuine and amazing people. I couldn't have predicted the changes my life took after a simple tea leaf reading invitation. Thinking of the moments that marked me, when my weekends consisted of rice and veggies and TV with Bosco. I never again would wish for things to be simple. If they were, I wouldn't have Caine and I wouldn't have Donovan, and I wouldn't have Kim, my best friend who started it all.

Inevitable and unable to sleep, I crept out of the basement without waking Caine or anyone else, though positive Donovan was pretending to sleep since I too was awake and our connection stayed as strong as it was in Diluculo. I grabbed the letter from my purse in the kitchen. I looked at it for a good fifteen minutes as I sat at the kitchen table and worried Nya's ring like it was willing me to open it.

I didn't want to read it. I didn't want to have that one-sided conversation with the dead woman who showed me the potential of my life, but delaying was ridiculous. So as the envelope seemed to gain in weight, I went outside into the warm summer night, illuminated by a small wall sconce and the moon.

Sitting cross-legged in the grass, I took a breath with my eyes closed, took a couple more, then opened them and the envelope, trying not to look at 'Salix' scrolled in fancy writing. Facing it as I should have hours ago, I sat and read Aunt Lacey's last words. Not the ones she imparted before she could no longer speak or the ones her separated soul spouted before she passed onto an unknown existence, but the ones she chose for me.

Under the stars and clear moonlit night, I absorbed every word while I cried for the woman I would forever miss.

———

Sign-up and stay current on book cover reveals, sales, giveaways, and more with S.J.'s newsletter! http://www.sjcairns.com/newsletter-sign-up/

———

Read on for DIVISION, SOUL SEER CHRONICLES, BOOK 3 teaser coming January 2023.

Division, Soul Seer Chronicles, Book 3

Death won.

We limped away bloody, but we lost big.

Olive's release and rise to heir of the Ballard Family Estate is the one outcome I can say I'm proud of.

But everything else is a mess.

No time to feel deflated.

Enemies are multiplying like feasting cockroaches and taking on strange forms, spouting old-world pledges of vengeance and making us second-guess how to deal with it all, including who we can count on when no one is trustworthy.

Safety at Donovan's began as a practical solution, but the arrangement overwhelms already strained relationships and carries weighty consequences I will have to live with.

No matter the enemy, or the last resort tactics meant to save our lives, I refuse to let death win again.

ABOUT THE AUTHOR

S.J. Cairns creates paranormal romance fantasy from her hometown in Southern Ontario, Canada. When S.J is not plugging away at her laptop on her comfy couch, you can find her chasing around her two-year-old daughter alongside her husband of twenty-one years or working in true chaos at the local women and family's homeless shelters and an anti-human trafficking safe house.

Website: www.sjcairns.com
Facebook: www.facebook.com/SJCairnsauthor
Twitter: www.twitter.com/SamiJoCairns
Email: samijocairns@gmail.com